MENACING ANGELS
THAT NIGHT

AVENGING ANGELS

Carolyn S. Tanner

CAROLYN S. TANNER

This book may not be reproduced or transmitted in any form without the permission of the publisher/author. In no way is it legal to reproduce, duplicate, or transmit any part of this document in either electronic means or in printed format. Recording of this publication is strictly prohibited and any storage of this document is not allowed unless with written permission from the publisher. This is a work of fiction. Names, characters, businesses, places, events, and incidents are either the products of the author's imagination or used in a fictitious manner. Any resemblance to actual persons, living or dead, or actual events is purely coincidental.

Book Cover artist: Mirela Barbu @ 99designs portfolio https://99designs.com/profiles/1328241.

Copyright 2023

All Rights Reserved

Carolyn S. Tanner

Dedication

To my cousin, Chasidy Tomlin. A heartfelt thank you and much love. You are a true heroine and a perfect match for the main character! So beautiful! Thank you for being the model for MENACING ANGELS THAT NIGHT!

Author's Note

Thank you, dear Readers, for taking the time to read the second book in the *MENACING ANGELS: That Night* series. I have finished the third book of the series, *TROUBLE WITH ANGELS*, which contains some levity. Though life can be hard, there are also times of joy even in the harshest times. I'm in the midst of the fourth book, *STOLEN ANGEL*—well, it is on the way as soon as I can get out of the parlor.

The next published book will be *CRIMSON ROSE,* a standalone historical romance not associated with *MENACING ANGELS.*

A word of caution—do not use any of the medical material within my books. These are old, not verified methods used during that time period and are not proven in today's medical field.

I hope my stories pull you in and you live with the characters, experience what they experience and yet come out with a different perspective of understanding that we do not know what others are going through in life or why they react in a certain way. We are individuals with different passions, reactions, and sometimes, the pain of living life. There's always the upside—life does get better when you step away from the past and forgive yourself and others. The light at the end of the tunnel sometimes seems very small, but the more you strive, the brighter the light becomes.

Again, thank you, dear Reader. May blessings fill your life and bring precious smiles to your face.

Carolyn S Tanner

CONTENT

Part III AVENGING ANGELS 1873-1874

Chapter 1   Faltering Steps
Chapter 2   Justice or Revenge
Chapter 3   Lawless Abode
Chapter 4   Heart of Ice
Chapter 5   Wall of Hate, Wall of Sorrow
Chapter 6   Fires of Hatred
Chapter 7   The Endless Pain of No Tears
Chapter 8   Mercy of an Angel
Chapter 9   Ride the Wind of Death
Chapter 10   Babes in Arms, Doll of Death
Chapter 11   Retreating Hearts

Part IV SAVAGE ANGELS

Chapter 1   Blood Red Sun
Chapter 2   Too High a Price
Chapter 3   Ice Fire Cannot Melt
Chapter 4   Savagery Among Angels
Chapter 5   Angels of Fate
Chapter 6   God is Good
Chapter 7   Death Angels
Chapter 8   A Mad Dog Must Die
Chapter 9   Sow the Wind, Reap the Whirlwind
Chapter 10   Tears Mend the Heart
Chapter 11   Weep This Heart of Mine

I Stood Outside the Gate

<u>Josephine Pollard</u>, *pub.* 1870

1. I stood outside the gate,
   A poor way-faring child;
   Within my heart there beat
   A tempest loud and wild;
   A fear oppressed my soul,
   That I might be too late;
   And, oh, I trembled sore,
   And prayed outside the gate.

2. "O Mercy!" loud I cried,
   "Now give me rest from sin!"
   "I will," a voice replied,
   And Mercy let me in:
   She bound my bleeding wounds,
   And soothed my heart oppressed,
   She washed away my guilt,
   And gave me peace and rest.

3. In Mercy's guise I knew
   The Savior long abused,
   Who often sought my heart,
   And wept when I refused;
   Oh, what a blest return
   For all my years of sin!
   I stood outside the gate,
   And Jesus let me in.

Cheyenne and English Translations

Ovaxehee	Dreaming Woman
Tsistsistas	The people
Heammawihio	The Wise One Above or The-One-Who Is-Always-There
Vo'evahtamehnestse	Cloud Walker, the medicine man, correct translation Walking In Clouds
Mahpevahee'estse	Standing In Water, the Contrary
Nestonevahtsete	Noisy Walker, father of Dreaming Woman
Epo'o	Gray, *Ovaxehee's* favorite mare
Hestoemestaa'e	Strange Owl
Monevata	Young Bird
Maehonene	Red Wolf, spirit guide
Tsehemesemetovestse	Grandfather
Neskeesta	Chipmunk
Meeskevotse	Baby
Hohnuhk'e	Speaking opposite of meaning.
Wunun	Sacrifice by starving.
Ho'neo'kaestse	Long Wolf's
Anestaeseva'e	Misty Woman
Ma'ena'evahe	Red Arm
Haa'hae'ameohtse	Wind Racer
Mo'eheso	Little Elk
Ese'he Ohnesesestse	Two Moons.
Nahtataneme	Brother

Wohksehhetaniu	Kit Fox Soldiers
Ehyophsta	Yellow Haired Woman
Heenevaahetanehee	Woman Who Is Man Woman
Nanasehamehee	Mountain Lion Woman or mighty above all the other beasts
Heoohtato	Water puppy or water dog
Hotohkohvq'komaestse	White Star

Part III: Avenging Angels

1873-1874

Chapter 1
Faltering Steps

THE BROWN SEA OF TALL PRAIRIE GRASSES with an occasional shrub or a small dead tree, outstretched in a seemingly endless mirage. The sky lengthened into boundless blue and the hot sun nearing the western zenith battered the small group. Nikki halted her mount and swept the black hat from her head, letting it dangle on the chinstrap behind her shoulders. Dismounting, she rubbed her forehead, wiping away sweat.

"We make camp here for the night," Nikki Pride commented when the women, the six-year-old LeeAnn, and the dog joined her.

While Tawnie Sands and Ginger Starr unsaddled their mounts, Kissa Loving rubbed her posterior, fighting the tears forming in her eyes. Besides her backside, her inner thighs hurt, so sore she could barely touch them without crying. Never so uncomfortable in her life, she swore every joint in her body ached. Over two weeks on the trail and she still wasn't used to riding for hours at a time. How did the others stand the constant riding? *It just isn't natural*, she thought, dropping the reins and loosening the cinch from underneath the mare's belly.

Her arm muscles straining, she pulled the heavy saddle toward her, bending backwards to pull it from the horse's back. Suddenly she was on the ground, the heavy saddle on top of her. Stunned, she sat there a few seconds, then burst into tears--the hard riding and living more than she could tolerate.

The others never helped her with the mare, explaining she had to learn and insisted she do it by herself, but she just wasn't strong enough. They constantly teased her about being able to hitch and unhitch a horse to a carriage and take care of the horse afterwards but couldn't even saddle her own.

"Da' blasted! Here we go again. Can't ya do a dang thang without cryin' like a baby? Heck, LeeAnn's got more guts than you do." Tawnie dropped her saddle behind Kissa, her face stony.

Turning to Nikki, she bellowed, "I told ya the baby don't have no business goin' on the trail with us. We're already havin' to travel too dang slow, plus divide her work 'tween us. She can't even pull her own weight around camp. Heck, LeeAnn helps more than she does." Turning, Tawnie stalked off toward the pack animals.

Weary, Nikki heaved the saddle from Kissa and dropped it nearby. Tired by the end of the day, tempers ran short, bringing with it bickering and tears, a constant occurrence with Tawnie's barbed remarks usually aimed at Kissa. Ginger withdrew inside herself after her night at Miller's Pond and LeeAnn spent most of her time with *Heoohtato* when they were not riding.

"I'm sorry, Nikki. I'm trying. I can't seem to do anything right! I've never even been out of Rustic before now!" Kissa wiped at her nose with the back of her sleeve, tears shimmering in her eyes. Pain seemed to find places she didn't know she had, and it made moving and helping around the camp excruciatingly uncomfortable.

"We all must pull our weight, Kissa, and you have to take care of your own mount. Just do your best. I know you can groom and bed a horse. After Tawnie and Ginger unload the pack horses, you could take care of the animals. None of us really like to cook or sew. *And* rounding up buffalo chips or firewood is not hard. You would be taking a load off us just helping in those areas." Nikki held out her hand and Kissa took it, allowing Nikki to help her stand.

"Everything on me hurts," Kissa sniffled.

Understanding, Nikki placed an arm around her shoulders, patting her. "Kissa, we all hurt after riding all day. It will take a while for our bodies to adjust, but we will."

"All of you hurt too?" Kissa's eyes widened with surprise, Nikki's words unexpected.

Nikki laughed. "Of course. Do you think any of this is natural for us?"

"But none of you act like you hurt."

Smiling wryly, Nikki compassionately patted Kissa's shoulder again. "We all do. We knew what to expect, but we take it in stride, ignoring the pain and our tiredness. We have to or we will never survive."

Glancing around her, Nikki noticed the horses grazing nearby with their loads laying close by the saddles. Remembering tonight was her night to cook, she turned to Kissa and suggested, "Kissa, if you want to fix the meal tonight, I will round up some buffalo chips and get a fire started."

"Yes, I can cook a meal out of almost anything." Kissa's cornflower blue eyes dried and a new strength entered her face, a tenacious smile curling her pouting lips, the first smile since before they had left Nikki's farm.

"I'll do it. I love cooking, and I'll help you find chips to show Tawnie I can pull my own weight." Kissa took a step, determined to help with gathering buffalo pads, then stopped and turned back toward Nikki. "Thank you."

Hearing the conversation, Tawnie hollered a suggestion, "Kissa, find a stick to beat the grass so ya can check for snakes. Give a little whistle afore ya do and the snakes will slither in the opposite direction."

Turning her back to Kissa, Nikki bit back a grin while gathering the dried buffalo chips hiding in the tall grasses. Her smile grew wider after hearing Kissa's soft whistle and the grass moving behind her, then Tawnie's and Ginger's soft chuckles.

The group sat around the campfire, their bellies full of the best meal they had eaten since leaving the farm. Kissa hummed under her breath while plying a needle to Tawnie's torn blouse while Ginger looked on with lackadaisical interest. Tawnie cleaned weapons and LeeAnn curled up beside Nikki and her dog *Heoohtato*.

The long, hot days with the sun beating down on them where even a whisper of wind was welcomed, produced its own miseries. Exhausted every evening, it depleted their remaining strength to unload and bed down animals, then gather wood or buffalo chips for a fire. Though they tried switching off cooking meals between themselves, sans Kissa, the days seemed to last forever before they laid down for the night, a night where one or more moaned in their sleep when *that night* invaded their exhausted slumber with nightmares.

Nikki leaned back against her saddle, holding a

steaming cup of coffee, and enjoying the new camaraderie in their group. With Kissa taking over the cooking, everything seemed to move quicker, easier, and a new empathy filled the group.

Moving the cup toward her lips, she glanced down into its depths and the form of Dane Travis' face suddenly shimmered in the black liquid. A soft sigh escaping her, she took a sip, drinking his image inside her, confused by her tumultuous emotions. One moment, she silently accused him for not protecting them *that night*, the next, her body yearned to have him near her again.

Grimacing, she tossed the remainder of the coffee, again fighting the divisions within herself. And it was a division, a division of her red and white blood, and her love/hate for Dane. It did not help when she doubted herself and wondered if she was doing the right thing by convincing the other women to join her on her quest for vengeance.

Staring at her empty cup, she pondered if she was as empty inside as it. With a soft, shaky sigh, she bent over to place her cup in the saddlebag, careful not to awaken the child. Moving her long braid to the front of her shoulder, she shifted beneath the blanket. LeeAnn moved closer to her warmth, and she opened her arms, closed her eyes and cuddled the child against her.

Nikki was almost asleep when the child rocked her blonde head back and forth, fighting her nightmare. Caressing the child's face and hair to soothe the distressed child, she whispered, "*Meeskevotse*, shush. I will protect you with my very life." The words echoed in her brain, her promise to Cari adding to the list of unkept promises and destruction. *Neskeesta, forgive me for not keeping my promise.*

Grey dawn faded into light and an array of birds thrilled to the awakening day. After eating a hastily prepared breakfast, the trail stretched out before them with Nikki keeping a careful watch for signs of roaming Indians. Riding along the banks of the North Platte River, the low, shallow river barely flowed through flat plains, the sandy banks bearing little to no vegetation or trees, and the blistering sun bore down on them, baking them in clothing stiffened with sweat and white dust. At night, they fill a bucket with the brown, silt-filled river water and let it set until morning for the silt to settle in the bottom before refilling their canteens.

Spotting a green patch a good distance ahead and nestled closer to the distant hills starkly outlined against the flat, dreary plains, the women kicked their heels against their mounts, setting a trotting pace, eager for even a slight tree shelter to shade their sweating bodies from the sweltering heat. Nikki set the stride carefully to not overheat the horses, acutely aware shimmering heat could mask the true distance. Slowing her mount, she lifted her hand to stop the entourage. When the women drew next to her, she pointed in the distance. "It will take another day to reach the area ahead. The sun is setting, so we'll camp here."

Eager to reach the tree-shaded haven, they broke camp just before dawn, kicking their heels against their mounts' flanks. By early afternoon, they rode into a section overgrown and surrounded by growing life where leaves of green and silver willow trees mingled with shrubs and cottonwoods, clinging together in impenetrable thickets. They were met by rushing silver water, teasing them with its coolness. Jumping out of saddles, the woman ran toward the river, their horses following them to the riverbed, and drank their fill.

Nikki left the group to scout the tree-lined river before going back and ordering them to mount up again and leading them deeper along the river's banks. Colorful birds sang in simplistic sweetness, darting through the foliage while deciduous trees rustled with the wind, sighing the women into drowsy somnolence.

Halting the group, Nikki allowed them to fill canteens with good water and wash some of the sweat from their brows before calling it a day even though plenty of daylight was left. Anxious to find the outlaws, she decided it was more important to take a well needed rest. Besides, she was tired of the group's rank body odor, especially her own. It might be days or even weeks before they found another place so welcoming during their journey; the flat, hot, dry plains still lay before them.

After unloading the pack animals and taking care of the animals, Nikki absently took the plate of food Kissa handed her and quickly down it. Setting the tin plate on the ground for the growing pup to finish the rest, she stood, and without a backward glance, walked toward the inviting water.

She divested herself of hat, moccasins, and weapons, then placed them in a neat pile close to the river's edge. Unbraiding her hair and shaking it loose, she swiftly slipped out of her stiff clothing to carry them with her into the river.

The cool water rippled across her legs, bringing with it a welcoming freshness and chasing away some of the heat. Holding her dirty clothing in her arms, she knelt in the water, letting the gentle rushing water caress her skin and soak her clothing at the same time. She almost wished she could drop her clothing and let them float away while she soaked, but common sense interfered. With a weary, yet content sigh, she began washing her clothing.

While scrubbing the clothing, she heard the shocked intake of breaths when the other women stared at her standing naked in the river's shallow water. The surprise only lasted seconds before someone joyfully hooted and the women copied her motions, joining her naked in the river to wash more than three weeks of dust and grime from their bodies and clothing.

A smiling LeeAnn and the puppy joined them, with LeeAnn copying them by washing her own clothing. The cool water refreshed their bared flesh, and after hanging cleaned clothing on the bushes, the women, child, and puppy played in the river.

Refreshed, Nikki stepped out of the water and entered the hastily setup camp. A bemused smile barely lifting her lips, she hoped the water dripping from the back of her hair would wash the sand sticking to the bottom of her feet, but it only made the sand thicker on her soles. Sitting on top of her hot saddle, she shifted her bare bottom on it until she could withstand the heat, then stretched her arms toward the heavens to enjoy the breeze prickling her flesh.

The others joined her and grabbed at saddlebags. Pulling a clean shirt out, Kissa asked, "Nikki, do you want your saddlebag?"

Nikki laughed, placing her hands against the saddle and kicking her legs upward. "No, thank you. This is marvelous."

"You're not gonna dress?" Kissa asked, shocked.

Tawnie dropped her saddlebag and lifted her arms, stretching, the golden hair underneath her arms catching the sunlight and sparkling. "Sounds good to me. Dang, you're right. This feels great!" Laughing, she did a squat, her knees outward.

"Tawnie!" Kissa cried in shock along with Ginger's giggle.

"Kissa," Ginger called over the laughter, "God created us without clothes. Didn't Adam and Eve go without clothing until they sinned against God?" She jumped upward, tossing the saddlebag back toward her saddle, laughing when her breasts bounced upward when she landed.

"I can't do that," Kissa cried, watching a naked LeeAnn play with the puppy.

"You are beautiful." Nikki glanced over Kissa's body, appreciating the chubbiness firming and redefining her body, the only imperfection the bite mark still red upon her right cheek bottom.

"What?" Kissa cried, turning several shades of red while placing her hand over the blonde patch above her legs and the other arm across her breasts.

"Relax, Kissa, and enjoy whut God gave ya. We don't have to have clothes on 'cause there ain't nobody around. How many times will we have to enjoy this type of freedom?" Tawnie stood with her legs apart, stretching again, loving the warm sun kissing her naked flesh.

Ginger tossed her wet hair over her back, also stretching. "Ah, the breeze feels so good. I'm so tired of being hot and sweaty. I'm going to enjoy this while I can."

Turning her smile to Kissa, Ginger repeated Nikki's compliment, "You are beautiful, Kissa, so relax and enjoy the cool breeze. So what if we're all naked? We're all females, and for once in our lives, we are totally free. Enjoy it while you can." Laughing, she sat on her saddle, then rose just as quickly, the saddle scorching her bare backside.

"I gotta go pee," Kissa suddenly exclaimed, dropping her saddlebag and shirt as she ran toward the trees, the twittering giggles of the women following her into the bushes.

Arriving back at camp, Kissa slipped a clean shirt over her head, the bottom edges coming just underneath her buttocks. At least she didn't feel so naked, and it provided a coolness she had been missing for what seemed forever. She did not realize that each time she raised her arms to reach for something, the shirt rose above her buttocks, giving the others another glimpse of her bare backside, a disheartening reminder of *that night* displayed on her rump cheek.

The next morning after loading up and riding a short distance along the banks, Kissa started squirming in the saddle with her thighs twitching distressfully against the hot leather of the saddle. Her hands tightened on the reins, inadvertently stopping the mare, chagrin turning her face the same color as her apple-red cheeks.

Nikki turned the gelding around and rode back to Kissa, pulling up beside her and watching with concern when Kissa burst into racking sobs while clawing at her hands, thighs, and between her legs. "What is the matter, Kissa?"

"Whut the hell's the matter now?" Tawnie sawed on the reins, a scowl solidifying the golden tan of her face and thinning her lips into a pale slash.

"I do not know." Nikki slid off the gelding, letting the reins dangle toward the ground, to help Kissa dismount. "Let me look at your hands."

Doing a little dance and holding out hands covered in a mass of red rash, Kissa rubbed her thighs together at the same time. Solicitude etched Nikki's forehead. "Where did you get into poison ivy?"

"Poison ivy?" Kissa wailed, looking down at her thighs.

"You did not?" Nikki asked, staring at her painful dancing.

"Ya wiped with poison ivy?" Throwing back her head, Tawnie guffawed. "Ah, hell's bells, what'll happen next if she don' know whut poison ivy looks like?"

Kissa's face turned all shades of red. "Help me! It itches so bad I can't stand it!"

Nikki's mouth twitched, fighting against her own laughter. "Get undressed and into the water, Kissa. Bathe every place the poison ivy touched and *do not* scratch yourself. I will search for some *mahkhanowas*."

Turning her attention to Tawnie and Ginger, Nikki ordered, "Setup camp for tonight."

Nikki rode away toward the plains, a good distance away from the other women before bursting out laughing. She giggled until her sides hurt and had to bend over to ease the stitch. Sniffing a few times to gain control over the humor of the situation, she slowly straightened and wiped her eyes.

Short bursts of giggles still attacked her every so often while searching for the poison-weed medicine, a plant closely related to the locoweed. It took a couple of hours for her to find some of the plants and longer still to build a fire to dry them more thoroughly, then ground it into a fine powder. By the time she had everything ready, the infected area of Kissa's body ran a watery substance.

Grabbing a blanket, Nikki motioned for Kissa to follow her, away from the others into some trees and brush. After sprinkling the powder over her hand sores, and to Kissa's embarrassment, Nikki ordered her to take off her pants and lie on a blanket.

Red flushed spread across Kissa's face when Nikki spread her legs and sprinkled powder along her thighs where the poison ivy touched, but when Nikki slipped between her legs and used her fingers to open her vulva wide, she shuddered, not only in embarrassment, but from the sudden wetness appearing, and the unusual and kind of exciting sensation with Nikki sprinkling the powder along all the itching edges.

"Gee, Kissa, this is pretty bad. For the next few days, you will have to sprinkle this medicine over the rash. Hope you do not mind, but if this gets infected, especially here, it can become very serious indeed," Nikki whispered under her breath so low Kissa barely heard her while she opened her vulva wider, peering at the sores.

Kissa sucked in her breath, chagrined, yet curiously aroused, the sensation not only itching horribly, but also stirring her with the new sensations down there. "All right," was all she could manage to say, confused by her reactions.

Nikki stood, shaking her head and compassion filling her. This was not a job she wanted, but for her friend's sake, she would ensure Kissa doctored the sores until healed. Uncomfortable and self-conscious over the way she had to administer the medicine, she could well believe it had not been any easier for Kissa, yet she had no other choice. Shrugging against the worrying thoughts, she was also thankful during their horseplay and carelessness near the river, no one else suffered the same discomfiture and itching.

Walking toward the river to wash her hands, she heard the soft rustle of clothing as Kissa dressed. "Tell the others we will camp here for a few days. We do not want you developing an infection from saddle sweat."

Irritated and stressed their quest was delayed yet again, Nikki was also relieved they were near vegetation and trees, staving off some of the heat. The experience turned out to be enjoyable with the group slipping out of their clothes and bathing in the river, then running around without clothing until either taking care of the animals or when the grey evening arrived with the mosquito swarms. The sheer freedom was something none of them had ever experienced before, and even Kissa joined them in their nakedness before leaving the area.

"We ain't gettin' nowhere. I bet we ain't traveled two hundred miles in three weeks." Tawnie dropped beside Nikki, the scowl turning her granite face callous. She glared at Kissa's form cuddled in a fetal position close to the fire, her body twitching in a discordant rhythm. "We've gotta do sumthang about her, ya know. She'll end up bein' the death of us yet."

Nikki sighed. "I know, but we have to make allowances for her. We cannot take her back and we cannot leave her here. We are stuck with her."

"We've gotta be the strangest group of avengers in the world. Four women, one who can't even wipe without gettin' into trouble, a mute six-year-old, and a half-grown puppy." Tawnie rubbed her chin, then fixed Nikki with a hard glare. "If'n ya pick up any more strays, count me gone."

Nikki laughed in self-defense, fully aware Tawnie was serious. "Keep your temper under control and I will promise not to pick up anymore strays."

"Ah, heck, ya know just where to hit a person where it hurts most. Guess we're even. I cain't no more control my temper than you can control takin' in strays." The aggravated lines of her face easing, Tawnie guffawed.

AFTER THREE DAYS, THEY WERE BACK on the trail with the heat bearing down on them in shimmering waves, distorting distance and landmarks. Perspiration and dust stuck to their exposed skin and clothing with irritating persistence. Nikki kept them riding, hoping to form some semblance of normalcy. The new peace short-lived, Nikki set a necessarily slow pace. Ginger's fair skin turned red with the heat, Kissa was almost constantly in tears, complaining loudly about the discomforts, and Tawnie's hard-bitten replies made matters worse.

LeeAnn now rode her own mare for most of the day and the growing puppy ran a longer distance each day to stay up with them where before they all shared letting LeeAnn ride behind them or hold the puppy in front on their saddle when they were too tired to follow.

Reaching Fort McPherson, Nikki asked around until she obtained information regarding the Mason gang: when they left and the direction they traveled. Afterwards, she kept the group riding hard, even refusing to take time to enjoy a pleasant lunch, her main concern for the animals, praying the horses could last a little longer before resting.

Toward the third evening, the wind increased until it battered them with stinging dirt. Nikki ordered them to wet their neckerchiefs with canteen water and tie them around their mouths. Grey clouds scudded overhead and blocked out what little light there had been. Lightning splattered the murkiness and danced on the ground, then jagged across the skies like wicked pitchforks. Within seconds, arid smoke drifted toward them on the strong wind.

Nikki halted the group.

"We can't stay out in the open," Ginger shouted. "Remember the last lightning storm back home? It went right through the new ranch hand and the horse, killing them deader than a doornail."

"There should be an abandoned fort close by. Follow me and stay out of high places," Nikki shouted back.

Uneasily, the group followed Nikki through the blasting wind which tore at their hats and clothing. Dirt particles stung unprotected areas of their faces and hands, bringing tears to their eyes while dust clogged their nostrils through the drying neckerchiefs. Plodding along in the near darkness, their eyes straining against the gloom to avoid pitfalls, they were conscious of hidden ground holes that could break a horse's leg, and it made the journey harder.

With lightning flashing across the vast prairie skies, Nikki gave a triumphant shout, pointing ahead. Two buildings stood close together, both in a dilapidated state of disrepair. One building sported a partially intact roof and the other, though roofless, was large enough to accommodate their animals.

The group unusually quiet while eating supper, Tawnie set aside her plate to hold a mug of hot coffee in wind-chapped hands. "Got any plans, Nikki?"

"Not yet. I will scout out the outlaw's hiding place tonight. They are so close; I can smell them. After I find them, I will come back for the rest of you. I should have a plan formed by then."

"Dang, I sure hope so. I'm ready for some action." Tawnie leaned against the weathered wall of the building and closed her eyes a moment, the uncompromising lines of her face showing her lassitude.

"And if you don't come back in three days?" Ginger asked, her voice soft in the fire's crackling noise.

Nikki glanced at each of them, fixing their tired faces in her mind. LeeAnn slept beside Kissa, *Heoohtato* at her feet. Kissa was strangely withdrawn after the poison ivy incident, Ginger withdrew back within herself, sitting alone and rubbing at her temples, and Tawnie cupped a steaming tin mug, her topaz eyes distant. "If I am not back within three days, head back to Rustic."

Tawnie threw the dregs of coffee toward the fire, her mouth narrowed. "Heck no! We'll go find ya."

Nikki calmly shook her head, a tired smile barely lifting her lips. "If I am not back in three days, I will be dead."

"Do ya think you're the only one who can lead us?" Tawnie belligerently threw the tin cup against the wall, the pinging sound of metal bouncing against the adobe wall accentuating the sudden tenseness.

"I did not say that, Tawnie. I was thinking about the rest of you."

LeeAnn awakened and sat up, her eyes widening with

fear and grabbing at the hand Nikki held out to her. When the child reached her, Nikki put an arm around her, soothing her with caresses on her blonde head, her mouth pursing with bitter fatigue at Tawnie's continued gladiatorial behavior.

"Welp, it dang sure sounded like ya were implyin' it." Her anger unabated, Tawnie grabbed the whip always close by her and let the loops straighten.

Planting a kiss on LeeAnn's forehead before easing her back down and drawing the light blanket over her shoulders, she glanced at Tawnie, a fatalistic demeanor drooping her shoulders. "I never asked to be the leader, Tawnie. If you want the job, you are welcome to it. I will gladly give up the responsibility of worrying where to find water, shelter, and information. If you know how to dodge unfriendly Indians and follow the trails of hiding outlaws, welcome to the job. And more importantly, welcome to the worry of keeping everyone together and safe."

Never taking her eyes off Nikki, Tawnie rolled up the whip and placed it back beside her. "Ah, heck! Benefits of bein' leader are too dang high for me."

Nodding slightly, Nikki accepted Tawnie's way of apologizing. "My main concern is you getting to safety. I never thought you could not carry on without me."

"We understand perfectly." Ginger stopped rubbing her temples to fix both Tawnie and Nikki with a calm look. "We'll do as you asked, but I'm warning you, dear friend, you better come back. You're the main reason we're here.

Ginger could have left the last unspoken; it already weighed heavily on her mind. Rising, Nikki glanced at each one before walking out the opening where a door had once hung. "I will be back."

Trepidation making her heartbeat faster, Nikki stood against the weathered wall. Violent winds blasted her, lifting the heavy braid and slapping it against her face and shoulder. Dust teared her eyes, blurring her vision. With a weary sigh, she left the insufficient shelter of the dilapidated building to walk across the prairie until she had an unimpeded view of the chained lightning displayed across the southwestern skies.

The wind whipped strands free from the long braid and she smoothed the hair from her face and mouth, holding it down so she could focus all her attention on the lightning storm in her desperate yearning to clear doubts from her mind. She was responsible for all of them, and if she led them into a gun battle and one of them got hurt or killed, she would never forgive herself. They were well aware of the risks involved, but it still did not make it right. It was her idea to go after the outlaws. She had almost forced Ginger and Kissa to go, and LeeAnn had no other choice.

She closed her eyes against the blowing dust, her need to punish the outlaws for their crimes against them undiminished. Opening her eyes, she lifted her hands heavenwards and prayed in a singsong voice, "*Heammawihio*, grant us strength, cunning, and courage to overcome our enemies. Help me to be a wise leader. Keep me true to myself. You are showing me your great power this night. Grant me just a little of your power so I may triumph over my enemies."

The wind blew the large, brown bear claw necklace against her shirt. She touched it for courage and strength before dropping her hands at her sides. Watching the lightning a few more moments, she turned and headed back into the building.

Riffling through her saddlebags, she took out a brush and two red strips of material, then sat on the ground Indian fashion. Unbraiding her hair, she brushed it before tying the red headband around her head and fixing the other piece of material into a cummerbund around her waist, the long ends hanging down her left side. Her eyes mirroring melancholy, she fastened her knife case and pistol holster into position.

Ginger watched Nikki load the pistol, leaving the first chamber unloaded. "I'll pack you enough supplies to last for three days."

"Thanks." Nikki left and headed for the roofless building sheltering their horses. Lifting the saddle by the horn, her muscles straining, she threw the saddle over the gelding's back, then cinched the straps underneath the belly. Turning when she heard footsteps behind her, she accepted the saddlebag and canteen from Ginger.

"Be careful."

A self-deprecating smile touched Nikki's lips. "I will be back." *I cannot die until all of those men are dead*, she added to herself, not needing the reminder.

The wind slackened, but still the ride through nearly pitch-black darkness was harrowing. In the brief flashes of lightning, she studied the land, then cleared all else from her mind to allow her sixth sense and the horse take over to guide them through the broken landscape.

After several hours in the saddle, she crested a hill and stared down into the valley below, recognizing the land. Shifting her weight, the saddle leather creaking, she stared down at an old Indian burial ground. Firelight flickered in shifting motions and the hum of voices obliterated by the howling wind, she discovered the outlaws were much closer than any of them realized.

Down below, Toad glanced up when a streak of lightning highlighted the skies, a frightened gasp escaping his throat. He rubbed his eyes and stared harder when another flash brightened the night. There it was again—a dark apparition astride a horse with thin black snakes for hair. He pointed at the spot. "Look yonder! A haunt!" But when lightning struck again, there was no entity there.

"The bastard's done gone loco on us," Mad Dog grunted, fingering his knife.

"Either that or someone really was up there. Mad Dog, go take a look." Jock eased the pistol out of his holster and cocked the hammer. "Get goin'."

THE WOMEN SURROUNDED THE OUTLAW CAMP by bellycrawling through the tall grass. Fear rose to choke Nikki and her hands trembled on her bow. She stopped and waited for Kissa, who breathed in loud gasps behind her, trying to catch up with her. Studying the camp, she nearly jumped out of her skin when one of the horses snorted close by her. Birds thrilled with the beginning of dawn, breaking the deathly silence. The fire had burned down to dull embers and the figures in the bedrolls lay motionless, too motionless for her peace of mind.

There was something not right about the camp, something amiss. The reality of no saddles, saddlebags or weapons impressing upon her mind, something suddenly flew up in front of them, the flapping noise nearly drowned out by Kissa's sharp cry. Pandemonium rang out and gunshots split the greying morning. Kissa screamed again and rose to her feet.

In seemingly slow motion, Nikki watched Jock Mason roll from behind a Spanish Sword plant, then come to a sitting position near them, his pistol aimed at Kissa. He was so close; Nikki saw the small scars across his left cheek where she had scratched him *that night.*

Nikki shouted a warning, did a quick roll toward Kissa, and knocked her to the ground a split second before a flash of smoke followed by a sharp boom shook the morning air.

Knocked from her feet, Kissa fell backwards over Nikki, her finger snapping on the trigger of the shotgun. The explosion scattered shot toward the sky and Kissa landed with a thud and a swoosh of air from her lungs. The shotgun knocked loose from her perspiring hand, skidded across the ground. She squeezed her eyes shut, fighting for breath while frightened little ear-piercing whines squawked out of her. Pulling her cumbersome legs from Nikki's back, she lay in a fetal position, her arms over her head and shaking so strongly her teeth rattled.

The fresh morning air awash with the acrid smell of gunpowder, rapid gunfire deafened them, and bullets kicked up dust, keeping them pinned to the ground. A creeping shudder tingling her spine, Nikki shifted on her elbows and drew the arrow back on the bow, glancing over her shoulder in time to spy Mad Dog duck behind the horses near her. She let loose the arrow about the same time she saw smoke erupt from his long barrel, six-shooter, the shot kicking up dirt beside her.

The arrow plowed into Mad Dog's shoulder. He let out a howl and grabbed at the shaft, breaking it off near the flesh. Lifting his gun, Mad Dog shot in her direction before jumping onto the back of a saddled horse.

Chapter 2
Justice or Revenge

NIKKI'S HEART BEAT A RAPID TATTOO against her chest. Both bullets missed her by a hair's breadth. The gunshots increased and when she next raised her head to squeeze off another shot, all she saw was the rising dust from departing horses.

She crawled toward Kissa who sobbed in near hysterical gasps. A quick glance did not show blood on her anywhere. "Are you hurt?"

"No matter what they have done to me, I cannot harm another human being!" Kissa sobbed, avoiding the question.

"Stay put while I find out what happened to the others. I will call you when the danger has passed." Nikki lithely rose to her feet, unable and unwilling to comfort Kissa this time. A bullet whizzed past her ear. "Tawnie! Ginger! For goodness' sake, stop shooting!"

"Is that you, Nikki?" Tawnie shouted.

"Yes, it is me!" Nikki yelled, stepping toward the dying fire and biting back the rest of the sentence she wanted to utter, annoyed by the stupid question. The outlaws had gotten away, and the only danger was from the nervous fingers of her companions. "Ginger! Where are you?"

Ginger appeared from behind a bush, her jade-green

eyes huge in her face. "I told you we'd be no match for men. They got away without a scratch."

Ginger shuddered and wiped her eyes. "Was anyone hurt?" Nikki shook her head, and Ginger breathed, "Thank God. I was afraid with all the bullets flying around us someone would be."

"It is a miracle we are still alive. Apparently, they were waiting for us." To prove her point, Nikki kicked at a bedroll. Prairie grass and dust puffed upward from the blanket.

Kissa joined them, and Tawnie turned on her, her booming voice sounding all the louder in the aftermath of gunshots. "Why in d' hell did ya squeal like a stuck pig? Ya nearly got us killed! Don' ya realize that?" She grabbed the frightened woman's shoulders and shook her. "Whut in the hell did ya think ya were doin'?"

"Don't, Tawnie! Please don't! I'm sorry," Kissa cried, her head wobbling back and forth with Tawnie's angry hands gripping her shoulders and still shaking her.

Tawnie shoved her, unconcerned the woman sprawled to the ground and lay with her arms over her head. "Whut happened, Kissa? Da' blasted it, whut happened to ya?"

Kissa sat up and held her hands in front of her, examining them as if she had never seen them before. "Some…something flew up in front of me and scared me."

"Hellfire and damnation, stupid! Better it scare ya than for ya to squeal and get us all killed." In disgust, Tawnie turned her back to Kissa. "I done told ya if she gets any of us killed it'll be on your head, Nikki. Do whut ya want. I'm goin' after the kid and the horses." Tawnie stalked off, her fist gripped tightly over the handle of the whip.

"I'm sorry, Nikki. I didn't mean to mess up. Truly I

didn't." Kissa shook with the weight of her cries.

Nikki wearily sighed, the bickering wearing on her frayed nerves. "You scared a prairie chicken which in turn probably saved our lives. It was your scream upsetting Tawnie. In another situation, it could of gotten us killed."

"You should of left me on the stagecoach. I can't do anything right! Just leave me here or shoot me, anything! If something happens to any of you because of me, I'll just die." Kissa cried all the harder.

Kissa's words struck a corresponding chord within Ginger, and it was she who knelt beside Kissa to offer comfort. "Don't be a silly goose. You're a part of our group and you are vital to our mission too. Besides, didn't you hear what Nikki said? They were waiting for us. You probably saved all our lives, regardless of what Tawnie thinks."

Nikki wiped at her red, aching eyes, the knot in her stomach growing and extending into a stomachache. Ginger gave Kissa a hand up and led her to the dying fire. With heads close together, the soft murmur of their voices mingled with the song of birds.

With a sigh, Nikki pulled the red headband from her forehead and shook the long length of her hair back from her face. The clamoring noise of Tawnie, LeeAnn, and the pack animals coming into camp, drew her attention to them.

"Dang it, is that brat still bawlin'?" Tawnie bellowed, letting the whip slide to the ground.

"Leave off, Tawnie. She's suffered enough." Ginger rose to her feet, her fist on her hips, her head tossed high. "None of us are perfect. In fact, we all fouled up. Or didn't you notice? For all our practicing and excellent shots, we couldn't hit the broad side of a barn."

"Heck, I never did figure out where all the bullets were comin' from." Tawnie frowned, then threw back her head and guffawed, her anger forgotten. "Ya know, you're right. Never even dawned on me! Shit fire and save the matches, we're a helluva group of avengers."

Ginger relaxed and laughed with Tawnie, her meadow green eyes sparkling with mischief. "All Dusty Joe's training didn't do a cotton pickin' good. I never did figure out why it was so important to learn how to fast draw."

"Coordination and spontaneity," Nikki softly replied.

"You always have the answers, don't you?" Ginger reflectively responded, then giggled. Settling on the ground, a brief flicker of jealousy sparked in her eyes. Rubbing her rough hands together, she exclaimed, "God, what I wouldn't give for a bath and smooth skin again."

"There's no time. Mount up before we lose their trail." Nikki turned toward the horses, but Tawnie's words stopped her.

"I ain't budgin' an inch till I've got sumthang in my belly." Tawnie plopped on the ground and waited for Kissa to take the cue and prepare breakfast.

Nikki ran her fingers through her hair, trying to ease some of the tangles free, then shrugged in resignation. "Have it your way."

Perhaps it would not have mattered one way or another, Nikki thought later, gazing out over the milling buffalo covering the plains. The outlaws had cut through the herd and there was no way they would be able to track them now. It seemed to be the outlaws' most common trick.

"What now?" Ginger asked, tying her neckerchief

around her mouth to keep out the pungent smell of buffalo and blowing dust.

"Head north to the Cheyenne."

SUMMER LEAVES WHISPERED AND DRIFTED toward the ground. Small animals scurried through the underbrush. Birds grew silent with man near its destination, and the wind bore the sounds of delightful giggles on invisible wings. The roan stallion nickered and received an answer.

Dane dismounted and led Renegade toward the sounds of splashing. Tying the stallion to a tree several yards away from the noise, he stealthily crept forward. The outlying trees and bushes hid him from the women playing in a nice sized pond a tributary had formed. Parting a bush, he stared at the scene before him like an invader in some mythical land watching water nymphs play in the pool of life.

Rising, he inched forward, then leaned back against a tree to enjoy the feast before his eyes. His stomach balled up into a hard knot and his groin ached while he inspected the perfection of womanly bodies before him. Nikki stood, her long, black hair floating on top of the water. Sparkling moisture clung to the rich bronze skin and displayed her slenderness of form, tiny waist, and gently rounded hips. Firm high breasts with hardened nipples peeked out between strands of hair.

Kissa shoved Nikki backwards, and Nikki landed with a splash, her long slender, well-shaped legs appearing above the surface of the water.

Kissa laughed and cupped her hands, squirting water toward Nikki when she surfaced. Nikki headed toward her, and Kissa ducked under water, her delighted giggles cut off in mid-sound. She surfaced, bobbing on top, her short curly wet locks a darkened blonde, and her full roundness shining in the sun. Full, bouncy breasts, also with hardened nipples, curved into a small waist, a rounded stomach, golden triangle, and plump, softly rounded legs, set off by shell pink complexion.

Ginger dove into the water and pulled Kissa's legs out from under her, then bobbed back to the surface in a jump, her strawberry-red hair darkened and weighed down with water, flowing to her waist. It emphasized the extreme tininess of her waistline and full, sensuous hips. High, firm breasts with hardened rose-colored nubs, enough a man could get a nice, overflowing handful, bobbed with her jump. Her legs were perfection, unlike the firm muscle tone of Nikki's, the extreme muscular depth of Tawnie's, and the soft roundness of Kissa's. Her pouting rosebud lips pursed in a hearty laugh and jade green eyes sparkled with mischievousness in an alabaster face.

Tawnie pushed Ginger from behind, then threw back her head and boomed with laughter while Ginger fought back to the surface, gasping. Tawnie picked up a squirming LeeAnn playing nearby and tossed her in the air.

LeeAnn landed in the water, sending sprays of moisture over the rest of them. She emerged sputtering, her eyes rounded with laughter. The half-grown puppy dogpaddling in the pool, barked excitedly, and the child splashed with the uninhibitedness and carefreeness of childish delight.

Tawnie was a golden girl or one of the fabled Amazon warrior women he had once read about. Everything about her was golden, from the mid-back length hair, tawny eyes, and the rich golden tone of her skin. Her womanly parts were over defined, from the wide shoulders, big, firm breasts with dark golden brown and hardened nipples curving into a womanly waistline and rounded hips. Glistening drops of water set off the overdeveloped muscles in shoulders, arms, legs, and buttocks, and her golden triangle was big and bushy compared to Ginger's lightly furred one.

A smile curling his lips, Dane acknowledged he had stumbled into paradise. His pants suddenly growing too tight, he shifted uneasily to ease the ache in his groin and to loosen the pants around his crotch. He watched them for quite a while in their joyful play; the bobbing breasts, the wiggle of hips, and the teasing glimpses of womanhood awakening a bestial mating call within him.

A creeping sensation sweeping through Nikki, she went stock-still, her sky-blue eyes pulled toward the figure slouched against the tree with his brown Stetson pulled low over his face, his hips thrust forward, and drawing her attention to the bulge in the front of his pants.

Soon, all their attention was focused on him. Kissa and Ginger ducked under the water, their heads the only thing showing. Tawnie stepped behind Nikki to cover most of her nakedness, and Nikki stood with her legs slightly apart and crossed her arms underneath her breasts. The mounds swelled over her arms and the dusky rose nipples played peek-a-boo over her forearms. She, above all the others, was not ashamed of her nudity and stood like a naked goddess, her face set in an emotionless mask and her light blue eyes startling in her dark tanned face. The gold locket caught a stream of sunlight and reflected back to him.

"Enjoying yourself, Marshal?" Nikki sarcastically asked.

Dane pushed himself from the tree and tipped his hat back with a forefinger. "Very much. And are you enjoying the water?"

"It is a pleasant interlude, Marshal," Nikki taunted. "Look your fill, then be on your way. We have no business with you." The water lapped around her thighs and the breeze pricked gooseflesh on her body while her lips tightened, and her eyes narrowed when he did not move. "Are you finished?"

"With the delectable flesh of goddesses? A man can never look his fill."

His voice was silky and too warm, conveying his desire in a low voice that carried over the rippling water and sending shivers of longing down her spine. Nikki uncrossed her arms and Dane watched, delighted with the bounce of her breasts. "Go away, Marshal."

"Ah, my dark angel, I do have business with you." He moved forward, pulled toward her by some invisible force. She held out a slender hand to stop his advance and shook her head, the wet strands of hair clinging, then sweeping free from her drying skin.

"I did not invite you in for a swim, Marshal." Her stance taut as a bowstring, she vibrated with the stretch of nerves. "I will discuss business with you only if you have the decency to allow us to dress in private."

Sweeping off his hat, he brought it toward his chest in a courtly gesture, then mockingly bowed. "Your every wish is my command, all except this one. I know you women too well, my dear. You'd have a gun in my back before I knew what was happening."

Her mouth compressing in distaste, Nikki shifted to the other leg, unaware of the provocative tilt of her hip. "You are a low-down mangy dog, Marshal. None of us will budge from this cold water until you leave. So, if I promise we will not threaten you with weapons, will you get out of here?"

He filled his eyes with her again, noticing the shiver running through her body. Turning sharply away from her, another image of her bruised flesh interfered with the present. "Then dress. I'll wait at your camp where I'm sure you can't leave without my knowledge."

Wondering at his quick turnabout, she watched him stalk off toward their camp. The other women made a quick scramble for their washed clothes hung out on the bushes. Nikki stood immovable as a statue; her forehead wrinkled with confusion.

The other women followed him back to camp, untrusting of the Marshal, but Nikki took time to soak her body with glycerin before dressing. Heading back toward camp, she pulled a brush through the tangled strands of wet hair, reaching the camp in time to hear Tawnie get in her two bits worth.

"Ya darn slimy worm, ya ever pull that stunt again, I'll geld ya like a horse. In fact, that's what I oughta do now."

"When you think you're man enough to try, ma'am, then come on," Dane answered, a glint of amusement gleaming in his eyes.

"Why ya son o' a whore, I'll…"

"I'll handle this, Tawnie," Nikki interceded when Tawnie raised her fist.

Tawnie hooked her thumbs under her wet pants' waistband, her hands balling into fists. Walking off, she grumbled, "The slimy worm oughta be taugh' some manners."

"Marshal, it is unwise to make an enemy of Tawnie. She has developed a powerful hatred for men and would geld you without a shred of remorse. She has already formed a strong distaste for you for some strange reason. She liked you at first." Nikki frowned slightly when he shifted his eyes from hers and his face tightened under her steady look. "Well, do we stand here offering banalities or do we get down to business?"

Dane glanced around the camp, tension showing in the women's movements and furtive glances. Tawnie watched him under lidded lashes, Ginger nervously searched through packs, glancing at him every now and then, and Kissa, red rushing across her face, sat on a fallen log pressing the frightened child against her bosom. The pied-colored dog sat at their feet, its eyes watching his every move.

He pulled the hat lower over his eyes, his chin lifting with determination. Taking Nikki by the arm, he led her toward a thick strand of trees. "You're a hard bunch to find. You nearly had me fooled. I guess you're the one who told your landlord you'd be heading to your tribe's summer camp."

"Too bad it did not work, Marshal," Nikki scorned, then shrugged. "It was worth a try. Now, what do you want?"

Perspiration popping above her upper lip and her insides shaky, she knew why he was here. She could feel his anger. Refusing to show fear, she unwillingly let him lead her away from the others. Stopping, she focused on him and blandly met his searching gaze. "Well?"

"Washburn was shot outside of Rustic soon after the trial."

"So?" she asked coldly. "Why should I care?"

Dane grabbed her forearms, pulling her nearer and holding her eyes with his. "Did you or any of your friends do it?" Frustrated with her limp indifference, his fingers bit into the tender flesh of her arms and he gently shook her.

Her head swung back and forth on a slender neck and the wet length of her hair slapped stingingly against her arm. Closing her eyes, she swallowed hard. His shaking made her nauseated, but she refused to answer him until his anger passed and he released his hold on her.

He stopped but did not release her. "Open your eyes, Nikki, and answer me!" Her eyes fluttered open, those extraordinary baby blues emphasized by the thick black lashes. A small pink tongue snuck between her lips to moisten them.

She sighed. "What difference would it make, Dane?"

Staring at her, he wanted to slap some sense into her stubborn head and kiss her at the same time. He had to stop her before it was too late! She had warned him if the court didn't do its duty, she would go after those men. Didn't she realize he was protecting her? Releasing her, he stepped back, lowered his face until it was on level with hers, and glared into her eyes, his voice low and cynical. "If you or one of your friends put a bullet in his heart, you have put yourself on the same level as he."

Nikki brought her arm forward and the flat of her palm connected with the side of his face, the sound reverberating through the sighing trees. Her palm stung from the contact, and she balled it into a fist, then anchored it to her hip. "Do not ever put us in the same category as those murdering animals," she warned.

His face jerked in the direction of the slap, and he straightened suddenly, his eyes widening in surprise and pain. Her handprint was white against the tan of his face, then turned a glaring red. He put his hand to his cheek, his eyes piercing her with their silver-blue intensity.

"Revenge is a nasty thing, Nikki, and in my books, it's the same as murder." They faced off like adversaries, their one night of love forgotten.

"If I were a man and went gunning for those murdering beasts, you would call it justice. But since I am a woman, is that revenge?" Nikki turned her back to him. He breathed heavily behind her, fighting to control his own anger. Taking a deep shuddering breath, she spun around on her heel. "Justice and revenge, Dane? Are they not on the same side of a coin? What is it your white man's Bible says? An eye for an eye. A tooth for a tooth?"

"Damnit, Nikki! We don't live in Old Testament days!" He watched confusion cross her face at his reference and amended, "I've told you before, let the law handle this. I brought in two dead members of the Mason gang before coming to find you. Besides, Judge Story has just about pulled his last stunt and flouted the law once too often. He'll be replaced and another judge will give you justice."

"Justice," she derisively snorted. "Tell me, Dane, what will happen to them if a good judge does sentence them properly?"

"Hang 'em," he answered promptly, taking off his hat and wiping his brow with the back of his arm.

"And how long will it take to get a fair judge?"

He shrugged; helpless he could offer no more.

"No, Dane," she harshly mocked. "How many more deaths will it take before you catch them, and they get hanged? Answer me, Dane. How many more people must die? How many more children must die, their little bodies torn to pieces by an animal, a mad dog?"

She grabbed a small tree branch above her head and pulled on it until it broke. Wrenching it in her hands, she plunged ahead, "Wake up, Marshal. Justice may never come and until then we will be spinning our wheels for nothing. Put yourself in our position. We were assaulted. I watched my brother cold-bloodedly shot down. And did I tell you those outlaws killed my father over some coins?"

Not waiting for him to answer, she finished her tirade, "I saw my mother commit suicide instead of suffering the violation of her body. And…" Her voice caught painfully in her throat. "And watched a monster force himself into my sister's little body. I could not help or save her like I always promised to!"

She bit her lower lip, her body shuddering with the memory. Forcing the picture of her sister's torn body from her mind, she said more quietly, "Ginger watched her husband killed and lost her baby the same day. Kissa was to marry the next month, but her fiancé broke the engagement—said he could not marry a stained woman. And Tawnie? It was a powerful blow to her pride and sanity. It took three outlaws to hold her down. We were laughed at, mocked, ridiculed, and said we were the blame for the violations committed against us. Women shun us on the streets and men spout horrible obscenities at us. Where does it end?" She shook her head, the pain too fresh to discuss rationally.

"Enough, Nikki," Dane ordered, but his demand went unheeded.

"Kissa's sister Kallie and Tawnie both got with child that night. Instead of bearing an animal's baby, Tawnie self-aborted and nearly bled to death. Ginger's father hated and despised her after all this. He called her foul names no woman should hear, especially from a father, and Kissa's family could not bear the shame. Her father was sending her and her sister away."

She fully met his eyes, searching the silver-blue depths and the embarrassed shame filling his face. "Oh, there's more that happened, Marshal. You tell me how we can live a normal life again. Tell me where it all ends."

Her deep-seated pain reached out to him, touching him with its despair, hatred, anger, and frustration. He replaced the hat on his head and rubbed the back of his neck, his head throbbing and pounding against his temples. Lord, help him! He did not know what to say, but he could not let her take the law into her own hands and end up getting killed. No, now was the time to end this charade before it went any further. He sighed heavily. "Did any of you kill Washburn?"

She rocked back on her heels and laughed, the sound a low, hurt-ridden chortle. "You do not give up, do you, Marshal?" Shaking the hair from her face, she turned her eyes away from his too piercing ones. "If you have to ask, then you have no clue who killed him, do you?" She met his gaze blandly, hiding her emotions behind a sneering mask. "Find your own answers. I will not make it easy for you."

His gaze locked on the thin line of her mouth; he pulled

her unresisting body toward him. He wanted to kiss her, but he was not yet able to clear the pictures she so vividly painted again from his mind and instead warned her, "Don't go after the Mason outfit, Nikki. The men in the Mason gang are so wicked even Quantrill's Raiders threw them out after one raid. Not only is Jock Mason the worst of the worst, but the one called Mad Dog is beyond evil. He believes nothing is sacred and would shoot a baby as well as sexually violate one. Let me handle them."

He realized his stern warning was not getting through her stubborn head and finished, "If you kill any of them, you better keep looking over your shoulder because I'll be right behind to stop you."

He released her so suddenly, she stumbled. "Remember what I said, Dark Angel. I'll follow you like a shadow, and if I have proof you killed any of them, I will bring you in to stand trial for murder."

"How so, Marshal? The Mason gang is wanted for murder and the wanted posters say dead or alive. We have as much right as anyone else to bring them in," Nikki taunted.

"I'm warning you again, don't do it, Nikki, if you value your friends' lives." In a sudden, impulsive gesture, he slammed her body hard against his and took her lips with his in a bruising, punishing kiss, then shoved her from him and stalked off in the direction of his tethered horse.

She stood motionless, watching him walk away and how his buttocks moved under his tight pants, then listened to the sound of retreating hooves, her lips burning from his kiss, her heart resembling a shattered piece of pottery.

THE DAY WAS GREY, THE SKIES BURSTING with rain so heavy, visibility beyond twenty feet was impossible. Barton, the proprietor of the stagecoach section of the combination bar, watched five riders trudge into the stagecoach station, their hats pulled low over their faces and long slickers shedding off the sheets of rain. A half-grown pit bull terrier stopped wearily beside the horses.

The men led their animals into the barn, and it was almost thirty minutes before they stepped through the station door. Their entry was almost silent compared to the stomping fanfare of the rough men frequenting the place. The lanky, awkward dog slunk inside, shook the rain from its coat, and headed straight for the warmth of the fire.

"Ain't it a mess out there? It could rain all day or stop in a few minutes. Cain't ever tell in these here parts. Even if it did stop soon, within fifteen minutes the ground will be dry as a bone." Wiping his hands on the towel hanging on his belt, Barton stepped forward and motioned toward the long wooden table near the burning fireplace. "Take yore slickers and hats off, boys, and sit yoreself here near the fire." A furrow lined his brow when the boys drew their hats lower over their eyes and pulled out benches to sit down. "What can I git ya?"

The tallest of the group answered for them. "Coffee and some milk."

Barton scratched at his balding head. "Ain't got no milk. How 'bout some sarsaparilla for the kid."

The tall boy looked at the child, then at the short boy

whose curly blonde hair showed around his face. "Make it two."

Pouring the sarsaparilla, Barton talked, not put off by their noncommunication. He had met all kinds in this business. "Yep, a real dreary day. Needed the rain though. It's been dry enough around here for a word to start a prairie fire."

Serving the sarsaparilla first, he then placed tin coffee mugs in front of the other three boys. He snatched the towel from around his waist to lift the coffeepot from a hook near the fire and poured the steaming liquid. With a nod toward the other end of the long room, he warned, "Dem boys over there are a rough crowd. It be best for ya'll to stay away from 'em."

"We didn't come lookin' for trouble, mister. Just a place to get outta the rain and warm up a bit," the tallest one stated.

"Didna figure you were, boy. You seem like nice enough kids, though for the life of me, I cain't figure out what yore doin' in these here parts. I jist wanted to let ya fellers know there's always trouble with that bunch over there."

"Maybe you can give us some information…"

"Let me give ya'll a word of advice, boys. Around here you don't know nothin' and you don't see nothin'."

Chapter 3
Lawless Abode

BARTON REMAINED STANDING AT THE TABLE, staring at the boy, a puzzled frown wrinkling his brow and balding head. Again, the boys drew their hats lower over their eyes and pulled their slickers tighter around their bodies.

"Need sumthang'?"

Barton shook his head. "No, no. You boys holler if ya need sumthin' else." He stood there a moment more, something nagging at his slow brain. "Got some stew cookin' over d' fire and got beds if'n ya'll need a place to sleep tonight."

The tall boy scooted back and walked over to the black kettle bubbling over the fire. Bending down, he sniffed at the stew and wrinkled his nose. "Ya call that food? Smells like a da' blame skunk." Straightening, he turned to the proprietor. "Beds got bugs?"

"Bugs?" Barton asked, stunned.

"Yeah. When's the last time ya cleaned the beddin'?"

"Damned particular, ain't ya, fellow?"

The boy shrugged. "When's the next stagecoach due?"

"Not for another week." Barton poured them another cup of coffee. After replacing the pot, he went back behind the bar at the other end of the room, still scratching his head in puzzlement.

Tawnie sat on the bench and cocked an eyebrow toward Barton. "Dang nosey feller."

"It will probably attract less attention if we act like boys while we wait for the rain to slacken, then we best get out of here." Nikki added a few grains of precious sugar the proprietor allowed them to the black liquid and absentmindedly stirred it while she cautiously snuck glances at the noisy men standing around the bar.

The other end of the room sported a long unfinished plank of wood propped up on beer kegs, serving as a bar. Armed, rowdy, and rough characters stood at the makeshift bar and drank from dirty appearing glasses. A poker game was in progress at one of the crude tables. At another table within the dark, shadowed section of the bar, a man with his hat setting low over his face and his feet propped up on the table, lounged against the wall. There was something vaguely familiar about him. Shrugging, Nikki brushed the feeling away. LeeAnn trembled beside her. Nikki took her hand and squeezed it. "Easy, little one. Be brave."

"Brave?" Kissa whispered, her voice catching in her throat. "I'm shaking too."

"It feels like trouble here." Ginger glanced nervously around the long room and spotted a lanky man of medium height, heading in their direction. "Trouble," she whispered again.

"Let us get back on the road. The rain will be safer." Nikki drained her coffee, then snapped the tin cup down smartly when the man stooped at the end of the table close by her elbow.

"Well, now. What've we got here? You boys look to be

a fer piece from home." He squatted down until he was on level with their hats, his colorless eyes searching the shadowed faces.

Tawnie placed the cup carefully on the table, shifted her flat-topped hat lower over her eyes, and scooted the bench slightly back. "We ain't looking for trouble, mister."

"Name's Bodine, son." He grabbed her wrist, holding her rooted to the bench. "Ain't no need to git in a hurry. It's still pourin' out there."

His crooked grin revealed rotted teeth and the stench of his breath nearly gagged her. "Lookin' for a group to join up with? Several of the different outfits got a boy or two here."

Tawnie barely shook her head, her mouth a white slash underneath the hat, recognizing the outlaw. She would never forget his dark brown hair and beady eyes, and thin lips with his crooked smile. Her hand dropping to her waist, she lowered it on top of her pistol. "We ain't got time to mess around with ya, Bodine."

"Perky son of a bitch, ain't ya?" Laughing, Bodine straightened to his full height and turned toward the boy sitting across from Tawnie. "Take your hat off and stay awhile, boy."

Before any of them could guess his intention, he snatched her hat, watching in amazement when her long black braid tumbled down her back and her eyes widened in alarm. Aiming to tease them, he stared with astonishment at the delicate oval face and the unforgettable light blue eyes. "Well, I'll be damn! I know ya!"

"Unless you want to be made into a gelding, you'll

back off and pretend you never saw us." Underneath the table, Ginger eased her slicker aside to reveal a pearl-handled pistol aimed at his groin.

The sharp click of the hammer being brought back erased the pleased astonishment from his face when the taller boy eased his pistol out of his holster and pointed it at him from across the table. Bodine's beady eyes narrowed in anger and a cruel smile barely lifted his thin lips. "Think so, ladies? I doubt if ya could hit a wagon at ten paces."

Ginger pushed the hat back from her eyes, her smile matching his. "I wouldn't bet on it if I were you, mister."

"I would. Care to prove it?"

Reading a challenge in his colorless eyes, Nikki shook her head. "We do not have time to mince words. Just ease back, then very slowly move away from us."

Closely watching the man's eyes, Nikki drew her pistol and cursed herself for suggesting they stop in here to get out of the rain. She never guessed it was a stopover for the lawless.

The room went silent except for the rain pounding on the roof. The other men moved closer to surround them, their faces an array of lust, curiosity, and aversion. Terrified by the advancing men, LeeAnn slipped her hand from Nikki's grasp and slid underneath the table. She huddled there with her arms around her drawn legs, making herself small as humanly possible, and buried her face against her knees.

Bodine ignored the growling echoing throughout the room. Turning slowly, he spun around so swiftly the women's reflexes were frozen and knocked the pistol from Nikki's hand. The growling abruptly stopped and

Heoohtato leaped toward him, his teeth bared.

Bodine screamed; the dog's powerful jaw snapped over the calf of his leg. Kicking at the dog, he freed his pistol hand and threw Nikki from him, who had grabbed his arm during the shuffle. With the pistol aimed at the animal attached to his leg, he squeezed the trigger. His arm was knocked upward, and his shot went wild, careening into the rafters. A shower of loose sod fell over them. He sent the person who had knocked his shot wild toward the table and with a muttered oath of pain and anger, turned his pistol toward her.

Nikki slammed against the heavy table, the edge of it sending piercing pain through her lower back and knocking the breath from her lungs. Death stared her in the face and her heart beat a wicked cadence. Her eyes went wide, and the color drained from her face, waiting for Bodine to shoot.

She jumped with the deafening explosion and experiencing no pain, looked up into the surprised eyes of Bodine. He slowly crumbled at her feet, and *Heoohtato* released his hold on Bodine's calf just before the man fell to the floor. Mingled with the crowd gathering around them stood Dane, a smoking .45 Peacemaker in his hand.

"All right, gentlemen, the fun's over." Dane motioned the men away from the table, the groves around his mouth deepening into compressed hard lines.

Ginger stared at the pistol in her hand, a derisive smile tightening her mouth. Everything happened so quickly, she forgot the weapon clutched in her hand until Dane's blessed interference. Tipping her hat back with the barrel, she stepped from the table and turned toward the men lined along one wall.

Ginger aimed the pistol in their general direction, barely glancing around when Tawnie slipped beside her holding her own pistol. "Now, gentlemen, very carefully ease your weapons out and lay them on the floor, then kick them over here. Easy now, I've a nervous finger."

Moving to stand with the women, Dane kept his eyes on the men, his granite jaw hard with suppressed fury. The women interfered with his arrest of Two Thumbs and Bodine who had entered the station just minutes ahead of them. "Ladies, get the horses saddled."

"Me and Kissa will get the horses. Guess we oughta saddle the marshal's, too. Stupid worm," Tawnie muttered under her breath.

Nikki took the pistol Tawnie handed her, shock freezing her throat. *Where had Dane come from?* She glanced at the men, then at the shadowy table at the back corner of the room. No one was there. *How could I have been so blind?* she thought, stepping closer to him. "That makes twice I owe you my life. Do not think I am grateful either, Marshal."

"I'd be a fool to think you'd be grateful for anything, Dark Angel, but one of these days I'm going to call in your due." He suppressed a grin when her mouth narrowed.

"You can call it in, Marshal, but do not count on repayment." Nikki tried to ignore the strong jut of his square chin with the clef in the center, the intense silver-blue eyes, and the way he stood alert and strong. Perhaps she had thought of him as rather weak, but the deadly calm surrounding him, and the dangerous glint of his eyes demonstrated a man she had never seen before.

"Take their weapons and throw them out in the rain."

Two Thumbs protested, but Dane quickly silenced him

by pointing the pistol in his direction. "Another time, Two Thumbs. You and I will have our little confrontation, but right now, I'm not going to have you gentlemen following us. And don't think just because these are women, they don't know how to use weapons. I can guarantee you *they are* crack shots."

"Such crack shots yore ruining our weapons?" Two Thumbs sneered, clenching his fingers, the stubs where his thumbs had once been not keeping him from being a deadly shot. He surveyed the women, a tight smile cracking his mouth when recognizing them.

Dane laughed, the sound without humor. "I'm just making damn sure no one else gets killed. In fact, protecting you."

The last emphasis on *protecting you* was not lost on Two Thumbs, a member of the Mason's gang who attacked the Pride farm. "Give me a break, whoever in the hell you are. Yore makin' 'em sound mean, and I knowed better." He eyed the pistol in Dane's hand and decided the man was too alert to make a dive for his weapon on the floor near him.

"Not mean, *yet*, just damned determined."

Nikki reclaimed her own weapon that had been knocked from her hand and replaced it in the gun holster at her side, then placed Tawnie's pistol she handed her, into the waistband of her pants before she and Ginger quickly gathered the weapons and dropped them into a puddle of water in the muddiest area along the side of the stagecoach station road.

"I guess we've impressed the marshal in spite of himself," Ginger mumbled, walking back inside.

When Dane heard the horses at the front of the

building, he nodded toward the door. "Nikki, you and Ginger get out of here."

"You are going to hold them off by yourself?"

"Get out! Now!"

Gritting her teeth, Nikki wanted to refuse his order. With a furious sigh, she pulled the bench from the table, grabbed LeeAnn, and held her tight against her leg as she and Ginger left the building with *Heoohtato* following close behind. Placing the trembling child in front of her on the saddle, she said close to the child's ear, "You are safe here with me, *Meeskevotse*."

Dane followed the women after a few minutes and slapped Nikki's mount on the rear. "Ha ya! Get going!"

TIGHT CONTROL SHOWING IN HIS JERKY motions, Dane unsaddled his stallion. Throwing the saddle on the drying ground, he turned toward the women and glared at them. "What did you girls think you were doing?"

"Doing?" Ginger rigidly drawled with his slurred emphasis upon *girls*. She turned to face the hard-jawed marshal, her slender white hands tightening on the bundle she had just taken from one of the pack animals. "It was perfectly clear what we were doing, Marshal."

"Yes, perfectly clear you were trying to get yourselves killed." His fingers tapping an angry cadence against his hips, his hard eyes pierced each woman in turn.

An angry red flush colored Ginger's face. Kissa and LeeAnn froze in their tracks, their huge, frightened eyes fixed on him. Tawnie grinned at him with contempt, and Nikki slowly straightened before turning toward him, her expression unreadable.

Ginger walked forward a few steps and deposited the bundle in the center of camp, then straightened, her shoulders defensively arching. "When they discovered we were women, Marshal," she explained, adding extra emphasis on *women*, "they had one thing in mind, and it was better to die than to suffer through another assault."

Her announcement startled Dane, but he quickly covered it. "It was better for you all to die, Miss Starr? Even the child?"

The ridicule in his voice grated on their sensitive nerves. "You shouldn't of been there in the first place."

"We didn't know it was that type of place, Marshal," Kissa softly assured him, her huge eyes shining with unshed tears. "We just wanted a place to get out of the rain." She suddenly sneezed, then sniffed.

The grooves lining his mouth deepened and an erratic tic beat in his jaw. "You've no business in this part of the country. You should be at home where you belong."

"What home, Marshal?" Nikki furiously shook back her hair. "We owe you no explanation or anyone else for that matter."

"Like hell you don't!" Dane nearly shouted at them, his head, chest, and shoulders popping forward to tower over them. "When I have to save some foolish women's necks because they try playing games with dangerous characters, you made it my business. For all the trouble you've caused, I've got to start all over again."

"I'm sorry," Kissa cried, tears streaming down her apple-red cheeks. "We didn't mean to cause you any trouble."

"Shut up, Kissa, and quit your blasted crying!" Nikki

shouted, her eyes blazing. She turned toward the marshal and crossed her arms protectively in front of her. "We did not ask for your help, Marshal. We would have done fine without it."

In two long strides, Dane bent forward over her. "Yeah, Nikki? You could not have gotten out without my help. They'd be burying you right now if it hadn't been for me."

She glared at him for a few seconds, then shifted her eyes away, turning her back on him. He was right and it tore at her gut, but she would not admit it.

Dane swept the women with one disdainful glance. "Let's see how useful you are and if you can set up camp without my help. I'm going to keep watch, so someone relieve me after you've got something fixed to eat." With one more contemptuous glance at the group, he spun on his heel and left.

Nikki unholstered her pistol and checked the chamber, watching him leave. Snapping the chamber back in place, she regarded her friends, before leaving in the opposite direction of Dane ordering, "Do as he said."

"Why is she so angry with me?" Her face crestfallen, Kissa stared after Nikki.

"She's not angry with you. She's angry with the marshal." A sudden revelation striking Ginger, her brows furrowed and her mouth compressed into thought.

"But she shouted at me. In all the years I've known her, I've never heard her raise her voice at anyone, especially me."

Ginger nodded in agreement. "The marshal does seem to raise her ire. I don't believe I've ever seen them together when she didn't get angry." She rubbed her chin, shaking her head at the disturbing thoughts running through her mind. "Surely it can't be."

"What?" Kissa stared at her, confusion crossing her face.

"They're in love."

"Love? Nikki in love with the marshal?" Kissa shook her head, her growing curls bobbing around her head. "No, that's silly. Love's supposed to be tranquil, affectionate. From the way they act together, I'd say it is more like hate."

"Is love tranquil?" Ginger asked thoughtfully. "No, it's the only explanation. Perhaps they don't even realize it themselves, but let's face it, Nikki is a totally different person around him. He touches her in ways nothing else does."

She shook her head again, everything about those two disturbing her. "Think about it a moment, Kissa. The marshal's like a stick of dynamite and Nikki's like the cap. Together they become explosive."

Ginger smiled slightly at Kissa's incomprehension. "Dynamite isn't an explosive without the cap and isn't dangerous, but once you've placed the cap on it and light the wick, POW!"

"What a horrible comparison!"

Ginger dramatically shrugged. "But truth and that's the way they are. Alone they're sane, intelligent people, but put them together and a tiny spark sets them off like fireworks."

Ginger tapped Kissa on the shoulder. "Let's get things unpacked and a fire going before they get back. Lord, I'd hate another explosion between those two. Besides, we don't want the marshal to think we're insufficient."

Fury nearly blinding her, Nikki stomped along the

prairie. *Who does he think he is giving us orders? Why will he not just stay out of my life? I do not need him or want him!* Her stomach did a strange twist, remembering all times he had played upon her mind and haunted her dreams, knowing she was drawn to him like a moth to the flame. Furious, she shook the straggling strands of hair from her face. "I will not let you get the better of me, Marshal. I will show you we can handle ourselves just fine without you."

DANE STEPPED TOWARD THE FIRE, HIS EYES aching from studying the land. He really did not think the outlaws would follow them, but he would not risk these women's lives by not posting a guard. Too many good men died from carelessness, and he was not going to let it happen to them.

Kissa met him with a variable feast. The cooking pheasant had teased his senses for seemingly hours. He accepted the plate of roasted pheasant, beans, biscuits, and a mixture of roots and wild onions. "Smells mighty good, ma'am."

"Have a seat and I'll get you some coffee." Kissa smiled at him. Humming, she turned to pour him a cup of coffee.

He sat near the fire, the tight groves around his mouth relaxing. Impressed in spite of himself, the women had the camp well laid out and had prepared a meal with quality and variety. Nikki sat near LeeAnn, ignoring him, her voice musical and soothing while urging the child to eat. Her eyes seeming to come alive, Nikki nodded and spoke to LeeAnn in mime. He sighed softly at the protective, motherly quality she had with the child and how the child responded to her, then his mouth tightened.

The night had a different chill to it, and Dane's eyes on Nikki made her even more uncomfortable. She pulled the blanket tighter around LeeAnn's shoulders, for the heavy rain put a bite into the night air. Trying to ignore him, she rose and kept busy cleaning and putting away the cooking utensils. After she was done, she prepared a bed for LeeAnn and bundled her up against the cold.

Kissa was more relaxed and calmer than she had been in months. She buzzed around Dane like a bee to honey—there with something before he could ask.

It irritated Nikki. For some strange reason, she wanted to shout at her to leave him alone, to get away from him. She folded her lips over tightly and hummed LeeAnn asleep, her soft, husky voice a sweet sound in the night air.

The meal had mellowed Dane somewhat, and though his mouth tightened with ire when Ginger left her post to get a cup of coffee, he did not say anything. Mentally shrugging, he decided if the outlaws at Barton's Corner had not come by this time, they probably would not. "How did you become friends?"

All of them looked at Nikki, but when she did not answer, Ginger nervously laughed while Tawnie spoke for them. "Ah heck, Nikki showed up one day outta the blue and wouldna tell anyone where she came from or anythang 'bout herself. Made me mad as hell 'cause I thought she acted like she was better than us."

"Nikki couldn't move without Tawnie doing something to her. I still don't know how she took it as long as she did," Ginger interrupted, settling in front of the fire and cupping her cold hands around the steaming mug.

"I figured she was chicken and that really rankled. Never could stand cowardice in any form," Tawnie added, staring at the cup of steaming coffee in her hands.

"Tawnie sat behind Nikki in school, the only year we all attended together, and one day Tawnie tied her hair to the back of the seat. Nikki couldn't get it loose. Our teacher, Miss Wilkson, came at Nikki with a pair of scissors in her hand, getting ready to cut it free." A bubble of giggles punctuated Kissa's voice, and she put her hand over her mouth to silence them.

"Lord, I thought Nikki was going to beat the teacher with her blackboard. She told her in no uncertain terms she better not come near her with those scissors." Ginger laughed merrily, vividly remembering that day.

"It took me awhile to untangle my hair and by that time I was so angry I could have bitten nails in half." The memory still rankled Nikki.

"I was terrified," Kissa stated. "I'd never seen her mad before and have rarely since."

"Yeah, we met at Miller's Pond. I ain't never met a boy or girl nor man or woman who could whup me 'til I met her. I thought since I was a head taller and outweighed her a good twenty to thirty pounds that it would be a cinch to nail her. Told her to come prepared to crawl home. I figured a good punch or two would knock her down to size, then I'd just sit on her."

Ginger giggled so hard she could barely talk. "Nikki moved in and out of range so quickly, Tawnie looked like a big bear swatting air. I don't think she ever did hit her. Then Nikki had Tawnie in an arm lock and had her nearly begging for mercy."

"Ah dang, it weren' that bad."

"No? It was worse."

"Well?" Tawnie countered in embarrassment. "I though; since I couldna whup her, I might as well make her my friend. Dang glad I did. I ain't never had a better friend."

Dane chuckled, easily imagining Nikki and Tawnie fighting. "And you, Kissa?"

Kissa looked at her fingernails, her face suffusing with red. "Well, Ginger and I stole old lady Gaskins' snuff one day and took it to the schoolyard. Tawnie dared us to dip some. Ginger and Tawnie were the first to try it and when they spit the brown stuff on the ground, I started gagging."

"Tawnie forced her to take a dip, and Kissa thought she was too much of a lady to spit, so she swallowed it," Ginger giggled, remembering the day.

"Yeah, then I told Ginger to push her on the swing. Instead, I took the seat of the swing and twirled her round and round," Tawnie interjected, laughing.

"Kissa's face turned green, then white, then back to green the faster Tawnie twirled the swing."

"I thought I was going to die before Tawnie let me up. I've never been so sick in my life. It was Nikki who came along and saw what was happening and made them stop."

Dane burst out laughing, trying to imagine anyone silly enough to swallow snuff. He wiped at his nose and tried to gather his mirth under control. "Ginger?"

Awe tinging her laugh, Ginger told her story. "Well, Tawnie and I got along pretty well. I never backed down and instead of fighting all the time, we became friends. When Nikki first came, she went out of her way to avoid horses. I accused her of being afraid of them, and she met my challenge. We met in a field after school and Nikki showed me some horse riding tricks I'd never seen before. She vaulted on the back of my horse, rode hellbent for leather across the meadow, then when she came back, she disappeared, only to reappear underneath the mare's belly and over on the other side."

"Your daddy came then. Ya never did tell us whut happened." Tawnie had always been curious how Nikki could ride so well when she never saw her on another horse after that.

Sobering, Nikki tried to shrug off the long-ago memory. "He told me to never ride again unless I wanted the people around there to figure out I was part Indian. He said if I did not care for myself, to think of Cari. It was painful to be around a decent horse. After we left the Cheyenne, my father sold nearly all our horses so he could buy work horses."

Nikki curled her legs underneath her and lapsed into silence, the day bringing back an aching memory she tried to forget. For a brief span of time, she felt alive with a powerful horse surging underneath her, the wind blowing in her face and streaming through her hair, only to have it end within fleeting moments.

After a few minutes, Ginger threw the coffee grounds into the fire and went back to her post. The happy memories had turned sour, bringing back a need for home and family, and the way it had been before that awful night.

Dane had a way of putting Nikki on edge, and it brought out a simmering inside of her, an anger making her defensive and uncertain of herself. He always seemed to be just around the corner waiting for them, but the rational part of her knew it was inevitable they would occasionally meet. After all, they were after the same men.

Under lidded eyes, she watched him spread his sleeping gear on the outside of camp and lay down, his nearness tantalizing and uncomfortable. After positioning the Stetson over his face, he put his hands behind his head, his biceps flattening the material of his upper shirt sleeves. His chest moved evenly, and his supple legs were slightly apart, drawing her attention to the joining. Her fingers curled over the blanket around her, desire itching at her lower belly. She rubbed her lips to dispel the memory of his kiss, wanting to cuss at him, rage at him, deny him, kiss him, and make love to him all at the same time.

Rising in a fluid motion, a wistful smile playing about her mouth while clutching the blanket tight against her breast, an unwanted, yet demanding ache settled between her legs, yet she did not understand any of it. Her rational mind and betraying body combated each other, with both yearning for him, but her mind tried to deny it. Even the horror of *that night* did not quench her desire for him. She still wanted him, still needed him to cleanse the stain to her soul, and he *was* the only one who could make her whole again, she admitted with shock.

Clenching her hands, she fought the impulse to soothe the lines from around his mouth. If he awakened, he would only refuse her, and she could not bear another refusal, could not endure the disgust that would harden his eyes.

What is it about this man that brings out my anger and desire, and yet makes me so determined to carry out my vengeance? The question was beyond her comprehension. Wiping dry, tired eyes, she forced her legs to move.

Chapter 4
Heart of Ice

DANE RELEASED A RAGGED SIGH WHEN NIKKI walked away. He had been vividly aware of her standing near him, and he desperately wanted her, but she had erected a wall between them too high to breach. This self-sufficient, complex, and uncaring woman was not the child-woman who begged him to make love to her nor the confused woman who cried in his arms. The force driving her was in direct opposition to his idea of law and order, completely and hopelessly against every grain of his being.

He flopped on his side and stared blindly into the flickering fire. *How can I reach the tender, caring part of her?* he asked himself a thousand times. *What will crack the iron core and bring her back to her senses before it's too late?* The lines around his mouth deepening, a germ of an idea wiggled around his head.

GINGER NESTLED AGAINST A BOULDER, THE RIFLE laid across her knees, her head tilted to one side, and her lips softly parted. A small smile lifting one corner of her mouth, Nikki touched the sleeping woman's shoulder.

Ginger bolted upright and clutched the rifle to her

middle. Relaxing, her blurry, sleep-filled eyes focusing on Nikki, a derogatory smile curved her lips. "Not a very good watchman asleep."

"I will take over. Go rest."

"Did you sleep?" Ginger stood and covertly watched Nikki's expressions.

Avoiding the too searching eyes, Nikki reached for the rifle Ginger held out toward her. Her hands closing over the stock and barrel, she whispered, "No."

Ginger released the rifle and pulled the blanket close around her shoulders. Wanting to say something else, yet afraid to, she instead sighed, "Goodnight."

The place vacated by Ginger still warm, Nikki propped the rifle on her knees and stared out over the shadowed land, trying to blank her mind. Her topsy-turvy world refused to subside and allow her a moment's peace. Memories—each detail, each characteristic of the outlaws' faces, the blood, the screams, the broken promises, the death—and Cari were forever a symbol of her helplessness, her memories screaming her failure. She was a warrior woman, the chosen one, *Ovaxehee*, Dreaming Woman, and she had always been proud of those accomplishments and her uniqueness. Her failure came as Nikki Pride, a white woman shamed beyond life or death.

And here she was, the leader of a band of unconventional, displaced women, a mute child, and a growing dog. Outcasts of society, stained women who had never known such brutality and savagery of men existed.

A leader, she thought mockingly, *of what? Of women destined to die in the wilderness or be killed by the very ones they were trying to kill? Oh, One Above, what have I done?* Her life ended the moment her family was murdered, but the others could still live full lives in another part of the country where no one knew them. Instead, they followed her on this quest for vengeance.

The shifting of rocks giving underfoot as someone climbed the steep trail, alerted her. Surmising someone came to relieve her of guard duty, she stood and stretched her weary back. She shifted to relieve some of the tension in her shoulders and bottom, expecting Tawnie or Kissa to appear. A quiet talk with one of her friends would alleviate her bitter memories.

"At least you're still awake and alert," Dane drawled, frowning when she stiffened. "I'm taking over Kissa's watch. I wanted to talk to you alone."

Nikki tossed her head. "We have nothing to discuss."

Taking the rifle from her cold hands, he leaned it against the boulder. More than anything, he wanted to smooth the tired lines from her face and hold her, though the act would only complicate things between them. "We've a lot to discuss."

Her spine snapped to attention and her lips tightened into white lines. "We will just be beating a dead horse, Marshal."

"Let it be as it may, Dark Angel. I just wanted to let you know I'm taking LeeAnn with me in the morning."

"Over my dead body."

"I'm not going to debate the issue with you, Nikki. I'm telling you what I'm going to do. The child deserves a home. Not this foolhardy chase through Indian infested country." The night lights sparkled in her strange colored eyes and the shadows emphasized the fatigue lining her face. He clenched his hands at his sides, stopping himself from pulling her against him and kissing her into submission.

"Do not try it, Dane. I have warned you once before. As you said yourself, no one else will have her. Besides, at least with us, she has four mothers who love and adore her."

"Four women who need to be bent over some man's knee and spanked until their bottoms are set on fire. No, Nikki, if you want to risk your fool neck over this revenge, fine, but I am not going to let you risk a child's life. It's bad enough you brought these other women on the same quest and double bad you brought someone as innocent as Kissa Loving too."

"Innocent, Marshal Travis?" Kissa stepped out from the darkness and stood a few feet from them. "Shall I tell you how innocent I am? I begged Nikki to get me off the stagecoach my parents put me on. I begged her to rescue me because I didn't want to go to Boston with my sister. Kallie's with child and she hasn't spoken or recognized anyone since that horrifying night. She needs me now more than ever, but I kept deluding myself into thinking she didn't. I didn't want the responsibility of taking care of her, Marshal. I didn't want to remember I should be like her instead of reacting this way."

Kissa sadly shook her head, her tears glistening in the moonlight. "No, Marshal. I'm not innocent, not anymore. If you take LeeAnn away from us, we will become almost as savage as those men. LeeAnn is our lifeline to sanity and to some semblance of home life. We love her," she finished simply.

Dane rubbed the back of his neck, Kissa's momentary lapse of innocence affecting him more sharply than all of Nikki's cold determination. "It doesn't change anything,

Miss Loving. The child deserves better."

Tears slipping past her cheeks, Kissa drew a shuddering breath. "Better, Marshal? Are we not good enough now? You said yourself no one else would have the child. We want her. She has become a part of us."

"And keep dragging her all over the country into nearly every danger known to man? What will you do when winter comes? Live in a cave? Drag her through snow drifts and let her freeze to death?" Dane argued, though Kissa's words knocked at his heart. Her words carried the depth of the women's love for the mute child and proved they were not savages. At least not yet. Could he risk the child to their care?

"You have a low opinion of us, don't you, Marshal?" Ginger asked, stepping into the small, tense group. "You can't seem to get it through your thick skull the child is ours. You gave her to us, and you nor anyone else will take her away."

"Ya heard 'em, Marshal," Tawnie snarled, following Ginger.

"I've never met such a hardheaded, stubborn group of women before in my life." Dane looked with exasperation from one woman to the other, wondering how to confiscate the child. Something inside him knew, in many ways, they were right—no other family wanted the child.

"Just hope like hell ya don't ever meet anyone like us again," Tawnie shot back.

"I'm warning you, Ladies, we are not through with this matter."

"As far as we're concerned, it is," Tawnie declared with finality, watching Nikki slip into the darkness.

Heoohtato lifted his head when Nikki walked into

camp, then rose, noisily stretched, and trotted off into the darkness. Nikki rubbed her bleary eyes and knelt beside LeeAnn who slept the sleep of the innocent. She brushed a lock of hair from the child's forehead and sighed. *Is it right to drag along a six-year-old child in our bid for vengeance?* They were constantly in danger, the child more prone to it than they. *But what are we to do? Who will want the child? We, at least, want and need her, but is it enough to make what we are doing right?*

Ignoring the sounds of the others filing back into camp, she wearily rose to her feet and walked out toward the prairie to answer a call of nature. She barely had time to fasten her pants when she heard someone coming toward her.

Dane stopped a few feet from her and searched her face in the darkness. "We still have not finished our conversation, Nikki. Maybe we can conclude it without your friends' interference."

"Go away, Marshal. Get out of my life!" She turned her back to him, suppressing shudders of frustrated anger.

"You can turn your back on me, Dark Angel, and you can pretend I won't constantly be on your heels, but you can't shut me out forever."

She swung back around, her hands on her hips, her eyes burning. "You are like a dog always snapping at my heels, Marshal. You are always there trying to be my conscience, but it will not work. I will not listen. I will do what I set out to do whether it is right or wrong."

He sadly shook his head, suppressing the rolling bubble of anger rising within him. There was something of a hurt, tormented child in her words. Her face and posture were defensive, and her chin trembled ever so slightly.

She bit back a shuddering sigh and tightened her chin with resolve. He *was* her conscience, she forlornly realized. Each time he came around her, she wondered once again if she was doing the right thing. It was right for her, but was it right for her friends? That was the main question, the main concern, the main frustration. Scuffing at some rocks with her toe, she broke her gaze from his and inspected the black shadowed land. She did not want him to see her turmoil.

"Dark Angel," he murmured softly, the warmth of his voice caressing her. "Let me avenge your family. Let me do it according to the law. Jock Mason is a cold-blooded killer and the Mason outfit is so low they haven't risen to the rank of bandits. They're ravishers and dangerous. I don't want you hurt."

She glanced up, her body going still. The two parts of her heritage fought within her; the white part screaming to let him take over and the red part demanding her to extract vengeance on her terms. The battle must have shown in her face for he grabbed her shoulders and pulled her toward him, capturing her lips with his. Her anger quickly turning to desire, she melted against him, pressing herself against his long length.

Hot liquid fire strummed through her blood veins, the defenseless womanly part of her yearning for his love and protection. She raised her arms to his shoulders, stood on her tiptoes, tangled her fingers in the hair at the nape of his neck, and held his head against hers. Her body vibrated toward his, each place molding itself to his. His lovemaking could force her to comply with his wishes, force her to submit to the desire rampaging through her body. She needed him, needed his strength, his wisdom, his love. Sometimes the burden of leading a group of inexperienced women was more than she could handle, and it weighed heavily upon her shoulders.

His fingers tightened in the long, thick braid of dark hair and every part of him desired her more than any other woman. He covered her face with kisses and his hand roamed toward the gentle swell of her breast. She turned slightly so his hand covered the soft mound.

His fingers trembled at the buttons of her blouse, the soft, hot flesh underneath sparking images of another time, a time she showed him the appearance of her defilement. The vision refused to withdraw from his mind's eye. With a muttered oath of frustration, he pushed her from him.

"Dane?" she cried brokenly before her voice hardened. "Am I still so repulsive? Will you forever remember what those men did to me?"

She turned her back to him, every part of her crying out in denied satisfaction. "You make my shame real and painful. You are the only one who makes me feel used and dirty. If you cannot forget and forgive, then I cannot forget and forgive either. You force me to carry out my vengeance."

She swung back around toward him. Holding her chin aloft, she squared her shoulders and hid her pain behind narrowed eyes. "I no longer care who must help me carry out my vengeance or what I have to do. You have shown me my vengeance is right and just."

He reached toward her, then dropped his useless hands, realizing he made a grave mistake. Angry with her and himself, he let it wipe all reason from his mind. This woman, this dark, forbidding angel, had taken away his manhood. "You've got a heart of ice, Nikki Pride. Let their deaths be on your Godforsaken conscience. But I'm warning you, if anything happens to the child, I'm coming after you."

Nikki rubbed her throat, already feeling the noose tightening around it. "It will be on both of our consciences, Marshal. You will be as guilty as I. Never forget that." She stepped past him and hurried back to camp.

THE WOMEN FOLLOWED THE CHALKY, SLUGGISH running White River, the banks dried and cracked in patterns of dirty white. The prairie was brown with dashes of green thrown in, and they were bombarded by ripe prairie aster seeds in a weird snowstorm. They followed the gently sloped hill, meandered up it, then stopped at the edge of a sharp precipice. Below them stretched canyons, gullies, ridges, peaks, and spires far as the eye could see. The dying sun cast red over them and changed the devil's den of colors with each passing cloud.

The dry, westerly winds blew constantly and the sun beat down on them in shimmering heat waves. Their tongues stayed swollen, and the blowing dirt filled their nostrils, mouths, eyes, and hair, and clung to their clothing with grey persistence. Tempers ran short and arguments were almost constant as they pushed forward into the desolate stretch of the Badlands.

Nikki selected a camp place surrounded on two sides by eroding dirt and rock, a place where the brisk blowing wind was lessened. They hunkered down around the pitifully small campfire to wait for the stew Kissa had prepared to finish cooking. The wind whistled eerily around the rocks, keeping a steady stream of dust blowing into the food.

"How much longer before we get out of this Godforsaken place? I'd think your Cheyenne would be preferable to this." Wincing, Ginger ineffectually tried to wipe her face clear of dirt. Their skin was red and chapped, their lips cracked and dried.

Tawnie spit near Ginger's feet, the brown stream landing in a glob of dirt.

"Dang it, Tawnie! Keep that crap away from me. I don't know why you started chewing tobacco anyway." Ginger moved from the mess, her heart-shaped face grimacing in disgust.

"Mind your own business, ya damn redheaded firecracker. I don' have to answer to you or anybody else." Tawnie wiped a droplet of spittle from her chin, then spit the whole wad toward Ginger.

Ginger sidestepped it just in time to avoid being hit with the brown mess. "You may try to act like a man, but you don't have the right equipment."

"And you barely got the righ' equipment for a woman," Tawnie snarled, reaching for her whip.

When Tawnie's hand closed over the handle of the whip, Nikki stepped between the women. "Enough!" We have enough trouble without your constant bickering."

"What do you mean?" Kissa asked, pulling LeeAnn closer to her.

"Remember the old camp we passed today? Apparently, we are heading in the same direction they are, and we are catching up to them. The camp ashes were only a day old and there are nine or ten riders in the group."

"Indians?" Kissa quavered, her cornflower blue eyes

going wide.

Nikki shook her head, the thick, long braid swinging against her bottom. "White. The horses are shod."

She fixed Tawnie and Ginger with a narrowed look. "And somebody's been following us all day. I saw dust rising behind us."

"Why in the hell didn ya tell us afore?" Tawnie yelled at her, her hand gripping the whip handle so hard, her knuckles turned white.

Nikki eyed the whip, then met Tawnie's eyes, her own conveying a warning. "What would have been the point? At the time I discovered it, you were picking a fight with Kissa and had her crying. Your waspish tongue has been too busy lashing at Kissa and Ginger to hear anything I say."

Nikki and Tawnie faced off, the tension building between the women. A flutter of doubt rippled through Tawnie. Nikki was slender and quick, hiding her multi-talented skills behind a cool exterior. There was something dangerous in her withdrawn, steel self-control, and the cold rage gleaming from her light-colored eyes, whereas her own anger was right under the surface, ready to explode anywhere, anytime. She released the death grip on the whip handle and leaned back against the warm rock wall, deciding the odds were too dangerous and deadly this time.

Her relaxed stance deceptive, Nikki was taut as a bow string and a tiny touch would start her twanging. "We are all tired, Tawnie, but for goodness' sake, you have done nothing but pick fights with Kissa and Ginger. You have even had LeeAnn crying. We still have a few days in these Godforsaken Badlands, and it will take all our wits to get out of them alive."

"And the way you're going about it, you'll all be killed before too many days pass."

The women spun on their heels toward the deep masculine voice, their hands going for weapons. A figure detached itself from the shadows, his Stetson pulled low over his eyes, ignoring the clicking of pistol hammers.

Nikki eased the hammer forward, then replaced the Remington .44 back into the holster. Crossing her arms underneath her breasts, she drawled, "Well, Marshal, what brings you to our humble camp?"

Dane pushed his Stetson back with a forefinger, stepped close to the fire, and hunkered down, rubbing his hands. "Smells good. Reckon I might have a bowl and some coffee? I've been living on beef jerky and hardtack."

"Make yourself at home, Marshal," Nikki sarcastically invited.

"I'll fix you some, Marshal Travis," Kissa offered, taking a tin bowl and cup from the pack beside her, ignoring Tawnie's and Nikki's snort of derision. She felt safer now since a man had joined their ranks in this desolate hell hole.

They watched him scoop the stew in his mouth with a big wooden spoon. When he held out his bowl for more, Nikki moved forward and took the bowl from him. "The rest of us have not eaten yet, Marshal."

"Pardon me. I figured since you were arguing, you had already eaten your fill." Dane sat back and cupped his hands around the mug, an amused smile pulling up one corner of his mouth.

Nikki knelt before the fire, her eyes never leaving Dane, filling the bowl she had taken from him. "You did not answer my question, Marshal. What are you doing here? And why are you following us?"

Crossing his arms loosely over his chest, Dane stretched his legs and relaxed against the rock facing. With nonchalance, he pulled a cigar from his pocket, bit off the end, and lit it. The pungent smell of sweet tobacco wafted across them. Taking a deep drag, he blew the grey smoke toward Nikki before answering. "I thought I'd save you a little trouble by joining up with your group. I noticed you're tracking some members of the Mason outfit. They were meeting to regroup when you girls had the run-in with Bodine at Barton's Corner." Taking another drag from his cigar, he missed the sideward glancing of eyes between the women.

"How so, Marshal?" Tawnie asked around a mouth full of hot stew.

Dane met each of their eyes. "I thought I'd deputize you until after we've caught them. I figure we'll catch up with them by tomorrow night." He shrugged off the nagging doubt about deputizing women. If any man found out he was doing this, he would be laughed out of the west. But then, after watching them practice shooting, he realized they were more accurate than most men.

"Deputize us?" Kissa whispered, the wooden spoon clanking against the plate.

Nikki kept eating. Dane was unaware he had answered the question of whom they were accidentally following. It was possible if he had not come along when he did, they would have stumbled onto the outlaws' camp. What could have happened afterwards, she did not want to ponder further.

She sensed her friends' thoughts without looking at

them. Tawnie was against it. She would rather kill the men on her own. Ginger was for it wholeheartedly. She had never gotten used to the idea they were going after the murderers. And Kissa only wanted the safe feeling of a man with them. They were waiting for her to answer for them, but she finished eating first. "All right, Marshal. We will accept your proposal—this time."

With the tip of his finger, he flicked the ash of his cigar, then met her gaze from across the flickering fire. "Follow my orders and we'll come out of this no worse for the wear. I want them alive, if possible."

"Alive?" Tawnie spat. "I'll kill the buzzards soon as I get close enough."

"If you're determined to kill them, the deals off. You've got one of two choices, be deputized and do it my way, or take your own risk and probably be killed in the deal. Take your pick." Dane knocked the fire off his cigar, then put his finger to the tip. Satisfied the fire was completely out, he stuck the stub in his pocket.

"Well?" he prompted after a lengthy silence. "Which is it?"

"All right, Marshal, we'll do it your way, but as soon as the job's done, get the hell outta our way."

A CUP OF COFFEE IN HIS HAND, impatient to be after the outlaws, Dane paced in front of the dying fire, cursing under his breath about slow females. Nikki sat on the ground with LeeAnn between her spread legs, braiding the child's long blonde hair. Tawnie cleaned her weapons, Kissa packed the gear, and Ginger applied glycerin to her face and hands.

Nikki tapped LeeAnn's shoulder with her fingertip. "There you go, *Meeskevotse*. Go get your things ready." After LeeAnn raced off to do her chores, Nikki rose and dusted the seat of her pants, cocking an amused brow at Dane.

Ignoring his impatience, she took her bow and tested the string, then grabbed an arrow from the quiver and notched it. An impish desire to shoot an arrow between his feet and stop his crazy pacing, prompted her to walk toward LeeAnn who was cinching the straps underneath the Calico's flanks, to get a clearer shot. Nearing LeeAnn, a warning rattle stopped her cold.

"LeeAnn, do not move," Nikki whispered, drawing the string back and releasing the arrow. It twanged through the air and thunked behind the rattler's head.

The soft swoosh of metal against leather swiftly spun Nikki on her heel. "Put your pistol away, Dane, unless you want the outlaws and any Indians in the territory to hear us. Sound carries far around here."

His mouth tightening in anger, he holstered his pistol. She was right and it disgusted him he had acted without forethought. Shoving the Stetson over his eyes, he watched her slide the knife from around her waist and neatly sever the rattler's head from its body. Afterwards, she retrieved her arrow and cleaned both it and the knife on the sparse brown grass.

To cover his embarrassment, he snapped, "Hurry up. We don't have all day and we're losing precious time." Throwing his coffee grounds on the fire, he stalked off, fuming from not only their slowness, but embarrassed Nikki had to remind him of the dangers.

It was near dusk when they spotted the trailing dust of the outlaws. Nikki, who had been bringing up the rear, rode ahead and galloped up the sharp-ridged hill, aware of Dane stopping his snorting mount next to her. "There are nine in the group. They look like they are slowing down. My bet will be they will camp on the open meadow yonder."

"We'll rest here and move forward soon as it's dark," Dane announced, having already surmised the situation. Turning Renegade, he headed back down the hill.

Nikki watched a little longer, her throat dry and her stomach knotting up with fear. Knocking the wide-brimmed hat from her head, she let it dangle on the string around her throat. Doubts assailed her once again if she might not be leading her friends into death. *Are we strong enough and proficient enough with weapons to handle this?*

Chapter 5
Wall of Hate, Wall of Sorrow

THE BRILLIANT COLORS OF SUNSET AT HER BACK, Nikki stood straight as an arrow beside the black gelding. Her midnight-black hair gleamed with blue highlights and the wind picked up the straight strands, wisping them around her back. She appeared dark and menacing in the black clothing relieved only by the blood red headband around her dark forehead and the one around her waist along with decorated knee high, leather moccasins hugging her calves. The only other color was her incredible light blue eyes fringed by heavy black lashes. She was the dark angel Dane called her; a heathen princess disguised by the civilization of white men.

Hauntingly beautiful and an aching sadness surrounding her, it tore at Dane's heart. He should be protecting her instead of allowing her to face the Mason gang. Was he any better than she in leading a group of inexperienced women against hardened criminals?

He was trying to shield her and the others, he reasoned, but doubts assailed him. He blocked his thoughts, wondering if perhaps he followed because he felt duty-bound to guard Nikki against herself. If one of them were killed, he would always blame himself for not doing enough, and yet, there was more to it. Nikki compelled him to discover things about himself he did not want to understand, examine, or acknowledge.

Shaking the morose thoughts away, he pulled his wistful gaze from her and addressed the women. "After we surround the camp, I'll give a bird call like this." He proceeded to make a burrowing owl call before continuing, "Hopefully we can do this without gunplay. Remember what I said, I want them alive if possible." Dane looked at each of them to make sure they understood. "Mount up and stay close."

"Yeah, stay close!" Tawnie gave a low gurgle of laughter. "Hell's bells, we'd know who we was a followin' by our noses. Lose the smell and your lost anyhow."

The cold face of the quarter moon watched the six riders wind their way among rocks which twisted and turned until the narrow path rose sharply. Dismounting, they lead their horses toward the cliff side of the hollowed rock wall where the rock curved up overhead and provided a perfect place to hide LeeAnn and the horses.

The voices of men drifted back to them on the wind and *Heoohtato* growled, the hairs on his back hackling. Nikki laid her hand on the top of his head, instantly hushing him. While the others crept forward to surround the camp, she knelt beside LeeAnn and touched the child's cheek in a soft caress. "LeeAnn, stay with the horses. *Heoohtato*, stay. Protect."

She strung her bow and slung it across her back, the string of the bow resting over her shoulder before she crept toward the sounds of murmuring voices and careless laughter. Uneasily glancing back over her shoulder, she inched forward, her heart beating a rapid rhythm against her chest and her palms growing sweaty.

Pressing herself against the rock facing, she bit hard on her lower lip to steady her nerves. Pebbles shifted underneath her feet and she stopped, her breath catching painfully in her throat, but the laughter and voices continued unabated. Filling her lungs with dry air, she crept forward again.

The red and yellow flickering campfire burned in the valley thirty yards in front of her. Dark shapes, almost a part of the shadowy landscape, moved and neared the fire. She stretched out on her belly, ready to move forward at the given signal when she heard a menacing growl behind her. Gunshots cannonaded through the valley. Jumping to her feet, Nikki turned and raced back to the niche where she left LeeAnn.

The yelps of a man and savage growls put wings to her feet. She rounded the edge of the rock, her bow ready, then stopped. *Heoohtato*'s white teeth bared and bright in the pale moonlight, pinned a man underneath his heavy body, his warning growl echoing and mingling with the rapid gunfire.

LeeAnn cowered close to the restlessly moving horses. Motioning her away from the horses, Nikki stepped toward the man on the ground. A flicker of light on the barrel of his pistol snapped her voice. "Attack!"

Heoohtato went for the man's throat, the outlaw's piercing scream ending in a gurgle. The smell of blood reached the horses, and they whinnied and tugged at the ground hobbles. She grabbed the reins and bore down on them to keep the animals calm while she soothingly talked to them and LeeAnn.

After the gunshots and the animals quieted down and she was convinced the animals were subdued, she stepped quickly to the prone, lifeless figure and searched his pockets. She pulled out several coins of gold and silver, and stuffed them into her own pocket, then took his weapons and ammunition. Without a moments regret, she heaved the body off the sharp, rock face. The body bumped and scraped down the sheer face and landed with a sickening thud at the bottom.

After hushing the frightened child and making certain she was unharmed, Nikki ordered her to stay with the horses and *Heoohtato*. She hurried back to the valley and arrived in time to hear Dane's angry shouts.

"You stupid assed women! I should have my ass kicked for even asking for your help. You haven't got the brains God gave a piss ant. I said I wanted them alive, not have them riddled with bullets. It was a damned massacre!" Slapping his hand against his legs, he growled, "That's what I get for trusting trigger-happy women."

"Massacre, hell!" Tawnie yelled back. "The bloody scumbags fired on us first. Was we to sit still and let them kill us?"

"You were shooting as much as we, Marshal. How can you be so sure we're the ones who killed them?" Ginger asked, her lips narrowed to keep the bile from rising to her throat.

Still hearing the pounding hooves in the distance and Kissa retching somewhere behind him, Dane pulled off his hat, then rubbed the back of his neck, staring at the three bloody bodies lying at his feet.

Nikki entered the camp, casting shadows around the dim glow of the campfire, and his anger exploded. "Where in the hell were you, Nikki? You weren't at your post and some of the ruffians got away! Well, are you just gonna stand there like an idiot or are you gonna answer me?"

Cold fury sweeping over Nikki, an unreal sensation clouded her mind and eyes. She pulled the knife from the wolf leather casing around her waist and threw it in his direction. The Bowie knife thunk into the ground between his feet and vibrated.

His eyebrow lifting in sardonic anger, he did not move for a few seconds, then he slowly lowered, pulled the knife free, and held the handle end toward her.

"Yell at us one more time and I will give you something to yell about," Nikki warned in a low, harsh whisper. The unreal sensation passing, she stepped forward and took the knife, then thrust it back into its casing before leveling her eyes to his.

"You miscalculated, Marshal. I could have stayed and attacked with you. Or…" She paused a moment for emphasis, "gone back to protected LeeAnn from the outlaw after her. My choice was easy and if you do not like it, you can choke on it."

She spun on her heel, swallowing against the lump in her throat. Reaching the edge of the campsite, she swung back around and ordered, "Tawnie, Ginger, check their pockets and take what money they have, then take their weapons and ammunition. We will need them later."

In an apparent better mood, Dane was joking with Ginger by the time Nikki brought LeeAnn, *Heoohtato*, and the horses into camp. LeeAnn, her face chalky white and her brown eyes huge in her thin face, clung to her leg, making it hard to walk. Nikki's main thanks was the dead bodies had been removed from around the campsite.

"I like things the way they are, Marshal. If I want to eat saltine crackers in my bed, I will. I don't need some man telling me I can't."

"Ginger, my love, I'd never kick you out of my bedroll for eating crackers."

Nikki's quelling look stopped the sharp retort on Ginger's lips and she ducked her head to unroll her bedroll. The cockeyed grin on Dane's face and his warm reply to Ginger pierced her heart. She should not care what he did or who he desired, but she did.

After leaving LeeAnn in Kissa's care, she crouched near the fire, eyeing him disdainfully. "Our business with you is finished, Marshal. You go your way, and we will go ours come morning."

He stood over her, his legs splayed and his hands lazily at his sides. "Depends on what you're planning, Nikki."

"The only thing I am planning is making it to the Cheyenne camp before winter blows in, if it is any of your business. Besides, if the rest of the Mason gang head in the direction of the Black Hills, the Cheyenne and Sioux will take care of them."

Dane crouched down beside her, his eyes narrowing. "You could save all of us some trouble if you and your friends remain deputies and joined up with me for a while, but this kind of carnage can't happen again."

"Marshal, if you were not so hardheaded, we might have thought it over. Thanks, but no thanks. There are three men in the Mason outfit I personally want to take care of and I do not want you around to stop me."

"You're a hard-headed bunch, Nikki Pride. If you or any of your friends get killed over this idiotic revenge, don't come crying to me." An angry tick worked in his cheek and the grooves around his mouth deepened.

"Marshal, I would not come crying to you if my life

depended on it," she snorted, watching him walk away.

Tawnie patted the stock of the rifle and motioned toward Dane with the barrel. "I'm takin' first watch. Told him I would. Reckon ya'll be up to takin' the next?" At her affirmative nod, Tawnie continued, "The marshal said to wake him after your watch." She spat toward him, her voice low, "I don' trust the mangy dog."

Nikki sighed. *Do we have any reason to trust him?*

Ginger squatted behind her and lifted the heavy hair from her neck. "I'll brush and braid your hair so you can get some rest."

"Thanks."

Ginger applied the brush to the straight black hair. "Don't you think we should take the marshal up on his offer? We can still get the outlaws and have extra protection with him."

"At what price, Ginger? He is a man and a man wants more when he is in the company of women. Are we to sleep with him just to keep him off our backs if we kill more of the outlaws?" She stared at his sleeping form lying on the outer limits of the camp, her brow furrowing. "What was he saying to you right before I arrived with LeeAnn and the horses?"

Ginger shrugged; thankful the darkness covered the red rushing to her face. "He was smarting off I should get married instead traipsing around out here. I think he was afraid if he didn't get in a better mood, you'd end up gelding him."

Nikki tried to relax with the soothing brushing of her hair, but the marshal's presence kept her tense, unsure, uncertain about everything.

Plaiting her hair, Ginger confided, "Nikki, I think the

marshal's figured out who killed Washburn."

Turning slightly, Nikki looked over her shoulder at her. "How so?"

"Well, when Kissa was throwing up in the bushes, he made a comment about vomit being found near Washburn's body." Ginger's hands stilled on the hair in her hands before saying, "I just looked at him and said, you do know Washburn made my husband watch while he assaulted me…" Her breath caught in her throat before she finished, "and my husband died watching him do it."

Nikki slept fitfully. She missed the warmth of LeeAnn's body against hers, but Kissa coaxed the child to sleep with her. Not that Nikki minded. Kissa needed the comfort more than she. The little blonde-headed child kept them careful, probably too careful while they tracked and attacked the outlaws. Somewhere in the back of each of their minds was the need to come back alive to protect the mute child. The child is what kept them from becoming savage as she suspected they could be; she was their anchor to reality.

The camp was never really quiet; every night one or more of them awakened the others with their moans or screams. Tonight, Ginger moaned in her sleep and called out Lyle's name several times, and Kissa cried softly in hers. Each were tormented, and one or more would moan and/or cry in their sleep every night when memories invaded their slumber.

They never really rested, Nikki thought, trying to force herself to sleep again. When she finally fell into a restless sleep, she fought to come awake when the recurring, blood-covered nightmare and the piercing screams of terror invaded her sleep. Would they ever be free of them?

Some instinct brought her quickly upright, her knife in hand.

"Whoa, easy now, Nikki. It's just me," Tawnie held her hand toward the knife.

Replacing the knife, Nikki kneaded the sleep from her eyes. "Rest well, Tawnie," she whispered, leaving to take over the watch.

She walked farther away from the camp than necessary until she found a nice sized boulder to sit upon. The ringing chatter of crickets and the musical whistles of a canyon wren sang to her, keeping her company, the night lulling her into a strange peacefulness. She needed time to herself, time to sacrifice to the spirits, and gain answers to the unanswered questions plaguing her. She withdrew more into herself as the days went by. The trust the others gave her put pressures on her and brought doubts. Was she doing the right thing by getting them involved?

"Nikki?"

She jumped, automatically going for the pistol at her waist, then stopped after she recognized Dane's deep voice. Resentful he interrupted her soul searching, she growled, "What do you want, Marshal?"

"To talk," he stated softly, sitting beside her. Glancing up at the stars, he then dropped his gaze back to hers, searching her face in the shadowy darkness. "I want you to reconsider my proposition."

"Why, Marshal? You have already said we did not have the brains God gave a piss ant and you ought to have your ass kicked for joining up with women." She shifted away to look at him.

"I said it and it's true. But for Christ's sake, Nikki, wouldn't you rather be working with the law than against it? It would still give you a legal right to carry out your revenge.”

“Will it, Marshal, or are you just wanting to get into bed with us?” she snorted, refusing to blush, remembering he pushed her away when she begged him to make love to her.

“Damn it, Nikki! Is this all you think about? Is this why you’re going to the Cheyenne camp—to a find a buck to sleep with?” he asked harshly. “If you had any sense at all, you’d have stayed at the farm and made a living for yourself and LeeAnn.”

His words hurt, but she would not let him see how much it hurt her. “How? What was I to do for money, Dane? There is only one place I can make enough money to support LeeAnn and myself. Is this what you want—for me to work on the south side of town? Would you prefer I spread my legs for any man who has the price?”

“I’d have given you the money to live on.” He disliked the guilt flooding him.

Her laugh was bitter. “To salvage your pride? No thanks. You see me as everyone else—a fallen woman. Even though you took my innocence, you have not touch me again.”

She stood, her back to him, a bubble of pain clogging her throat. “You like virgin territory, Marshal, but only if you are the only one who has been in it. Which is fine, but when someone else trespasses on it, you do not want to have anything else to do with it.”

She did not speak aloud the thoughts running through her mind that he probably would have never come back to court her as he promised during the picnic. She was ruined goods, unclean, damaged, and unworthy after the night of the attack.

Moving in front of her, he stared into her eyes, searching for hidden truth. "You're wrong, Nikki."

"Am I? You are the one who makes me feel dirty. The others do not matter. They never touched me the way you did."

He flinched at her accusing voice, his anger mounting in strides. "Now wait a damned minute! If you were any kind of a woman, you would've stayed and tried to make a home for LeeAnn. You wouldn't have led her and these other women on this damned foolhardy, dangerous chase."

Hating him for bringing her doubts into the open, she drew back her hand and aimed for his face. He caught her wrist in midair and jerked her up against him, his face a bare inch from hers.

"Don't try to slap me again, Nikki or I'll break your wrist."

"Let me go, Dane! I do not need you. I never did." Her voice ragged and her throat hurting, she did not say what else tore at her heart—that he had the power to hurt her, did hurt her each time he was around her.

Pulling her closer, he anchored her hands between them. Her fingers splayed across his chest, he cupped a hand behind her head and held it so she was forced to looked into his face. "Damn it, Dark Angel, you don't make anything easy, do you? I've thought about my inability to make love to you until I've nearly driven myself crazy. I thought I was somehow less than a man. It wasn't another man touching what I claimed as mine so much as it was you."

"Me?" she cried in disbelief.

"Yes, you!" he growled. "You're not the same person

I made love to. You're a hard, cruel woman, Nikki Pride. You're trying to use me to get back at those men, and you don't care what happens to you or your friends. All you have is this deep driving need to kill, to avenge if you will. With this need you don't give a damn who you hurt in return. If you did, you wouldn't have dragged a little six-year-old girl and women who have only known comfort, on this Godforsaken, idiotic chase."

She tried to pull away from him, but he held her tight. "Even the little bit of kindness you do show toward any of them is an unconscious act, not from the heart."

He shook her, rage coloring his vision red. "You've got ice for a heart and the fires of hell couldn't melt it." He shoved her away and clenched his hands at his side, fighting the need to strike her, the thought of striking a woman a second time, disturbing him.

Falling in a heap at his feet, the stones scratching her hands and poking into her knees, she raised her head and glared at him. "I will not let you hurt me anymore, Dane."

Something in her low voice touched him. He knelt in front of her and grabbed her upper arms. "You're building a wall around your heart, Dark Angel, and it's getting taller and thicker. One day you'll find yourself alone hiding behind your wall and without a friend in the world. Then what will you do? What comfort will you get in your lonely, cruel world? You're not letting anyone close to you."

He brushed a stray wisp of hair from her face, ignoring her stiffening and pulling away from him. Realizing his love was one-sided, he tried to hurt her to hide his own growing love for her. She left no room in her heart for love, just bitter hatred influencing everything in her life, and it thrust them on different sides. They were both too stubborn to bend to the other's will. Their one night of passion was not enough to bind them, to nurture the attraction and the spark of love between them. *Now*, he thought sadly, *we're after the same men, but on different sides of the law.*

Nikki's throat ached and her eyes burned, but the tears refused to come. Things were building up inside of her with no way to release the pressure until one day she knew she would explode and there would be nothing left of her. "Go away, Dane," she painfully whispered. "Stay out of my way and my life."

He caressed her cheek, then clenched his fingers. Her eyes remained unrelenting, and he did not know how to reach her. Standing, he looked down at the crumpled heap at his feet, his insides churning with regret. "Don't keep pushing me away, Nikki. You'll push once too often and I'll not be there when you really need me."

"Need you?" she whimpered, glancing up at him. "You once told me what we had together was probably the beginning of love. What do you say now, Dane? It was the beginning of hate?"

She turned away from him and stared out over the dark land. "Please, Dane, leave me alone. I cannot take any more. Just get out of my life."

She was like a hurt child, bravely holding back the tears, and there was no way he could bring the child back to the present to infuse with the woman in her. Turning on his heel, he realized she would not let him help her. Sticking his hands in his pockets, the leather strip of her 'chastity' belt filled his hand. Pulling it out of his pocket, he brought it to his nose before turning around and letting the length dangle between them.

Standing, she made a grab for it, but he wrapped it around his hand. This may be the only chance he had to reach her, and his deep voice rose softly between them, "Nikki, you are my wife per Cheyenne customs. You and your father accepted my bride gift."

"No, we did not," she disagreed with him, watching him slip the proof back into his pocket, shocked he even knew about the custom.

He wanted to pull her closer to cup her face with his hand, instead he tenderly answered, "Your father and I agreed on five quality horses who were already saddle broke. You, Kissa, and the child are riding three of them. You're using the other two as pack animals."

"No, that is not true," Nikki answered, shaking her head. Her father would not do such a thing without telling her.

"Your father and I had a talk the day before the picnic. He agreed to our courtship, but it was your mother who thought we should also do it the Cheyenne way, and your father and I agreed," he explained, moving slightly toward her, then stopped when she lifted puzzled eyes to his.

"No, Mother would not have said a word. No one was to know of our Indian blood."

Dane stopped her with his next words, "Your parents and I discussed your Indian heritage many times before that, Nikki."

Shaking her head against the startling revelations, she cried, "You do not speak truth. Ginger took the horses from her father's herd."

"Go ask her where the horses came from, Nikki, if you do not believe me."

Trying to ignore the fluttering of her heart, she stalked past Dane to find Ginger, wondering why he was bringing this up now. Her confusion increased and she could not help but worry about his sudden disclosure. What was his purpose, his reasoning, and where was he going with this?

Motioning Ginger to follow her, she turned and walked away, Ginger behind her. Stopping and turning around, assured the others could not hear them, Nikki faced her. "Ginger, where did you get the horses you brought with you?"

Ginger glanced at her in surprise before her eyes shifted away from hers. "Ah, I never did explain it, did I?"

"Tell me now, please. It is important."

"Well, Dusty Joe brought it to my attention that I would be stealing horses from my father when I told him to gather four or five horses from my father's herd, even though I knew my father was already furious with me. Dusty Joe said my father ordered him to take those five saddle-broken horses to your father, and it would be better if I took them instead. I agreed only after he promised to put saddles on them. It was part of our bargain."

Nikki covered her face with both hands, rubbing her forehead and eyes before dropping them to her sides, the distress on her face obvious. "Oh, God, what next?"

"What's going on?" Ginger asked, concerned with the stress lining Nikki's face.

Nikki brought her hands to her face once again, shaking her head. "I cannot talk about it now." Turning, she walked away into the darkness of the night.

DANE WAS NONE TOO HAPPY THE WOMEN took the

weapons, money, and outlaws' horses, leaving him one horse for the bodies and his own mount, but there was not much he could do about it when looking down the barrels of their weapons.

Nikki refused to speak with him after his revelation last night. Now, watching them ride off, he wondered what to expect next. The women were a hard-headed bunch and determined to do everything their way.

He ran his fingers through his hair, uneasily aware of the dangers they were letting themselves into and his own inability to make them see reason. "Damn it all!" he muttered. They could have had what they wanted if they had gone along with him. He would make sure the Mason gang received their due punishment.

Jamming the Stetson on his head, he mounted Renegade. He knew one thing; he would have to keep the women from entering his mind or he would grow careless following the five men who escaped from the camp last night.

DEEPLY AWARE OF THE NEED TO BE WITH her people, Nikki kept them traveling hard and fast. The noon sun beat down on them and the wind whistled through the branches of the ponderosa pines as she led them into the higher reaches of the Black Hills. She had been aware of a scouting party following them since yesterday afternoon but had not mentioned it to the others. She did not want them to become nervous and end up doing something stupid.

With the ponderosa pine trees growing denser, she stopped the group and called LeeAnn forward.

"*Meeskevotse*, ride behind me for a while."

She gave her a hand and swung the child up behind her. After LeeAnn grabbed Nikki around the waist, they started forward again.

Ten warriors appeared before them like they had solidified from the trees. Nikki halted the group and rode toward the warriors, speaking haltingly in the Northern Cheyenne dialect. "*Ese'he Ohnesesestse, Nahtataneme.*"

"*Ovaxehee, Vo'evahtamehnestse* has been expecting you," Two Moons answered, his mouth tightening when she called him her brother.

"My Grandparents?"

"They are well. *Haa'hae'ameohtse* is still peace chief." Two Moons looked behind her, studying the women in the group. "I do not see my brother. Is *Mo'eheso* well?"

LeeAnn gripped Nikki's mid-section and she hid her face behind the sheltering back. A violent shudder ran through her, causing the black gelding to nervously shift.

With LeeAnn's fear apparent, a hard lump came to Nikki's throat, and she patted the child's hands around her waist. "*Mo'eheso* is dead. I am the only one left. I will explain everything when we reach my grandfather's lodge, then I will repeat it no more. You will be there?"

"I will." Two Moons' face hardened, his oblique eyes piercing hers and understanding more from her eyes than she said. "Follow me. We have a long ride in front of us before we reach camp."

She nodded, then spoke to the members of her group. "Cloud Walker has been expecting me. The warriors will escort us to the camp. Ginger, rope *Heoohtato* and keep him near you, especially after we reach the camp. We do not want him killing any of the camp dogs when we go in."

She waited until Ginger had the rope around *Heoohtato's* neck before she kicked her heels in the gelding's sides and followed the scouts.

Chapter 6
Fires of Hatred

WINDING TOWARD THE HIGHER REACHES of the mountains, a discernible tension developed between the Indian scouts and the women. The air grew crisper and cooler, the land a fertile green, and birds chattered merrily, flitting from tree to tree while small animals ran underbrush.

LeeAnn tightened her fingers around Nikki's waist until weariness and the steady stride of the horse lulled her to sleep. *Heoohtato* loped beside Ginger's mount, not lagging nor running in front, or the rope around his neck would tighten.

With the setting sun, a crimson ball lowering against the changing background sky colors at their back, the riders stopped and dismounted. Nikki nudged the sleeping child enough to awaken her, then helped her slide to the ground. Leaving LeeAnn in Kissa's care, she walked toward the shadowy figure separating from a tree.

A tired, happy smile creased her lips when the Cheyenne medicine man, Cloud Walker, appeared. Longing to hug him, she acknowledged he had not changed much in six years: wisdom lined his wrinkled face, his hair pure white, and his body thin and now bent, yet still strong. "I counted each passing sun until I could come once again to my home."

"*Ovaxehee*, you surpass the sunset in beauty, but there is a deep sadness in your eyes. Come, walk with me. *Ese'he Ohnesesestse* will take care of your ponies and your women."

Sitting on the ground, the lingering light quickly fading, Cloud Walker opened the pouch at his side, withdrew a pipe, and filled it, carefully tapping down the tobacco with an index finger. After lighting it, he thoughtfully puffed while he studied her face. "You are troubled, child. Tell me why you travel with strange companions on a long and perilous road."

"I am like the baby who was weaned too quickly from the breast and has come once again to be suckled," she quietly answered.

"Once the babe has been weaned, the mother's milk dries up and can no longer suckle the child, but the mother can enfold the child close to her breast and offer comfort. Is this why you have come?" A wisp of smoke rose between them.

"Yes, and more. I need answers to many questions and my friends need guidance and training."

"Tell me what has happened, *Ovaxehee*," Cloud Walker encouraged, laying his arms, palms upward over his crossed legs. One hand held the pipe carefully, his fingers holding the bowl over his palm without the pipe touching it and with the upright stem pointed to the east.

"Many things have happened, friend, but I wish to speak it once and only once in the presence of my grandparents. My heart can no longer repeat it for each time I do the pain goes deeper." She tenderly touched his forearm, letting her eyes reveal her sorrow.

Cloud Walker took another puff, blew the smoke heavenward, then met her eyes. "Despair fills you, *Ovaxehee*. I know your words will bring great sorrow to *Haa'hae'ameohtse*. Being your mentor, it is I, a man of the tribe, who should be telling him your story."

Silence deepening between them, she considered Cloud Walker's wisdom. Her grandfather was peace chief and could claim no vengeance against anyone or anything. If he showed anger or tried to organize a war party to seek revenge, he would lose respect and his position within the tribe.

The wind picked up an errant strand of hair and blew it across her face. Inhaling the fragrance of pines and clean mountain air, she pushed the hair around her ear. Slowly, she told her story, carefully leaving out any mention of Dane Travis.

A watery glean in his sharp eyes, Cloud Walker waved his blue-veined hand in front of them. "You and your warrior women go after these Long Knives?"

At her nod, he continued, "You wish us to teach them, yet you have taken no notice of the signs, *Ovaxehee*. The caterpillar's band is wide and the ground squirrels collect seeds early this year. Anthills are higher, the bark on the trees is thicker on the north side, and the owls hoot at midnight. There are other signs which say to prepare for a hard winter." He paused to let her digest the information. "Times will be hard when the snow falls."

"Are you saying we cannot stay?" she asked, her throat raw and tight.

"I am saying you have been gone a long time and the people will look at you with suspicion. It will not be as it was before, *Ovaxehee*. You and your warrior women will have to prove yourselves. Still, many braves will want to claim you and your friends as their women instead of helping you."

He took another puff of his pipe, considering her with sharp, intelligent eyes. "I will help you until the first snow falls, then you and your warrior women must leave."

Her eyes blazed, then dulled. The Cheyenne season was in the last moon of *Hiviutsishi*, the moon where the buffalo bulls are rutting. Nikki calculated the time in the white man's calendar and decided it was late July, and if winter was coming early, they would need to leave by the end of the plum moon, September or possibly early November. It gave them about two months of training—such a short time to learn the skills needed to fight and survive.

Standing, she turned her back to him and stared sightlessly into the darkness. The chilled wind blew strands of hair around her head and cut through her clothing. Wrapping her arms around herself, she remarked sadly, "It is as before. I am being driven from my home and my people. Why can I not stay with my people this time?"

He shrugged away her question. "Life goes in circles, *Ovaxehee*. After you and your family left, many of our friends, the Sioux and other *Tsistsistas* died from the white man's diseases. Because you cared so much for us and did as *Maehonehe* ordered, our tribe was spared."

He carefully held the stem of the pipe, letting neither his palm nor the ground touch the bowl. "Tell me what you feel, *Ovaxehee*."

Gripping her arms across her chest, she remained silent

a few moments. She searched for appropriate words, her confusion a bubbling mass within her. This was not the homecoming she had imagined, but Cloud Walker had always been her friend and mentor, his quiet patience and wisdom adding strength to her topsy-turvy world. Shaking the hair from her face, she focused hurt-filled eyes on him.

"A big fire burns inside of me glowing bright and hot, but each day the flames grow dimmer until one day not even a speck of light will remain. I will then plunge into darkness with nothing left of me but grey ashes. It does not matter anymore. After I have had my vengeance, I will be ready to die—for I belong nowhere, to no people."

"You are *Tsistsistas*! Never forget! Remember your path in life is not with us. You were sent to us for a purpose, and at its completion you must leave. Darkness surrounds our beloved Black Hills and war will follow against the Long Knives who come into our land to hunt for the yellow rock."

"Gold," she spat contemptuously to hide the pain closing around her heart.

Staring off into the blackened landscape, she twined a strand of hair around her finger. The wind whistled through the pines, crying with the same tone of despair matching the sigh of her voice. "I am like the wind— always moving with nowhere to go. Yet I have a child whom the spirits have taken her tongue, three inexperienced women, and a fighting dog. How do I survive my destiny, yet take care of them? I wish the One Above had taken my life also."

Her pain touched and saddened him. "Do you wish you all were dead, and you had no responsibility? What would you say to your loved ones in *Seyan*?"

He pointed toward *Ekutsihimmiyo*, the Milky Way. "The Hanging Road bears the footsteps of many. Would you have it bear your footsteps—the footsteps of a coward? And the one the spirits have touched is like the eaglet we found long ago. Do you remember, *Ovaxehee*? It had a broken wing, and I was going to kill it, yet you took and nourished it until it healed, then you set it free. So must you do with the child when it is time. Be generous with your spirit."

"Words, old man," she spat, sitting beside him and leaning close, her eyes cold. "They are nothing but words. Look at me! I can feel nothing. I have no heart left in me. I am the crimson and white rose of my dreams, drifting in the icy cold spring waters with nowhere to go, always drifting until I wither and die."

"All things pass in their season, *Ovaxehee*, and so shall you. Remember hate rots the soul. You are too proud and strong for hate. You must rise above this and learn to bend with the wind. Do what you must do, then forget it." He studied the weary slump of her shoulders, the pain-ridden eyes, the bitter twist of her mouth.

"Life is what we make of it, *Ovaxehe*e, whether it be sweet, content, or bitter. Take time to sacrifice to the spirits, fortify your soul, find peace with nature. You will discover all is not dead inside of you. A person with a cold heart does not take in a parentless child nor ponder if she leads her friends into danger. Think, child. You have shown friendship and love to your warrior women in their time of need and shall again."

Her mouth caustically twisting, she remembered Dane's contradicting words.

CHIEF WIND RACER AFFECTIONATELY PLAYED with
the damp length of his granddaughter's hair while he
waited for the women to finish eating. His wife, Red Leaf
Woman, took their bowls, then sat behind Nikki, her
curiosity vivid in her brown eyes.

The women had entered the village unnoticed during a
bewildering, torrential rainstorm which swept upon them
without warning. After they had unloaded their animals
and put their supplies away in the lodge her grandmother
had previously set up for them, they were directed to Wind
Racer's lodge.

A smile creasing his pleasant face, Chief Wind Racer
watched the dog they had brought with them poke his head
through the flap, then crawl inside and position himself
behind his granddaughter and the little yellow-haired
child. The child put her hand on the animal's huge head
and absently patted it. "*Nisha*, you have been away a long
time. The child beside you is not *Neskeesta* Two Moons
told me about."

Nikki put her hand on the child's knee. "No, *Namshim*.
This child was given to me to raise. The spirits have taken
her tongue."

"You travel with strange friends, Grandchild."

She shifted uncomfortably, the smell of leather, food,
and smoke filling her nostrils. Beds with their headrests
filled with everyday things, lay along the edges of the
lodge. The lodge was the same as she remembered, but she
felt out of place, strange.

With the rain passing and the sun lowering, the camp

noises increased with people coming out of their tipis. Someone shouted an invitation to a feast and children went to and fro across the circle carrying the message. The best horses were staked out in front of the owners' lodges and the rest driven back to the hills.

"Why did not *Mo'eheso* come with you, *Nisha*?" Wind Walker released the damp strand of her hair, his dark eyes watchful.

"He is dead. I am the only one left alive," Nikki said in a lifeless, low-pitched voice. She heard the soft intake of breath from her grandmother and then her sobs while Cloud Walker explained all Nikki had told him. His oblique eyes fastening on hers, he read from her eyes and posture what she had carefully left unsaid earlier.

She kept her eyes on her grandfather's gentle eyes, her heart aching with the same sorrow deepening the lines of his face now. Wind Racer had been one of the fiercest warriors in *Tsistsistas* history, but the years of being generous with his possessions and spirit were firmly etched into his face.

She watched a flare of anger flash into his eyes, then disappear just as quickly when her grandmother rested her hand on his arm. All their children were dead. Her uncles, Heart of Buffalo and Flight of the Eagle, were killed in battle before she had left her people. She had never been able to conquer the guilt pertaining of her uncles' deaths. The dreams had been symbolic, hiding the dangers the hunting party rode into when they went in search of deer, and instead ran into a war party of Utes.

After Cloud Walker finished speaking, Two Moons jumped to his feet, his face fierce. "*Haa'hae'ameohtse*, I will lead a war party to avenge my brother in your place. I will kill many white faces when they come into the Black Hills to look for the yellow rock.”

Nikki rose, every nerve in her body strained. “No, *Nahtataneme*. I have my own war party. We seek the men responsible, not innocent lives.”

“These?” Two Moons scorned, motioning to the women on either side of them. “They should be in lodges having babies.”

“Yes, these. The one with the hair the color of sunset is *Mo’eheso*’s woman. They are all warriors.”

Two Moons’ lips pulled back in a snarl. “*Mo’eheso* was my brother and I have the right to avenge his death, not you and your *meeskevotses*. Even you have lived the white ways too long. You are no longer *Tsistsistas*.”

Hurt anger washing over her, Nikki clenched her hands at her sides and her feet anchored firmly on the ground. “I am *Ovaxehee*, a Cheyenne warrior. I went on four war parties and counted many coups. I took no lives,” she almost shouted, jabbing a thumb at her chest. “I demand respect!”

Cloud Walker held out his hand, stopping words better left unsaid. “What is it you want, *Ovaxehee*? How might we help you?”

Pulling her eyes from Two Moons’ indignant face, she sat beside Cloud Walker. “Guidance. I hoped *Ese’he Ohnesesestse* and some warriors from his society would teach us the skills only the *Tsistsistas* can teach.” She faced Two Moons. “I will pit my friends against any of yours, *Ese’he Ohnesesestse*.”

You wish members of *Wohksehhetaniu* to fight women,” Two Moons snorted.

“Yes.” She leaned forward, her eyes hard and sure. “If

your soldiers can beat them at their own skills, we will leave. But if we beat yours, then you will teach them?"

Two Moons remained silent, so Nikki tried another tact. "You are a respected member of *Wohksehhetaniu* and the bravest, *Nahtataneme*. I will match my skills to yours. If you win, we will leave, and if I win, will you then ask your society?"

A flash of resentment tightened Two Moons' face. "I am not your brother, *Ovaxehee*. Have you forgotten so much you do not remember a brother many not look or speak to his grown sister?" He watched her bow her head and harshly continued, "It is my place to take you and *Mo'eheso 's* woman to mate."

She raised her head, her chin lifting a notch. "I will be no man's woman, *Ese'he Ohnesesestse*."

She glanced around her; her friends shifted impatiently, uncomfortable in the confines of the tipi and the long conversation. She had tried to explain earlier the Cheyenne's code of manners demanded a wait before the real business of the visit could begin. That code had been a reprieve, and yet a torment for her. Closing her eyes for a moment, she faced Two Moons. "Do you avoid the question I asked?"

"I will think it over, *Ovaxehee*."

Full darkness set in by the time they left Nikki's grandparent's lodge and went to their own. Bright firelight shone through the yellow lodge skins around camp and sparks flew out of the top of one of the smoke holes from someone mending a fire. Music of a dancing song called young men and women for a social dance. It mingled with the quicker, more lively music of the gambling song from another lodge. Over the camp, the hum of voices was broken by the neigh of a colt and the barking of dogs. A yelp of excitement was followed close by the shout of an old man calling a friend to a feast. The musical laughter of women and the distant shrill howl of coyotes added to the cacophony.

The women crawled through the flap toward the inviting fire blazing inside. Nikki sat on the fur draped bed along the wall and leaned back against the headrest, her mind a jumble of incohesive thoughts.

Ginger left the group of women and knelt behind Nikki. Taking a brush from the saddle bag, she went to work the tangles from Nikki's long, ebony hair. "What happens now?"

Nikki relaxed, her troubled thoughts disappearing with the soothing strokes of the brush. "We wait."

LeeAnn moved over to them and laid her head in Nikki's lap, her brown eyes watching her closely. Managing a small smile, Nikki smoothed the hair from the child's face. "*Meeskevotse*, you will like it here. The Cheyenne will treat you well."

"What does *meeskevotse* mean?" Ginger asked, separating Nikki's hair into three strands to braided it.

Nikki smiled again, running her fingers across the child's cheek. "Baby."

LeeAnn smiled and cuddled closer.

Exhaustion took its toll on the women and they slept the sleep of innocent children. Nikki watched the smoke disappear up the smoke hole, her thoughts in turmoil. Doubts pressed down on her, disorienting her and shaking her confidence. Her two bloods fought with each other, crying out to belong to one people, one race. *Why can I not cry?* she silently moaned. *Why am I different?* But she was different, had always been different, a fact she once knew how to live with.

It was several days later before Two Moons announced the Kit Fox Soldiers had agreed to the contest. Word went around the village; some of the warriors mocking and ridiculing Kit Fox members. Tensions ran high, and Nikki was aware of the mistrust directed toward her. She felt out of place, dissociated with the Cheyenne life, and it was tearing at her already bruised heart and pride. She had been so positive she would always be at home here. To discover she belonged nowhere quickly chipped away her knowledge of self.

THE WOMEN WERE NERVOUS, CONSCIOUS THEY must perform well, or Nikki would be disgraced in front of her people. They bunched together; their weapons close at hand. It was up to Nikki to ease the tension and she did it with aplomb, notching an arrow and shooting the feather off the pole set up at the other end of the field. Excited warbles rose, the Cheyenne approving of her excellent marksmanship.

She pulled another arrow from the quiver, notched it and sighted down at the piece of hide on a round hoop. The wind blew the hoop back and forth on the pole causing it to swirl, making it a hard target. She waited for the target to begin its backward swing before she released the arrow. It whistled through the air and struck dead center through the hoop.

His face split in a wide grin, Two Moons clasped her forearms with his. "You are still warrior woman,

Ovaxehee."

"Do you match my skills with your bow, *Ese'he Ohnesesestse*?" she softly asked.

Two Moons threw back his head and laughed. "I am a member of the *Wohksehhetaniu* and do not need to prove myself."

Biting back a challenge, she laughed, elated Two Moons let her skill speak for itself. He could have made the challenge harder, hard enough for her little used skills to fail her. The pride gleaming in his hard-black eyes was enough to tell her he wanted her to succeed.

Tension easing in most quarters, Ginger entertained the tribe members with fancy rope tricks, her brilliant strawberry-red hair catching the bright sunlight and shining like fire on top of her head. The Cheyenne watched in awe as Ginger spun the rope and gracefully went in and out of the hoop. Milky white mounds of breast showed above her lime green blouse and brought teasing glimpses, and her musical laughter enhanced her appeal.

A match for the bright sunlight with her golden good looks, Tawnie rolled up her shirt sleeves to display the long, muscular length of her arms. She flexed biceps with each flick of the whip, a smile big as Texas on her thin lips. The Cheyenne had never seen anyone like her, more man than woman, yet somehow retaining the appearance of a woman.

A golden Amazon, her rectangular face and tawny brown eyes crinkling in exuberance, Tawnie was in her element and the line of men around her brought out the flirtatious woman. She glanced at one of the smaller men of the tribe and gave him a wink before flicking her whip and snapping one of the middle feathers from the pole several yards in front of her. None of the other feathers moved so much as a breath. A yip of approval rose, and Tawnie placed her fists on her hips, threw back her head, and boomed with laughter.

Kissa's aura of innocence seemed to protect her from the worst life had to offer. She had an uncanny knack of blending with any group of people, and she quickly made friends with Running Deer Woman. Their heads leaned close together as Running Deer Woman explained in halting English how to make pemmican. She took Kissa with her each morning in search of plants while imparting her knowledge of plant life and their properties. In the afternoons, Running Deer Woman showed her how to tan rawhides and explained how to store food for long periods of time. None of the Cheyenne seemed to notice she did not display her weaponry skills. It was a blessing in disguise. Kissa was barely adequate with the shotgun, missing almost as much as she hit.

LeeAnn's fear of men slowly dissipated and she showed an inordinate attachment to Nikki's grandparents, following them around like a lost puppy. Collective war whoops and cheers went up around the group of braves surrounding *Heoohtato,* and LeeAnn clung to Chief Wind Racer's leg.

A frown wrinkling her forehead, Nikki forced her way toward the front where growls and yelps came from the center. *Heoohtato* fought a brown camp dog twice his size and weight. *Heoohtato's* powerful jaws opened and caught the camp dog's front left leg, easily snapping the bone.

Trying to get away, the animal's yelping filled the air around them. Before the camp dog could move more than a couple of inches, *Heoohtato* caught its other leg and snapped it in two. In moments, *Heoohtato* ended the animal's life with a powerful clutch at the throat.

Nikki started forward, determined to end the dogfight, but someone caught her arm. She swung around on her heel, her mouth open to berate the person who had the audacity to stop her. Her grandfather stood in front of her, his hand still on her arm. "This is cruel. I cannot stand by and watch them fight these dogs."

"Who is it cruel to, *Nisha*? Not to *Heoohtato*. He enjoys fighting. And not to the other dogs, they enjoy it too." Wind Racer watched the changing expressions on her face, his eyes serious and gentle.

"But—it is wrong," she argued.

"Is it?" Wind Walker gently asked. "*Heoohtato* is like a *Tsistsistas* warrior. He fights for the enjoyment of it and with all his abilities. Do you want him less than *Tsistsistas*? The braves honor him—proud of his fighting spirit."

He stopped her from speaking with a light shake of his head. "Let *Heoohtato* fight, *Nisha*. His ability to fight well may one day save your life."

The impact of what her grandfather said made her realize just how long she had been away from the *Tsistsistas*. The fighting spirit—was that not what she had? "I wish no harm to *Heoohtato*."

Wind Racer softly laughed. "*Nisha*, three of our camp dogs could not harm your *Heoohtato*. Look at the depth of his chest and the power of his jaws. He is an animal to be proud of."

A whoop ascended from another group, and curious, she left her grandparents.

An old friend of Nikki's, who was with her during her

wuwun, wrestled with Tawnie, and was several inches shorter than the tall woman. Young Bird pinned her to the ground, exerting pressure on her wrists, his arm muscles bulging with the effort and leaning his face close to hers. Her face red with exertion, Tawnie pushed upward, then slyly smiled. She raised her head and kissed him on the lips. Young Bird drew back in shock. Tawnie flipped him over and was on top of him before he could recover his composure. Laughter rippled through the spectators.

Finding himself in the same position he had Tawnie earlier, Young Bird pulled her trick. Tawnie drew back, slightly releasing her hold, only to find herself flat on her back. She relaxed underneath him and boomed with laughter. Young Bird lithely jumped off and gave her a hand up. Looking down at the short brave, Tawnie laughed and slapped him companionably on the back, almost knocking him to the ground.

Cloud Walker stood beside Nikki, watching the wrestling match. "Your warrior women have proven themselves. The *Wohksehhetaniu* have honored them." Cloud Walker nodded toward Kissa. "She is *Ehyophsta.*" He pointed at Tawnie, then at Ginger. "She is *Heenevaahetanehee* and she *Nanasehamehee.*"

"You honor *Nanasehamehee* greatly by saying she is the best of all. Will you tell me why?" Waiting for his answer, she watched Ginger patiently show a brave how to draw a pistol.

"I named her, *Ovaxehee.* I see great depth in her. She will be a friend above all others to you and help you in ways that will prove their worth later. Never underestimate her."

He glanced toward the west, drawing her eyes the same

direction. "The time will come soon when I will take you to the sacred mountain for your *wuwun*. Be ready."

Darkness covered the land and the drums pounded out for a feast. The women bunched together, their eyes shining with euphoria. "How'd we do?" Tawnie asked, speculatively eyeing Young Bird. Young Bird stood near a group of braves, gesturing wildly, and describing their earlier fight.

"Very well. You were honored with names," Nikki proudly answered. She looked up at Tawnie and stated, "You are *Heenevaahetanehee*–Woman Who Is Man Woman."

Tawnie repeated the name the best she could in the Cheyenne syllables, then threw back her head and laughed. "You'll have to help me later with sayin' it right." She laughed again, "Well, who'd thunk that'd be my name—Woman Who Is A Man Woman."

Nikki turned her attention to Kissa and Ginger. "Kissa you are *Ehyophsta*–yellow Haired Woman, and Ginger, you were honored most of all. You are *Nanasehamehee*—Mountain Lion Woman which is also means mighty above all the other beasts."

Chapter 7
The Endless Pain of No Tears

THE KIT FOX SOLDIERS TRAINED THE WOMEN hard, teaching them skills of knife fighting, riding, shooting bows and arrows, lances and using other war weapons, including hand-to-hand combat, tracking, and making war. Nikki translated when hand motions and mime did not convey messages, but as time wore on, the women learned to speak a smidget of Algonquian and learned the hand motions and mime, seldom needing her help.

Nikki watched her friends grow more confident and secure in their skills. Even Kissa took time to train with the warriors when she could free herself from Running Deer Woman. She watched a Kit Fox warrior patiently teach Kissa how to hold the shotgun, training her to fire the weapon with a skill Nikki and Ginger had failed to teach her. *It is good*, she thought, pleased with the drills going on around her.

She did not notice Two Moons until he stepped beside her and his voice interrupted her thoughts. "*Ovaxehee*, your women do you proud. They have learned much from the *Wohksehhetaniu*."

"Yes, I could not have done it without your help,

Ese'he Ohnesesestse," she stated softly yet proudly. Unconsciously, she fingered the large bear claw necklace around her neck, pulling Two Moon's attention to it.

"I wish to take you as my woman, *Ovaxehee*. It has been my wish since we were young. Stay with me and I will also take *Mo'eheso*'s woman as mine. Your women will have a place here as well. *Monevata* has already stated he wishes to make the big one his woman. Your warriors are well respected and many warriors have said they would be proud to make them theirs," Two Moon said, his voice soft yet confident.

Turning to face him, Nikki placed her palm over the bear claw, her hand too small to completely cover it. "*Nahtataneme*, it can never be. We have been ordered to leave when the first snow falls."

Two Moons glanced at her slender hand covering the bear claw necklace, wishing it was him she clasped so tightly against her breast. "I will speak with the chiefs, *Ovaxehee*, and request you and your women be allowed to stay."

Shaking her head, Nikki released her grasp on the bear claw and laid her hand on Two Moons' forearm, touching the puckered scars where the bear's claw swatted him many years ago, the necklace one trophy from their kill hanging around her neck. "No, do not interfere for it will bring death to our people. Neither of us wish this to be."

"Then our time is short. I will teach you all you have forgotten and train you on what you still need, *Ovaxehee,*" Two Moons stated, searching the azure eyes staring up at him. His stomach roiled with longing and it flickered briefly in his eyes before he glanced away. "Come so we may learn again."

Time passed quickly with the women mingling with the *Tsistsistas*, enjoying and learning from the constant interaction and training. It was a time where the past could not reach them. They were allowed to be their true selves without the shame of assault negatively overshadowing them.

Tonoishi, the cool moon, had arrived and the leaves began changing colors, turning green leaves to an array of golden-yellow, red, burnt orange and brown, to shift in a falling pattern with the wind and settle on the browned grasses around their trunks. Their season with the Cheyenne was quickly ending.

The days shorter and the lowering sun proclaiming the end of the day, Cloud Walker informed her in two rising suns he would take her to where the sun goes over for her *wuwun*, giving Nikki time to strengthen her body to endure the three days and nights without food, water, and only light covering for the cold nights.

Nikki sat with Ginger and Kissa while LeeAnn petted *Heoohtato* who rarely left the child's side. Kissa had a Bible in her lap, training LeeAnn to read, her voice soft within the sound of the crackling fire, while reading Romans 12:9. *"Let love be without dissimulation. Abhor that which is evil, cleave to that which is good."*

Nikki sucked a shuddering breath, the words hitting something within her. Taking her gaze from the pair, she glanced around her. "Where is Tawnie?"

"Probably with Young Bird. She said something about going with him to pick out some horses from his herd." Ginger glanced up from tightening a screw in her pistol, curiosity sparkling in her eyes. "Why do you ask?"

Nikki stood up, groaning, "Oh, no. I have to find her

now before it is too late."

"Too late for what?" Kissa asked, looking up from her reading. "She disappears with Young Bird every evening. What is wrong?"

"Every evening?" Nikki cried. She had been so involved in listening and talking about Cheyenne skills and working with Two Moons, Cloud Walker, and her grandfather Wind Racer, she never noticed Tawnie's disappearances.

Without waiting for an answer, Nikki slipped out of the lodge door flap and ran toward the open land near the edge of the forest hiding the village from sight. Hearing the horses before seeing them, she rounded a small hill and looked down at the herd, her eyes searching for Tawnie and Young Bird. After spotting them, she ran through the herd, spooking the ponies who skittered or jumped out of her way.

Nikki neared them, breathless, and Tawnie looked at her with surprise. "Whut's wrong," Tawnie asked, leaving Young Bird's side.

Holding up her hand, Nikki bent forward to catch her breath. After a few seconds, she croaked, "Have you taken any ponies yet?"

"How'd ya know 'bout that?" Tawnie suspiciously asked.

"Have you?" Nikki asked again, urgency in her breathless voice.

"I was fixin' to, not that it's any of your business."

Nikki took another painful breath before standing straight to meet the suspicious golden-brown eyes. "Do you know why you were told to pick ponies from his herd?"

"I don't know why ya think it's…"

Nikki interrupted her, "Tawnie, he is asking you to pick ponies from his herd for a wedding price."

"Whut ya talkin' 'bout? Weddin' price?" Tawnie sputtered, not understanding.

"You have no family here, so for him to take you for his woman, he is offering you the wedding price by allowing you to pick out his best ponies for yourself."

"Woman—wife? He's a wantin' to marry me?" Tawnie stared at Nikki in disbelief, then glanced at Young Bird in amazement.

"Yes, I wanted to make sure you knew what was happening so you could think about it and make the right decision. It will be too late if you have already accepted his ponies."

Tawnie shuffled her feet, suddenly unsure if she understood the implications, then glanced at Young Bird who stood close beside her. "Ah shucks," Tawnie said softly, looking away from Nikki, a glimmer of tears wetting her eyes. "Ah shucks," she repeated. "Tell him…"

She stopped, trying to gather her thoughts. Clearing her throat, she replied, "Tell him I'm honored that he wants me to be his woman, but…but…we've been ordered to leave when the first snow falls."

"You are free to make your own choice," Nikki reminded her, her own voice soft noticing the big woman glance at Young Bird with eyes clearly exposing her desire to accept the warrior's offer.

"Tell him whut I told ya," Tawnie ordered with a shaky, tear-filled voice.

Tawnie listened to the guttural sounding exchange, gazing longingly at Young Bird, unable to hide her emotions. Slowly, she pulled her eyes from him and turned to Nikki when she spoke.

"Young Bird says he will take you to another tribe so you can both live together. He wishes to be mated with you," Nikki explained.

Tawnie shook her head, meeting Young Bird's eyes, her answer plain. "Tell him I cain't! If it had been some other time, some other place, we might've been all right, but I cain't. I cain't get any plainer than that."

Nikki spoke to Young Bird, but before she could finish Tawnie's answer, Tawnie interrupted her, "Tell him I want to be with him while I'm here, but I gotta go when you do."

Nikki nodded and spoke to Young Bird in Cheyenne. "*Heenevaahetanehee* will be your woman only until the first snow falls, then she must leave with us. Will you agree to be hers until then?"

Young Bird looked up into the golden-brown eyes of his woman, a yearning for her tearing at his heart. She was a pleasant surprise, one who fulfilled him in ways he had not known were there before now. He knew he could agree to her short-term proposal or walk away forever. Looking into the golden-brown eyes intriguing him so, he made up his mind, "*Heenevaahetanehee*, I take you for my woman until you leave with your warriors after the first snow falls."

CLOUD WALKER CAME FOR NIKKI BEFORE dawn and led her up the slopes of the Black Hills, past the thick foliage of autumn-colored trees. She listened carefully to his instructions, then watched his slow, meticulous descent to the bottom of the hill. He would wait for her there while she sacrificed for three days.

Throwing her arms wide to implore the spirits for a vision, she subconsciously chanted the slow, rhythmic medicine songs, reminded of another time when she was nine years old and received her vision in much the same way, but in a different place. That day was close to her now—the child she had been and her separate bloods, and she mourned for the lost child. She had been an important person in the tribe. Now she was a confused, hate-ridden person with no home or people to call her own.

Pushing the painful memories behind her, she became *Tsistsistas*—Dreaming Woman. With her white blood crying out against the abuse of her body, her vision blurred, and her voice grew raspy.

Vaguely, she thought she heard Cloud Walker's soft voice chanting a death song, but the wind whipped the sound away. The color burst dimming into shades of dusky purple, she dropped exhausted onto the bed of white sage, pointing her head toward the east.

Shivers racking her slender frame, she lay in a fetal position to reserve body warmth. Her sleep was uneasy from the aches in her body and the crisp fall night. Hunger cramped her stomach and her water-parched tongue swelled like cotton in her mouth.

At the closing of the third day, her legs trembled with weakness and her head swam dizzily. She briefly wondered how the war party, which included Tawnie, Ginger and Kissa, was progressing, praying the women passed their initiation without incident and returned glorious and proud of their accomplishment. If any of the women or the Kit

Fox Soldiers were killed, the guilt would always lay heavy upon her.

Shaking the thought from her mind, she laid upon the bed of white sage. A tingling crept to the tips of her toes, up her legs, through her spine, and on to spin her head. Suddenly, she was plunged into a crimson void, the visions sweeping across her eyes with increasing intensity.

"Ovaxehee, rise." The faintly familiar voice rustled like dead autumn leaves.

Dreaming Woman knelt on shaky knees and rubbed her grit-filled eyes. Taking the water Grandfather handed her, she drank slowly, the old ritual a poignant reminder of days past. Drinking her fill, she placed the water gourd cup close to the fire before gazing into the Grandfather's kind, wrinkled face, a reminiscent smile playing about her mouth.

"Your pain has reached us in Seyan, Daughter. I come to give you hope and courage for the trials you face. Watch and learn, Ovaxehee." Praying in a croaky singsong voice and invoking the spirits of things to come, Tsehemesemestovestse lifted her upward, through the air along the star-strewn path of the Milky Way, stopping in the middle of the heavens, and releasing her hand.

She glanced at him, but Grandfather was no longer beside her. Red Wolf stood there instead, his huge reddish-brown body blocking out part of the stars. "Maehonehe, do you answer my questions?" she hesitantly asked.

"I show you what is, what will be, and what has been, Ovaxehee. The sum of it all will answer your questions. Take this message to your people. Listen with your heart, eyes and ears, then come no more to visit the Tsistsistas."

Suddenly back on the hill, she sat on the ground and

Cloud Walker sat beside her. The hilltop rose to the heavens where the air around them was sweet and pure, and stars surrounded her in the peace reigning place. "What do you see, Ovaxehee?"

Events happened in a flashing streak, vividly showing each detail. From the beginning of time to the future, images moved with lightning speed across the screen of heaven, barely impressing her memory as she tried to describe them; an ancient people moving across the land, speaking in a language she did not understand, but was somehow able to interpret, on how they were from the lost tribe of the one true God, then viewing the changing landscape and the changing tribes until she recognized the near future. "Food is scarce. White hunters have killed all the buffalo. Braves leave before sunrise to find food to feed the hungry children. White soldiers attack! So many killed."

A cry of terror rose to her lips. Screams, gunshots, shouts, trampling horses, and blood were everywhere as children, women, and old people were mowed down by the pale faces' fire.

The scene changed rapidly, and Cloud Walker encouraged her to tell all she saw. "We fight many battles with the Long Knives and many die. Many tribes come together for the Sun Dance. White soldiers appear and the tribes are victorious at the Little Big Horn—no white soldier survives the battle. But other white soldiers come, killing many in the different tribes and our people. There is hunger and the people have no lodges. To save our children, we must live on the Long Knives' reservation, a small piece of land outside our own land. The White Father says if you do not like it there, you can go back to the Black

Hills. Beware! He does not speak truth!"

"Our brothers, the Southern Cheyenne, do not want us. They call us Sioux and accuse us of stealing. Many Northern Tsistsistas sicken and die, but if we must die, then we die in our beloved Black Hills."

"We escape to the Black Hills, but our Sioux brothers try to force us to go back by giving us no wood for fire nor food for our hungry children. They betray us by delivering us to the white soldiers. Pale faces put us in tipis which have no walls and many poles set around it so we cannot leave. We would rather die close to our home than go back to the desolate, unfriendly country of the Southern Cheyenne.

"The white soldiers steal our women and children, dividing us even more. Still, the warriors will not go back. No more, they say. We will live in our beloved Black Hills. Oh, One Above! The blood! The blood!" Red covering her vision, she violently shuddered, all she had seen taking away her voice. Whimpers tore from her throat.

"Tell me what you see now, Ovaxehee." Cloud Walker leaned close; his gentle face streaked with tears.

She breathed deeply. The vision changed to a peaceful scene, the unhappiness and despair easing. *"They go back home to the Black Hills to live and die. They are home! And yet, the distant future shows the tribes coming together and praying with the Long Knives to their God, the God who gave them the land to overcome a great evil spreading over it and the world. Our voice becomes one with theirs and defeats the evil for this land has become all our land."*

The visions stopped and the hilltop slowly lowered to earth. She turned to Cloud Walker, the stress of all she had seen lining her face and eyes. *"Tell me what it means."*

He touched her cheek with a finger, erasing the pain from her face. "You cannot come back to the Tsistsistas to visit, Ovaxehee. Know you are always a part of them and your life parallels with theirs. From one people to another, by each you feel betrays you, but you will find your home after much pain and death." He ran his fingers along the silken length of her hair, then turned and walked toward the heavens.

Dreaming Woman came to her feet and reached toward him. "Cloud Walker, where are you going?"

He turned around and Nikki screamed; across his throat was a huge black gash.

Her scream bringing her out of the vision, she found herself kneeling with her hands outstretched toward the dawn with her eyes and mouth opened in terror. "No!" The birds fluttered from the trees below her at the shouted denial.

She never knew how she reached the bottom of the hill and found Cloud Walker's dead body with his throat slit. She fell on her knees beside him, wailing a spine-prickling sound eerily like a strong wind finding crevices in a tipi.

Two Moons and a party of warriors found them that way, Dreaming Woman's voice a hoarse whisper while she keened, her eyes strangely dry and empty. Two Moons led her away while the braves tied Cloud Walker's body in his robe and laid him on a *travois*.

LEEANN CURLED UP BESIDE NIKKI, and *Heoohtato* moved close beside LeeAnn to lick the wounds he had received during the latest dog fight. While absently caressing the child's cheek, Nikki stared at the ivory bow with the wolf leather grip Cloud Walker had given her before she left for her *wuwun*. Over to the side of the lodge were four bundles, each filled with twelve black and red striped arrows plus Cloud Walker's parfleche of medicines.

She should have recognized the signs when he gave her his personal medicines and herbs. He knew beforehand he would die on that lonely hill. She remembered snatches of the death song she heard during her *wuwun and* berated herself for not stopping to check on Cloud Walker. Now it was too late.

In the two days since Cloud Walker's death, she spoke to no one. Even if she had wanted to speak, her throat was so raw and swollen, and swallowing hurt. *Oh, One Above, why? Must death dog my every step? Do I bring these deaths with me? Tears…just grant me tears, I beg you!*

Conflicting emotions tore through her, and she buried her face in her hands. *Death and destruction!* She was truly the dark angel, the angel of death!

Kissa poked her head through the door flap. "Nikki, Running Deer Woman says a war party is bringing in some white men."

Nikki nodded, then gently settled the child in the robes, and rose before belting the gun holster around her waist and slinging the arrow quiver across her back. Taking the larger new ivory bow, she glanced at the sleeping child and decided not to awaken her. She would need her sleep—for none of them would sleep this night.

The returning war party pranced through the village on decorated ponies and a warbling rose from the people. Two white men with ropes around their necks and their hands bound by leather thongs in front of them, stumbled through the village. The white men were a scraggly lot with dirt hiding most of their features and their hair dirty and matted. The first man's shirt had been torn from him, his chest and back a mass of bloody scratches. Already there were women and children beating them with sticks, rocks, or with their hands.

Nikki pushed her way through the gathered people. Two Moons stopped in front of her, the badge on his buckskin shirt catching the sunlight and sending blinding rays of light toward her. Recognizing the badge, she glanced at the man on the end of the noose rope Two Moons held in his hand. The prisoner lifted his head and looked at her with piercing silver-blue eyes.

"Dane," she whispered, a warning shiver shaking her. He gave her a weary, half smile. *No, it cannot be!* she wanted to cry out. During her time with the *Tsistsistas* she once witnessed a man tortured for days on end. He did not have a chance unless she found some way to free him. They may have their differences, but she would not stand by and watch him tortured and killed.

She turned to Two Moons and softly demanded, "Let him go."

Two Moons looked at her, his triumphant face showing surprise, then it hardened. "He dies like the other, *Ovaxehee*. He is a long knife."

Her face unrelenting, her stance proud and determined, she covered her throat to ease the ache speaking caused it. "He did not kill Cloud Walker. He is one of the white lawmen after the men who did kill him."

Glancing at the other prisoner, she remembered him. He was one of the members of the Mason gang and was with the outlaws at Barton's Corner. She nodded toward him, her voice a low-pitched sound of hatred. "The other is one of the men responsible for my family's deaths. Do with him as you wish but let this one go."

"You lived too long with the Long Knives, *Ovaxehee*, and think like them. I captured him and I will either release him or torture him. I have decided he will die."

Tawnie walked up behind Nikki and gave a contemptuous snort. "Well, if'n it ain't the high and mighty Deputy U.S. Marshal Dane Travis. Fancy meetin' ya here. I reckon this will be the last time we'll have the pleasure of seein' ya alive."

The warriors tied the prisoners to poles driven into the ground. Nikki turned away to search for her grandfather, refusing to watch the women and children torture them with sticks and rocks. She found him near the edge of people. "*Namshim*, order Two Moons to let his prisoner go. He is not responsible for Cloud Walker's death."

Wind Racer's eyes sad, he answered her. "I can do nothing, *Nisha*. You know the laws of the tribe."

"But you are chief! The most respected man of the tribe!" She touched his arm, imploring, "He is after the men who killed our family. Please, *Namshim,* it is wrong to torture him!"

"Cloud Walker's death demands a life in lieu of his life." He held out his hand to stop her stuttered words. "I can do nothing, *Nisha*. It is up to you to find a way to protect his life if it is your wish."

Hiding her disillusionment, she spun on her heel and moved purposely to where they had tied the white men. Two Thumbs strained against the ropes, kicking out at the women and children who tortured him, his eyes wild with fear.

Dane stood motionless, his eyes fastened toward the skies when he was hit and beaten. Ignoring him, she drew her pistol and shoved her way in front of Dane, her legs spreading out in a protective, fighting stance. Brandishing the pistol in front of her, the bow slung across her back bumping against her bottom, she gestured wildly at the people.

Ginger, Tawnie and Kissa stared at her in shocked bewilderment for a few moments before they drew their weapons and took positions around Dane. Feeling the tension, *Heoohtato* loped up beside her and bared his teeth. a low growl issuing from his throat when the people stepped too close to the women.

Tawnie waved the rifle in front of her, forcing the people to back off further. "Are ya tryin' to get us killed?"

Nikki shook her head, uncertain why she was defying the very people whom she most needed approval. "I cannot let them torture him, Tawnie."

"Ah, heck, Nikki, at least the worm won't be on our asses."

Chief Wind Racer and Two Moons stepped in front of Nikki. "Why?" Two Moons angrily asked. "He is a long knife, our enemy. Do you go against tribal ways? Must you become an outcast among our people?"

"I am an outcast," she sadly answered. "Cloud Walker told me we must leave when the first snow falls and to come no more to the *Tsistsistas*. I have no home, no people, yet I avenge my family's death and my dishonor. But I will not stand by while you torture an innocent man."

Two Moons moved a step closer and stopped when she cocked the hammer on her pistol. "You will kill me, *Ovaxehee*?"

"I hope we do not have to find out."

Two Moons shifted uneasily, aware of the hard glint in her eyes and the determined tilt of her chin. Part of the girl he had known long ago, the hard part which was brave and very much *Tsistsistas*, would accomplish and carry out her subversion. "You can kill me, *Ovaxehee*, and many more of our people, but in the end, you and the rest of your warriors will be dead alongside this Long Knife you protect. Is this your wish?"

"My people?" she softly cried, the hurt in every intonation of her voice. "You said I was no longer *Tsistsistas*!"

She shook her head, the long length of hair flying around her. "I wish no harm to you or anyone else. Still, I will not let you torture him for something he did not do."

"How can you be so sure he did not kill Cloud Walker?" Two Moons leaned close to her, his eyes hard and questing.

"Do you question my powers? I am *Ovaxehee*, the chosen one! I have been the seeing eyes of our tribe for many years until Red Wolf commanded me to leave."

"It was long ago," Two Moons softly reminded, though his face belied his words and held respectful awe as she steadily pointed the pistol at his heart. Her stance regal and her azure eyes shining with pride, she became a dark pagan goddess carved from living stone. The ivory bow and arrow quiver swung across her back, her black and red clothing, and her long ebony hair indicated her as a warrior of renown.

Her soul swelling and filling with glowing blue light, she held out her free hand, palm upward toward Two Moons, and slowly closed it. "It is I who holds the future of our tribe. I have seen what was, what is, and what is to be. From the beginning of time to the ending of time." She pointed at her head. "It is all here, *Ese'he Ohnesesestse*, respected member of the *Wohksehhetaniu*. Do you risk your life and all here by destroying me and what I have seen?"

The mystery of who she is settling around her, she holstered her pistol and held her hands toward the heavens. She was a Cheyenne enigma, something great, horrible, and unreal. "Do not tempt me to call down evil spirits on our tribe, *Ese'he Ohnesesestse*."

"If you evoke evil spirits on anyone, it should be me!" Strong and brave warrior he was, Two Moons experienced fear. He had known *Ovaxehee* most of his life and he had never grown accustomed to the spirits taking over her body and her tongue.

She pointed a finger at him. "Evil spirits destroy everyone who hears my words, *Ese'he Ohnesesestse*. I have no power over what comes. Hear me and hear me well. One last time am I to give a message to the *Tsistsistas* and I am to come no more. Do not put your lives into jeopardy by going against me."

Dane refused to believe the power emanating from Nikki or the sudden heat from her body blasting him where she stood in front of him. He gave her credit for putting on a great performance, but if she overplayed her hand, she could cost all of them their lives. New energy invigorating his body and a growing sensation of danger racing along his spine, he shouted in Algonquian, the Cheyenne language, "*Haa'hae'ameohtse!*"

"Speak," Wind Racer demanded. The people grew restless when the spirits departed from his granddaughter, but the fear still lingered, the sense of something terrible she had seen in her vision burning into his mind.

"I am an adopted member of Black Arrow's tribe. I am *Hotohkohvq'komaestse.*"

"He cannot be *Tsistsistas.* He has no scars on his chest!" Two Moons interrupted, the bonds holding him in frightened veneration, breaking loose. Glancing at Dreaming Woman, he saw the spirits who had taken over her body were no longer there. Instead, she was once again a beautiful young woman, stubbornly determined. Still, he was unwilling to give up his prisoner even if *Ovaxehee,* a legend in the tribe, had become the mystery she had once been.

"Release him," Chief Wind Racer ordered.

Nikki quickly cut his bonds, frowning when he sharply whispered, "I didn't need your protection, Nikki, even if it was a damned good performance."

When he shouldered past her, she sputtered, "You ungrateful...I should have let them torture you, White Star!"

Dane ignored her. "It is true I have no scars, Chief Wind Racer, but I am willing to undergo the Sun Dance."

Two Moons sarcastically snorted. "The Sun Dance is past and I say you do not speak truth."

"Let him prove himself. *Ovaxehee* will pick the trial." Chief Wind Racer turned to his granddaughter; his eyes carefully guarded against his thoughts.

"Will you also go the test?" Dane asked Two Moons in Algonquian.

Two Moons' nod was abrupt.

Biting on her bottom lip, she glared at the men, furious she was required to choose the trial, but she could not, in good conscience, refuse. "Then let them be tested at the swinging poles."

Two Moons drew back, his face a mask of rage. "You ask this of me, *Ovaxehee*, knowing I swung to the poles to tie the bond of friendship and brotherhood with *Mo'eheso*, your brother?"

"Yes, I ask it. No, I demand it! *Haa'hae'ameohtse* ordered me to pick the test and I have done so. Ask no more of me."

Pivoting on her heel, Nikki took two steps forward before she spotted LeeAnn standing transfixed, her thin face drained of color and her brown eyes wild, reflecting the appearance of a trapped animal. The child stared with horror at Two Thumbs and her mouth opened in silent screams. Supplying the screams for the mute child, *Heoohtato* howled with bone chilling effectiveness.

Nikki ran to the frightened child and pulled her stiff little body against hers. Holding LeeAnn against her breast, she blocked off the child's view of Two Thumbs. "Hush, *Meeskevotse*. He will never hurt you again."

LeeAnn sobbed in big hiccupping gulps and her thin body shook with fear. Nikki soothed her, wishing somehow, she could protect her from the past. Looking over the child's head at Dane, she transferred all her hatred for Two Thumbs to him.

Dane shrugged helplessly. "I was bringing him in when your friends captured us."

LeeAnn wiggled free and made wild gesturing motions with her hands. She pointed at Nikki, then the man, then back at Nikki, making a gun with her hands and pulling the trigger. "He shot your mother?" Nikki asked.

LeeAnn nodded, then motioned at Nikki again, her

mouth working frantically, but no sound came out. She slapped her hands together several times, then made a motion across her neck. Nikki shook her head, not understanding. The child made the motions several more times.

"Your sister?" Dane softly asked. LeeAnn vigorously nodded. He turned to Nikki, his face tensing with anger. "She's trying to say Two Thumbs assaulted her sister, then cut her throat."

Nikki picked up the child and held her close. "Mercy, Marshal? Can you honestly want to show mercy to those animals? Perhaps you can understand a little of what this child and we have been through. Look at her," she almost shouted at him. She nodded toward the child in her arms who shivered so hard her teeth chattered. Not giving Dane a chance to speak, she sidestepped him and steered LeeAnn quickly toward their lodge.

Chapter 8
Mercy of an Angel

SKELETAL FINGERS OF NIGHT CREPT ACROSS the land and passed in a grey cloak, swiftly turning black, bringing with it bone-chilling cold. Gusting wind howled through the trees and wiped away the smell of burned flesh, then the smell grew oppressive and brooding when it stilled again. The moon hid her face from the follies of man, and the stars drifted in and out of grey clouds, the clouds slowly building tears.

Tsistsistas victoriously danced around the big bonfire in the village center. The rhythmic beat of drums, the chu-chink of rattles, the excited babble of voices, and bloodcurdling screams, echoed through the hills.

Nikki shivered, not so much from the chilled wind, but from the screams coming in undulating waves. The food bowls rattling in her hands, she neared the lodge where Dane rested before his trial by swinging pole in three days' time. After risking the enmity of her people to save him, she wanted to stay far away from him. She would have if her grandmother had not forced the issue of a wife's duty upon her.

With a toss of her head, daggers of dread and anguish swept over her after discovering Dane had informed her grandparents of the bride price accepted by her father and unwittingly by herself. Drawing a shuddering breath, she ducked under the lodge flap, resenting her grandmother pressuring her to move her things in with his.

Staring into the fire and trying to block out the screams, Dane barely glanced in her direction when she deposited the food in front of him. Without taking his eyes from the fire, he grabbed her wrist, knowing if he exerted a little more pressure, the fine bones between his fingers would snap like dry twigs. Slowly, he turned his head to look into the shadowy, expressionless depths of her eyes. "Listen to the screams, Dark Angel. Is your hatred so strong you would have him scream for days before death overtakes him?"

She tried to pull away, but the hand on her wrist tightened, making her wince with pain. "I can do nothing. I have already risked my life for you. I cannot for him too—not for that murdering beast." Her face hardened, hiding how the stridulous noise affected her.

"You can do something. Kill him. Put him out of his misery." He jerked on her wrist, forcing her to sit beside him.

Shaking her head, the long length of her hair sweeping the ground behind her, she scorned, "I am not ready to die, Marshal, especially not for one such as he. If you cannot bear the screams, I will bind your ears, but do not ask the impossible of me."

"You're savage, Dark Angel, savage as them. Does it make your blood run hot to hear another's torment?" Dane captured her chin with his free hand, exerting enough pressure to make her cry out. "Answer me, Nikki! Have you picked someone tonight to cool your hot little body? Is Two Moons the buck you've picked?"

"Let me go!" Her eyes widened with the new slice to her already butchered heart and she pulled back, but the pressure on her wrist and chin increased. "Why are you doing this to me? I have done all I can!"

Releasing her chin, he dug his hands in her hair and pulled her closer, the steady screams driving him crazy and wearing on his frayed nerves. "Does your blood boil, Nikki?"

A whimper sneaking past her lips, she caught her hair underneath his hand to ease the pressure. He frightened her with his insane conversation and the glazed look in his eyes. She wanted to join her screams with the outlaw's, drown out his with hers, anything so she would not have to listen. "Please, let me go!"

He jerked her roughly against him until her face was a bare inch from his. "Has hatred drunk every single drop of compassion you once had, Dark Angel?"

A shiver ran through her with his raspy, accusing voice, and she clenched her teeth, hearing them grind. Surely, he did not think she enjoyed the torture, but in his silver-blue orbs she saw an endless whirlpool of death.

Pulling her closer still, he ground his lips against hers, searching for a way to drown the wails of the tortured man from his hearing. He forced her on the blanket beside him and his hand traveled toward her breast. A soft, inviting mound filled his hand and he squeezed it, bringing a yelp of pain from the woman underneath him. "Will you tell your grandparents we are mated and share this lodge with me? Then I will cool your hot little body, Dark Angel."

The metallic taste of blood filled her mouth and her breast hurt where he forced his anger into her. Struggling against him, fear wrapped her in its deadly claws. *Where is the gentle man I once knew? Why is he doing this to me?*

She managed to pull her mouth free and spit blood onto the ground, some blood trickling down her chin. "Will you become one of those monsters who ravished me?" she rasped, pushing ineffectually at his chest, ignoring his question since she already knew he had broken their secret. He abruptly released her and sat up, his eyes going back to the fire's dancing lights, the screams a bizarre background.

Sitting up, she rubbed her bruised breast and lips, then wiped the blood from her cheek and chin. "You are acting like an animal, so why should I let you touch me, much less tell my grandparents we are mated?"

He glanced at her, wanting to say he was sorry, wanting to explain why he had reacted so violently, but he did not understand it himself. The pain in his head resembled someone beating it with a sledgehammer. God help him! He wanted to hurt her, destroy her the way those screams were him, yet realizing she was not responsible for them, but he blamed her anyway. With palms pressed against his ears, he almost groaned in despair with the memories whirling around his head.

A shred of compassion easing into her heart at his despondent position, she reached toward the thick mat of light brown hair, then stopped with his next whispered words.

"I was riding with a fellow named Tom Brown, a U.S. Deputy Marshal, and Johnny Raspin, a 17-year-old who was learning the ropes. My uncle sent me with them since he was going after another lawless individual. He thought he was sending me on a safe pursuit."

Drawing a shuddering breath, he paused, then

swallowed hard before speaking again. "We were captured by Comanches."

Compassion filling her, Nikki leaned forward a little to hear him better. Comanches usually roamed the Texas plains and were known for their cruelty, and sudden understanding flashed in her heart.

"I was ten at the time and forced to watch the Comanche warriors staked Tom spreadeagle and naked on the ground." Staring into the depths of the fire, his voice deepened with the memory, "Comanche women and children sliced off sections of his skin and his ears and stuck burning brands against his body. They kept him alive for days, but when I was forced to watch my friend Johnny go through the same thing…"

Wincing, he fought the images flying through his head: his friend's screams, the smell of burning flesh, the cackles of the Comanche women. "They kept him alive, torturing him for almost a week."

Lifting haunted eyes to hers, he finished, "They kept a rope around my neck and my hands tied in front of me, pulling me forward after stripping me of my clothing when my friend's screams ended with his death. It was my turn to be staked out naked."

Unable to help herself, she placed her hand on his, but he pulled away, his troubled silver-blue eyes still focused on the fire. "Somehow, a visiting Arapaho brave saw something in me and bargained with the Comanche for my life, buying me as his slave before adopting me."

"I…" she stopped, words escaping her with her sudden understanding how he understood the Algonquian language, the chastity belt, and marriage bargaining. The Northern Cheyenne and Arapahos spoke the same language, and their customs were very similar.

When he lifted begging eyes, pleading for sympathy within them, she shook her head, rose, and left the lodge, not able to deal with his past much less her own. They all had their demons to conquer this dark night.

She walked toward her lodge, trying to keep her eyes from straying toward the fire and the man tied to the pole. Sobs and retching erupted with the screams of Two Thumbs, and she found Kissa with her face streaked with tears, kneeling close to the tipi. Nikki knelt beside her and smoothed the hair from her face.

Kissa rubbed her mouth with her shirt sleeve, then clasped Nikki's shoulders. "They burned his eyes out and now they're sticking burning brands to his body! Nikki, Tawnie joined them. Please, make them stop! Make her stop!"

"Come. I will help you back to the lodge." Nikki placed her arm around Kissa's waist and helped her stand. Something within her desperately wanted to push her away and shove the words down her throat. *What do they think I am? Some kind of superhuman and all I have to do is snap my fingers to make everything all right?*

Almost pushing Kissa through the flap, she watched her crawl toward the fire and huddle there, her arms wrapped around her drawn up knees and her face hidden against her them.

Ginger held a crying LeeAnn, her own face streaked with tears. "I hate the wretch, hate him with my whole being, but even I don't want him to die this way. How much longer will it last?"

"All night, a day, two days." Nikki shrugged. "They can keep him alive for days."

"You've got to do something," Kissa shrilled, lifting her face a moment, then burying it back against her knees.

"Perhaps we can do something." Ginger pulled the child closer to her to still the shivers pricking the hairs along her neck.

"There is nothing we can do." Smoothing the hair from her face, Nikki looked around, not really seeing her surroundings, only her friends' tortured faces and teary eyes.

"Tawnie's out there watching," Ginger informed her under her breath, rocking the child back and forth while holding LeeAnn's head against her shoulder and covering her outer ear with her hand.

"Stay inside. I will close the flap so you cannot see what is happening." Surreptitiously slipping her smallest ivory bow from the leather covering, she hid it underneath her arm and exited the lodge. Frozen with fear and indecision, she wondered what she should do now. She knew the consequences of killing a prisoner during a ritual like this, and the very thought quaked her stomach. *Why me?* she wanted to scream. *Why must I find a way to end his torment?*

Silent and stealthily as a bobcat, Nikki snuck around the back of the lodges, heading for the arrow makers' lodge. Fear and remorse filling her, she almost groaned out loud with the thought of stealing an unpainted arrow. She was breaking a deep moral code instilled by the Cheyenne—to never steal.

Her palms sweaty, she clutched the arrow to her breast, slipping in and out of shadows. At the edge of the village, behind a temporarily unoccupied tipi, she slumped with her hands on her knees and breathed deeply to steady her nerves. She only had one chance, and if she failed or someone caught her… She shook her head, unwilling to explore the possibility.

With the arrow notched, she stepped from the tipi's cover, brought the bow in front of her, and stretched the string back, the muscles in her neck, back, and arms straining.

Staring at the people surrounding the man tied to the pole, Nikki caught sight of Tawnie beside Young Bird, a burning brand in her hand. Remembering Two Thumbs' head buried between her friend's legs, she pulled the string back further, aiming the arrow at the outlaw's heart.

Voices from the past whispered in her ear, then became louder. Cari's face rose before her, *you will always protect me, won't you, Nikki?* Then her words flowed toward Red Wolf, d*o you call me now to make me the angel of death?*

Each person in her life flashed before her mind's eye, their voices accusing with Dane's deep voice loudly proclaiming, *you're savage, Dark Angel, savage as them.*

With shaking hands, she bit her bottom lip to steady herself, her eyes blurring with Cloud Walker's voice sounding behind her, *you cannot come back to the Cheyenne, Ovaxehee. But know you are always a part of them and your life parallels theirs.*

Holding the bow and arrow steady, the power of tongue settled over her and she slowly eased the pressure off the string, allowing the arrow to anchor between her fingers. Lowering the bow, she remembered the Bible verse Kissa read to LeeAnn, *let love be without dissimulation. Abhor that which is evil, cleave to that which is good.*

Dropping her gaze to the ground, she heard herself proclaim, "Let justice be weighed against Two Thumbs,

Wise One Above, and deliver your verdict."

A shrilled, frightened, horrific scream rent through village, and Two Thumbs slumped against the pole, the sudden silence as piercing as the screams.

Nikki quickly replaced the stolen arrow at the Arrow Maker's lodge, then hid the bow inside her bed, relieved Kissa and Ginger had not noticed her when she reentered the tipi.

The early chirping birds mixed with the excited babble of voices reached her, the words indistinct. Drawing knees to her chest, she wrapped her arms around them, and laid her chin on top, fighting the fear threatening to tear her sanity in half.

The nerve-racking sounds wiped away Kissa's and Ginger's memory of Nikki leaving, but it was Tawnie's excited voice which brought them back to their surroundings. "That whore's son just dropped dead, and they think sumbody killed him. The Cheyenne are madder than a disturbed hornet's nest. I'd hate to be the mongrel that put that dog outta his misery, especially when those people out there get their hands a hold of him."

THE CAMP GROWING QUIET FOR THE NIGHT and her friends asleep, Nikki crept out of the lodge, slipping between the rows of tipis, and making her way toward the river. Maneuvering through the tall trees, she reached the river's edge, barely noticing the night creatures were strangely silent. The moon reflected silver in undulating waves across the surface, the sweet murmur of rippling waters moving across the sands and rocks, trying to pierce through her heavy heart.

Leaning her head back to gaze at the stars above her, she observed a shooting star pass across endless dark skies. She lifted her arms upward, her voice a bare whisper in the wind, "Strengthen me, One Above. Give me courage and strength for all the days of my life."

Lowering her hands, she bowed her head. A crushing weight lay across her, sapping her strength and energy. *Who am I kidding? No one is up there to hear me or give me what I need. Though surrounded by people, I am all alone.*

Tawnie moved in with Young Bird after selecting ponies from his herd, and she rarely saw her, the couple having secluded themselves in a tipi outside the village. Nikki avoided Dane, refusing to transfer her things and herself into the tipi set up for him, though her grandmother often strongly suggested she take her place by his side.

No one guessed she put Two Thumbs out of his misery, but the guilt laid heavy on her conscience: guilt not so much for the mercy killing, but for using her power of tongue. Nikki took the trust instilled in her and used it against her people to save a man who could save himself, and then used it to kill a man who raided her farm, freeing him from her people's judgement, and it weighed heavy on her soul.

Stripping out of her clothes, she waded into the stream, the icy water slapping against her flesh, chilling her. She hurriedly bathed, then waded back to the shore and dried with the clothing she wore to the river. After dressing in her ritual clothing and placing the robe Cloud Walker painted for her years ago, around her shoulders, she sat beside the stream and waited for morning's light.

Dawn erupted over the land, but she did not enjoy the beautiful splashes of color folding into bright light. Instead, she headed for the hill where Dane and Two Moons would be sacrificing to the spirits, showing them honor per her ceremonial apparel.

"Now walk this way and back four times."

Finding a large rock nearby, she sat on top so the people could witness she honored the men. Scrutinizing Dane, gratification swelled within her; the way he kept his face from showing pain and kept a steady beat with the music while striving against the swinging pole. The top part of his body richly tanned and his legs starkly white, the muscles in his legs, back, and neck bulging, he labored against the ropes with his face tightening in concentration, confirming a man she did not give enough credit to his character.

She nodded to herself, agreeing with her thoughts. *Yes, there will be a feast soon to celebrate Dane's and Two Moons' show of strength and courage.*

Noticing the shift in the wind, a bitterness different from before, she lifted her eyes to the glaring blue sky. Grey clouds banked in the north and scudded across the skies. She nodded her head again. *It is nearly time to leave.*

SOMEHOW DANE ENDED UP IN THE LODGE and Nikki sat beside him, spreading some foul-smelling ointment on his chest. She was unaware he watched her, and it gave him a chance to study her. Her face was a perfect oval, her loss of weight showing in the protruding high cheekbones. Long black lashes swept across the top of her cheeks, then fluttered when the medicine stung her eyes. Dusky rose lips pouted with her concentration, and he wanted to grab the long length of raven black hair and kiss her, to celebrate his triumph.

He must have made a sound for she turned her head and met his, her eyes light blue and clear as a summer sky. Lashes lowered to cover her thoughts, but not before he glimpsed approval in them.

"If you will rise, I will bind your chest," she softly demanded, shifting her eyes back to his.

Her hands warm against the flesh of his back, he eased himself up and smothered the groan rising to his lips. He silently watched her bind white strips across his chest, then sit back on her knees.

"How do you feel?"

He managed a weary smile. "Exuberant."

"Good. In two days, they will honor you and Two Moons with a celebration. It should give you enough time to heal some." Her hands tightened on her thighs to keep from smoothing the haggard lines from his face.

"I'll make it, Dark Angel."

There was so much to say, but neither knew how to begin, so they sat there in silence, staring into the flickering fire. She shifted uneasily, preparing to rise when he stopped her with a light touch on her arm.

"You're the one who ended Two Thumbs' life the other night," his voice conveyed his thanks the only way he knew how. His jaw tightened and flexed when she pulled her arm away and rose quickly to her feet.

"Do not try to make me into an angel of mercy, Marshal. I had nothing to do with it." She spun on her heel and was out of the lodge before he could open his mouth again.

She headed toward the outer limits of the village, her jaw aching from clenching her teeth. *What is the man doing to me?* She had stolen for him and lied to him, abet she did replace the arrow, but it was something she had never done before in her life. For him, she had gone against some of the most sacred teachings of the *Tsistsistas. What is happening to me? Why does his presence disturb me and why do I think about him when he is not near me? It makes no sense. Nothing makes any sense anymore.*

"Ovaxehee," a deep voice called behind her.

Turning slowly, she dreaded facing Two Moons. *"Ese'he Ohnesesestse,* should you not be resting?"

"I will, but let us walk to the river," he invited, coming up beside her. They walked beside each other, silent until reaching the riverbank. *"Ovaxehee,* I saw you the night the pale face died."

Nikki stopped to face him, anxiety widening her eyes and wondering where the conversation was headed. "What are you getting at?" she asked, studying his bland expression.

"I saw you at the village edge with an arrow aimed at the captive, then the spirits filled you. Did you speak his death?" Two Moons searched her eyes, probing for the truth.

"No, I did not, *Ese'he Ohnesesestse,"* she assured him.

"He died soon afterward. I followed you and watched you replace the arrow you took from the arrow maker."

Flushing with shame, she nevertheless kept her gaze on his. "Yes, I took the arrow and was about to end his life, but I could not. I could not bear the disgrace of going against my people yet again nor the dishonor of taking something not mine."

"What did you say? His screams changed right after that and turned to absolute terror."

Stepping closer to him, she placed her hands on his upper arms, keeping her gaze locked with his to verify her honesty. "I asked *Heammawihio* to pronounce his judgement."

Relief flooding his face and searching her eyes with his, Two Moons raised his arms and placed his hands on her upper arms. "I did not want to reveal your part in his death to the others and now I have no reason to divulge this information."

His hands tightened a little on her upper arms, wanting to pull her closer. "I did not want to see you suffer the tribes' justice."

Weak with relief and her eyes softening, she recognized the warmth in his eyes, still desiring her as his woman. He drew her slightly forward, released his hold on her arms and slipped them behind her back before pulling her against his body, his arms wrapping around her and capturing her arms between them.

Relaxing slightly against him, her heart broke because she could not return his affection. She shook head, her eyes still locked with his, and regretfully whispered, "No, *Ese'he Ohnesesestse*, I am no longer free. I am *Hotohketana'otse* woman now."

He did not release his hold but drew her closer to him. "You do not share a lodge with him, *Ovaxehee*. How can this be so?"

With a heavy sigh, she moved back from him, keeping eye contact. "My father accepted his marriage price of five ponies. I did not know about the arrangement because my family was murdered before I was told. I did not know when my friend, *Mo'ehes*'s woman, brought five ponies to my home afterwards that they were the marriage price until not long ago. I inadvertently accepted them."

He tightened his arms around her again, searching her face. "You can agree to separate, *Ovaxehee,* and return the bride price. You have not stayed in his lodge."

Gently disengaging herself from his embrace, she stepped back, her face filled with unhappiness. "Even if I wanted to, we can never be. I have been ordered to leave when the first snow falls."

FEATHER LIGHT SNOWFLAKES SWIRLED AROUND the dancers performing around the fire. Nikki sat beside Two Moons, her thoughts a million miles away. She and her friends presented the gifts of the outlaws' horses, the ponies from the raid, and weapons taken from the outlaws to the members of the Kit Fox Soldiers who had trained them these last few months. Tawnie also returned Young Bird's ponies back to him. With a heavy heart, Nikki informed the group they would leave at dawn. The Cheyenne would move the day after for their winter camp deeper into the Black Hills.

Two Moons spoke to her several times before she heard him. "Did you tell He Who Walks Away, the medicine man, what you saw in your vision?"

"I told him." Her answer was short and blunt, dreading the next question.

"Did you see me in your vision?"

She turned toward him; her eyes shielded against her thoughts. "Your bravery is great when you fight many battles." She touched his arm, shaking her head. "It is all I saw about you."

Silent, she stared into his black incessant eyes. "I cannot leave without trying to heal the rift that has come between us. I will always think of you as my brother. We did share blood after killing the bear."

"I never wanted to be your brother, *Ovaxehee*. I planned to ask your brother again for his permission to take you as my woman. We can fight the Long Knives side by side." But he already knew her answer.

"I am already taken, *Ese'he Ohnesesestse*. I ask you to be my brother. It is all that can ever be between us. And even if I wished it different, the spirits are against us. *Maehonehe* and *Vo'evahtamehnestse* ordered me to leave and never return."

Two Moons turned his attention back to the dancers, his face granite hard. "I said you were *Tsistsistas* no longer and I did it to hurt you, *Ovaxehee*. Forgive me and I will be your brother." He lifted his face to hers, his eyes widening ever so slightly before he reached across to touch the bear claw necklace he had given her long ago hanging around her throat.

"There is nothing to forgive," she said softly. "You were right in part. I have lived with the whites too long and my strength is not strong anymore." She clasped his forearms with her hands, gripping them tightly. "Say a little prayer for me."

"Go in peace, *Ovaxehee*."

Placing a quick kiss on his cheek, she rose and dodged the people lined around the dancers, hurrying toward her lodge. The longer she put off going, the harder it would be for her to leave. At dawn, ten warriors would escort them out of the Black Hills.

Watching her leave and making his excuses, Dane followed her, catching her before she entered the tipi. "Nikki, wait. I want to speak with you."

The brilliant bonfire at his back illuminated her face, and the flames reflected in those hauntingly beautiful azure-blue eyes. The straight, proud nose and strong impudent chin were thrust upward with unbending pride, but it was her mouth capturing his attention. Clearing his throat, vividly aware of his need to hold her and kiss the stubbornness away, to thank her for ending the tortured outlaw's life, and maybe even salvage part of his pride, he commented, "I heard you and the others are leaving at dawn."

"The first snow has fallen." She did not explain further when confusion crossed his face.

"Where are you going?"

"Why should it matter, Marshal?"

"Nikki, for God's sake, talk to me!"

"Why, Dane? What else is there to say?" She coolly brushed his hand from her arm. It did not matter what she wanted. Her revenge was more important than them both.

One Above, help me! She wanted to be in his arms, for him to tell her nothing mattered except the passion between them, and they needed to explore it more fully before she destroyed everything good in her life. She needed something. Sacrificing to the spirits had not been the answer. She felt empty, used, and lonely, and did not know how to combat any of it.

He read nothing from her carefully schooled face. He

wanted to spank her, make her angry, make love to her, anything to put some emotion into her beautiful, but empty body. "My offer of making you and your friends deputies still stands. Will you at least consider it again?"

Knowing her answer would never change, she nodded slowly, then turned on her heel. He placed a hand on her arm, stopping her.

"Don't leave."

Her shoulders wearily slumped. "Why, Dane? So, we can hurt each other more?"

He stared at her uncompromising back and how her luxurious coal-black hair hung past the bend of her knees with the red wolf tail flowing with the silken strands. Touching a fine-spun tress, he willed her to turn around. "I need you, Dark Angel."

Chapter 9
Ride the Wind of Death

THE VIBRANT CARESS OF HIS VOICE pulled Nikki toward him, and an aching hunger trembled her knees. Without words or conscious effort, she slipped her hand into his. A frightened, appealing purse quivered her lips, her wish to break the spell failing to form into a coherent thought. Conflicting emotions fleeing across her face, she let him lead her around the tipis to his lodge.

Dane gently pushed her inside, and Nikki wet her lips, trying to speak. *What am I doing? He only brought me here to hurt me or try to talk me out of the mission which cries out for vengeance in my dreams. He has refused to make love to me, has gone so far to say it is my fault he could not. What is the matter with me? Am I a glutton for punishment?* Dane pulled her into his arms, molding his lips to hers, and her anguished thoughts went no further.

The steady cadence of the drums pounded in their eardrums and pulsed through their blood. Snowflakes drifted down the smoke hole, the fire hissing with the contact. A dog yipped and the haunting melody of a love song serenading lovers rose around them. He slipped the headband from her brow and dropped it at their feet. Digging his hands in the silken, midnight-black mass, the scent of pine and the fresh outdoors teased him, enveloping him in a sense of lovers' springtime.

The cold seeping from underneath the hide edges of the tipi heightened the sensations when he pulled her forward and lowered his head. She met his lips, opening her mouth to his questing tongue, knowing she was lost under the assault, especially when he dropped his hands to cup her bottom, pulling her closer against him.

While caressing her buttocks, he gently moved her buckskin dress upward until the cold hit her in the places his hands did not cover. Dropping one hand down his side, she wormed it toward his breechcloth, moving aside the leather before cupping her hands between his legs. Fondling the sac, playing with one nugget, then the other, she enjoyed feeling his sac grow tighter with her ministrations. She moaned when his hands moved upward, dislodged her hands and pulled the dress over her head, dropping it beside them.

They slipped out of the remainder of confining clothing and lay on a bed of fur, the softness caressing their naked flesh. Pulling her shivering form close to his, he fitted each curve and indentation to the muscled length of his body, showering her with feather light kisses on her temples, eyes, nose and stubborn chin before capturing rose petal soft lips with his.

Their breath met and mingled, tongues moved in and out suggestively, hands explored satin smooth flesh. The wind picked up and whistled eerily through the lodge, invoking phantoms of past, ill-fated lovers.

She moaned against his lips, a surging of hot blood enlivening nerve endings and flowing to the secret center of her. "Yes, love me. Cleanse my soul and free the loathing fear and consuming hate from me."

He rose slightly above her, interweaving his fingers in the straight length of her hair, and gazed into her desire-lowered eyes. "You're mine, Dark Angel. You are my wife now and forever."

Kissing her eyes closed, he filled his hand with the inviting mound of her breast, ran his tongue from the corner of her mouth, along the long column of her neck, over her shoulder to the rosy nub of her other breast. The faint taste of soap and camp smoke magnified the sensitivity of his tongue. He played upon her sensitized globe, sucking, nipping, and running his roughened tongue across the love tip while slipping his hand between her legs.

A sob catching in her throat, she arched against him. Her fingers slid through his light brown hair and closed around the thick, coarse locks, holding his head captive. Desire, hot and demanding, surged through her with each beat of the drum, becoming insistent, constant, begging for release as he caressed her until she bucked against his hand.

She touched his shoulder, pushing with enough force to free his mouth from her nipple. Pressing him on his back, she rose above him, her heavy hair falling across them in blanketing darkness. Running her fingers across ridged, smooth skin, she bent, tasted and teased his man nipples with a questing, inquisitive tongue.

A wisp of her hair tickled his nose and mouth, the essence of him throbbed against her stomach, insistently demanding release from this bittersweet torment. His breath caught in his throat when her tongue traveled along the indentation of his chest, past the bandages down to the rough hair of his stomach and along the line of hair toward his pelvis. Ensnaring his hands in the long length of her hair, he stopped her journey of excruciating delight and forced her upward toward him.

His touch intoxicating, she wanted to be one with him, somehow pull him into her body and keep him there forever. She could no longer think, only feel each delicious thrill rampaging through every part of her body. Rising slightly, she caressed his smooth shaft, running her tongue over her lips while lifting upward and straddling him, placing his hardness at her entrance.

Sighing with pleasure, she settled on top, shivering with intensity as it filled her. Leaning toward him, she captured his lips with hers while moving her hips with his, each stroke building inside her, his groans against her mouth sending even more pleasure racing through her.

Entwining her hair around his hands, he gently forced her on her back, parted her legs, and plunged into her welcoming moist, velvety folds. "You'll never be free of me, Dark Angel. Never!"

Matching her rhythm with his, whimpering moans broke past her lips, every delicious sensation centering between her legs. Drumming bliss rose increasingly stronger until she cried his name over and over, riding the wind of yearning toward the Milky Way and crashing over the top to float back to earth securely in his strong arms.

She fell asleep with his arms wrapped around her, and he awakened her more than once with his exploring caresses, their need for each other insatiable.

Instinctively knowing dawn was near, she waited until he fell asleep before slipping out of his embrace and dressing. It was with misgiving that she left his side when everything within her wanted to stay, but her family's blood cried for vengeance, a mandate that demanded she avenge them and eliminate the horrible men who destroyed all their lives. Making her way back to her friends on wet ground where it had snowed and melted, she entered the lodge just as birds began their pre-morning song.

Tawnie jammed a shirt into the saddlebag, turning when Nikki entered, wondering briefly about the soft, sleepy droop to her eyes. "What ya gonna do with the kid?" She nodded to the sleeping child along the edge of the tipi, trying to hide the swelling of her own eyes.

"Leave her with my grandparents. They will take good care of her." Suddenly, small arms captured her waist behind her, and she turned to look into the wide frightened eyes of LeeAnn. LeeAnn violently shook her head back and forth, pointing at herself, then at Nikki.

Her throat tightening and her heart beating an unsteady tempo, Nikki knelt in front of her and held her still. "*Meeskevotse*, you will be safer with them than with us. My grandparents will adopt you."

LeeAnn shook her head, her blonde hair flying around her, and her big brown eyes filling with tears, her hurt palpable.

"Please understand, little one. It is not because I do not love you. It is because I want you to be happy. I want you someplace where you will not be on the dangerous road we will be traveling."

The child grabbed her around the neck and held on, her sobs shaking her small body. Nikki had debated this issue since Dane and she had such fierce words after the trouble at Barton's Corner. After much soul searching, her decision had been reached. Last night's lovemaking had firmly entrenched the plan in her mind, arguing it was the right thing to do even though the child's sobs broke her heart.

NIKKI HUGGED HER GRANDPARENTS, THEN LeeAnn, her eyes growing distant when the child cried and held onto her like a lifeline. With misgivings and a bruised heart, she gently pushed the child into her grandmother's arms before she mounted.

With the grey fingers of dawn touching the land, the small group of women and braves left the camp. She was afraid if she looked back, her resolve to leave LeeAnn with her grandparents would break. The child was better off with them, but each time she thought it, her conscience received a sharp pang of regret.

Heoohtato lagged behind and whined. He darted toward LeeAnn, then stopped when Nikki called his name. He whined louder, then with one last look at LeeAnn, turned and trotted after Nikki.

Nikki kept her eyes straight along the path, her heart lurching with each beat of the horse hooves, the anguish of leaving LeeAnn fighting against her longing to have the child still with her. Somewhere within her, she blamed Dane for her decision even though it was her choice. She tried to reenforce the knowledge that LeeAnn was much better with her grandparents, but several times she had to restrain herself from going back to reclaim the little girl.

Toward midday, Young Bird informed them someone was following. They dismounted and melted into the trees, their weapons ready.

A huge roan stallion and calico pony broke into view carrying Dane and LeeAnn. A mirthless chuckle slipping past her lips, she slid the pistol back into her holster and stepped from the concealing trees. Hands on hips, her head tossed proudly, she glared at Dane, not understanding why he brought the child with him. Could he not understand how hard it had been to leave her? Angry more at herself than him, she scorned, "You follow us like a thief in the night."

Dane pulled on the reins, his eyes narrowing at her sudden appearance. LeeAnn jumped from the pony's back and ran with the agility of a frightened fawn into her arms. The child nearly knocked her from her feet, and a soft swoosh was forced from Nikki.

"Hey, *Meeskevotse*. Take it easy or we will both be on the ground." Hugging the child close, she was unable to hide her pleasure. She had missed the mute child during the short interval they were separated, and her heart ached with her absence.

Suddenly, she and LeeAnn were knocked to the ground, and Nikki emitted a short cry of surprise. The ungainly, near-grown puppy yelped excitedly and delivered sloppy licks to the child's face. "*Heoohtato*, get off before you smother us."

LeeAnn scrambled up and wrapped her arms around the dog. Nikki's laughter suddenly stopped. Dane stood over her, his hand outstretched to help her up, a hard gleam in his silver-blue eyes.

His hand closed tightly around hers and he roughly jerked her upright. He had awakened to an empty bed and wondered if the soft, giving woman he had made love to last night had been a beautiful dream. It had taken a little while to convince himself the dream had been real, only to have it destroyed when he discovered LeeAnn crying at the edge of the village and Nikki gone. "I made a terrible mistake trusting the child in your care, Dark Angel. I will remedy that right now. I'm taking the child with me."

Guilty hurt flashed in her eyes, but it was Ginger who answered. "Lay off, Marshal. She left the child for her own safety. You saw how improved LeeAnn was with the Cheyenne."

His eyes narrowing, his eyebrows meaningfully drew together. "Thick as thieves,"

"Ya stupid worm, it was you who kept sayin' she needed to be with a family and not with soiled women like us," Tawnie snapped, wanting to knock those beautiful white teeth down his throat. "Ya don't know whut in the hell your wantin' 'cept to cause Nikki pain. You're a sorry scumbag. Cain't you see she's tryin' her darndest to do right by that child? Do ya think she'd leave her with just anybody? That child had it made in the shade with the Cheyenne just 'cause she cain't talk none."

An angry, embarrassed flush rose to his face. In Tawnie's rough, hard-bitten way, she came upon a truth he had not realized himself until she said it; he *was* trying to cause Nikki pain, trying to make her see reason when all the time he knew she would never do anything right in his eyes if she persisted in going after the Mason gang. *And why is that?* he wondered morosely. *Do I blame her for the assaults and the deaths? God help me, I don't know what's going on in my own mind anymore.*

Gazing into her disturbingly sober eyes, he knew last night had been no dream. The light blue depths dulled with the slash to her shattered heart and held a longing—a need for his understanding.

He slowly walked toward the stallion and mounted, then turned his eyes toward her. "I'm giving you another chance, Dark Angel. Don't fail me again."

THE NEARLY FLAT PLAINS OF GRASSLAND, cactus, and endless skies gave way to rolling hills and low scrub brush foothills after they separated from the marshal and headed toward the Colorado Territory. The only amusement lifting her firm lips was watching Tawnie and Young Bird say goodbye. Tawnie grabbed Young Bird and lifted him up against her to passionately kiss him goodbye. She was startled when Tawnie snuck a hand underneath his breech cloth before setting him on his feet.

They were a sober group after parting company with the Cheyenne. Nikki barely spoke to her friends, and her wintery blue eyes grew distant, constantly praying for the tears which never came. Anguished hurt opened more wounds in her already shredded heart and the glacial center of her wept frozen tears with her need to escape back into Dane's arms.

Growing gaunter and more reserved each day, Nikki reasoned they never had a chance, not now, perhaps never. It did not stop her yearning for life to be different, and in her confusion and doubt, she found she could not justify anything anymore.

Riding toward the higher reaches, the landscape gave way to ponderosa pine interspersed with groves of aspen and lodgepole pine whose trees were splendidly arrayed in autumn colors. The wind, soft and far off, rustled through the trees, building with intensity until the breeze reached them. The breeze ruffled their hair and blew splashy fall leaves in swirling pools, then all was silent.

Birds called to one another overhead in trees reaching toward the heavens. Mountains rose on all sides. Bedrocks gave the water a brown appearance with silver waves, but the stream was sweet and pure. A flash of iridescent silver wiggled through the water, then the fish disappeared.

"It's breathtaking," Kissa whispered in awe. "It's a whole different world out here!"

"You will be cussing all this beauty before we get out of the Rockies," Nikki darkly predicted. "Keep moving. There should be a mining town close."

The tired, chilled group rode into the bustling mining town and none of them ever asked for the name. The busy dirt and mud road was bulging with people and all types of horses and wheeled wagons. They dodged overzealous miners, dray wagons, and horses. After settling the horses at the stable, they walked to one of the nicer appearing clapboard hotels.

So used to the various types of people out to make their fortune, the clerk barely raised an eyebrow at the pant-clad women or the dog staying close by LeeAnn's and Nikki's side. "Community beds fifty cents a night, private rooms five dollars. Got two private rooms left. What'll it be, Ladies?"

Nikki glanced at her companions, then with a devil-may-care attitude, decided to splurge. They needed a treat. They had spent the last weeks sleeping on hard ground underneath the open skies. Besides, the community beds probably only contained smelly men. She plunked down the coins and heard an ecstatic sigh behind her.

"Please have plenty of hot water and a tub sent up."

The clerk took the money, turned the register book toward her, dipped the pen in ink, and handed it to her. "Don't have bathing facilities. There's a bathhouse down the street."

Nikki took the keys and mumbled thanks in a clipped tone before she led the group up the rickety stairs. They entered the first room and plopped their gear on the floor.

Kissa headed straight for the bed and laid down. "Heavenly! I had forgotten what it felt like to lie in a real bed."

"Don't get too comfortable. Let's get a bath first," Ginger warned, pulling at her blouse and wrinkling her pert nose with the smell.

"And scented soap? Wouldn't it be nice to smell and dress like a woman again? And LeeAnn needs a new dress. She's grown so much." Kissa laughed, fluffing the still unstylishly short locks. "And pretty hair ribbons."

Tawnie snorted. "I'll go for a bath, but I ain't gonna put on no darn skirt. These pants are a helluva lot more practical."

"Nikki?"

"Get LeeAnn the dress and the furbelows, and restock our food supply, enough for several months." She grudgingly handed the money to Ginger, then laughed at herself.

"Oh, good grief, let us enjoy this night to the fullest," she intoned, flipping more coins into the pile before giving them to Ginger. "I will leave it up to you to get us all a winter coat, gloves, long underwear, and blankets."

"Long underwear like men wear?" Ginger queried.

"We will need them. Get whatever you think we will

need for extremely cold weather."

"And scented soap?" Kissa hopefully asked.

Nikki laughed. "And scented soap. While you three are at the general store, Tawnie and I will ask around. Maybe we can pick up a lead."

"I'll ask around the saloons," Tawnie added. "Meet me at the bathhouse in an hour. I'll stop by and make sure there ain't no men around when we bathe."

SETTLING IN WARM WATER, FIVE TUBS lined in a row, Kissa made a big production out of handing them the scented soap. "The storekeeper said he kept it stocked for some…uhm…ladies in town. Ginger, I got you attar of roses, Tawnie—honeysuckle, LeeAnn—strawberry, I got myself lilacs, and Nikki…" She handed it to her a bit shyly, eagerly waiting for approval, "spice and wild roses."

Nikki brought the soap to her nose, nostalgia sweeping over her with the heady fragrance reminding her of springtime in the Black Hills. "It is perfect, Kissa. Thank you."

None of them were too eager to get out of the warm baths. It was a special treat after shivering in cold streams, but with skin wrinkling and the water growing tepid, they forced themselves out of wooden tubs. Dried and dressed with their precious soaps packed away in pockets, they headed for the hotel restaurant, slightly awkward in long skirts again.

After a hearty meal of buffalo steaks, fried potatoes, beans, biscuits, and precious eggs and milk, Nikki reached into her pocket, searching for the pouch containing their money. "The money! It is gone!"

"But how… "

"The bath," Nikki angrily decided. "I had it with my clothes when we went to bathe."

"Why that son of a gun!" Tawnie growled, rising from the chair. "I'll meet ya later in the room."

"Where are you go…" Kissa stopped as Tawnie stomped out without a backward glance, then she turned to Nikki. "Was that all our money?"

"Every cent." Grimness whitening her mouth, she found it hard to meet their eyes. She had been the guardian of the money and she had failed her responsibility.

"I've some money left from buying supplies. I hid it in my shoe." Ginger slipped out of her shoe, hiding what she was doing underneath the table before handing the coins to Nikki. "It'll get us by for a while."

"It will have to do." Nikki hesitantly took the money, then handed it back to her. "You take care of it." With a frustrated, self-deprecating sigh, she rose from the table. "I will report the theft to the sheriff."

IT WAS A SUBDUED GROUP LEAVING the next morning. The sheriff laughed in Nikki's face, saying women didn't have any business out traipsing around the countryside without men, then made a few suggestions to her that burned her ears.

Tawnie headed back to the bathhouse, but the lights were out, and the door locked, and no amount of pounding on the door brought the proprietor to answer it. She salvaged part of her pride by breaking the expensive pane glass windows and shooting holes in the water barrels out back. If she could have burned the bathhouse down without burning the rest of town, she would have. The only saving grace of stopping in town was information gleaned on one member of the Mason gang.

As they winded their way through the higher reaches of the mountains, the air grew thinner and colder, propelling them to thank Nikki for her insistence on wearing men's long underwear. Breath puffing out in frosty clouds, they gathered heavy ponchos closer around their chilled bodies while glancing nervously at the sky. It was still a clear blue, but winter would soon hit the mountain region.

Nikki proved an excellent scout, deftly leading them around miners and bands of Indians, an increasingly difficult feat for the trees thinned out and the ground became rocky. Only once did they run across a band of Indian scouts.

Nikki remained calm as a morning breeze and spoke with them in sign language. The others watched in amazement when the scouts gave her gifts, then left. No number of questions or pleading forced her to disclose what they said or what had transpired.

Pulling the black gelding to a halt, Nikki examined the sheared drop off in front of her. The silver thread of the Arkansas River writhed through the lower reaches. Scattered pine groves of lofty lodgepole and ponderosa growing on both sides of the rocky incline gave way to a smattering of pinon pine with gnarled branches and squat bushy profiles while the barely discernable, narrow path winded haphazardly along the rock sides, and on the other side were shear drop offs.

"Where do we go from here?" Kissa asked in a short, frightened gasp. She already knew, but she hoped she was wrong.

"We follow the path." Nikki pointed to the grey path below them. "It is the only way. We will have to dismount and lead the animals down. If we watch our step, there should be no trouble crossing."

"Can't we wait until morning?" Her stomach doing a weird quaver, Kissa was willing to put it off long as possible.

"Might be too late. Weather has a tendency of changing without warning. Besides, we have most of daylight still left."

Nikki dismounted and took the lead, Ginger followed behind, and Tawnie brought up the rear, leading the pack animal. The footing hazardous, they carefully descended the sharp incline while rocks shifted and tumbled into the abyss below. The tortuous path narrowing, the cold wind buffeted them, and ominous storm clouds gathered overhead dulling the bright sunlight.

Nikki placed each foot carefully, feeling out the ground, but the threatening snowstorm impelled her to hurry with less caution. If they were caught in a blizzard on this narrow ledge, the results could prove disastrous.

Her frozen face tingling from the icy wind, she reached up to wipe a droplet of mucus from her nose, then with a frightened gasp, she felt the loose soil shift underneath her foot. Before she could adjust her balance, the side crumbled, and her hand released the reins.

Trying to find her balance, she nevertheless plunged over the edge of the mountain. The sky and earth twirled in crazy titillation, her breath tore from her lungs, and her heart raced madly while she frantically grabbed, her arms flailing thin air, then hard rock. The wind whipped around sounds of frightened screams and barking above her; her hand caught and held onto something, jerking her body to a popping, bone jarring stop.

She hung helplessly in midair, sharp leaves and rough bark biting into the palm of her hand, her legs hanging uselessly, and she thanking the One Above who directed her hand.

Swinging her free hand above her head, she felt the branches and took hold, then rocked back and forth, swinging her legs toward the rock face. The scraggly tree groaned, and small rocks and dirt fell, blurring her vision. Her hold precarious, she remained motionless. Glancing below her at the dizzying distance to the bottom of the mountain, she grew lightheaded and her stomach lodged in her throat, making breathing difficult with the wind battering her in eerie shrieks.

"N..i..k..k..i..!"

Her name echoed throughout the wide canyon and mingled with someone crying. Pebbles rushed down from twenty feet above her, stinging her head and face. "Help me!" she yelled back, then caught her breath when the tree shifted.

She kept her eyes from focusing on the rock wall hundreds of feet below her. Lifting her vision upwards, she saw Ginger's face as she leaned over the edge above her.

"Thank God, you're alive. Hold on a little longer. I'm lowering a rope. Try to get it around your waist and we'll pull you up. Tawnie, can you make it up here?"

Tawnie gingerly crept along the outside of the animals, and more rocks and dirt fell from above. Nikki ducked her head to avoid them falling into her eyes while her arms and bleeding hands strained against their sockets.

The rope snaked down several feet to her right side. She reached toward it. The unstable tree groaned and gave again. Frantically grabbing a branch, she held on. "Swing the rope toward me!"

After several tries, the tree giving a little after each until the roots were showing, the rope passed close enough for her to reach it. Carefully, she reached into the loop and caught hold of the upper length, her position too dangerous to slip it around her waist. Before she could free her other hand, the tree gave way.

She remained suspended in midair, dangling securely by one hand where the noose had tightened around it while roots slashed at her face, and the loosened dirt choked and clogged her nostrils.

"Nikki!"

She could not answer—all her concentration was on staying alive.

Chapter 10
Babes in Arms, Doll of Death

NIKKI STRAINED TO PULL HERSELF UPWARD with one hand to grab the rope with her free one. A panicked sob forced past her lips with the rough texture rubbing against her fingers. Grabbing the rope above her suspended hand, another cry escaped her. Her breathing labored; she swung herself toward the face until her feet levered against the sheer rock wall. "Pull me up!"

Gazing upward instead of the dizzying distance below, Nikki focused all her attention on living. Fear rose so hard she swallowed several times to keep from crying out loud when the small niches her feet found loosened dirt and rocks. Numerous times the earth broke loose, and she slammed against the rock face.

She had no feeling in her right hand anymore, and her shoulder ached from the strain, but the fear of falling and ultimate death kept her fingers firmly rooted on the rope. After several mishaps, hands grabbed her upper arms to pull her to safety.

Nikki slumped forward in Ginger's arms, relief seeping the remaining strength from her and every muscle and joint in her body aching. Everything frozen inside, she accepted Ginger's hug before she gently pushed the woman away to lift her face toward the fluffy white flakes falling around them. The stinging abrasions where the snow landed assured her, she still lived. "Give me a moment to catch my breath; then we better get going."

"But…" Ginger fell silent.

"We ain't got a choice. We can't afford being on this path any longer with it snowin'," Tawnie gruffly answered, already starting back to her former position.

It was a torturously slow crossing, and with Nikki's near-death experience, assured each was doubly cautious following the narrow mountain pass. By the time they made it to firm, safe footing, snow covered the land in pristine white, the temperature sharply dropping with the lowering sun. They stopped for a brief rest and traded their ponchos for coats and gloves. As Nikki predicted, Kissa cursed the mountains and their treacherous beauty.

THE STEADY, DOWNWARD CLIMB FLATTENED OUT, and the near-frozen and exhausted group stopped at the edge of semi-evenly paced trees. Late afternoon sunlight glistened on the snow and nearly blinded them. Horses shifted uneasily underneath them, the creaking leather sounding loud in the unnatural calm. A cabin, surrounded by other buildings, nestled inside the meadow, the first sign of human life they had seen in weeks.

Waiting for Nikki to issue instructions, the group shifted uncomfortably while Nikki studied the homey place in front of them. Woodsmoke mingled with the scent of pine, a cow lowed, and a bird called, but nothing else.

The outhouse appeared to contain several seats, indicating a good-sized family, but it was too quiet, too still for this time of day. It snowed again at midmorning, but no footprints appeared in the snow. It was near supper time, and children should be playing outside or someone working around the barn.

Tense, the group held their breath against the unknown and waited. There was something out of place, not quite right. After a while, a man came out of the cabin carrying a mail-order catalog under his armpit and headed for the outhouse situated at the back of the house.

"I know him," Ginger harshly breathed. "He killed Lyle."

"Yeah, I recognize the buzzard too," Tawnie said quietly, slipping the rifle from the scabbard. "He's called Toad, and he's the one I heard about in town." Her face turned red with her memory of him abusing Kissa as well as killing Nikki's brother—Ginger's husband. Hatred filling her, she turned her face from the others so they could not read the revulsion and pain in her eyes. It was Young Bird who showed her what real making love was about, and damn if she didn't miss him. She shifted uneasily in the saddle, mortified with the sudden sensations evading her womanliness.

The outlaw's face firmly planted in her memory, Nikki watched the man pull the door shut behind him. She slipped from the saddle and motioned for the others to do the same. "Kissa, stay with LeeAnn and the horses. I will leave *Heoohtato* with you. Tawnie, prop the outhouse door shut, then check the shed. Ginger, check the barn and examine any horses you find. I will search the house."

Nikki split from the other women and sprinted across the meadow in a low crouch, heading for the single window in the one-room log cabin. Through the crack in the window's wooden shutter, she spied a man lying on the dirt floor with blood covering his shirt.

Nearby, a woman was tied to a chair, her skirts pushed up around her waist and slumped forward. Three small children lay in the one bed along the opposite wall, and a baby crib sat at the bed's foot. She waited several minutes before deciding no one else was around, then slipped to the door.

Easing the door open, Nikki stepped inside and quickly shut the door softly behind her. The woman lifted her head and opened her mouth. Nikki put a finger to her lips in a bid for silence before walking toward the bound woman. The woman's eyes grew large with Nikki slipping the Bowie knife from her belt. "I will not harm you," Nikki whispered, cutting the ropes binding the woman.

The woman smoothed the bunched skirts from around her waist to her feet before rubbing at her wrists. Closing the ripped edges of her blouse over her swollen breasts, a faint blush rose in her pale cheeks. With jerky, uncertain movements, she sat up in the chair and glanced at her children, a single tear slipping down her cheek.

"How many men are there, ma'am?"

"Just one. He kilt my husband and did unspeakable things to me in front of my sick kids." Tearing her gaze from her children and meeting Nikki's eyes, her eyes held a wild look.

"All these years, I've gone crazy 'cause of Injuns always watchin' us and comin' to the house a beggin'. I'd fear of bein' captured and tortured by those savages. 'Stead it was a man of our own race who did this to us, and in front of my sick kids too," The woman's voice cracked with her wail, her eyes darting back and forth around the room.

"We will take care of the man. What is your name?"

"Lucinda, Lucinda Ashton."

Nodding, Nikki knelt beside the man on the floor and placed her hand on his chest. "Your husband is still alive. Are you well enough to take care of him and your children?"

Two of the children huddled together, tears streaking their fevered faces. The other child lay too still for comfort.

"I'll take care of my own."

A coal oil lamp hung by the door, and Nikki took it as she left to meet Tawnie and Ginger in front of the cabin. "Round up wood and brush and place it around the outhouse. Do it quietly," Nikki ordered, her foreboding lingering.

After Tawnie and Ginger carried out her order, Nikki sprinkled coal oil from the lamp over the wood around the outhouse, then set the lamp on the ground. Her heart skipped a beat when the man inside yelled in a gravelly voice.

"Who's there? Is anybody there?"

Nikki did not move. After a few minutes, the man seemed satisfied and started singing an off-key ditty.

"Now what?" Ginger nervously whispered.

A branch on the snow-covered ground dropped when they placed wood and branches around the outhouse. Nikki knelt to retrieve the branch, then soaked it with coal oil before lighting it like a torch. Motioning to the big quarter moon cut in the front of the outhouse door, she whispered, "He can slip his pistol out the hole. All we have to do is make him."

"How?"

Checking her rifle, Tawnie morbidly grinned. "Just watch, Ginger."

"Toad, throw out your weapons or we will set the outhouse on fire," Nikki called.

Gunfire erupted inside the outhouse, and bullets pinged against the ground, but Nikki bade the others to hold their fire. "Throw out your weapon or burn. It is your choice."

The door rattled, then banged. Explosive curses sounded inside the outhouse. "Who the hell's out there? Answer me!"

"Some of your victims demanding justice." Nikki held the torch so he could see it, then drew back her arm to throw the firebrand at the outhouse.

"All right, damn it," Toad growled, his pistol coming out of the cut moon. Suddenly he gave a blood-curdling scream. "What the hell's going on? Open the door. Damn it, open the damn door!"

The women looked at each other in confusion before they noticed smoke curling from behind the outhouse. Lucinda Ashton came around the side, lighting the oil-soaked wood and chanting, "Burn, burn in hell. You kilt my husband and soiled me in front of my children. Now you can burn in hell."

"God in Heaven," Ginger cried, standing and taking a step forward. The outhouse burst into flames outlining the crazed woman in an eerie orange and yellow glow.

Lucinda grabbed the pistol the outlaw had tossed out and pointed the gun at Ginger. "Don't move. Let 'im burn in hell!"

Toad screamed, and Lucinda cackled in madness. The sickening odor of singed hair and burned flesh gagged them except Lucinda. She only cackled loudly and rolled her eyes toward heaven when Toad screamed in pain. "Yes, burn, burn in hell!" she kept repeating.

"We've got to do something," Ginger said under her breath. "We can't let him die like this."

"And get killed for that sorry piece of crap." Tawnie's scorn held a touch of satisfaction. "No thanks."

The screams abruptly died. Engulfed in flames, the outhouse crackled and hissed, and within seconds the roof fell in with a loud crash. Gunshots blasted over the sounds of the fire.

Ginger, Tawnie, and Nikki dropped to the ground and covered their heads for protection. The women looked around them to pinpoint where the shots were coming from before they realized the bullets came from inside the outhouse, probably from the outlaw's gun belt. The bullets were exploding and flying in all directions.

Lucinda's cackles still rang over the noise of the fire, then stopped in a gasp of pain. Nikki watched Lucinda clutching at her breast before she fell flat on her face. Blood grew in a widening pool in the back of Lucinda's blouse and tinged the white snow pink around her.

Nikki groaned. There was nothing she could do except protect herself from the exploding bullets. Her stomach churned with the stench of death and smoke burned her eyes. After the bullets ceased to explode, Nikki, in a low crouch, made her way toward the demented woman's body to check for signs of life. Turning to her companions, she shook her head. "There is nothing we can do for her. Let us look after the living."

Silent and shaken, they entered the cabin. Ginger went to the cradle at the foot of the bed, Tawnie to the children, and Nikki to check on Mr. Ashton. It was too late for Mr. Ashton.

"Oh, God, this baby's been dead for days." Clutching the edge of the baby crib, shocked tears slipped down Ginger's cheeks.

"The littlest boy is dead, stiff as a board." Tawnie looked around and spied a shawl hanging by the door. Retrieving it, she wrapped it around the tiny body and took the boy outside.

Ginger wiped tears from her cheeks and went to the two children huddled in the bed. Even from a distance, she felt the heat of their fever. She touched the oldest boy's forehead, then the girl's. Their skin was like parchment, and their eyes were fever dulled. They were so thin she wanted to cry again.

Nikki filled a bowl with fresh water and found some rags, throwing them in the water before taking them to Ginger. Squeezing excess water from one of the cloths, she placed it on the boy's forehead, then drew back the covers from the children. Lifting the child's nightshirt, she saw tiny red bumps covering his body. The children were so ill she doubted either would survive the night. Scarlet fever had already taken its toll.

"Nikki?" Kissa asked from the doorway, stopping and staring at the children in the bed.

"Stay outside with LeeAnn. These children have scarlatina. I doubt we can catch it, but LeeAnn can." Nikki rubbed her pounding forehead. "Better yet, set up camp where you were before. We will check on you every so often while we take care of the children."

"Can't I help here?" Kissa asked, wiping at the tears forming in her eyes.

"You will be by taking care of LeeAnn. Now, please, take her away." Nikki spoke more sharply than she intended, the horror of the day wearing on her already tattered nerves.

A couple of hours later, the little girl died. Nikki wrapped the tiny thing in a quilt and carried the body outside to lie next to the other children's bodies. Lifting her face, the cold night air cooled her fevered brow. With a weary sigh, she noticed the outhouse fire had burned to embers. Along the edge of the snow-covered meadow, Tawnie stabbed uselessly at the frozen ground with a shovel.

The little boy died the next morning. It nearly crushed Nikki, even though she knew the children were already too ill for them to help, but she had hoped and had prayed somehow the children might still live. With Tawnie and Ginger's help, Nikki laid the family side by side on the house floor. Bowing their heads, each said a little prayer.

"Now whut?" Tawnie asked after a few minutes.

Nikki looked over her shoulder, her lips grimly folded over her teeth. "Burn everything, the family included. Have Kissa lay us some clean clothes near the stream. We will bathe there and boil our clothes before joining Kissa and LeeAnn. But, whatever you do, do not go near Kissa, especially LeeAnn."

Taking another deep breath, she faced Ginger. "Free all the animals from the barn. Hopefully, with the animals free, some will live."

THEY WERE AN UNUSUALLY QUIET GROUP that night.

After setting fire to the cabin, they broke a hole in the ice and bathed in the freezing water, washed their clothing in boiling water from the pot Kissa had also left, and threw the wet clothing in a saddlebag. Mounting horses and gathering Kissa and LeeAnn, they rode until the sunlight faded into dusk. Still, the smell of woodsmoke and the sickening odor of burned flesh was strong in the night air.

It was Kissa who broke the silence. "I feel so helpless and useless. We should have been able to save at least some of the family."

"The children were too far gone, Kissa. We all must understand death is a way of life, especially around here. The sooner we accept it, the better off we will be." Nikki shoved the barely eaten plate of food toward the fire, the meal Kissa prepared, the first meal they had eaten since before riding into the farm.

"Yes, but to lose a whole family in one day," Kissa persisted.

"Yeah."

"Oh, Nikki, I'm sorry," Kissa cried, suddenly aware of how thoughtless her observation had been. Grief-stricken, she lapsed into silence.

"What were you going to do if the outlaw had forced his way out of the outhouse, Nikki?" Ginger softly asked.

"Do?" Nikki shrugged. "I had not thought that far ahead."

Tawnie laughed, the sound derisive and amused. "Let's turn in and get outta this mountain range first thang in the mornin'."

Nikki sighed in agreement. Pulling the covers from LeeAnn, Nikki prepared to get into the bedroll beside her. Her mouth opened and shut—the child cuddled a bedraggled doll. "Kissa, where did LeeAnn get this doll?"

"I don't know. She had it yesterday." Kissa stopped, her face blanching. "Do you think…

Nikki was already shaking LeeAnn awake. The sleepy child opened her eyes and stared at her, clutching the doll closer to her chest. "LeeAnn, where did you get the doll? Answer me!"

Wide, frightened eyes staring up at Nikki, LeeAnn pointed toward the burning house.

"Give it to me." Nikki held her hand toward the doll.

LeeAnn shook her head and held the doll tighter.

"I will buy you another one in the next town, *Meeskevotse*. Just let me have this one." No amount of pleading, cajoling, or demanding would entice LeeAnn to give up her treasure.

"Let her keep the blasted doll," Tawnie grated, LeeAnn's tears and the possessive need for it grinding on her rattled nerves. After witnessing a whole family wiped out, especially the children, she did not need to witness a big production over a simple rag doll.

Nikki shot Tawnie a cold, narrowed look and reached toward the quivering LeeAnn. Regret, yet determination filling her face, Nikki forcibly removed LeeAnn's fingers from the rag doll. The child grabbed it, tears streaming down hurt-filled brown eyes. Weary, Nikki shook her head and pushed the grabbing LeeAnn back into the bedroll.

"No!" Kissa gasped, but it was too late. Nikki had already thrown the rag doll into the fire. "You're cruel, Nikki, a savage for doing that to her."

With hands on her hips, Nikki stood firm. She shouted at Ginger when she headed toward the fire. "Leave it! Do any of you understand the danger of her having the doll?"

The women shifted their eyes away from hers in disapproval.

"Oh, blast it all!" Nikki mumbled, walking away from the fire. She knelt beside the weeping LeeAnn, but the child threw the covers back and scooted away from her. Rising to her feet, LeeAnn turned and ran toward Kissa.

"What did ya expect? Dang it all, Nikki, what harm was it?" Tawnie pulled the blanket tighter around her shoulders and laid down, turning her back to them.

A fresh wave of pain swept over her, and Nikki watched Kissa cuddle the child to her breast, offering her blanket to her. *I did the right thing*, she assured herself. *I had no other choice. Scarlet fever is too volatile a disease for children.*

The camp lapsed into an uneasy silence, broken only by the sounds of LeeAnn's sniffles and the cackling fire. LeeAnn's and her friends' reactions hurt her more than any would ever know. Closing her eyes, Nikki pulled the blanket over her head and fell into a troubled sleep, the surface of her nightmares splattered red.

DURING THE SUCCEEDING DAYS, THE TENSION grew. None spoke to Nikki unless necessary. The normally active child gradually faded into lassitude and refused to eat. She completely avoided Nikki to the point of hiding her pale, tear-stained face against Kissa or Ginger.

Concealing her bruised emotions behind a passive face, Nikki kept them steadily plodding through snowdrifts, fighting to keep alive in subfreezing temperatures. If another snowstorm hit before they found permanent shelter, the heavy snow would change the appearance of the land and hide dangerous pitfalls. If that happened, a hazardous journey awaited them unless they froze to death first.

They had been traveling for five, half-blind and frozen days when Kissa pulled her mare to a stop and confronted Nikki. "LeeAnn is shaking like a leaf, and she's motioning that her head hurts." Kissa drew the child closer to her body for warmth and laid her cheek on the trembling child's fevered brow.

Dismounting, Nikki plucked the stubborn LeeAnn from Kissa's lap. She had no more set LeeAnn on her feet when the child fell to her knees and vomited. Dread seeping into every fiber of her being, Nikki absently took the neckerchief Ginger wetted with water from a canteen to bathe the child's forehead and mouth. LeeAnn leaned heavily against her; every muscle in her body suddenly turned to water.

Checking the child over, Nikki tenderly laid the child's head on her shoulder, deeply disturbed by the swollen, inflamed throat and heavily furred, cream-colored tongue. She took the blanket Ginger handed her to bundle around the child, explaining meaningfully, "The rag doll. She has scarlatina."

The shocked group looked accusingly at Nikki, but she shrugged. "I tried to warn you. It is not my fault, so stop blaming me." A flash of bitterness showed briefly in her eyes. She had tried to protect the child from the disease, which is why she had taken the doll away. The question was, when had LeeAnn gone into the cabin without their knowledge? With a weary shake of her head, she uneasily realized she did feel responsible for the child's illness. She was responsible for all of them.

Glancing overhead, another weary sigh escaped her lips. The grey overcast skies warned of another snowstorm before dusk. The shelter was the primary concern now. Tenderness and worry vivid on her face, Nikki handed LeeAnn to Ginger. "We do not have much time before the snow falls. We must make a shelter to protect LeeAnn."

IT WAS A SOMBER GROUP WORKING side by side. Even though the women barely spoke to Nikki, it was apparent they still trusted her for they followed her directions to the letter. Ginger administered to the ill LeeAnn, and Kissa gathered enough deadwood to stock a fire for several days.

Ginger tried to start a fire and a burst of angry words accented her voice each time the fire did not light until finally, a tiny burst of flame lasted long enough to get the fire going. Kissa found long aspen poles and brought them into camp while Nikki and Tawnie cut pine boughs.

Nikki and Tawnie set up a tripod with the straightest of the poles, then the women placed the other poles around it and intertwined the pine limbs, starting from the bottom and working their way upward around the shelter.

After sweeping the snow from inside the shelter with a pine bough, more pine was cut and placed around the firepit Ginger had dug inside the shelter. With Ginger and Kissa taking care of the increasingly ill LeeAnn, Nikki and Tawnie fashioned a lean-to for the horses. Dusk and snow fell by the time the group finished. To Nikki's relief, the women were once again talking to her.

Ginger smoothed the hair from LeeAnn's face, sighing. "What do we do now? LeeAnn is getting sicker by the minute."

"And we're running low on food, Nikki," Kissa remarked, digging through the packs.

"This wickiup will provide shelter for a short time, but it is not enough to live in all winter unless we fortify it." Sighing, Nikki searched their tired faces, wondering if she could teach them to survive winter in the mountains. She hoped so. "We cannot travel with LeeAnn ill. And even if there is a town close by, which there is not, we would be quarantined because of scarlatina."

"So, whut are we gonna do?" Tawnie stopped cleaning her rifle long enough to look at Nikki.

Nikki ran her fingers through her tangled hair, trying to keep her hands busy while she tried to find the right words to explain the problems they faced. "It will be a miracle if we survive the winter in the mountains, Ladies, and even more so if LeeAnn survives scarlatina."

With infinite care, Tawnie placed the weapon beside her. "Nikki, I want the outlaws much as you do, if not more, but ya know, I'd give it up and become a momma if'n it means LeeAnn's life."

Her statement was followed by Ginger's and Kissa's, "Me too."

"So, if LeeAnn lives, we stop our search and find a place to raise LeeAnn?" Nikki asked, knowing she would give up everything to save the child's life. Her heart did a tug-of-war, but she squelched the doubts. The child's life *was* more important than their revenge. Nodding, she accepted the women's voiced agreement.

"In the morning, I will show you how to prepare for

harsher weather to come, then I will go hunting.”

DAWN BROKE TO GREY SKIES AND ANOTHER snow. After Nikki explained what needed to be done to the wickiup to reinforce it and how to gather sap from the trees, she checked her weapons, then saddled the black gelding.

Heoohtato's whimper drew her attention to him. The dog was lying halfway out of the wickup door, looking at her and whining. “No, *Heoohtato*. I need you to stay with LeeAnn and the others to protect them. I will be back in a day or two, no longer than three days.”

“Ya better be,” Tawnie growled, coming up behind her. “We ain’t got a snowball’s chance in hell if ya don’t.”

Mounting, Nikki looked down at Tawnie. “If I do not find the game and a deserted cabin soon, none of us will have a chance.” With her last spoken words, she kicked her heels in the gelding’s sides and rode away.

Chapter 11
Retreating Hearts

DEEP SNOW COVERED THE LAND in pristine white, whitewashing all colors, the only evidence of humanity in the marring and disruption through its perfection. A black gelding lunged through the snowy banks, the motionless, frigid air stoking color into the rider's cheeks and her hair streaming down hers and the horse's backs in a silken banner, the wolf tail flagging a symbol of her heritage.

Searching the layout of the land, Nikki cleared her mind of all doubts and focused on the teachings of Cloud Walker to allow Mother Earth to speak to her, to whisper the ways of the elk, and direct her toward the correct path.

Horse and rider's labored breaths formed frosty clouds, and frozen pine needles broke loose by their passing, pricking them like miniature daggers. Breaking into a small clearing, Nikki sawed on the reins. Eyes sharpened by Cloud Walker's teaching, she searched the area around her, and satisfied man nor beast was nearby, she slid to the ground. It was near dusk, and though she again searched the white ground around her, she observed no tracks indicating large game. She wasted no time building a small wickiup and starting a small fire inside.

Settled for the night, the wickiup's warmth lulled her into somnolence. She used the time to think, to send her spirit upward the way Cloud Walker taught her, to commune with nature, search, see, and listen in the *Tsistsistas* way.

She needed that comfort now. The valley she spotted earlier this afternoon was still another day's ride away. With her legs crossed in Indian fashion, she rocked back and forth, singing a prayer for good hunting until she finally lay on her side, cuddled within her coat, poncho, and blanket, and fell asleep.

Up before dawn, she drank fresh snow warmed to water, then sang once again to the four cardinal directions, the Spirit Above and Mother Earth below. Mounting, she headed toward the direction of the valley, enjoying the steady warmth the further she traveled down the mountainside. It was mid-afternoon when she reached the snow-covered valley. Dismounting, she slipped the poncho over her head, draped it across the saddle horn, then unrolled her leather robe and slung it across her back.

After tying the leather thongs around her throat, she faced the sun and threw her arms wide. She chanted her medicine song in a rhythmic, singsong voice imploring the spirits to come to her aid, invoking it four times as advocated by the Grandfather in her vision, before beginning her prayer. "Hear my prayer, *Heammawihio*. Grant me strength, courage, and wisdom to overcome my enemies..." She stopped, her face pinching up in bitterness.

"Why must I do everything the way you taught, Grandfather, when it does no good? *Naehonehe*, why do you not come in my dreams and tell me what I must do?"

She cried softly into the stillness. "Help me save the child! Give me power and wisdom because I cannot face life again if I lose LeeAnn. Can you not understand?" A rabbit, startled by the soft murmur, darted from the trees and leaped away.

Watching grey clouds cover the sun's face, a smothering silence enveloped her. "Answer me!" she groaned in frustration. Swiftly, she pulled the knife from around her waist and slashed the palm of her left hand. In bemused anguish, she watched blood rise to the wound and slip down into the snow, turning it pink where it landed and spread. Rising her hands upward again, she prayed, "My blood, my sacrifice for the child's life."

Closing her eyes against the grey skies mirroring the desolation inside of her, she moaned and whispered, "Cloud Walker, what have I done? Was I allowed to come to the *Tsistsistas* just so you could die? What good am I but to bring death to my loved ones? Help me."

"*Ovaxehee.*"

The rustling voice mixed with a shiver of wind, and she wondered if she imagined it. Afraid she was dreaming, she hesitantly opened her eyes. She made out Cloud Walker's wavering form, the outline of his body barely discernible, standing before her in front of the winter-cloaked trees. "*Vo'evahtamehnestse*," she breathed joyfully, stepping forward.

"Come no closer, *Ovaxehee*." He lifted his hand, his palm toward her and stopped her in mid-stride. "We felt your pain in *Seyan*, and I have come to help you."

"Help me?" She cried, a sudden ache gnawing at her heart. "I am the one who caused your death! Oh, *Vo'evahtamehnestse*, please forgive me!"

"Forgive you for what, my child? My time had come. Why do you think I gave you my parfleche of medicines?"

"But…"

"Listen to me, *Ovaxehee*. I do not have much time." His form dimmed, then grew a little stronger. "Reach down and take a handful of snow, then hold it in your bleeding hand."

Snow crunching underfoot, she knelt, following his instructions. Rising, a shadow of pain, not from the wound but from her inner turmoil, dulled her eyes. She held her fist toward him and waited.

"When you lived with the *Tsistsistas*, I took you under my wing and taught you all I knew. I was training you to be Shaman, a Medicine Woman. The knowledge is still within you though you have let the white ways overshadow your *Tsistsistas* blood. *Ovaxehee*, remember all I taught you."

The wind blew, lifting strands of hair from her back, whipping them across her face and obscuring his fading form. His sibilant voice whispered about the medicines and their properties. Mentally compiling the list within her tortured brain, her hand grew numb with cold and ached from holding it out toward him.

"Open your hand, *Ovaxehee*."

Opening her hand, she let the blood-tinged snow drop to the ground.

"Remember nature. All *Heammawihio* gives us we can use to make us well again. The snow also has its healing qualities. See how the bleeding has stopped?"

His image quickly faded, and he hurried with his last instructions. "Take the child and pack her in snow, then wrap her in robes and keep alternating these until the fever breaks. Feed her the sacred herbs. Rub the *hohaheanoistut* on her chest to chase away the bad spirits occupying her body."

His voice faded in the distance. "Remember, treat the body, mind, and soul."

His form faded completely, and his voice was a bare whisper. "Look to your right, *Ovaxehee,* and know I will always be with you."

"*Vo'evahtamehnestse*! Wait!" Crestfallen, she stared at the spot where he had stood, but no tracks marred the perfection of the snow.

A dry sob lodged in her throat with his disappearance, then movement caught the corner of her eye. She turned her head slightly to face a bull elk, his rack of antlers nearly four feet long. He was poised on the brink of flight, his big brown eyes fastened on hers, his head lifted in majestic splendor, his nostrils quivering.

Holding the elk's gaze with her own, she remained motionless except for her right hand. She slowly slipped the pistol from her holster; any sudden movement would startle the animal, then aimed it at the animal not more than ten feet in front of her.

Mother Earth has fed you from the bounty of her bosom so you might live, Great Elk. Now, I must take your life so we may live. Your beauty and majestic presence awe me, yet it has come down to either let you live and we die or you die so we might live.

For such a wild animal, Nikki was stunned by its soft brown eyes, its poised flight, and its wild fight for life during rutting season. Lessons were learned from the mighty elk—its flight to fight another day, its endless energy in running, and its strength in combat.

She drew a soft breath and pulled the trigger, regret reverberating within her as the sound echoed through the mountains. The elk fell to its knees, the shot slamming into his head. Shaking his impressive head, he rose clumsily to his hooves and bound away, leaving a trail of blood in the pristine snow.

Nikki took a deep breath, grabbed the reins, and jumped onto the gelding's back to track the elk. The elk did not get far before his life drained out, and he crumbled on the snow, weakly flaying his legs to rise.

Dismounting, she quickly walked to the animal and slit its throat to end its agonized death. With eyes lifted upward, she sang, "I thank you, great elk, for giving up your life to feed us so my people may live. Wise One Above, thank you for providing food for us so we will not starve."

Within minutes, she had the hind feet tied together and a length of rope thrown over a sturdy branch. After wrapping the rope's end around the saddle horn, she backed up the patiently waiting gelding until she had the elk high enough so marauding creatures could not get at it. After tying off the rope, she proceeded to bleed and gut the animal.

She unsaddled the gelding and rubbed him down before allowing him to feed off the sparse remains of grass sticking its head above the snow. Within an hour, she had another wickiup built; then she built a travois to transport the elk back to the camp. She planned to be up before dawn to load the elk, and hopefully, if she pushed hard, she would be back with her sisters before darkness set in tomorrow.

WITH NIGHT QUICKLY FALLING, NIKKI FOLLOWED the smell of woodsmoke back to the camp. She heard *Heoohtato* barking long before she made it to camp and was met by three women with loaded weapons pointed straight at her. Nikki did not give a greeting. "How is LeeAnn?"

"Lord, Nikki, you gave us a fright," Kissa declared, lowering the shotgun. When Nikki did not reply, she finished, "LeeAnn's delirious."

"Kissa, set some water boiling. Ginger, get a pan and put some live coals in it, and Tawnie, bring LeeAnn outside and pack her in the snow," Nikki ordered, dismounting.

"Whut in the hell for?" Tawnie stared at Nikki, wondering if she was demented.

Crawling into the wickiup, Nikki ignored the immovable woman. She grabbed hers and Cloud Walker's medicine parfleches and backed out of the doorway. She was relieved they had made a long firepit in front of the wickiup to reflect heat into it, per her earlier instructions. Kneeling in front of its welcoming warmth, she removed small leather pouches inside the parfleches, smelling and tasting each. "Kissa, bring me a cup."

Tawnie pushed at her shoulder to get her attention. "Whut the hell are ya doin', Nikki?"

Nikki set a leather pouch to one side before lifting her eyes to flashing topaz ones. "I am trying to save the child in there! Any objections?"

"Ya dang right, I'm objectin'! Ya ain't gonna use none of your heathen concoctions on her," Tawnie growled, stepping in front of Nikki and bending down until she was at eye level with her.

Nikki sat back on her haunches; her head lifted with furious pride. "Am I a heathen now, Tawnie? Or am I only a heathen if I want to use the healing plants I learned from the Cheyenne?"

Confusion narrowing her eyes, Tawnie lifted her square chin in impotent fury. "I ain't gonna stand by and let ya try out no da' blasted savage superstitions on that kid."

Nikki pulled out another pouch and checked it, her mouth narrowed in white lines and a shadow crossing her face. "We have little choice, Tawnie, unless you would rather stand by and watch the child suffer as she dies. If we do not do something soon, she will die like those other children. Is this what you want?"

"Let her try, Tawnie," Kissa begged, holding an empty cup toward Nikki. "It's our last chance. And besides, her medicine for poison ivy worked on me."

"If the kid dies after ya try your heathen medicines on her, I'm gonna take it outta your hide. You understand that?" Tawnie waited for Nikki to answer, her hands on her hips, her golden-brown eyes fastened on Nikki's, the hardness reinforcing her warning.

Nikki barely glanced at her. "She will not die if it is in my power to prevent it, Tawnie."

Tawnie's slow rising drew her gaze back toward her, and Nikki nodded toward the wickiup door. "If you cannot stand to watch my administrations of heathen medicines on LeeAnn, then you and Ginger can cut up the elk *this savage* shot two days ago."

Ginger carried LeeAnn out of the wickiup in time to hear Nikki's last statement. "We'll do it unless you need us here."

"Kissa can help me." Nikki turned her full attention to the medicines in front of her. "This is *towaniyuhkts*, and it reduces fever." She handed the pouch to Kissa. "Take some of this and mix it with grease to rub on her body. It will help bring the fever down quicker."

Taking another bag, she opened it. Putting pinches of the dried plants into the cup, she explained them to Kissa. "This is *wikiiseeyo*. It will make the tea more palatable, and this is *moeemohkshin*, good for a weak heart which by this time she may have developed because of the fever, and this is *mohktawiseeyo*. It will soothe her throat. After you steep the medicines, let it cool. I will pack LeeAnn in snow. Then we will wrap her in blankets and take her back inside."

Satisfied Kissa understood her instructions, Nikki took LeeAnn from Ginger's arms. The fever-wasted child was so light in her arms it tore at her heart. With a tenderness she had not felt since carrying her little sister to her grave, she stripped the blanket from the child, laid her in the snow, and began to pack it around her.

After sprinkling *meemiatun*, a sweet-smelling fungus, on the live coals to strengthen the medicines, she ran her fingers over the child's forehead to soothe her. Her other hand packed the snow Kissa dumped from a wooden bucket around LeeAnn's shivering body.

They worked through the night, piling snow on the freezing child, then wrapping her in warm blankets. Crowded into the wickiup, Kissa, Ginger and Tawnie placed their hands on LeeAnn and prayed to their God for her recovery, each fervently praying this time her fever would break and she would start on the road to recovery.

Heoohtato continuously whined, refusing to budge

from the foot of the child's bed. He only left for a call of nature and barely ate enough food and drank enough water to keep him alive. The mute child, so much a part of them, had succeeded in worming her way into all of their hearts, and her illness was a mortal blow to their close-knit group.

They took turns working with the child, praying against hope the fever would break and LeeAnn would live. It was a slim chance, but the women did not give up and worked through the softly falling snow through the night. By the time the sun reached midday, Ginger's cry LeeAnn's fever had broken had all the women shouting with joy.

NIKKI TAUGHT THE WOMEN HOW TO CUT the meat and smoke it into jerked strips, then store the pieces in the intestines of the elk, along with how to use nearly every part of the elk so there was no waste. It was basic survival.

The women understood and appreciated the Indians' ingenuity. Kissa had learned enough from Running Deer Woman to try her hand at cleaning and tanning the hide while LeeAnn grew marginally stronger each day, but the child was still too ill to do much more than lay on the pine-bough bed.

Nikki decided with her gone, her friends could finish preparing the elk. She would leave some of her precious herbs with Kissa in case they were needed.

Nikki saddled her horse, aware she had trained her friends well and they would not starve, nor would LeeAnn be without medicine for months. LeeAnn still would have nothing to do with her, and she wanted to leave before the others saw how much it wounded her. She had no other choice. LeeAnn had impressed the necessity for her to disappear from their lives very well.

They had never forgiven her for the child's illness nor would the child for destroying the silly doll. The least she could do was find a town close enough to send someone to bring them out of the mountain.

Strapping her few belongings on the back of the gelding, she heard someone walk up behind her but did not turn around to see who it was.

"I never figured ya'd run out on us like a dang, two-bit coward."

Nikki rolled up a pair of pants and crammed them into the saddlebag before turning toward Tawnie. "You are better off without me. I brought so much danger with me, and I cannot afford to harm my friends anymore. You will not starve now. I will make sure someone comes to bring you down from the mountains before a month is gone."

"Thanks a lot. Ya led us to these Godforsaken mountains at the beginnin' of winter, then ya desert us? Have ya gone totally loco?" Tawnie leaned against a pine tree, watching the distressed woman struggle with her conscience.

Nikki pushed a wisp of hair from her cheek, her eyes distant. "I had to destroy the awful rag doll. I had to! I did not want her to catch scarlet fever, but it did not work. Now, she will have nothing to do with me, and the rest of you blame me, too." Nikki's voice cracked, and a fresh wave of sorrow washed over her.

Tawnie pushed away from the tree and moved toward Nikki, speaking in an irritated snarl, "Hell yeah, we blamed ya, still do 'cause that stupid doll made us realize that we ain't let LeeAnn be a kid. We expect her to take the same thangs as us when all the time she's just a little girl. Hell, yeah, Nikki! It hurt all of us to realize we ain't worth crap when it comes to motherin'."

Nikki smoothed the sleeves on the shirt she folded, her eyes startled. "She does not blame you. I am the one who destroyed the doll. I am the one who lost most of our money at the bathhouse."

Tawnie's laugh was a strangled bark. "Lost our money? Like hell! Most of the money was yours to begin with, by God, and the rest we took off the dead outlaws!"

"Ours," Nikki corrected, shaking her head. "It was all of ours." Turning away, she stared sightlessly at the crystalline frosted landscape.

"I failed, Tawnie. I have made a mess out of everything. What right do I have in leading all of you into danger? What right do I have in asking you to help me avenge my family's deaths?" She leaned her head against the gelding and sighed. "I do not know any more if what I am doing is right."

"Gawl darn, son o' bitchin', mutter…" Tawnie stopped, fighting to gather her temper under control. She slammed her fist into a tree, then brought her smarting knuckles to her mouth. "Dang it all, Nikki! That ain't you talkin'. That's that da' blasted marshal talkin'. Whut in the hellfire did ya do the night afore we left the Cheyenne camp? Did ya bed him?"

Nikki's mouth tightened with fury; her back jerked ramrod straight. She might dislike Dane Travis but would not stand for someone else to call him names. "Leave him out of this, Tawnie. He has nothing to do with it."

"Like hell! He's got ever'thang to do with it." Her square face hardening and her eyes blazing, Tawnie crossed her arms in front of her chest. "Do ya think you're the only one who lost sumthang that night? We all did! Dang it, Nikki, we wouldna of followed ya if we didna want to. Ya didna force us to come, but if'n ya want to run out on us now when we need ya most, then get the hell outta here, and I hope to God I never see ya again."

Nikki slowly faced Tawnie, a shadow of remorse turning her eyes a shade darker. "How can you still want me after I have made such a mess of everything?"

Tawnie's face relaxed, and her eyes softened. "'Cause we trust ya. We may have our differences, but God help us, we're still a part of each other. Without each other, we cain't raise that little girl in there fightin' for her life."

Nikki glanced at the black shirt neatly folded in her hands, her mind churning with turmoil. She needed them! The One Above only knew how much she did. They were her family now, and her heart ached with the knowledge she had to leave.

"Look, I ain't much for makin' people see reason, but it'd be a dang mistake for ya to leave here." Tawnie shoved an old, bedraggled rag doll in front of her face. "Give this to the kid. Maybe, it'll help." Her face bloomed with color when Nikki looked up at her. "It's the only thang I've got left of my momma's. It's a silly thang for a grown woman to keep."

Nikki took the doll, recognizing it from the one she had briefly seen on Tawnie's bed in the Sands' shack. She clutched the doll to her breast with a bare smile shading her lips. She realized if Tawnie was willing to sacrifice this small piece of herself, then she could do no less. Handing it back to her, she promised, "I will come back if you give it to her, but first, I must find a better place for us to live and somewhere to pick up more supplies. It is possible we cannot survive the winter in this wickiup, much less LeeAnn. Hopefully, when I do come back, LeeAnn will be strong enough to make the trip."

Ginger stepped out of the shadows and took Nikki's hand, pressing something against it. Nikki closed her hand around it, then brought it upward. Their remaining money lay in the palm of her hand. "Ginger?"

"Tell us what we must do while you are gone, Nikki. And take the pack horses to bring back the supplies. We will wait for you. Just come back, my friend. We all need you, even LeeAnn."

Part IV: Savage Angels

Chapter 1
Blood Red Sun

UNDERNEATH LIGHT BLUE SKIES with a scattering of white clouds, the panoramic view of mountain ranges, their treeless, rocky tops covered in snow and their bases ranging from dark blue to different shades of purplish-blue, swooped downward toward heavy forests of pines, junipers, firs, and spruce interspersed with aspen trees bearing slender white trunks and spreading goldened-leaved swathes throughout differing shades of green, then lingering outside of brown, grassy meadows.

It had not snowed since Nikki left the higher reaches of the mountains, but with the coming snows stretching toward the lower ranges, the land would turn into treacherous beauty, hiding dangers at every pass and turn, and with the winter deepening, it would become even more hazardous.

Nikki followed the South Platte River her group had been following even though it curved from its southwestern course to a northwestern one. The river churned over rocks, forming picturesque ice patterns along its edges even though freezing temperatures grew warmer the further she descended toward the valleys below. Each passing day filled her with concern for her friends' safety, and most particularly LeeAnn's. Sleep came only after tossing and turning most of the night and she awoke cursing the sun for its slow rise and early decent.

Discovering a barely discernable trail underneath the snow, hope grew within her for the manmade path led to civilization. Luck had been with her so far and she prayed the snow would continue to hold off until she could make it back with supplies; her only disappointment, she had not found an unoccupied cabin or a miner's shack along the way.

Cresting a sparse tree-covered peak, she stared at the valley below. Wood and coal smoke plumed upward in spirals, darkening the sky, the town resembling children's toys in the distance. With a weary shrug of her shoulders, she headed the gelding and pack animals down the mountainside toward the open land below, perceiving she had several more days' ride before she reached town.

The almost flat appearing valley made traveling easier. Impatient and bone weary, Nikki kneaded the gelding forward onto the road full of potholes and mud. Snow patches dotted the brown grasses, and the bustling town in the middle of the valley cried welcome.

Long before she reached town, she saw squat tents and the skeletal forms of construction rising from the charred ashes of previous buildings with newly built false-fronted structures lining the main street. Heavy dray wagons, burros, and an occasional horse plodded through the mud-covered streets. The wind carried sounds of the tinny clang of a piano and construction hammering.

In her hellbent-for-leather ride from the upper reaches of the mountain, this was the first sign of human life she had seen since leaving her friends. Perhaps, with luck, she could get the supplies back up to camp and still have time to bring the group to civilization, but only if LeeAnn was strong enough to travel. There were too many variables—*ifs, ands*, and *buts* determining their future.

Lifting her face toward the sun, she judged it early afternoon. She should be able to load supplies and head back before the sun lowered. The sooner she got back to her friends, the better. Even if they could not make it back to civilization, at least they would not starve with the elk she killed and the supplies she would bring back. It could be worse, much worse, she knew.

Passing the mine and surveyor's offices, she stopped the gelding and pack animals in front of the false-fronted general store. After she secured the animals to the hitching post, she stepped up on the only boardwalk in town. A man crossed in front of her and tipped his hat.

"Ma'am," he intoned. "Haven't seen you around here before. I'm Sheriff Watkins."

"Sheriff," Nikki acknowledged. "I came down to gather supplies."

"Minin'? That's a mighty rough adventure for a woman." The sheriff's eyes drifted from her face to the front of her black blouse and lingered.

Self-consciously, Nikki laid her hand over the brown bear claw necklace. Before entering town, she had forgotten to hide it under her blouse and jacket. "I reckon it is," she agreed.

The sheriff lifted his eyes back to her face. "Sorry for starin', Ma'am. It's an unusual necklace." He held out his hand. "Didn't catch your name."

"I did not give it." With a moment's hesitation, she shook hands with him. "Nikki Pride."

"Nice meetin' you, Miss Pride. Welcome to Fairplay.

If I can help you with anything, you just give me a holler. My office is down the street a ways," he said, nodding toward the other end of town. "And…" he paused, "please wear a skirt. I'd hate to have to arrest you for wearing men's clothing."

"Sheriff, I will be in town only long enough to buy supplies, then I will be gone before the day is done. Good day to you, sir." Nikki turned toward the door of the general store, uneasiness slipping down her spinal cord. Shaking her head to dismiss it, she opened the door and slipped inside, closing it behind her.

The interior contained a narrow walk space through the middle, the different types of products displayed in sections of mining tools, tools of trade for building and farming, housewares with cast iron skillets, pots, different types of eating utensils and plates, and a small section offering different bolts of material, threads, and furbelows with a selection of boots and other types of clothing. The very back and the other side of the building stored food supplies, small drawers comprising smaller goods, and a long counter with a glass top shielding the more expensive items. There was only one other customer in the store—a miner paying for a shovel and pickax. The store clerk took the customer's money before turning his attention to Nikki. The customer gathered his purchases, nodding to her as he left the building.

"Ma'am," the proprietor greeted her as though he saw women clad in pants every day. "May I help you?"

A slight smile lifted Nikki's lips. "I will tell you what I need, then we can go from there, sir."

"Sounds good to me. So, what can I get you?"

She had repeatedly played the list in her mind and

rattled it off to him. "Beans, flour, salt, dried fruit, rolled oats, coffee, sugar, ammunition, and oats for the horses to start with, and maybe some matches. If there is any money left over, I have a few other things I would like to purchase. Please hurry, sir. I must get back up the mountains soon."

"Not to be nosy, Ma'am, but are you minin' around here?" he asked, examining the money she handed him.

The man had a kind face, and for some reason, Nikki said more than she intended. "No sir, I have three women and a very sick little girl waiting for me to return with supplies."

"Alone? You left them alone in the mountains? Where's your husbands?"

"Husbands?" Nikki stared at him blankly, trying to decide what to say.

The store clerk did not wait for her to answer. "Killed in minin' accidents, huh? It happens, Ma'am. Hear tell of men around here gettin' killed nearly every day."

Looking at the money she gave him, he cleared his throat. It was insufficient to cover the inflated prices of the supplies she ordered, but something about the desperation in the woman's eyes softened him. He dealt with rough men and other kinds of ladies all the time, but this was a real lady, apparently a lady taking care of others, including a child. "I'll round this up right quick. I see you're in a hurry. You've enough to get those extras you was a'wantin', so what'll it be?"

"Maybe some glycerin, a few spools of colored sewing threads, a shovel maybe, and a chaw of tobacco." A glass jar filled with red and white peppermint sticks sat on the countertop. Lifting the lid, she took a peppermint stick and laid it on the counter. "And this for the child."

He nodded and collected the items, placing the smaller items in a large burlap sack and placed it along with the larger items along the edge of the boardwalk. Entering the store again, he added more peppermint sticks to hers before wrapping them in brown paper and tying twine around it to keep them secure. "Take this to the little one. Now, anything else? Do you ladies have plenty of blankets?"

Without waiting for her to answer, he added two blankets to the pile. "Now, ma'am, you go git them women and that child down from the mountains afore the snow gets any deeper. If'n you don't, you ladies will be stuck up there all winter and at God's mercy."

Picking up the remaining bundles from the countertop, he replied, "I'll get this loaded for you. That *is* your pack animals out front, isn't it?"

He did not wait for her to answer but nodded toward the men who entered the store. "Be with you gentlemen in a moment. Let me take care of this little lady first." Turning back to Nikki, he stared momentarily at the top of her blouse. "Peculiar necklace you got there, Ma'am. Is that a bear claw?"

Her hand covered the necklace again, disturbed this was the second time since entering town someone noticed it. "Yes, sir. It was a present."

"From your husband? Right peculiar, ma'am," the proprietor stated before turning and taking the last of her items toward the pack animals tethered outside the store.

From the corner of her eye, Nikki glimpsed the men who entered the store. Disinterested and her mindset on other things, she ignored them. The peppermint sticks sacked in a small brown wrapping, sat on the countertop and she picked it up to put in her saddlebag later.

Turning, she ran into a solid body. She barely glanced up to apologize to the man, but it was enough to show the smirking face of one of the outlaws. "Oh," she gasped, her hand going to the knife at her waist. *No! Stop!* her brain shouted. *You made a promise not to hunt down any more of the outlaws if LeeAnn was spared. But*, she reasoned, *I am not hunting them*. In reflex, her hand tightened around the knife handle. Before she could draw it, an arm wrapped around her neck, and a big, hairy paw closed around her hand holding the knife.

"It ain't nice to pull a knife in a general store," the voice behind her mocked. "Now, unless yore wantin' yore neck broke, you'll move yore hand away from the knife."

Nikki released her grip, then held her hands upright, one hand still holding the sack of peppermint sticks to indicate her surrender. The voice grating in her ear spurred recognition and hatred spread through every pore of her body. Mad Dog!

The hard palm against her back pushed her forward, and she lurched toward the other outlaw. Something cut into her throat, choking her, then broke free, the momentum from the sudden release slamming her body against the other outlaw. With disgust, she pushed away.

"Well, Injun Bill, didna we have luck today? Told ya I was a'feelin' lucky," Mad Dog snickered, dangling the bear claw necklace in front of her nose.

Nikki lunged for the necklace. Hands gripped her upper arms near her shoulder blades, turned her body toward the front door, and slammed her backside against him. Held securely against Injun Bill, she glared at Mad Dog.

Everything about the man disgusted her from his beady little eyes, his pockmarked face, the scar running from his right eye across his cheek to his chin, and his lank, grey-black hair hanging in his eyes. His evil laugh only increased her revulsion.

"Ump," Injun Bill grunted, holding her tightly against his front.

"We'll have more fun when she tells us where her friends are," Mad Dog answered, swinging the bear claw necklace in front of her face, taunting her.

Her eyes narrowing, Nikki gave him a slight smile. "They are not with me, Mad Dog."

"Well, now, I can see that, stupid. Where're dey camped?" Mad Dog twirled the thong around his finger, then with another turn of his hand, unwrapped the thong with a quick turn close to her face.

Instinctively, Nikki moved her head to one side, dodging the sharp claw. With a sarcastic laugh, she answered, "I would be stupid if I answered you, now would I not?"

Mad Dog swung the bear claw toward her again so quickly, she did not have time to duck. The sharp claw caught her underneath the chin. "Don't git smart with me, gal, or I'll use this 'ere bear claw to git the answers from ya."

Nikki gasped, raising her hand toward the wound, but Injun Bill's hands on her upper arms stopped the momentum. The injury was not severe—it was his reaction and the sudden stinging surprising her. Her palm itched to reach her knife, but the men were too alert. *Maybe I can distract them*, she reasoned, looking around the store for some kind of diversion.

"Hang on to her," Mad Dog ordered, moving in front of Injun Bill. "I plan on gittin' some answers from d' witch. 'Sides, the arrow wound she give me never did heal up righ'."

Hands left her shoulders and big arms closed underneath her breasts. When his buckled knees started straightening to force her feet off the ground with his height, she used the body holding her from behind to brace herself, kicking upward with both feet. Her right foot landed squarely in Mad Dog's face, and she kicked him hard again using both feet, propelling him backward at the same time she and Injun Bill tumbled to the floor.

Rolling over quickly, she dropped the peppermint stick package down the front of her blouse and rose in a crouched position with her bowie knife in hand. Injun Bill scrambled to his feet, a knife appearing in his hand, almost grinning when he turned to face her.

Injun Bill stood and when his arm came down and forward in a slicing action, Nikki stopped his momentum with the top part of her knife, stepping backward, then twirling the knife's cutting edge toward the back of her forearm, and spun away from him, still in a crouching position before pivoting back toward him and slipping underneath his arm close to his legs before he could correct his slicing motion toward her.

With a backward pivot, she brought the knife up behind her, turned, and stabbed him in the hip joint. The knife point cut through flesh and into his joint, enough to disable and off-balance him. He grunted and suddenly slumped forward, knocking pots and pans from the shelving.

Mad Dog stumbled backward, hitting a large barrel sitting close to the door, his surprised expression quickly turning to rage. Straightening to his full height, he lifted the knife from his belt and headed toward her. "Dat weren't nice, liddle lady. Do ya think ya can really fight me and Injun Bill and win a knife fight?"

Smiling tightly, she twirled the big bowie knife from one hand to the other, then lifted her free hand and held it near her shoulder in a defensive posture while positioning herself in the middle, a descent distance from both.

"Gentlemen, drop your weapons and leave the lady alone."

Both men turned to stare at the proprietor. He aimed a rifle at them like he knew how to use it and would use it if provoked.

"Now, mister, we was jist a'funnin'," Mad Dog sputtered, not taking his eyes off him. Dropping his knife when the proprietor drew back the rifle hammer and pointed it directly at his heart, he proceeded to dust his backside, his stance and hard eyes showing displeasure his amusement with Nikki had been interrupted.

Straightening, she held the knife in front of her, motioning for Mad Dog to move further away from the door, alert to even the slightest move. She slipped past him and moved to the proprietor's side.

"Ma'am, your pack animals are ready with your supplies. Go now. I'll hold off these varmints long enough to let you get a good start." He barely motioned toward the door with his head, his eyes never leaving the two men.

Nikki lightly touched his arm. "Thank you." Without a backward glance, she left the store, patting the bag of peppermints inside her shirt, surprised they had not broken.

Untying the reins to the gelding, the pack horses' ropes

still securely tied to each other and the gelding, she vaulted on its back. Wasting no time getting out of town, she kicked her heels in the horse's flanks and raced as if the hounds of hell were chasing her.

A gunshot kicked up mud in front of her and the gelding reared, nearly unseating her. Her eyes widening, she turned toward the direction of the gunshot.

A man with a big red and grey-streaked bushy beard stepped onto the street, holding a pistol. "Hold on there, stranger. When you go through this here town, slow down so folks can get a look at ya."

Afraid the man would notice she was female, she pulled the hat lower over her eyes, kicked her heels in the gelding's flanks, and galloped out of town, leaving the man staring at her departing back.

Nikki pushed the animals hard to put distance between herself and the outlaws. Hatred boiled in her stomach and rose to her throat, choking her. Her mind shouted against the fates, man, animal, anything her mind conjured because she knew, she had promised, she had sworn her revenge would be no more if LeeAnn lived.

She rode the gelding, the pack animals trailing behind, until there was barely enough light to see in front of her. With a muttered oath, she decided against a fire—she was in an open meadow, and a fire would be too easily discernable. She contemplated unloading the heavily packed horses but decided against it, surprised the small amount of money she paid had bought so much. The only place to put the supplies was on the ground, and it would be too easy for roaming or hunting animals to find. At least the horses would alert her if any animal was close.

Unrolling her bedroll, she folded the blankets in a

triangle around her, hoping it was sufficient to keep her warm enough to sleep.

It was a long night, too long for her peace of mind. Sleep did not come easy, and when it did, nightmares plagued her. The only thing she remembered about her nightmares was one scene burned across her brain—buzzards circling overhead with four howling black wolves outlined against a bloodred sun. The image bothered her, not just because the wolves were howling at the sun instead of the moon, but because of the symbolism. She shook off the dread and promptly forgot the dream. Long before dawn, she fed the horses and packed her gear, anxious to be off again.

Over two weeks, two long, drawn out weeks, she traveled the upward slopes toward the camp. Heavy grey skies overhead mocked her, interrupted by flashes of lightning and thunder, a natural phenomenon in the Rocky Mountains. Snow fell before half the morning was gone. She knew she was close to camp. She could feel it, but her instincts warned if the snow came down any harder, landscapes would change and she could go around in circles, never finding camp.

Clamping down hard on her fear, she turned her eyes inward, her mind outward, and kept going. It snowed harder, coming down so fast visibility over ten feet ahead was pushing the status. Darkness fell sooner than usual with the winter storm in full rage, but she did not stop.

With the temperature steadily dropping, Nikki constantly moved her body, especially her fingers, toes, shoulders, and head to keep from freezing. She could not stop now. She had to stay alert. Falling asleep or stopping would be disastrous.

After a while, she could not feel her fingers or toes. Wind whipped tears in her eyes and icicles formed on her eyelashes. Snow covered the blanket she used to cover her lower face and hair. She wondered if her mind had frozen too because no thoughts formed in her mind—just the need to get back to camp and not fall asleep, but not falling asleep was the hardest part. Several times, she jerked awake to the freezing chill and numbness of her body.

The snow fell around her in thick blankets until she could barely see, and trees seemed to suddenly loom up in front of her. The only sound was the eerie whistling of the wind and the only visibility the steady stream of whiteness mixed with black. Some instinct drove her onward. She had no thought of the horses or herself, just the need to get back to camp.

She was close, she knew she was close to the camp— she could feel it. So close, she almost rode the gelding through the snow-covered wickiup. If it had not been for *Heoohtato's* sudden appearance and happy barking, she would have ridden through it.

Ginger, Tawnie, and Kissa appeared before her, their exclamations of surprise and happiness garbled in her ears. Nikki was so cold she could not speak. Hands reached out to help her dismount. The tug, then pull brought a startled cry to her frozen lips. Tawnie's voice came from a far-off distance.

"Easy, she's frozen to the dang saddle. Kissa, go git the fire goin' good."

"My Lord, she looks like a snowman," Ginger exclaimed, frantically separating Nikki's pants from the saddle. "How in God's Heaven did she make it back through all of this? I can barely see my hands in front of me!"

Nikki felt herself lifted from the saddle. If her feet touched the ground, she did not feel it. The next she knew, she was lifted upward and carried, then shoved into welcoming warmth, and that was when the shivering started. She shivered so hard; her teeth rattled. The more she thawed, the worse she shivered. Her skin tingled and stung until she wanted to cry with the pain, but if the tears were there, they froze somewhere inside before they made it to her eyes.

Nikki had little memory regarding the rest of the night. Somehow her clothes were stripped from her and dry ones put on, blankets placed around her, a mug of hot coffee shoved into her hands, and then blessed blackness. She could not even call it sleep—just welcoming blackness.

She slowly opened her eyes and stared around her. It took her a few moments to identify her surroundings—and—she was warm.

"So, you're still with us," Tawnie greeted her.

"LeeAnn?"

"She's a doin' better. Been slippin' in and out of fever since you left, but we're thinkin' its past now." Tawnie crawled the small distance between them to help Nikki sit in an upright position.

Gratefully, Nikki accepted a cup of coffee from Ginger. "The horses?"

"We took care of them. We did get a corral and a better lean-to built while you were gone." Ginger smiled, her concern darkening her eyes. "We were worried about you. You've been out for nearly two days."

"I said I would be back." Nikki sipped the coffee, looking around her. LeeAnn slept peacefully against the opposite wall of the wickiup. Though the wickiup was small, probably not more than ten feet wide, the women had made it into a somewhat homey place. And it did feel like home, a safe haven. "My saddlebags?"

Tawnie motioned toward Nikki's head, then reached over her and placed them in her lap.

"Thanks," Nikki said quietly, handing her empty coffee cup to Ginger. "I have brought presents for everyone."

"Presents?" Kissa chimed, a smile lighting her face.

LeeAnn sat straight up in bed, kneading her eyes. When she saw Nikki, a smile lifted her thin mouth. Within seconds, she ran and jumped into Nikki's open arms, her small, thin arms closing around her neck and tightly hugging her.

"*Meeskevotse*!" The joy in Nikki's voice was unmistakable. LeeAnn's welcome made the hard journey to and from the mining town worth it. Not even being able to carry out her revenge made it worthwhile. Taking the child by the shoulders, she moved LeeAnn back enough to reassure herself the child was well. What she saw nearly broke her heart. The child had lost all the weight she had gained since living with them and now was thin to the point of emaciation, her eyes huge, and her cheekbones prominent in her drawn face. But even the child's fragility could not erase knowing she had finally forgiven her for taking away the doll.

"Goodness, I haven't seen her move that much since she got sick," Kissa exclaimed, kneeling close to the group.

Nikki hugged LeeAnn, hiding her distress over the child's appearance. *You have a lot to be thankful for*, her mind asserted, *she is alive*. Placing a tender kiss on the child's forehead, she gently moved her away, only slightly, and placed a hand over her heart, her eyes softening. "I love you." LeeAnn smiled and placed her hand over her heart, then moved it to touch Nikki's hand still across her chest.

The snow continued unabated for three days. By the time it quit snowing, the snow packed around the wickiup, adding extra insulation. Nikki spent special time with the child, working with her to increase their sign language or playing with her hair while Kissa read the Bible to them. *Heoohtato* never left the child's side except to answer nature's call, and at night, he slept at her back, keeping them both warm. *It is good to be home, home with my family.*

The day woke bright and clear, the blue skies finally appearing. It took two of them to shove the door against the snow to allow them to squeeze out of their cozy shelter, and afterward, the women had to dig a trench outside the door and clear a path to the firepit. Stepping outside, they surveyed their surroundings of new snow whose depth was nearly high as their waistlines within the vast whiteness, and the only other color showing was dull juniper green underneath snow-covered tree branches.

"This pretty much seals our fate," Nikki commented, gauging the deep whiteness around them and realizing it would be months before the snow began melting. "We are stuck here all winter now. We better prepare for the worst."

"How do you plan for us to do that?" Ginger glanced at the wickiup, wondering how they were to care for LeeAnn. The child was still weak though they noticed minuscule improvement each day.

Nikki's laugh was deprecating. "Well, if I remember correctly, there are several windblown groves of lodgepole pine and aspen trees around here. We best start finding them and bring them down to build a cabin."

"A cabin? You can't be serious." Ginger looked from one to the other, surprise and astonishment showing on her face.

"Why not?" Tawnie asked, a grin splitting her face. "I'd say we can do just 'bout anythang we want. If men can do it, so can we." Guffawing, she suddenly choked.

Nikki slapped her back so hard, Tawnie fell face down in the snow. Her coughing stopped, but when she rolled over on her back, the surprised expression on her face was enough to send the other women into giggling fits.

"Da' blasted, I swallowed the whole chaw of tobacci."

Chapter 2
Too High a Price

LAUGHTER IS GOOD FOR THE SOUL, her grandfather used to always tell her, and Nikki agreed. They needed the laughter Tawnie unwittingly provided. None of her friends realized how dangerous it was to be trapped in the mountains during winter, or if they did, they did not admit it. Somehow, someway, she was going to make sure they were not on the *frozen-to-death* or *starved-to-death* causality list.

With a mental shake of her head, she turned her attention to building a cabin. "If we bring down approximately six logs a day, providing the weather holds, we should be able to start building a twelve by twelve-foot cabin in a month or so, depending on the weather and our ability. The river nearby will provide the clay we need to chink it with."

"How are we going to measure it?" Ginger shifted her feet in the snow, then wrapped her arms around herself to provide extra warmth against the subfreezing weather.

Nikki laughed. "Well, since Tawnie is six feet tall, we will use her as our measuring stick."

An uncontrollable giggle erupted from Kissa, and she had trouble speaking. "Well, if she keeps swallowing tobacco and you keep slapping her on the back, it won't take long to measure the whole thing."

Giggles burst from the women, and it took a few moments to stop laughing enough to finish the discussion. Nikki cleared her throat to get their attention, her mouth quirking with the need to laugh again. "The next thing we need to decide is how to build the cabin."

"I thought we had decided on a log cabin," Kissa interrupted, looking confused.

"Heck no, Kissa. We can build it with rocks if ya wanna dig them outta the snow." Tawnie motioned to the deep snow, her face showing disdain.

"Oh, leave her alone, Tawnie. She's from town and doesn't understand a lot of this." Ginger wondered if she understood. They had hatchets, and she comprehended the technique of notching logs, but were they strong enough or capable enough to build a cabin? That and the weather could prove it to be an insurmountable task.

Nikki pointed to a nearby sloped hill. "Kissa, what I am trying to ask is whether we want to dig into the side of a hill and use it as one of the walls or do we find flatter ground?"

"The hill would take less wood," Ginger agreed, "but how do we…"

"That is the next problem," Nikki interrupted. "If we dig into the side of the hill, we will have to shovel off snow and warm the ground with coals. By the time we finish bringing in logs for the day, it should be warm enough to dig out part of the surface. How much we accomplish each evening will depend on how deep the ground is frozen."

"Sounds like more work than we've got time for," Tawnie stated, staring at the hill, calculating the time and effort needed. "Either way, we're gonna need to shovel snow. That's another problem we're gonna have to solve, but I'm a thinkin' we can figure out how to make crude shovels to go along with the one you brought back."

"Shovels are not the only thing we have to make. We need to gather enough limbs to make snowshoes," Nikki stated.

"Snowshoes," Kissa asked, confused, looking down at the lower half of her body and measuring the depth of the snow in her mind.

"They are shoes to enable you to walk on top of the snow. Without them, we will be as we are now, wading through waist deep snow."

"Oh," Kissa commented, still looking confused.

"I will show you how to make them and then you can try them out. And..." Nikki looked at Tawnie and Ginger to get their approval. "I think you should stay with LeeAnn while we bring down the logs. You will have time to make pitch sticks with the sap I had you gather before I left."

"Yep," Tawnie agreed. "That'll keep her outta trouble and outta our hair."

WIND WHISTLED EERILY THROUGH THE WICKIUP, the red embers outlining the four young women, the child, and the dog in a reddish amber glow. Snow filtered through the cracks and powdered them in white. Nikki lay with her head on the saddle, her long hair flowing around her in a tangled mass, the shake of her head accompanied by soft moans. Her spirit drifted toward the crimson maelstrom, and she entered it, swirling downward, descending into the dream world.

Wind blew leaves across the barren ground, sweeping them in front of the rough grey timbers of a dilapidated and boarded house. Swept by the wind around the rundown house, she entered a garden overgrown with weeds.

With steady heartbeats reverberating in her ears, she was drawn to the thorny bush devoid of leaves and roses standing sentinel in the middle of the weed-congested garden. Four roses of pink, red, golden yellow, and crimson with white streaks lay on the ground, wilting.

The steady heartbeats increasing in volume, the wind blew petals from the roses, then lifted the roses upward and blew them out of the garden into the frozen reaches outside. She followed the path of the roses, the wind drifting her along with them. The roses, out of place in the frozen winter terrain, were the only splashes of color on the pure white snow.

Toward her right, a snorting herd of buffalo drew her attention. Sadly, she watched the buffaloes run in a circle, unconcerned when members of the herd fell dead around them.

The wind blew the roses further afield into a fall landscape of trees clothed in red, orange, yellow, and brown leaves. Increasing in strength, the wind picked up the fallen leaves and roses, swirling them. Heartbeats grew stronger, louder, and the whirlwind landed the roses by a bear and her cub. The roses hovered there, watching and waiting. The heartbeats increased in tempo, then beat in irregular rhythms, growing fainter with each beat.

At first glance, she observed the cub was weak and ill, knowing it would never make it through the winter. She watched the sow tenderly lick her cub several times, then with a quick bite to its throat, instantly killed it. The irregular heartbeats stopped, the silence ear-shattering as the heartbeats had been.

The wind blew again, picking up the roses and carrying them further into a windswept area toward a cave mouth. Landing on the ground, the roses turned into wolves, their heads lifted toward the moon, and in an eerie, mournful symphony, howled.

After a few minutes, the wolves lowered their heads and started playing together. The lead wolf issued a bark, then a growl, and the pack surrounded him, watchful, waiting. The leader turned and the pack followed him to pursue a whitetail deer. Nikki admired their beauty, gracefulness, and the perfect coordination of attacking wolves until their prey was downed.

Soon, the wolves turned back into roses. The wind swept the white streaked crimson rose upward, buffeting it around in circles. Above it, a star twinkled and winked, trying to give the wandering rose some direction.

"Maehonehe," Nikki screamed, covering her ears against the whining wind.

"Ovaxehee," Red Wolf snarled greeting, appearing in front of her.

"You bring me to a bleak place," she stated calmly, sitting at Red Wolf's feet. Fall leaves shifted around her and the wind lifted her hair, swirling it around her head. She brushed the tresses from her face, noticing for the first time she wore a deerskin dress, leggings, and moccasins. A single white feather flapped beside her face, attached to a waving strand of hair.

"Ah, Ovaxehee, you do not greet me with fear or anger this time. It is good." Maehonehe's yellow eyes gleamed

approval. With his tongue, he licked the salvia running down his jaws, exposing huge white teeth.

"I am in need, Maehonehe," Nikki quietly replied, holding her hair back with her hands.

"I have already shown you what you need, Ovaxehee. It is for you to discover the truth of the symbols." Red Wolf leaned toward her, his paw coming out to touch her head.

"Use your intelligence, Ovaxehee. Tell your warrior women your dream and let them help you unravel the symbols." Without another word, he turned and walked away.

"Maehonehe!" Dreaming Woman stood, ready to run after him, but he turned toward her and snarled, "Ovaxehee, your road is still long and dangerous. Remember the animal kingdom and do likewise."

Suddenly, she was blown back into the crimson vortex.

Nikki opened her eyes and sat straight up, glancing about the wickiup. Her friends and LeeAnn lay asleep around the red embers of the fire. Only *Heoohtato* lifted his head to look at her.

ANOTHER SNOWSTORM HIT, THE HEAVY FLAKES keeping them captive inside seated around the fire and listening to Kissa read from the Bible, her finger moving along the passages, showing LeeAnn each word she spoke, *"Behold, how good and how pleasant it is for brethren to dwell together in unity! It is like the precious ointment upon the head, that ran down upon the beard, even Aaron's beard: that went down to the skirts of his garments; As the dew of Hermon, and as the dew that descended upon the mountains of Zion: for there the*

LORD commanded the blessing, even life for evermore."

"What a beautiful passage!" Ginger exclaimed, smiling, her expression wistful.

"Very appropriate," Nikki responded, glancing at each of her friends while lying her hand on LeeAnn's knee. "As long as we work and live together in unity, we *can* and *will* survive anything."

"Yep, I agree. Gotta give the good Lord credit. He always knows how to touch your heart." Stretching, Tawnie leaned back against her saddle and closed her eyes, her face relaxing.

WITH SNOWSHOES STRAPPED ACROSS THE FRONT of their saddles, Ginger, Tawnie, and Nikki headed for the grove of downed trees closest to the camp Nikki remembered spying before the snowstorms. Each was heavily dressed, donning their ponchos over their heads where Kissa had sewed the edges together to protect their heads and faces, leaving their eyes uncovered.

Reaching the area, Nikki examined the snow-covered landscape, suddenly understanding their quest would not be easy. The deep snow appeared evenly surfaced and without definition underneath its weight. She looked at the shovel in her hand, knowing that it was useless unless she figured out exactly where and how the logs lay underneath the snow. Jamming the shovel in the snow, she faced Tawnie and Ginger. "Any suggestion how we find the trees?"

"Maybe," Ginger replied, walking toward a large spruce tree, cautiously testing different branches before pulling out her knife and sawing through one of the lower, longer and thicker branches. After stripping it down to a bare branch, she walked around the area, pushing the stick down into the snow until she finally used her knife to make a mark around the branch to indicate the depth of the snow. Walking around the area pushing the branch into the snow, and leaving poke marks around a large area, she finally stopped and shouted, "Bring the shovel and try here."

Tawnie grabbed the shovel jutting in the snow and walked toward Ginger, then began shoveling snow around the spot Ginger marked. She dug deep until she stood on top of a fallen log, but instead of stopping there, she kept digging the hole wider. Literally crawling out of the snow pit, she clambered to her feet to stand close to the edge. "Welp, we hit the jackpot. I found three here close together. Now whut?"

Nikki grabbed the rope hanging around her saddle horn and walked toward them. After taking off her snowshoes, she jumped into the hole and struggled to get the rope around the most prominent trunk. After getting the rope underneath and around the tree trunk, she took her gloves off for better dexterity in tying the rope before laying the other end on top of the snow around her. "Ginger, get your horse, tie this to your saddle and start pulling the log."

Ginger complied without luck. Nikki put her gloves back on and dug the hole larger and longer around the trunks before jumping free and motioning Ginger to try again. With a mighty pull, the log pulled free, collapsing the hole as it was forced out of its snowy grave.

"This ain't gonna be easy." Tawnie walked around the hole, evaluating how much longer it would take to clear the other two logs out of the snow. "Don't reckon this gonna be worth our time."

"It will be if no other reason than to keep the fires going. If not, we will freeze long before we run out of food anyway." Forehead wrinkled in thought, Nikki jumped into the hole to remove more snow until the other two logs were cleared.

Laying the shovel on top of the snow, she crawled out to face her friends. "I've been thinking if each morning we take a stick to find the logs like Ginger did, then one can dig while the other two look for other possible places for logs. It may take a little longer, and we may or may not find one, but it is a start. What other choice do we have?"

"We only have one shovel. I thought about us trying to make shovels, but the snow is too heavy. I'd say it will be a day-by-day endeavor." With each in agreement, Ginger finished, "By the time we get the other two logs out of the snow, it will be time to take them back to camp and call it a day."

Nikki fastened the rope around the saddle horn, took the rein to urge her gelding forward. Her triumphant shout echoed through the hills when the gelding broke the dead tree loose from its hoary imprisonment. From there, it was relatively easy for the horses to pull the logs toward the camp.

"Gonna be slow," Tawnie remarked later in the afternoon, looking at their pitifully small bounty of three logs.

"Tomorrow should go faster since we almost know what we are doing." Ginger patted Cinnamon. "You'll get an extra ration of oats tonight, boy."

"All the horses deserve extra rations, but we have to conserve them. We do not know how long we will be trapped up here." Nikki looked around her, searching for an area with ground flat enough to build the cabin, her main worry providing winter shelter for them.

"Ya know, Kissa could be notchin' out the logs while she's watchin' LeeAnn." Tawnie rubbed her gloved hands together, dreading the notching part of the project. Her hands were so frozen now she could barely feel her fingers.

Ginger laughed. "If you want to take the chance, go ahead and show her how to do it."

"She could do it if we explain it while showing her how," Nikki agreed.

"And if she screws it up? Nah, better if we do it," Tawnie reluctantly decided. "'Sides, she keeps busy with the kid and cookin' for us, 'sides doin' all the home-type stuff. And talkin' about cookin', I smell supper and it's remindin' me that I'm starvin'.'"

It was hard work getting the logs to camp. Some days, they were only able to get three trees to camp, and a couple of those logs measured approximately 30 feet in length. The most they dragged down in one day were six logs, and some days they had absolutely no luck finding a log underneath the heavy snow. They had to go farther from camp each day to collect the wind-blown trees. There were days the weather and snowstorms prevented them from doing anything except sit in the wickiup and listen to either the whistling wind or total silence. It was Kissa's daily practice of reading aloud from the Bible every night, carefully running her index finger along the words while LeeAnn sat beside her, which provided normalcy in their chaotic and difficult situation.

Nikki thought again about trying to get them to town.

Realistically, she scratched the ideal. The snow had changed the appearance of the land and contained hidden traps. Also, there was the possibility of getting caught in a snowstorm and freezing to death. *No*, she decided, *we are better off here*. The wickiup at least blocked most of the bitter cold and provided an adequate measure of warmth. Also, the trimmed branches from gathered fallen trees provided extra firewood.

A long log fire was burning in front of the wickiup, reflecting heat back into their living quarters. The only time the fire was not burning was when the snow fell so hard, it succeeded in smothering the fire. Besides, they did have plenty of water and food along with the elk Nikki had killed before she left, which hopefully would supply them with enough meat to last the winter.

TAWNIE, GINGER, AND NIKKI SAT ON A LOG they had earlier succeeded in pulling free from the snow. Resting, they took time to eat the pemmican Kissa had made from elk meat and dried fruits. "Where's your bear claw necklace?" Ginger asked. She had noticed the necklace gone weeks ago, but by the end of the day, she was too tired to think about anything except eating and sleeping.

Sighing, her hand automatically going to her neck, Nikki explained her run-in with Mad Dog and Injun Bill.

"You're sure they didna follow ya?"

"If they did follow me, the snowstorm wiped out my tracks. Besides, if they did not freeze to death in the storm, they would have been here before now. It's been at least a month since it happened." Nikki hoped so but did not let doubts show on her face. They had other problems to worry about, particularly the big log they were trying to pull free.

They took turns shoveling snow from around the tree until all were too tired to shovel more. Tying their ropes to the log, all three horses were used to pull it out of the snowbank, but the fallen tree had not budged.

Wiping her hands on her pant legs, Nikki stated, "I think after we get this log freed along with the others we have collected, we should have enough to lay the foundation and start building the walls. From there, we should be able to judge if we have enough logs or if we need more later. I will take the log we are sitting on to camp and bring Kissa back with me. With her and her horse, we should be able to pull the other one free. It should not take long, and LeeAnn and *Heoohtato* will be fine staying at the camp during that time."

Nikki deposited the log close to the others, then rode the short distance to the wickiup. Stopping, she stared around her in surprise—all their possessions lined the spaces around the wickiup. Kissa backed out of the door, carrying more items outside. "What in the world are you doing?" Nikki asked, staring at the freshly washed and frozen clothes hanging on some evergreen trees.

"I thought since it was a reasonably nice day, I'd wash." Laying the blankets across the makeshift corral, Kissa looked up at Nikki.

"I scrubbed every dish we have and left them in the sun to dry until I finish redoing the inside. LeeAnn's asleep and I guess *Heoohtato* is hunting. I figured since I have the wickiup stripped, I'd start cutting fresh pine boughs because it really stinks in there. Don't worry, Nikki. By the time I get a new floor laid and a fire burning full blast, our wet clothes will dry soon enough inside."

Nikki laughed. Kissa was stuck all day with LeeAnn and if she wanted to clean their wickiup, then so be it. It *was* an unusually pretty day even if it was still bitter cold. "You will have to finish it later, Kissa. We need your help, so saddle your horse and grab your shotgun. I will tell LeeAnn we will have you back in a little bit."

While Kissa readied herself and her horse, Nikki whistled for *Heoohtato.* She heard its distant bark and whistled again before the dog appeared. Nikki reached down to pet the enormous head, and the dog wagged its tail in welcome. "Sorry, *Heoohtato.* You will have to finish hunting later. I need you to stay with LeeAnn." Giving the dog another pat on the head, she crawled into the wickiup.

Kissa had her horse saddled by the time Nikki came out of the wickiup. After slinging a saddlebag over the back of the saddle and strapping it down, Kissa grabbed her shotgun.

"Why are you taking a saddlebag?"

"I thought you might need ammunition to go hunting today. It is a pretty day, and a rabbit would add a little variety to our meal tonight."

Nikki laughed, thinking it was not worth mentioning the saddlebag contained all the ammunition for their weapons. "All right, bring it. I will go hunting after we get the log."

The large lodgepole was firmly stuck in the snow. The women added Kissa's rope around the tree trunk, and with their horses, all pulling in the same direction, slowly dragged it from underneath the high banks of hard, frozen snow. They gave a jubilant shout and patted each other on the back.

"Let's get the ropes off," Ginger pronounced, already loosening the ropes from the tree trunk.

"Kissa, take the tree to camp so you can get back to LeeAnn. Ladies, I have orders from Miss Loving to go hunting. She thinks we need a little variety in our meal tonight," Nikki laughed, helping Ginger with the ropes.

Suddenly, a loud boom exploded the air and reverberated through the mountains. Snow from branches above them sifted fine powdered snow over them.

"Gunshot," Tawnie stated, mirroring their thoughts. Tawnie, Kissa, and Ginger threw off their snowshoes and headed for their horses.

"Stop!" Nikki shouted. "We cannot run back to camp unprepared. We need to be logical." After getting their attention, she knelt in the snow. "Look, we are here," she stated, making a mark in the snow. "The camp is here. Kissa, ride to the west side of the camp and tie your horse to a tree, then take your shotgun and carefully come in from that direction. Tawnie, ride north around camp and come in from the back. Ginger, take the south side. I will go into camp from the east. Do not enter the camp until I give a whistle signaling all is clear. Now, go."

Her heart beating an unsteady tempo, Nikki threw her snowshoes over the saddle, every thought and emotion centering around LeeAnn and her safety. Surely the outlaws did not track her here. *But what if they did*, her mind argued. *I made a promise not to kill any more if LeeAnn lived.* Shaking her head to rid herself of the errant thoughts, she knew deep down she would do anything to protect the child, including giving up her own life.

Her heart beat faster with each lunge of the gelding through the deep snow, the ride seeming to take forever. Close to camp, she halted the gelding and tied the reins to a tree, then crept forward, pistol in hand. Something drew her attention toward a clump of trees, and she froze. Hidden in the grove, she spotted one of the outlaws about the same time he saw her. Barely thinking, she lifted her pistol and fired.

A bullet slammed into a tree trunk close to her, and she ducked, then poked her head around the tree. The outlaw had fallen backward in the snow, his blood marring the perfect white. Now the outlaws knew they were coming.

Creeping forward around a small thicket of trees, Nikki barely glanced at the downed outlaw, then stopped behind a brush, peeking around it at the wickiup. Through the thicket branches, she watched LeeAnn appear before the door opening, clutching the rag doll against her naked chest, shivering, not only from fear, but from the ice-cold air. She jerkily moved forward, seeming to refuse to move but being forced.

Smoke began pouring from the side of the wickiup. LeeAnn took several more steps forward, her eyes huge in her shrunken face. A head appeared behind her, then she was shoved outside, and the half-clothed Mad Dog appeared behind her. He lifted her body against him and stepped from the doorway, drawing a knife close to her throat.

Hiding behind a thicket of bushes, Nikki did not move and carefully aimed at Mad Dog's head, waiting for the perfect shot. The fire in the wickiup grew, highlighting them in a red-yellow glow. From her peripheral vision, she noticed another fire lighting the sky in the same direction the logs they had pulled from the snow were stored, the smell of burning wood and the crackling sounds an ominous sign of things to come.

Mad Dog stepped further from the burning wickiup, tightening his grip on LeeAnn's waist, the knife held closer to her throat. "I know yoren out there. Step out and throw yoren weapons toward me."

Nikki kept her weapon pointed at his head, realizing one small movement from either could offset her shot and hit LeeAnn instead. Keeping silent and perfectly still, she watched him look around, not knowing exactly where she hid. He inched LeeAnn forward and to the right toward a horse standing nearby.

"Throw yoren gun over here," Mad Dog threateningly commanded, moving the knife closer to LeeAnn's throat while inching closer to the horse.

Nikki froze, watching. He would have to turn his back to her if he tried to mount the horse or force LeeAnn into the saddle. *Patience*, she admonished herself, knowing she only had one shot and it had to be perfect. The child's tears fell from huge, brown, tear-filled eyes and LeeAnn's gaze settled on the bush Nikki was hiding behind, and Nikki wondered if the child saw her.

"I know yoren out there," Mad Dog growled, edging closer toward the horse's head.

With the rag doll clutched against her bare chest with one hand, LeeAnn lifted the other hand toward the bush Nikki was hiding behind, crying, "Momma Nikki!"

"Throw yoren weapons out and come out now with yoren hands above yoren head," Mad Dog commanded, threatening and pulling LeeAnn even tighter against his chest, the knife still at her throat.

An arrow tipped with fear pierced her heart with LeeAnn's first terror-filled words. She started to move forward but remained motionless, knowing it would only endanger LeeAnn even more. "Don't hurt her, Mad Dog. Have your way with me, but let the child go," she called out, never moving.

Another round of shots sounded and reverberated through the valley. The arid smell of smoke grew stronger, drifting toward her, and everything within her sank. *No!* her mind screamed; *they are burning everything!* But she knew it was too late. Powerless, she kept her focus firmly on Mad Dog and LeeAnn.

"Nice gesture, but too late. I'll finish what I should of done in the beginnin'—kill ya all. You're a burr in my side and it's time to end it," Mad Dog growled, moving the knife closer to LeeAnn's throat for emphasis.

"You can take my life. I don't care, but the others?" Nikki let the last sentence hang in the air. Another explosion of gunshots broke the stillness close by, then the only sound was the crackling of flames.

"Enough!" Mad Dog shouted, slamming LeeAnn tighter against his bare chest. "Throw yoren weapons out afore I cut this one's throat."

Realizing she was in a *damn if I do, damn if I don't* situation, Nikki smothered her disgusted sigh and stood, throwing her pistol in front of her and raising her arms. "Let her go and leave, Mad Dog, while you still can."

With a smirk upon his ugly face, Mad Dog threw the suddenly limp form of LeeAnn from him several feet away and turned.

Nikki cried out and dove for her pistol. Luck was with her; her hand landed on the pistol's handle. She rolled upright with it in her hand to level the gun at Mad Dog, then pulled the trigger.

Mad Dog jerked backward, the shot careening against the side of his head and leaving a long streak just above his ear, taking part of his hair where the bullet grazed his head. Grabbing the wound in surprise, he leaped on the back of his horse and jammed his heels in its flanks.

Nikki ran after him, getting off a couple of more shots before he raced off into the trees.

Flames rose around her, licking at everything they had worked so hard to prepare for the winter. The whole camp was on fire, and there was no sign of the outlaws.

Whistling, she turned to run back toward LeeAnn at a dead run. She stumbled and fell face down in the snow. Picking herself up, she kept running. "LeeAnn!"

Dropping her pistol hand, she dropped to her knees and turned toward LeeAnn's form lying in the snow, pulling her limp form against her, desperately checking for life. She lifted her head, smothering the wail of pain rising within her.

The child was dead.

Chapter 3
Ice Fire Cannot Melt

FIRE SPREADING ALL AROUND THE CAMP and smoke rising toward the sky, Tawnie broke into view and ran to Nikki's side, taking the limp child from her arms and moving her further away from the fire before laying her in the snow, shaking her head in shock.

"Get the fire out! Now!" Nikki yelled, her voice filled with urgency while she struggled to her feet. Running toward the makeshift corral, she pulled a frozen blanket from the fence and started beating the flames.

Tears streaming down her cheeks, Tawnie grabbed objects close to the fire and moved them further away before grabbing a blanket to slap at the flames.

Kissa's moaning scream alerted Nikki she had discovered LeeAnn's lifeless body. By the time she reached Kissa, Kissa sat in the snow holding the painfully thin, naked child in her arms, blood smearing them both. "They cut her throat, Nikki!"

"Put her down, Kissa. We can do nothing for her now." Nikki wanted to cry, to scream against the fates, to express the grief and anger raging within her, but the tears were lost somewhere inside her. The knowledge LeeAnn spoke her first words since she had been assaulted echoed in her memory, '*Momma Nikki.*' Those two words were enough to saturate her soul with morose mingled with guilt and unfathomable hatred for the outlaws because she knew she was the reason the child had been murdered. She was the one who had left her in camp by herself with only the dog to protect her.

Moaning, Kissa continued to rock the child. A shiver went through Nikki, watching Kissa and LeeAnn outlined against the eerie red-orange-yellow backdrop of the burning camp. The memory of her rocking Cari's dead body in much the same way almost brought her to her knees.

With a muttered oath, Nikki hardened her heart and stepped forward, slapping Kissa. Kissa's head rocked with the blow, shocking the tears from her eyes. Taking the dead child from her arms, Nikki roughly demanded, "Kissa, we have to put out the fire or we will all be dead. Get up and move!"

Another exchange of gunfire broke through the crackling sounds of the fire. Realizing Ginger was not present, Nikki forced her attention back to the blaze and their immediate survival yet wanting to run in the direction of the shots, but her instinct warned her against it. If the fire was not contained soon and grew any larger, it could start a winter forest fire, a fire none of them would survive.

Kissa stumbled to her feet and faced Nikki, tears streaming down her cheeks. "You're savage, Nikki! Don't you feel anything anymore?"

Kissa did not realize just how much Nikki wanted to cry and wail her sorrow, but there was nothing to be done for the child. Surviving themselves was now more important, and the only way was to distinguish the fire and salvage what they could. "Move, Kissa. Move it now or I swear I will knock your teeth out!"

With her last words, Nikki turned away and laid the dead child in the snow. Running toward the corral, she pulled another frozen blanket from the corral fence to beat the flames.

Something must have pierced Kissa's mind for she grabbed one of the frozen blankets to help Nikki and Tawnie fight the raging fire. It was a useless battle. Nearly everything was burnt, even the logs they had collected. The saving grace was Kissa had decided to clean the wickiup and had taken the saddlebags, blankets, and an array of personal items, along with the furs the Cheyenne gifted them outside to air. Each of them had kept their weapons with them and were safely on either their horses' backs or close at hand.

They surveyed the blackened remains of their home, thankful the snow proved deep enough to contain the fire enough to prevent it from spreading.

"They took the pack animals," Tawnie remarked, glancing at her blistered hands.

"The pack horses were probably used to carry the food they stole from us," Nikki informed them. "Look up at the trees. It's all gone."

Staring at the pitiful small bounty in front of them, they barely glanced up as Ginger rode in dragging one of the outlaws behind her.

"Oh, my God!" Ginger cried, nearly falling off her horse to get to them.

Tawnie looked Ginger over, searching for any injury, then focused her attention on the outlaw with his hands tied behind his back and a rope around his neck. "I was hopin' ya was still alive, Ginger. Didna know yet and didna have time to check. That bloody buzzard Mad Dog killed LeeAnn and torched our camp. Dang whoresons used the torch sticks Kissa worked on for weeks to destroy nearly everything."

Viewing the destruction of the camp, Tawnie added, "I shot one of the mangy dogs righ' tween the eyes. Too easy a death for him."

Her eyes hard, Ginger slowly moved toward them, jerking on the end of the rope. "Well, I brought one back with me. I wounded him while he and two other men were leaving. I shot his horse out from under him, then shot him in the leg to keep him from running away."

Nikki recognized Injun Bill, and everything within her grew hard and cold, the very brittleness edging out all human emotion. From the corner of her eye, she saw Kissa grab the shotgun and aim it at the outlaw. "No, Kissa, put your gun away. We do not want his death to be too easy."

"I want him dead. I want him tortured the way the Cheyenne did Two Thumbs, only worse!" Kissa lowered the shotgun, the dried tears replaced with a hardness none of the women had ever seen, narrowing her eyes.

"Good thinkin', Kissa." Tawnie slapped Kissa on the back, then took two steps backwards when Kissa lifted angry, hard eyes, the rigidity of her face stunning Tawnie.

Tawnie swallowed hard before saying, "The whoreson is bleedin'. We don' want him bleedin' to death, at least not yet."

Sauntering toward the outlaw, Tawnie grabbed his hair, and jerked his head backward. "Ya bloody buzzard, your gonna wish Ginger had killed ya back there."

"I want him so tortured he pays for what they did to Leeann with every scream," Kissa grated between clenched teeth.

Ginger turned her attention to the small body clutching the rag doll Tawnie had given her, lying on top of the snow. "They defiled her again?"

Tears forming in her eyes, Ginger wanted to rage against God. Had they not promised they would become mothers and forget their revenge if He saved her? And He did save her from the scarlet fever only for her to again suffer the act which had taken her voice in the first place. To keep from crying with rage then shoot the lone captured outlaw, Ginger's eyes swept over the camp. "Where's *Heoohtato*?"

"I will look for him while you and Tawnie tie Injun Bill to the trees. After we take care of LeeAnn, we will deal with him. Kissa, get LeeAnn ready for burial."

Kissa grabbed Nikki's arm none too gently when she turned, spinning her around to face her. "No, I will look for the dog. You take care of LeeAnn, Nikki, because you're the one who caused this."

Shocked, Nikki stared at Kissa's retreating back, her words a powerful blow settling in the pit of her stomach, all her self-doubts crowding her mind and squeezing her heart. She was the one to blame and she did blame herself. Her heart physically ached until she could barely breath, everything within her frozen and dead. She did not feel the hand laid on her shoulder and refused to turn around when she heard Ginger's voice.

"She's hurting, Nikki, and said it in anger. Don't think about it."

"She is right, you know. I am the one who led you through these godforsaken mountains and got us stranded here," Nikki muttered, shaking the hand from her shoulder. "And I am the one who got LeeAnn killed." Guilt-ridden, she moved toward the naked, abused body lying alone on top of the snow.

Nikki tried to clean the body and prayed for tears to help release the pain and the overwhelming hatred from her heart. The child had been defiled, beaten, and abused, and her life ended with her throat cut. *It is my fault and my fault alone. What have I done*? The one small twinge of compassion and love she had so desperately clung to sputtered and perished with the child clinging to an old, ragged doll.

Nikki cleaned the dead child the best she could and wrapped her naked body in one of the burned blankets, but she knew there was nowhere to bury her—the ground was too frozen. Blurry-eyed, she checked the bullets in her pistol, then put her snowshoes back on before leaving the solemn group to find Kissa.

Calling for *Heoohtato* and Kissa and searching the surrounding area, Nikki heard a whine toward the western limits of camp. She found *Heoohtato* lying under some evergreen trees around the camp's perimeter, blood streaming from his head. A bullet had grazed the top of his head and apparently had knocked him unconscious. "It is all right, boy. Stay."

A man's scream echoed through the camp, but Nikki ignored it, for some reason finding pleasure in the tormented shriek.

Working swiftly, she fashioned a travois and then loaded the dog upon it. She thought about carrying the big dog back to camp but knew the only place to lay him was on the snow. Instead, she laid the dog on the travois and pulled it toward camp.

"Kissa," she shouted and received no answer. Tawnie and Ginger were out of sight, but she heard their voices outside the camp where they had forced Injun Bill.

"Ain't seen her," Tawnie shouted back.

Nikki searched the fire-ruined campsite and located her medicine pouches near the corral. Breathing a sigh of relief they had not been destroyed, she knelt beside the injured animal. After cleaning *Heoohtato's* wound and sprinkling some herbs over it, Nikki patted the animal, running her hands along his side to reassure him. He must have tried to protect LeeAnn if he was shot. "Brave *Heoohtato*, you tried, did you not? If only…" she stopped the thought before it could form. *If onlys* never got anyone anywhere.

"Stay, *Heoohtato*," Nikki ordered, rising, then shouted, "I will look for Kissa. She has not made it back to camp."

"Don't bother," Kissa retorted in an unusually hard voice, appearing through the thick trees along the eastern border of camp and leading their three horses behind her.

"Glad you found the dog," Kissa replied, dropping a gun belt with two long barreled pistols, a thick woolen shirt and a winter coat beside her.

"Glad you are back," Nikki acknowledged, staring at the items Kissa had dropped beside her. Brief flashes of Mad Dog shirtless with no guns around his waist and standing only in pants and boots while he held a knife to LeeAnn's throat, played before her eyes. Her stomach tightened and churned, realizing why she had come across an unprepared Mad Dog.

Turning without speaking, Nikki headed toward the direction Ginger and Tawnie had taken. She found them standing in front of their handy work. The outlaw was suspended upside down and spreadeagle between two trees.

"I got his wound to stop bleedin'," Tawnie remarked, watching Nikki and Kissa walk toward them. "Put a chaw of tobacci in it. The son o' perdition screamed like he was on fire."

"Yes," Kissa muttered, a wild look in her eyes. "Fire, build a fire underneath him."

Tawnie started to slap her on the back again, then decided against it. "Good thinkin'. I'll get one started, just high enough so he don' cook none."

Turning from the group, Nikki forced herself to return camp and the dead child wrapped in a partially burnt blanket. She needed to mourn the loss, to accept the fact she had failed once again.

Kneeling beside the body, she wanted to cry, but the tears refused to squeeze past her closed eyes, yet hurt, sorrow, and hatred clawed deep at her insides.

Tenderly, Nikki uncovered the child's head and gazed down into the forever stilled face. Horror froze the tiny features into a grotesque death mask and the cut around her throat emphasized the terror.

Something about the cut troubled her and acting instinctively, Nikki picked up some snow and cleaned the gash more thoroughly. Studying the wound, she observed the cut was not deep and only cut across the front, not near deep enough for a knife to be drawn across it. Her dream rose before her, the steady cadence of heartbeats turning erratic, then growing fainter.

Shaken, Nikki fell to her knees, the picture of LeeAnn's limp body being thrown to the side suddenly making sense. They had spoken about how tired and feeble

LeeAnn was and worried about her failure to gain strength or weight, and now it appeared perhaps LeeAnn's heart had given out, and she went limp, her head falling forward over the knife blade. Was it possible?

It was logical since she had never witnessed Mad Dog pulling the knife across her throat, only him tossing her limp form away from him and turning toward his horse, an unusual gesture considering the circumstances at the time.

Setting her suspicion to the side for now, Nikki gently covered the face again and stood. Throwing her gloves and coat to the snow-covered ground, she lifted her arms toward the heavens. "*Heammawihio*, hear my prayer. Let my voice carry to you on the northern wind and echo through the heavens. Why have you taken this small one? This child kept us whole, kept us human. Why did you make our vows into a mockery? Must death follow me everywhere, even for the ones I swore to protect?"

She cried out in anger, bewilderment, and sorrow toward the towering trees overhead. "*Maehonehe*, your warning came too late, and the symbols were too hidden."

Her voice caught on a dry sob. "Once again, *Heammawihio*, I offer my blood for their blood." She grabbed the knife from around her waist and cut her wrists.

Watching the blood well up and flow down her arms, she lifted her arms upward. The blood stained the white snow, the drops slowly dripping from her wrists. "Give us courage, strength, and cunning to find the animals and punish them."

Her husky voice rising and falling, Nikki sang a haunting melody that trembled through the snow-covered trees and waft toward the heavens. Storm clouds gathered overhead and quickly covered the sun, spreading over the skies in pregnant grey. The north wind whispered at first, then blew harder, sending its freezing fingers through them. "I am accused of being a savage, so now I am savage. Let the savagery begin. I have no heart, no soul, only hatred and anger no amount of your cold wind can blow away."

Sometime during her cry to the heavens, her friends surrounded her, staring at the small body wrapped in the burnt blanket, tears on everyone's face but her own. Snow fell from the skies and the wind whipped it around them, freezing them to the bone while her voice rumbled from the depths of her soul.

In a long-drawn-out whine of pain and loss, she sang a Cheyenne death song for LeeAnn. The wind picked up the rhythmic sound and whipped it away, carrying her voice into the heavens. The knife still in her hand, she stared at it, then lowered her arms and knelt beside LeeAnn, her head lowered.

"I want to bury her in a town. I don't want her left in the mountains all alone," Kissa cried through racking sobs.

Nikki shook her head, unable and unwilling to debate what to do with the body now. "We need to build a wickiup before we take care of Injun Bill. And we will need to build a travois for LeeAnn and hang it up in the trees so the animals cannot get to her."

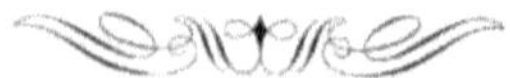

GREY MISTS OF FALLING SNOW WASHED across the white landscape intermitted with evergreen trees. Snow fell daily, almost constantly, over the near treeless slopes. None of them voted to stay in the destroyed camp since the place had become haunted with their painful memories.

Cold, tired, and hungry, the women tracked onward. They had little choice but to make it to civilization: their camp and all the food supplies were destroyed or stolen. The pemmican they had in their saddlebags ran out long ago and they survived on the few rabbits they were able to kill. Larger game had left the higher reaches toward warmer climes weeks ago.

It was a silent group. Little had been said since the day LeeAnn was killed. All their concentration was on staying alive—survival, the ultimate feat in the snow-packed, isolated mountains.

They had been traveling for three weeks and had not eaten anything in the last week. Their bellies growled with hunger, their heads ached, and freezing cold seemed to penetrate every part of their bodies. The sun had not shown through the overcast skies in weeks, and the mountain valleys were hidden in the overhanging grey haze. All that lay before them was a snow-covered wasteland where few evergreens survived.

Nikki did not tell her friends she was lost. Perpetual fog covered landmarks while they traveled through valleys and had hidden the sun, not indicating direction. Somewhere, during a heavy snowstorm, they had wandered away from the frozen river, their only guide toward civilization. They were like a wandering band of gypsies, alas, lost, hopeless, and constantly moving.

Nikki called a halt near dusk. After getting a wickiup built and struggling to build a fire with wet wood, the women cuddled inside. Snow particles sifted through the crevices and hissed in the fire. Smoke filled the small space of the wickiup, and every so often, one of them coughed.

Her face gaunt, Kissa pulled her knees against her chest. "I can't take anymore," she mumbled to no one in particular.

Nikki looked into the haunted eyes of Kissa, then at Ginger and Tawnie. She wondered if her face and eyes looked forlorn as theirs. Cheekbones showed prominently in pale faces, and clothes hung on rapidly diminishing frames. "We have to keep going," Nikki softly stated, trying to give them some reassurance.

"Go on?" Kissa looked up at Nikki, a glimmer of tears sparkling in her eyes. "I still hear Injun Bill's screams in my ears."

Kissa looked down at her hands as if seeing them for the first time. "I felt nothing, just hatred flowing through me when I put burning brands against his skin. I even burned his eyes out. So why do his screams still plague me?"

"Don't think about it, Kissa." Tawnie put a hand over Kissa's, her voice soft instead of the usual harsh rumble.

"I can't help it. I wanted to torture him for what they did to LeeAnn. I felt like a Cheyenne warrior. Now I understand how the Cheyenne felt when they tortured Two Thumbs, but I can't get his screams out of my mind."

"Enough," Nikki harshly ordered, trying to stop the flow of words before too much soul-searching was done. She did not need the group to splinter apart now. Too much was at stake.

"No, we need to talk about it. We haven't said anything since that day," Ginger declared, straightening her legs out from underneath her buttocks. "Kissa, at least you just hear his screams. I still smell the burning flesh. It seems to be in the very air I breathe."

"I don't know how we did it." Kissa searched each of their faces. "He deserved it, but still…" Her voice ended with a whine of fear and aversion.

Nikki turned her back to the group and bowed her head onto her knees. What good would bringing up their actions help in erasing their guilt. She fought hard to put the memory of their wild dancing around the fire and their savage yells from her mind. Hurt, anger, savagery, and hate had come to the surface with all of them, and she did not want to remember their responses because she knew, given the same circumstances, she would do it again.

Tawnie's laugh was bitter. "Yeah, we kept the bloody whoreson alive all day and night while we tortured him, and at the time, I enjoyed it. I can still feel my whip biting every inch of his flesh." Tawnie looked at her fingers, rubbing them together in a savory motion, yet the depths of her eyes mirrored bleakness.

"I cut off every one of his fingers, then cauterized the wounds. I had planned on making a necklace with them." Ginger blanched and her stomach roiled with the memory. Gagging, she knew her stomach was not the only thing empty.

Nikki lifted her head and turned back to them, her own troubled thoughts clouding her mind. "Do not talk about it. We did what we had to do. Now leave it alone."

"No, Nikki, we did not have to torture him," Ginger reminded softly. "It doesn't really matter. I will do it again soon as we find Mad Dog and Mason, only worse."

Kissa eyed Ginger with surprise. "You would?"

"Hell, yes!" Tawnie leaned toward Kissa, holding her

eyes with hers. "We all would. If I can hang Mad Dog and Jock Mason by their toes and slowly strip the hide from them, I will."

"But…"

"But nothing," Ginger interrupted. "They deserve to die a harsh, agonizing death. Those animals killed men, women, children, and animals. They abused women and little girls. They burned homes and robbed the defenseless. They tortured and burned…" Ginger stopped, unable to go on with her tirade. Words horrible enough to describe the outlaws refused to enter her vocabulary.

"Do not dwell on it anymore," Nikki ordered again. "Our main concern is staying alive long enough to bury LeeAnn."

"But you're used to this type of barbarity," Kissa argued, staring at Nikki with surprise. "You lived with it."

Nikki turned hard eyes on the group, her mouth narrowing. "Do you understand why Cheyenne torture? They do it so a man's spirit cannot go to what you call heaven. Do you think Indians are the only people who torture? All races do. Look at what your people did during the Salem witch trials. And do not forget the heresy trials of Europe. And that is just some of the things the white race has done, not counting the evils other races have done as well. As a whole, we are all a savage people. It is built within us, but most of the time we never have to see that side of ourselves. But with us, Ladies, we have seen it, we are living it, and we will continue doing it. Now, shut up." With her speech finished, Nikki wrapped the furs and blanket tight around her shoulders and laid down, closing her eyes. *Heoohtato* crept up beside her and laid down at her back.

Something within her knew too close an examination of what they had done could be detrimental to their survival. It only stood to reason if a person looked too deeply within herself, she would find something she disliked or hated. Nothing could erase what they had done.

It was better to put it behind them and get on with survival. That one incident could splinter their group, and right now, they needed to be sane and alert to stay together, working as a group.

Finding a more comfortable position, Nikki took a deep breath and sighed. The wickiup was quiet, the crackling fire and one of her friends sobbing the only noises. She envied whoever was sobbing. Tears were a great healer, but tears refused to come to her eyes. Hatred mounted over hatred until the walls within her isolated everything good and soft in her life.

Images of Dane popped into her mind, but like everything else, she forced the memories behind the closed doors of her memory.

NIKKI LOOKED OUT OVER THE HAZY valley below. They had been traveling for weeks and hunger clawed at their bellies. Not even a rabbit poked its head from the snow. After their one night of revelation, the group remained silent, speaking only when necessary. At night they were too tired, hungry, and cold to talk.

Nikki worried about Kissa. Kissa seemed to withdraw inside herself more each day and her eyes held an unnatural light. Nightmares tormented Kissa and she woke the group with her moans and screams. Many times, Nikki heard her sobbing. Of them all, Kissa was the most tenderhearted and ethical, but sometimes her natural innocence refused to protect her.

Shaking her head to dislodge the disturbing thoughts, Nikki knelt in the snow and pointed below. "It is very important we do not shoot at anything, talk, laugh, or shout. The conditions are perfect for anything to set off a snowslide. We must get across this area and find a cave to hole up in for the night. It looks like a forest fire burned nearly everything in this area."

Searching their faces, Nikki continued, pointing below them, "See how the land slopes upward toward those trees? We are headed there."

"I will take the lead. I am the most familiar with horses," Ginger informed them, looking down at the steep snow-covered mountainside.

"Tawnie will follow you with *Heoohtato* across her saddle, and I will follow Kissa and the travois." Motioning *Heoohtato* toward Tawnie, Nikki nodded at the slope. "Let us go then."

The memory of how wolves traveled flashed across her mind. They were traveling the same way, the watch and the strongest at the forefront, the weakest in the middle, and the leader bringing up the rear.

It was a slow descent down the mountainside. For the most part, the women allowed the horses free rein. Nikki kept a close eye on Kissa, afraid the woman would scream with the horse's sliding lope and the nearly horizontal position she had to take across the horse's back. A grim smile lifted her lips with approval. Kissa had learned much since they had left Rustic, Kansas, and even more from their time with the *Tsistsistas*. She rode nearly as well as

Ginger and Tawnie.

They had almost made it across the valley when rumbling sounded overhead. Nikki looked toward the mountaintop. Waves of white snow rushed downward toward them. "Go!" she shouted. She did not need to repeat her command—the women slapped the horses with reins and lunged through the snow.

Chapter 4
Savagery Among Angels

WITH A MIGHTY LUNGE, THE GELDING lurched forward, floundering through the snow. The rumbling increased, the sound deafening. Nikki was afraid to look up: she needed all her attention to get out of the way.

Not much further, she said to herself, watching the others race toward the small line of evergreen trees on the upward slope, praying the trees and incline offered some protection to slow the avalanche's momentum.

Suddenly, the gelding slipped underneath her. With a startled oath, she tightened her legs around the gelding's sides, struggling to keep her seat. The horse lunged upward, almost dislodging her when it regained its balance. With a kick to its flanks, she raced the horse toward the opposite hill. The mishap had put the other women at a considerable distance in front of her.

The rumbling, crackling noise grew louder, and she glanced upward. Waves of snow and debris rushed toward her. Within seconds, the white mass slammed into her, knocking her off the gelding's back. Tumbling head over heels, the snow covering her, she fought toward the top of the white waves and swam them like swimming water.

The massive snow drifts lessening in strength, she crested a wave, then sunk with the rollover. Suddenly, she slammed against something solid, and pain shot through her side, her ribs cracking with the impact.

Gasping, Nikki held onto the boulder while the white mass swept over and around her. Everything happened instantaneously, and she did not have time to think or react. Basic survival overtook her and each time a wave hit, she lost her breath, not only from the weight of the snow but from the pain in her side, while clinging to the boulder. Finally, the rumbling noise decreased, and the avalanche trickled around her.

Digging her way out of the heavy snow took more effort than she thought she had. Pain pierced her side constantly, robbing her of precious air. Finally, Nikki dug through the snow and lifted her head above it. The screams of her gelding broke through the distant rumbling noise further down the slope.

She searched the landscape. Down the mountainside several hundred yards from her, she saw the gelding buried in the snow with only his legs kicking above the snowline. Its right foreleg drew her attention. The mangled leg was covered in blood and white bone shown through its hide.

Despair filling her, she watched the gelding fight to free itself. His head popped above the whiteness, then his flanks, but he could not make it to his hooves.

Blood dribbling down the corner of her mouth, she gasped with pain when lifting her hand to wipe the blood away, then drew a painful, harsh breath. She bent forward and clutched her right side, holding it while rising to her feet and struggling over the snow. Air refused to fill her lungs and each breath ripped her in two.

In a scrambling motion, she slid, fell, and sank deeper into the snow. The horse screamed in pain, and she knew she had to put the horse out of its misery before its screams started another avalanche.

With a backward glance, Nikki saw her friends safe on the other side of the path the snow slide had taken and now they were headed toward her at a dangerous gallop. She fell in the snow again. Painfully, she picked herself up and kept going. She reached the gelding about the same time her friends reached her.

"Nikki, thank God you're alive," Ginger greeted her, jumping from her mount.

"You're hurt," Kissa declared, watching Nikki struggle to her full height with her hand holding her side.

Tawnie nodded acknowledgment of Nikki's physical state, then lifted her pistol toward the gelding.

"No," Nikki quietly ordered. "The shot could start another snowslide. I will take care of my horse."

Taking her hand away from her side to draw her knife, Nikki doubled over with pain. She gritted her teeth, pulled the knife from its casing, and stumbled toward the horse's head. With a quick, determined slash, she cut the animal's throat. The squealing stopped only to be replaced by gurgling, then the gelding lay still.

Kissa was at Nikki's side. "Let me see how badly you're hurt."

"It is more important to get everything off the gelding except the saddle. We must get out of here as fast as we can." Already snow fell on them, increasing in thickness.

Tawnie reached Nikki in two long strides. "Sit and tell me where you're injured."

Wiping blood from the corner of her mouth again, Nikki leaned forward, trying to relieve the discomfort. "My ribs are broken. I need you to set them before I can ride. I think one is puncturing my lung." She drew in a painful breath, gasping for air. No matter how much she breathed, it was hard to pull in enough air to fill her lungs.

"Tell me whut to do." Tawnie leaned over the woman, her face showing determination.

Nikki grabbed Tawnie's hand and placed it over her broken ribs. "I need for you to take the palm of your hand and slam it against my ribs here."

The only sign of doubt Tawnie displayed was her strong white teeth gnawing on her bottom lip. "Hold her upright, Ginger." When Ginger was in position, Tawnie slammed the palm of her hand against Nikki's ribcage.

Intense agony stole her breath away. Nikki slumped forward, praying for tears to help release the pain. Her vision darkened around the edges before finally clearing. She caught a harsh breath, then gritted her teeth. "Again, harder."

"Dang, Nikki," Tawnie sputtered, searching her eyes before she slammed the palm of her hand harder against Nikki's ribcage.

Sharp, excruciating pain rocked Nikki against Ginger, and black crept over her vision as she felt her ribs slip back into place. Gasping, she watched Kissa kneel beside her holding a long patch of material she had cut from her own shirt to bandage her ribcage.

It took every ounce of willpower for Nikki to sit still while Kissa wrapped the material tightly underneath her breasts and wound it close to her waistline. If she had any tears left inside her, she would have gladly cried with the pain. Instead, she focused her attention on Ginger and Tawnie, watching them strip her saddlebags and weapons from the dead horse.

"The small bow's broken," Ginger stated, slinging the equipment onto the back of her horse. "Don't know how the larger bow survived."

Nikki nodded, happy at least one of her bows survived intact. "Help me to Tawnie's horse," Nikki breathlessly demanded.

Worry etching her thin face, Kissa helped Nikki to her feet, then placed her arm underneath her shoulder to support her. Nikki leaned heavily against her, each step jarring pain to her side and her legs sinking into the snow drifts.

Nikki grabbed Tawnie's outstretched arm and swung up on the back of her horse, a cry slipping past her lips. The impact stole her breath and sent shafts of agony through her side. Gritting her teeth, she moaned, "Go."

Several times during the ride, Nikki wiped blood from the corner of her mouth. Each bump of her body against the horse's shot anguish through her ribcage. Nikki clung to Tawnie's waist, fighting the edges of blackness.

By the time Ginger, with *Heoohtato's* help, had found a cave, snow fell thickly around them. Ginger and Kissa helped Nikki dismount. Dizzy and weak, Nikki fell to her knees, gasping for breath, a red haze of pain blurring her vision.

"Get her inside," Tawnie ordered, unsaddling the horse.

"Check the cave first, Tawnie. Have your rifle ready to shoot anything that moves or doesn't move. Ginger, follow her and do likewise." Nikki struggled to her feet with Kissa's help.

The cold, dark cave was uninhabited and big enough to accommodate the women, the dog, three saddles, and the saddlebags. It took a while for them to find enough wood to start a fire. It took longer still to get a blaze strong enough to light the wet wood.

Ginger moved the travois carrying LeeAnn's body toward the cave mouth and buried it underneath the deep-packed snow while Tawnie staked the horses close by the cave.

"There's not many trees to strip the bark from to feed the horses. Looks like the other animals already stripped them. I did the best I could, and I cut some pine boughs to block the cave mouth too. It's not much." Her eyebrows drawn together with worry, Ginger slumped down beside Nikki.

Kissa and Tawnie brought in the pine boughs and positioned them against the cave mouth. The wind howled through the cave and snow blew in through the thin layers. Nikki leaned against the cold wall, too weak and pain-ridden to help. Kissa had put a fur hide around her earlier, and Nikki drew the edges close to her neck and shut her eyes.

Cold, tired, and hungry, Ginger, Tawnie, and Kissa stared at each other through the flames and smoke before shrugging their shoulders. Without saying another word, each unrolled their bedroll and laid down to rest.

Nikki drifted in and out of a pain-ridden sleep. It was uncomfortable to stand, sit, or lay with her broken ribs. Only her unnatural tiredness forced her to sleep for short durations. The wind whistled eerily through the cavern, bouncing off walls and echoing in her mind.

Heoohtato crept close to Nikki and laid down beside her, whining. Usually a big muscular dog, his ribs showed through his hide, reflecting the women's appearances. By morning, the storm continued unabated. The interior of the cave was dim and drafty but still better than being in the storm.

Kissa huddled close to the fire, her face drawn and dark shadows outlining her sunken eyes. "I'm so hungry. We've got to find something to eat soon."

"We will kill one of the horses soon as the snow stops enough to see outside," Nikki vowed, her own stomach cramped with hunger.

"We'd be better off killin' the dog and eatin' him." Placing another stick over the fire, Tawnie glanced at *Heoohtato.* He sat close to Nikki with his head on her lap while Nikki absently patted its head.

"No," Nikki answered, moving slightly and gasping with the sudden sharp pain. "He is our last option. The horses first."

Heoohtato lifted his head and slunk toward the mouth of the cave, growling. His hackles rose and his lips curled back to reveal strong, white teeth.

"Dang, I think the dog understood me." Tawnie reached for the pistol at her waist, but Nikki laid her hand over hers, stopping her.

"Listen." Nikki leaned toward the cave mouth, but nothing could be heard above the howling wind. The wind seemed to take a breath to blow again, and she heard the horses whinnying. Grabbing her pistol, then slumping with pain, she drew a breath before saying, "Something is wrong with the horses." Without another word, she was on her feet and walked, favoring her right side, toward the cave mouth.

The wind blew thick snowflakes in her face, the force of it propelling her back inside. Fighting against the strength of the storm, she leaned forward and crept outside again.

The low growl of a mountain lion stopped her. With the snow biting into her face and stinging her eyes, Nikki could not see beyond a few feet. Freezing, she motioned for the women behind her to do likewise.

Thrashing sounds and the frightened screaming of the horses sounded above the wailing storm. A blurry flash appeared at the corner of her eye, and Nikki was knocked backwards as one of the horses raced past her. Within moments, the other two horses broke free and disappeared in thick falling snow, but it was too late to do anything. Between the storm and the mountain lion outside the cave, she knew finding the horses again would be next to impossible. With a weary sigh, she painfully rose to her feet and turned toward the cave, motioning the women inside.

"Whut..." Tawnie sputtered as Nikki pushed her toward the cave.

"It is too late. The horses are gone," Nikki explained.

"But..."

"A mountain lion scared them away and may be nearby. We cannot risk it attacking us." An added weight of worry slumping her shoulders, Nikki watched Tawnie reposition the branches over the cave mouth after the dog slunk inside.

Kissa backed up to the far corner of the cave, her sobs breaking over the howling wind. Ginger sat in front of the fire, staring into the flicking flames, and Nikki stood looking at them, wondering about their chances of survival.

Dead silence fell upon the group until Tawnie glanced

at the mouth of the cave, muttering *paybacks are hell*, then looked around at her friends. "Welp, there goes supper."

"What else can happen?" Ginger quietly asked, staring into the fire.

Nikki watched the reflection of the flames dance in Ginger's green eyes and the hopelessness etched across the fine-boned planes of her gaunt face. The same feeling of hopelessness settled in the pit of her stomach and grew with each passing moment. *What have I done?* she wondered again. *All of this is my fault. My friends could have been at home, warm, safe, comfortable, well-fed, and—miserable because they had no life anymore, only shame.* She shook her head against the last thought. *But at least they would be alive. I cannot promise them we will get out of this alive.*

It was the last sobering thought prompting her dream vision to pop into her mind. "Before LeeAnn was killed, I had a dream—a vision. Red Wolf commanded me to tell you the vision and you would help me decipher the symbols."

A fleeting hope lifted Nikki's last words. They had nothing else to lose except their lives. If the vision could help them or show them what to do or expect, would it not benefit them?

"Tell us your vision," Ginger prompted when Nikki grew silent and thoughtful.

Nikki sat straighter and met each of their eyes, searching for approval. "I think I figured out the first of the dream. In my vision there was a house with its windows boarded up and the roof falling in. Four roses lay in a weed-choked garden. I think the old house symbolizes our former lives and each one of the roses symbolizes us.

I am the red rose streaked with white. Ginger, you are the red one, and Tawnie, the golden yellow." Nodding toward Kissa cuddled against the wall, she added, "Kissa is the pink rose."

"It makes sense, I guess, but it doesn't tell us much." Ginger crossed her legs in front of her and sat Indian fashion.

"I heard heartbeats beating in a strong, regular rhythm, and then I saw a herd of buffalo running in circles. Someone was killing them."

"Buffalos in a circle?" Ginger asked, confused.

"Yeah, buffalos run in a circle 'round their young'uns to protect them." Tawnie's face showed a new excitement. "That's us protectin' LeeAnn."

"Heartbeats? What can the heartbeats mean?"

"LeeAnn," Nikki softly answered, closing her eyes a moment to remember each detail of the vision. Missing one detail could alter the whole vision. "The roses blew toward a bear and its cub. That is when heartbeats grew softer and started thumping erratically. The mother bear killed her own cub because it was not strong enough to survive the winter."

"Do you think the cub and the heartbeats really mean LeeAnn?" Ginger slightly drew back, her face mirroring her thoughts. "I once read if a child lives after having scarlet fever, the child suffers from hearing loss or a weak heart. Do you think LeeAnn had a weak heart? She never did regain her strength and she tired very easily."

"Makes sense to me. I'm thinkin' that maybe it wouldn't of matter whut we did to protect her. If your dream is correct, LeeAnn would of never made it anyhow."

"I did not tell you before," Nikki started, leaning back against the wall to relieve the pain in her ribs. "I don't believe Mad Dog killed LeeAnn by cutting her throat. The wound was not deep enough. I believe her heart gave out and her head fell forward on the knife when she died."

"What? Why didn't you tell us before?" Ginger cried.

Nikki helplessly shrugged. "There was so much happening, mainly just keeping alive."

Kissa stopped crying, rubbed her eyes, and in a stricken voice, proclaimed, "No, he killed her when he violated her again."

"Gotta agree with that, but no matter, she weren't gettin' any better. Don't think she'd of made it much longer anyhow. Still, the whoreson killed her no matter which way he done it." Tawnie leaned forward to impart her meaning, her hand clutching the handle of her whip.

"Tawnie's right and he deserves to die for his crimes." Ginger glanced at each of the women, meeting their eyes and recognizing they all felt the same way.

"Since we all agree, go on, Nikki, with your dream," Ginger urged, fascinated with the vision.

Nikki nodded, her eyes rolling upward in memory. "The roses were blown toward a cave."

"We're in a cave!" Ginger exclaimed, interrupting Nikki's story.

"Yes, yes," Nikki agreed, excitement tinging her voice. "The roses turned into wolves and howled at the moon. Soon, though, the wolves started playing together, then the leader of the pack barked, and the wolves went on a hunt. They attacked a whitetail deer in perfect harmony."

The wind howled through the cave; each woman lost in her own thoughts. Ginger broke the silence, "Are we the wolves or will we encounter wolves? I don't know how a wolf pack acts."

Kissa lifted her head, her sunken eyes widening in horror. "Do you think we will be attacked by wolves?"

"I do not know. I do know wolves raise their young until they are about two years old. They have a pack leader and hunt together. Each wolf has its own job to do during the hunt, even when traveling."

"Could be either way," Tawnie grunted. "Either we work together, or we get attacked by wolves, or maybe both."

"But what about the white tail deer?" Ginger asked thoughtfully.

"I do not know." Nikki searched their faces, but none could figure out a symbol for the white tail deer. "Perhaps it means nothing," Nikki concluded.

"Is there anything else you remember that might help us?"

"Nothing else, Ginger, except Red Wolf did tell me our road is long and dangerous. He said to remember the animal kingdom and do likewise."

"It doesn't really tell us anything," Ginger commented, crestfallen. "It doesn't tell us how we are to survive."

"Or does it? When we traveled down the mountainside before the snowslide, we were going down the mountains the way a wolf pack would." At their blank expressions, Nikki explained, "The watch and strongest ones take the lead, the weakest is in the middle, and the leader is always last."

"We're gonna die here and nobody will care," Kissa darkly mumbled before curling up into a tight ball and closing her eyes. Her sobs echoed through the cave.

SNOW SPREAD A WHITE BLANKET ACROSS the makeshift door of pine boughs, keeping the blowing snow outside and closing them inside. A pitiful small amount of firewood remained to keep them warm. Hunger growled their stomachs, but they were too weak and dizzy headed to pay any attention to the rumblings.

"I can't take anymore," Kissa mumbled over and over in a discordant eulogy. "I should've gone with Kallie. How could I be so stupid to think I could make those men pay? I want to go home."

Sobs tore at her throat, but no one answered her or spoke. "I'm so tired. My stomach hurts because I am so hungry, and I'm cold. I don't even remember what it feels like to be warm."

Kissa shifted, looking at the other women between her tears. Focusing on Nikki, she screamed, "It's your fault, Nikki! We're gonna die here and no one will ever know or care."

"Shut up, Kissa," Tawnie growled, having heard enough even though Kissa's words mimicked her own thoughts.

"No, Tawnie. I've been quiet too long. The only time we talked was about the stupid dream Nikki had. We don't even have enough energy to fight among ourselves anymore." With a cynical laugh, Kissa swept her hand toward them. "I doubt very seriously any of us will get out of this cave alive. We're starving to death and lost. All the horses are either dead or run off. So, if you want to kill me, go ahead. I don't care anymore."

"Ya little shrew, I oughta kill ya," Tawnie growled,

coming to her feet.

"Stop it!" Ginger yelled. "We have enough to worry about without you fighting."

With a hysterical cackle, Kissa rose to her feet. "We're getting paid back for torturing Injun Bill. You know that, don't you? We're slowly being tortured to death."

"You're acting crazy, Kissa. Our situation has nothing to do with it." Ginger closed her hand around the pistol handle. Uneasy, she stared at the scarecrow figure standing before them. Kissa's eyes held a wild, deranged light in their depths. Her skin stretched tautly over the bones of her face and her cupid bow mouth drew into rigid pursed lines. The once blonde hair straggled in wild, dirty ringlets to her shoulders.

"I'm not crazy, Ginger. I'm hungry." The knife at her waist suddenly appeared in her hand, and with deadly intent, she crept toward the dog. "It's time to eat dog stew."

Nikki positioned herself between Kissa and the dog. "Sit down, Kissa. No one is killing the dog. He does not have enough meat left on him to feed us."

"Even a little is better than nothing," Kissa stated, still advancing.

"Dang it, Kissa, sit down and shut the hell up. You ain't the only one hungry. Nikki's right. We ain't killin' the dog. It's helped us too much already, and he's probably the only reason we're still alive." Tawnie jumped up, determined to shut the woman up one way or another. The strong bones of her face tensing with anger, she grabbed Kissa by the arm and raised her fist.

Suddenly, sharp pain sliced through her forearm. Gasping, surprise crept across her face. Tawnie covered the area with her hand and watched blood seep between her fingers. "Ya stabbed me, witch. Now, I am gonna kill ya."

Tawnie reached for her pistol, but before her hand could close on the handle, Kissa dropped the knife, and in a quick, desperate grab, took Tawnie's pistol from her holster. Her action was so fast, Tawnie did not have time to react. Grinning crookedly, Kissa cocked the hammer and leveled the barrel against Tawnie's nose.

"We'll see who kills who first," Kissa cackled, her eyes narrowing. An unnatural light gleamed in her eyes and her mouth twisted in a weird display of determination.

Heoohtato growled, his hackles rising. The tension within the confines of the cave crackled. Nikki made a quick quieting motion to him, then with a flick of her wrist, motioned him to leave the cave. With another growl, *Heoohtato* moved the branches back with his nose and slunk out of the cave.

"Put the gun down, Kissa," Nikki softly demanded soothingly, inching forward. "We are in this together. I promise you we will make it out of here alive. Just put the pistol down and listen."

"I've listened to you long enough, Nikki." With a quick motion, she turned and leveled the pistol toward Nikki. Kissa pulled the trigger at the same time Tawnie knocked her arm upward.

The shot went wild, careening through the cave and reverberating through their eardrums, setting their ears to ringing. Tawnie grabbed the pistol and wrenched it from her hand. With a backward slap, she caught Kissa across the mouth, slamming her into the cave wall.

"Enough!" Nikki shouted. "Ginger, take care of

Tawnie's arm." Her knees weakening with relief, she placed her hand against the wall to keep standing. Emotions swirled inside of her, fighting for control—fear, distrust, hurt, resentment, horror.

With a deep breath, Nikki stared at Kissa crying on the ground, her arms over her head, and lying in a fetal position. She reached out a hand toward the woman, then withdrew it. No, they all had their demons to fight, each in their own way.

Turning, she glanced at the flickering flames of the fire. The wood they had gathered would run out before morning. With a pain-filled sigh, she gathered the ropes and tied the ends together, then tied one end around her waist. "We need wood. Do not let the rope run out. I may need help finding my way back here."

Ginger finished tying a strip of material around Tawnie's forearm. "Be careful," she unnecessarily ordered.

Kissa glanced over her forearms to watch Nikki leave the cave. Tawnie and Ginger sat with their heads together, whispering. Neither of them noticed her grabbing the knife laying on the ground where she dropped it earlier nor her crawling toward the door. Standing, she made a mad rush toward the rope. She grabbed it and cut the rope in two. With a hair-raising cackle, she screamed, "That's one less mouth to feed."

"Oh, my God," Ginger cried, diving for the quickly disappearing end of the rope. The rope end slithered outside and disappeared before she could reach it.

Tawnie rose to her feet, hands on her hips, and faced Kissa. "Whut have ya done?"

Kissa lifted her head, her weird, madness-filled chortle

bouncing off the walls. "Both dogs are gone, Tawnie. We don't have to worry about feeding them." With another wild giggle, she sneaked toward the cave mouth and slipped past the astonished Ginger into the blizzard outside.

"Don't let her go," Ginger cried, moving toward the door.

Tawnie grabbed her arm, spinning her around. "Let her go, Ginger. We can't help her now. We'd only risk our lives tryin' to find her."

"But Nikki and Kissa…

Shrugging helplessly, Tawnie dropped her hand, her eyes mirroring Ginger's despair. "Ain't nothin' we can do. Just pray they find their way back."

Chapter 5
Angels of Fate

KISSA KNEW LEEANN'S BODY WAS STORED close to the cave. Food, any kind of food would do! LeeAnn was dead and she would not mind feeding them so they might live.

With an unholy giggle, Kissa cried in the blowing wind, "We might as well eat you, LeeAnn. You're dead, and we're going to starve to death if we don't eat soon."

Now, only three mouths remained to be fed. LeeAnn's small body should feed them enough to survive. Tittering in demented shrieks, Kissa dug into the snow with her knife, the thought of food spurring her onward. Her knife struck something solid, and with another cackle, she dug the snow from around the travois.

Greedily, she grabbed the ends of the travois, and pulled and tugged it inside. She did not see the surprised and disgusted looks on the faces of Ginger and Tawnie when she reentered the cave.

Hurriedly, hungrily, Kissa pulled the frozen burnt blanket from around LeeAnn's ice-covered body, ignoring the crackling of the blanket when she pulled the frozen edges away. Raising her knife, it was the deathly-white, motionless, yet terror filled face of LeeAnn that stopped Kissa. With a horrified scream, she threw the knife against the cave wall and fell beside LeeAnn's body.

"No! No! No!" she screamed over and over. "What have I become? What am I doing?" With ear-shattering screams, she rocked back and forth, praying, hoping death would come. She was an animal, a killer.

Protective arms soon surrounded her, and soft whispers broke through her screaming. Everything broke inside her, and with racking sobs, Kissa buried her face against the warm shoulders. Ginger and Tawnie encircled Kissa with their arms, their own faces wet with tears. The howling wind softened and decreased in respect for the women's sorrow.

Nikki moved forward, the rope giving easily with each step, too easily. Worried the ropes had slipped one of the knots she had tied, she stopped momentarily, then sighed.

Even if the rope slipped its knot, they still needed wood. Hunger was not the only problem they faced. Giving a sharp whistle, she stood still, pausing for *Heoohtato*, praying he heard her above the howling wind. While waiting, she pulled the rope toward her. She did not have to pull far before the rope end was in her hand. Staring at it through the blowing snow, horror filled her— the rope had been cut.

She wanted to scream with frustration and fear while the wind whipped stinging blasts of snow against her. Frost and snow covering her face, she wiped her face with a gloved hand, then felt something brush against her leg. Looking down, she saw the dog rubbing up against her. She bent to pet him, her whispered words encouraging, not only for him, but herself. "It will be all right, boy. Help me find wood."

Nikki had to keep busy, had to keep her body and mind

occupied so she would not speculate on who cut the rope. Even with her suspicions, she did not want to believe she would do this to her. *Is madness the last emotion before death? Will we all go mad before death overtakes us? What have I done?* she wondered once again.

Lifting her hands upward through the swirling snow, she cried, "Why are you doing this to us?"

Suddenly, Nikki felt the spirit enter her, and looking up through the snow where it was snowing so hard the skies were hidden, she proclaimed, "Wise One Above, we will live through all this and find a safe haven before long to winter the rest of the season. Let it be!"

The snow seemed to lessen, and the wind blew less fiercely. She did not know how long she stayed outside looking for wood. Everything on her was frozen and numb. She found a log barely sticking from the snow. With the help of *Heoohtato,* they dislodged the log, then she tied one end of the rope around a branch.

Ignoring the pain in her side, she shifted a small bundle of wood under one arm and lifted the rope over her shoulder. Straining against the weight and struggling for breath, she tugged and pulled the log, relying on the dog's sense of direction to get them back to the cave. Fire lanced through her side and spread through her chest, but she ignored it. She had to make it back to the cave, and she would make it back, she promised herself.

Her face, hands and feet felt frozen before the dog gave a happy bark, and a sigh of relief passed her lips. Through the sheets of snow, she saw the dark mouth of the cave loom in front of her.

Nikki dropped the smaller pieces of wood near the fire, the rope still in her hands. Tawnie and Ginger gave a cry of happiness and hurried to her.

"We didna think ya were gonna make it after Kissa cut the rope." Tawnie gave her a bear hug, then apologized when Nikki sharply drew in her breath.

Ginger lightly hugged Nikki, then nodded toward Kissa. "We've got a problem. Tawnie and I hid her weapons. I think today was more than her mind could take. We have to find some way to help her." Ginger took the rope from Nikki's hand, staring at it in confusion.

"I have a log tied at the other end," Nikki explained, edging toward the fire. Sitting, she lifted her hands toward the flames, wanting nothing more than to warm herself and sleep.

"We'll take care of it," Ginger promised, pulling on the rope.

Kissa lifted her head toward Nikki, her eyes darting back and forth, fear etched within the blue depths. "Are you going to kill me?" she asked softly, clenching her hands. "Go ahead and kill me, Nikki. I don't care anymore."

"I am not going to kill you, Kissa," Nikki reassured her.

"You should. I deserve to die." With a shudder, she focused on Nikki's face a moment before her eyes darted away again. "I want to go home. I want my momma."

"Kissa..." Nikki stopped.

"I have demons dancing on my shoulders. Do you see them?" Kissa leaned forward, motioning to her shoulders. "They laugh and play. They run around in my head and talk to me, mean things, dirty things. I can't shut them up." The sound of a hatchet slamming against the log broke through her muttered words.

Ginger knelt beside Nikki, speaking so softly only

Nikki heard her. "We don't know what to do. I think she's lost it."

Nikki watched Kissa draw herself up in a fetal position, her sobs barely sounding over the banging. "I have an idea if you and Tawnie will help me."

"What do we need to do?"

After Tawnie had chopped some of the smaller branches from the log and placed them near the fire, Nikki explained her idea to Tawnie and Ginger, each glancing at Kissa's cuddled form.

After a few minutes, with all in agreement, Nikki walked toward Kissa and knelt by her side. "Kissa?"

Kissa raised swollen yet sunken eyes to Nikki but did not speak.

"Do you trust me?"

Kissa nodded.

"Good. I was trained by a very powerful shaman. You remember Cloud Walker?"

Kissa nodded again.

"He showed me how to get rid of demons. Will you let me get rid of yours?"

Kissa lifted her head, her eyes growing hopeful. "You can do that?"

"Yes, if you trust me."

"Yes, yes. Make them go away. I don't want to listen to them anymore. They are in my head. They burn my shoulders when they dance there," Kissa cried, rising to her knees.

Nikki reached out her hand to Kissa. "Come and sit by the fire. We will perform a ritual to rid you of the demons."

With Kissa's hand in hers, Nikki led her toward the fire. Tawnie had built up the flames until heat filled the cavern. She handed Nikki a charred stick soon as Nikki had Kissa seated.

Squatting in front of Kissa, Nikki mumbled a prayer in the *Algonquian* language while she painted Kissa's face with the black remains of the stick using wavy lines that did not connect or touch each other.

After finishing Kissa's face, Nikki turned to Tawnie and Ginger to paint their faces with circles, squares, and triangles, closing each mark so the ends were connected. With the charred stick between her fingers, Nikki ground it into her palm, then completely blackened her own face.

With a slight nod of her head, Tawnie beat upon the log she had pulled into the cave and joined her voice with Ginger's in a Cheyenne song Nikki taught them earlier. The light soprano of Ginger's voice joined with the deeper, almost baritone of Tawnie's.

Nikki threw the robe Cloud Walker had made for her across her shoulders, then began to dance around the fire in rhythmic beats, ignoring the sharp pain in her side. The bone rattle she found in Cloud Walker's medicine pouch was in her hand, and she shook it first at the sky, then at the earth, praying the ceremony would work. Cloud Walker had taught her for a ritual to be successful, the inflicted person must believe it would work.

Swaying and lightly leaping around the flames, then shaking the rattle around Kissa's body, Nikki danced until she gasped for air and her side burned with excruciating pain.

Holding the rattle above Kissa's head and fiercely shaking it, Nikki demanded, "Be gone, wicked spirits! Inflict this one no more. Be gone, demons of hell!"

With her last words, Nikki tossed granules on the fire

behind her back so Kissa could not see her actions. The fire jumped upward in flames of yellow and red, the wood hissing.

Kissa screamed and fainted.

Ginger knelt beside Nikki and Kissa, her voice barely above a whisper. "Do you think it worked?"

Nikki shrugged. "I hope so. Cover her and let her sleep now. We will see if it worked in the morning."

Ginger nodded for Tawnie to join her. Covering Kissa with blankets, she and Tawnie knelt on either side of Kissa, placing their hands on her, bowing their heads, and praying to their God for her healing.

Nikki watched, leaning against the walls of the cave, holding her painful ribs and struggling to breathe before bowing her head, praying if there really was a God of the white man, he would heal her friend.

Sometime during the night, the blizzard blew itself out and all was calm. The women slept fitfully. Nikki felt *Heoohtato* stiffen beside her. Soon, he growled deep within his throat, his hackles rising. Petting the dog, she whispered, "What is it, boy?"

Heoohtato's snarl did not lessen. He stopped growling before jumping to his feet and running from the cave, his barks waking the other women. *Heoohtato's* bark-growl was heard over another growl.

"Wolves. Get your guns." Nikki was already on her feet with her pistol in hand.

Kissa crouched in front of the fire, her eyes still wild-looking, searching for the shotgun. Tawnie reached beneath her bedroll and pulled the shotgun from underneath. She handed her the gun, a silent warning in her eyes.

Snarling and the sounds of animals fighting broke over the silent group. Without another word, they ran toward the cave's mouth.

Heoohtato and a wolf fought, snapping, snarling and running at each other. The other wolves circled them, some sniffing close to LeeAnn's body Tawnie had taken out of the cave and reburied in the snow.

With a snarl, Kissa shot at them. The buckshot sprayed the wolves and they slunk away, whimpering. The wolves watched the women for another chance to attack LeeAnn's body.

Nikki shot a wolf, watched it do a flip-flop, and with a whining howl, the wolf crept away. The wolf *Heoohtato* fought, turned and ran. *Heoohtato* snapped at the wolf, running after him.

"*Heoohtato*, stay," Nikki commanded. Moments later, they heard the wolves' distant howling. *Heoohtato* lay in front of Nikki, licking his wounds. "Come inside, boy, and let me clean you."

Nikki glanced at her friends. "They will be back. They are after LeeAnn's body. We better post a guard near it for the remainder of the night."

"I'll do it," Kissa volunteered. Tawnie and Ginger looked at each other, uncertainty marring their faces.

"Don't worry," Kissa said, intercepting their look, "I'm sane now."

The rest of the night crawled at a snail's pace. None could sleep. They took turns watching over LeeAnn's body for short periods of time in the freezing cold, shooting periodically at the wolves venturing too close. With morning, the sun peeped its head from the greying mist for the first time in weeks. *Heoohtato* whimpered and stared at the opening.

"Go," Nikki encouraged, watching him disappear outside.

Toward midmorning, *Heoohtato* appeared back at the cave and deposited a dead rabbit in Nikki's lap. "*Heoohtato*," Nikki cried, hugging the dog before lifting the rabbit and looking at it.

"Have you eaten, boy?" Soon after asking the questions, Nikki laughed. Flecks of blood covered the dog's chops.

The roasting rabbit awoke the other women. Tawnie stretched and growled, "Dang, I was havin' such a good dream. I can still smell the rabbit I was eatin' in my dream." Glancing at the fire, she cried, "It's ain't a dream. Food!"

The women did not give the rabbit time to cook. They ate ravishingly, devouring every tidbit of the half-cooked meat, then sucked the marrow from the bones. "You ladies can thank *Heoohtato* for breakfast," Nikki commented, licking her fingers.

"I could eat ten more," Ginger cried, her stomach still rumbling.

"Well, since we have whiled away the morning by sleeping, I suggest we go hunting while the sun is up." Nikki patted the dog's head, eager to be in the sun. "Another rabbit might give us enough strength to head out again, providing the weather holds."

LIZZIE NELSON LAID A WET CLOTH over her husband's forehead, at a loss on how to help him. It was week yesterday when he fell off the barn roof and broke his left leg and arm, and she suspected several ribs. She did not know how many times she had begged him to forget the roof until spring, but he insisted the barn be finished for the animals before the snow grew any deeper.

He was lucky to be alive. She just didn't know how much longer he would live if the infection continued to grow worse. Her limited medical ability was not enough to prevent the infectious pus from settling in the wounds or the red streaks running through his leg. Though she had tried, she was unable to set the bones.

Lizzie had heard the crash when he fell and had found him lying at an odd angle across the woodpile, unconscious. At first, she thought he was dead, but his moans soon assured her he was alive. It was no easy task for her to drag him into the house. She took care of his wounds the best she could, then saddled a horse to ride to the neighbors for help. Between her being big with child and the snow closing off the passages, she soon had to turn back. Since that day, she had been fighting off the nagging pains in her back and front.

Bad luck seemed to follow her and Cal since those terrible men came through late last spring. They should have packed up and left then. She begged him to leave, pleaded to be sent to her family up north, but her stubborn, beloved husband convinced her it was just bad luck. He often said, '*Surely, the Lord cannot hate us so much to allow anything else bad to happen.*'

It hurt to watch her husband lying so still in bed. Sweat poured from him and he moaned in pain, half delirious. In all the years she had been married to him, she had never seen him cry until now. Cal had not cried when they lost all their children, one in infancy and the other two by those horrible men.

While gritting her teeth, she was forced to watch the many times he banged himself up against the wall to reset his own bones. Afterwards, he cried in pain, drained of all strength. He never wanted her help, never asked for it, and refused it when she did offer, though she had forced it on him anyway. It hurt his pride more than anything else to allow her to help him back to bed.

Lizzie wanted to forget the day she lost two of her children, wanted to erase it from memory, but the memory lived with her every day, all day long. Late last spring when the passes cleared, Cal went to Denver to buy supplies. She and the children worked on the garden plot by breaking the soil and then planting.

And then those terrible men came and trampled her young son, Jacob, underneath their horses' hooves. One of the outlaws grabbed her and kept her from reaching her son. Another outlaw with a scar across his cheek grabbed little Sarah, and… She blanked out the rest, knowing if she allowed the memories, she would go insane.

The outlaw holding her forced her to the ground. She did not remember her clothes being torn from her. She just remembered being molested by those men and fighting to get to her little girl whose screams sounded over the grunting noises of the men. Her son's screams had already stopped.

She remembered hands closing around her throat, then nothing else. Apparently, the men thought she was dead, *she wished she had died*, because they were gone when she regained consciousness. The destruction the men had left behind was more than any person should have to bear.

With her hands cuddling her enlarged stomach, she sighed, fighting back tears. She did not know if the baby she carried was one of the outlaws or her husband's. The baby was due anytime now, but with her husband unable to move from the bed and she unable to get help, how was she to deliver her own child and save her husband too?

Her husband moaned in fitful sleep. Tenderly, Lizzie placed a soft kiss on his forehead, then left the cabin. The animals needed to be fed and the ice broken off the top of the water troughs. Firewood needed to be chopped—she stopped her thoughts. Too much to do.

At least they had plenty of food for the winter, more than they could ever eat in one winter and spring. God had been merciful and provided them with a bountiful crop last summer as if apologizing in a small way for the destruction of her family.

Looking back once over her shoulder toward the room where she and her husband slept, she opened the door and closed it behind her before waddling through the snow.

Instead of taking care of the animals first, she trudged through the deep snow to the fenced plot toward the valley's northern edge. Three crosses buried in the snow with only the flat tops showing, beckoned her forward.

My children, all my children are gone except the small one I carry. With God's help, hopefully this one will make it to adulthood. She touched the first cross, her voice soft and her breath billowing out in front of her. "Jeremiah, my baby. I didn't get to hold you more than three days."

Lizzie touched the second cross close by. "Jacob, my little lad. Still a toddler, almost two years old when you…" She stopped talking, moving between the second and third crosses. "My babies, my little Sarah. You turned four a few days before that day."

Tears filling her eyes, she knelt in the snow and lifted her eyes toward heaven. "Father Whom Art in Heaven, you test my strength and sanity every day. Cal is so ill and in so much pain, and I don't know what to do for him. You saved him by keeping him in Denver from those men who took my other two children's lives. I need him now, Father. I need your help. Please send me a miracle. I can't do this alone."

The sun peeked its head from the grey skies, sending a weak ray of sunlight over the treetops lining the edge of the little graveyard. Lifting her head toward the sun and opening her eyes, she gasped. Before her, highlighted by the sun, stood four apparitions, one with a dog. The dog looked half-starved; its bones showed starkly through its winter coat. Eyes fright-widened, she stared, then an inexplicable calm surrounded her.

"If you wish to take my life and my husband's, Father, then I will not fight it." Rising, she stared at the figures before her. It was hard to tell much about them with their bodies wrapped in heavy furs and blankets, and their faces covered. The shortest of the group pulled a travois carrying something wrapped in a blanket. The next apparition to the tallest specter kept her gloved hand on top of the dog's head.

"Whatever be thy will, Lord," she mumbled, stepping forward to greet the strangers.

The next to the tallest removed her hand from the dog's head and pulled the wrappings from her face. Lizzie stared at the apparition. The high cheekbones looked as if skin had been stretched tautly over them and the strange light blue eyes were sunken in the thin face.

Nikki stepped forward. "Ma'am, we will not harm you. My name is Nikki Pride. This is Ginger Starr, Tawnie Sands, and Kissa Loving."

"Women?" the woman asked, walking closer.

"Yes, ma'am. We were snowed in the mountains for a while. After we lost all our food supplies, we had no choice but to leave." Nikki stepped forward, holding out her hand.

"Lizzie Nelson," the woman said, taking Nikki's gloved hand in hers. She placed both hands on Nikki's, looking into the light blue eyes. "I was visiting my children's graves and praying God would help me. My husband broke his leg and arm a week ago yesterday and I can't get help. The passages are snowed in."

"I am very sorry about your children, but maybe we can help your husband," Nikki assured her.

"You ladies look frozen and starved near to death. Come inside." She eyed the travois behind Kissa.

"Our little girl died up in the mountains. I didn't want to bury her where she will always be alone, so we are taking her back with us." Kissa turned her head slightly to look at the travois, a stray tear slipping down her cheek.

"Oh, my dear, I'm so sorry. Why don't you put her body in the icehouse, then we can talk about it after you've eaten." Lizzie touched the grieving woman's shoulder. "You will come and eat, won't you?"

"We'd be much obliged, Mrs. Nelson," Ginger said, moving forward to shake the woman's hand.

"Call me Lizzie."

After leaving LeeAnn's body in the icehouse, the women followed Lizzie to the house. Opening the door and stepping inside, Lizzie bent forward, a sharp pain piercing through her mid-section. She held her swollen stomach and drew a ragged breath, waiting for the pang to pass.

"Lizzie, are you alright?" Ginger placed her arms around the woman, concern lighting her dull green eyes.

Lizzie patted the hand holding onto her shoulder, then straightened to her full height. "I'm fine. It's my husband who needs help."

Nikki slipped her furs off and handed them to Kissa. With a quick look around her, she slung her medicine bags over her shoulder. "I will look at your husband's leg, Lizzie, if you will allow me."

"Yes, if you can help, I'd appreciate it." Lizzie untied her cloak and placed it on a peg behind the door, turning when she heard the other women's gasp. Placing her hand protectively over her stomach, she smiled.

"You're in labor?" Ginger's question was more a statement.

"The pain will go away soon enough. It has been doing this for a week now." The words no more left her mouth when another cramp hit her. Bending over, a cry rose to her lips and water ran down her legs.

"I don't think it's gonna go away this time." Tawnie followed the direction of Lizzie's startled eyes to the floor where a puddle of water formed underneath her feet.

"Nope, not this time." Tawnie crossed the small distance between them and placed her hands on Lizzie's forearms.

"Let's get ya to the rockin' chair by the fire." Noticing the dog had snuck in with them, Tawnie ordered, "*Heoohtato,* you need to go outside."

Lizzie shook her head, "No, let the dog stay. He looks cold as you ladies and starved. I've some scraps by the stove I was saving for the hogs. Feed them to your dog. He needs it more than those ornery things."

"Let's get ya seated, then I'll take him and the scraps outside." After Tawnie settled the woman in the chair, she crossed the living space to the stove and grabbed the bucket of scraps, envying the dog. She was so hungry, she almost grabbed herself a good handful to stuff into her own mouth.

Nikki moved the hair from her face, then looked down at the medicine pouch in her hands. "Ginger, you and Kissa will have to help Lizzie while Tawnie and I tend to Mr. Nelson," Nikki stated, watching Tawnie tease *Heoohtato* with the food scraps while leading him to the door.

"What if the baby comes before you finished doctoring Mr. Nelson?" Kissa asked, her eyes going wide.

"Well, I've helped deliver calves and colts. I guess delivering a baby shouldn't be much different," Ginger commented, forcing her glance from the pot of stew boiling over the stove to Lizzie. The delicious smell of food wet every taste bud in her mouth and nose, and salvia formed in her mouth until she swallowed several times to keep from choking. Her stomach growled so loud, she covered it with her hands, her face turning beet red.

Lizzie apparently heard it. "My husband and I will wait."

The rocking chair swinging backward with her rising, Lizzie walked to the big pot steaming on top of a big cast iron stove. On tiptoes, she reached for the plates stacked neatly on a shelf close by. "Sit down and eat so you will have enough strength to help us. You ladies look to be in worse shape than my husband or me."

"Ginger and Kissa can eat. Tawnie and I will tend to your husband first, then we will have time to eat."

"No, I insist. Come eat first, please." Lizzie saw the hunger in their eyes and faces. Whatever these women had been through was etched on their faces and in the dullness of their eyes. If the Lord provided angels to help her, then she was determined to remember her manners first, and these women needed food.

Chapter 6
God Is Good

NIKKI'S GAZE SWEPT AROUND THE NEAT, homey cabin; the large rock fireplace built along one side of the room, its fire burning brightly and filling the room with blessed warmth, surrounded by a couple of rocking chairs and a lovely dark green velvet Biedermeier sofa settled into an oak frame with minimal decoration, its sides curving into the wooden armrests and proudly displaying round tube pillows nestled under inward curving wood directly over the seat cushion with another two square toss pillows at the back of the couch. The elegant yet simple sofa flowed along the interior back wall of the cabin offsetting the beautifully smooth and polished interior logs.

On the kitchen side of the room, somewhat close to the stove, sat another rocking chair, and on the wall behind it bore wooden pegs bearing different types of outdoor wear and hats. A large cast iron woodburning stove trimmed in silver burnished to almost a bronze color was positioned near the center of the kitchen wall. The elegant stove contained an oven with four separate burners on the top and a warming area above the stove bearing the proud name of Garland etched several times within the surfaces. A smoke pipe connected to the back of the stove rose along the wall where it blew its smoke outside.

Along the corner of the kitchen, a narrow L-shaped table with shelves over and under them, provided room for working and preparing food, and the shelves contained an array of different types of cooking and eating utensils.

Nikki watched Lizzie place deep bottom plates full of stew and a plate of cornbread on the kitchen table, the top, a beautiful handworked wooden planks burnished to a shine where six equally handmade chairs set.

Hunger clawed at her belly so hard, Nikki felt faint. With a nod, she agreed to eat first and sat on the stove side, noticing a colorful blanket hanging over a door at the back wall of the kitchen where she suspected Mr. Nelson lay; the moans came from the same direction. Nearby, a ladder led upward to a semi-open loft, the open edges encased with narrow tree poles forming a low, small fence.

The smell of beef stew overwhelming, Nikki admitted somewhere in the mountains, they lost their manners. They dug into the stew without allowing it to cool off enough to eat, and though it burned her mouth and throat, Nikki had never tasted anything so delicious in her life, especially with the addition of fresh buttered cornbread.

Lizzie curiously watched the women shoveling food into their mouths, barely chewing like they had not eaten in a month of Sundays. *Perhaps they haven't,* she thought, staring at their clothes hanging on their starkly thin frames. The thought barely crossed her mind before another pain hit her.

"She ain't gonna wait long to have the baby," Tawnie grumbled, shoveling the last spoonful of food into her mouth. "Clear the table, Kissa. We're gonna have to work hard for this supper." With a laugh, she winked at Lizzie.

"Ma'am, tell Ginger and Kissa where ya keep your thangs. They'll help ya with the baby."

Lizzie sat at the table, waiting for the agony to subside. "I think you are right, Tawnie, isn't it? I've already made a mess on the floor, so I might as well make a mess on the table." She tried to laugh, but another pain hit her.

Kissa had already found everything they needed before Lizzie could direct her. She spread a quilt on the table Nikki had cleared, then spread cloths on top. The women helped lift Lizzie on the tabletop. Between Lizzie's moans and the moans coming behind the curtain, *Heoohtato* added his howl to the clamor.

"*Heoohtato, quiet!*" Nikki yelled at the dog outside the door of the cabin before she turned her attention to the women. "Ginger, Kissa, call if you need help. I think mine and Tawnie's patient is calling."

Pushing the hanging blanket back from the door opening, Nikki gagged with the sweet, sickly smell hitting her full in the face. A man lay in the bed, restlessly tossing, his dark hair sweat-matted across his skull. The covers were draped across his midsection and legs, leaving the nightshirt wet across his chest. Nikki gulped back the nausea churning her stomach and went to the man's side.

"Lizzie?" the man weakly called.

"No, Mr. Nelson. My name is Nikki, and this is Tawnie. Your wife is having the baby, so we are here to help you."

"The baby?"

"Yes, sir. She has help now. Please relax and let me look at your leg." Nikki moved the covers aside to reveal his bandaged leg. The smell even worse, she sharply drew a breath, almost afraid to breathe.

Working quickly, she removed the bandages from around the man's leg. The wound wept yellow pus and red streaks ran along his calf and upward toward his thigh, and white bone was exposed through the skin of his lower leg.

Nikki drew her Bowie knife from its sheath, holding the blade and offering the handle to Tawnie. "Put the blade in the fire and heat it almost red hot, then bring it back to me. While you are doing that, please set some rags to boiling to bring later."

Tawnie took the knife and headed for the blanket curtain, stopping when Nikki said, "Make sure you close the curtain too, Tawnie, please."

The leg swollen thrice its size, looked ready to burst, and his left arm was swollen and covered with blue and black bruises. Gently running her fingers over the arm, she felt the disconnect in his forearm bone. Still engrossed in her examination of the damage to his body, she barely lifted her head when she heard the curtain move.

Nodding when Tawnie handed her the knife, Nikki ordered, "Hold him down while I open the wound. We have to drain the poison before we can set his leg. While I am draining it, see if you can find several straight pieces of wood. He has a broken leg and a broken arm."

"Dang, bet he's in pain." Tawnie grabbed his shoulders and pushed him against the tick mattress. Biting into her lower lip, Nikki positioned the knife tip against his leg close to the infected area, then pressed it into the skin and slit the leg about an inch in depth and width. Mr. Nelson groaned but was too weak to do more than flinch.

"I need those hot rags now." Nikki concentrated on squeezing blood and pus from his leg and wiping it with a clean cloth she had taken from the rocker's seat close to the bed.

Releasing her hold on his shoulders, Tawnie closed her eye against the bead of perspiration running down her forehead. Wiping her eye and forehead free of moisture, she quickly left the room. The stench set her stomach to roiling and she swallowed several times to keep from losing her supper.

A sharp cry from Lizzie brought her attention to the kitchen table. Kissa held Lizzie's clutched hand in hers and crooned comfort while Ginger crouched between the woman's legs, her face tense with concentration.

"Push, Lizzie. I see the head." Ginger placed her hands between Lizzie's upraised knees, crooning, "A little more. There…the head's out."

"Dang," Tawnie muttered. "It's a bloomin' nut house 'round here."

With a shake of her head, she swept around the table to the fireplace where a big cast iron pot with water was hung on a metal arm, and pulled the boiling rags out of the pot with a long-handled spoon and placed them in a big bowl. With the steaming bowl balanced in her hands, she stopped long enough to watch Ginger pull the bloody form of the baby from between Lizzie's legs.

The baby's cry erupted through the room and Ginger's cry with it. "A boy! You have a son, Lizzie!"

"Tawnie!"

"I'm a'comin'," Tawnie replied, shaking her head and muttering an oath before she stepped behind the curtain. "Here," she snarled, handing the bowl to Nikki.

"Hold him down a moment while I put these hot rags on his leg."

Tawnie had no more placed her hands on the man's

shoulders when he bucked and screamed. "Heck, those rags musta hurt worse than ya cuttin' his leg."

Mr. Nelson uttered a moan, then slipped into unconsciousness. Tawnie released her hold. "I'm gettin' those sticks. I gotta get out of this place for a bit. It's a bloomin' nut house 'round here."

Nikki glanced up, noticing Tawnie looked a little green around the mouth, which was grimly puckered up, suppressing anything from coming up and out. "Go on, Tawnie, but hurry."

"I'm outta here."

Not taking time to grab covering against the cold, Tawnie opened the door, stepped outside and closed the door behind her. She lifted her face, breathing the clean, crisp mountain air, needing something to wash the smell of blood and putrid flesh from her nostrils.

Heoohtato looked up from the bucket of food he was devouring, his tail wagging a rapid beat of happiness. In the distance, Tawnie heard the cows lowing, the horses neighing and chickens clucking their disapproval. "Dang animals need to be fed," she muttered, "And I ain't got time to take care of 'em yet. At least you're a happy, well-fed boy," she remarked, bending to pet the dog on the head.

Nikki kept changing the hot rags on Mr. Nelson's leg, hoping to draw the infection to the surface. Mr. Nelson had thankfully passed out and she was glad since she had no whiskey to help relieve his pain.

Pressing the point of her knife against Mr. Nelson's leg, she punctured the calf, making a new incision when Tawnie appeared and dropped the wood near her. "If you will take these rags and boil them again, we will set his arm first, then see if the poison has drained enough to set his leg."

The full force of the putrid, festering smell hit her full in the face and with a muttered oath under her breath, Tawnie drew back the colorful blanket, slipped under it and hurried to drop the filthy rags in the boiling water.

"Look, Tawnie," Kissa cried softly, holding the bundle close to her breast. "It's a little boy. Isn't he beautiful?" A tender expression on her face, Kissa held the baby toward Tawnie.

Tawnie looked at the red, wrinkled face of the baby, thinking it was the ugliest thing she had ever seen. "Yeah, beautiful," she agreed, but the baby was not what was so beautiful in her eyes. It was the light of life gleaming from Kissa's. Kissa should be having babies instead of helping them search for a band of outlaws. Having babies would erase the horror and loss from her cherub face and revert her back to her natural innocence.

Kissa laughed uneasily under Tawnie's thoughtful gaze before she turned around to place the baby in his mother's arms. She didn't want to know what Tawnie was thinking. She was too happy; bringing a new life into the world is a joyous time. And the world will be safe again after they get rid of the monsters who took Cari's and LeeAnn's lives and all the other innocent people with whom she had no name or face to identify them. Well, maybe not the world, but at least they would wipe out some of the evil in the western territory. The tiny form somehow reassured her, she was doing the right thing—she was helping provide a safer place for children.

Tawnie stirred the rags, waiting for them to boil again. She felt itchy, anxious to get out of the cabin and feed the animals. The surprisingly spacious cabin seemed to close in on her, something which surprised her. "Been out in the woods too long," she mumbled to herself.

"Kissa, stir these rags and take them to Nikki after they start boilin'. I'm gonna go help her." With her order, Tawnie turned from the pot and headed for the front door to spit brown tobacco juice onto the pure white snow before heading to the curtained-off door.

"Let's set his arm 'cause somebody's gotta feed them critters. They're bawlin' for their supper."

Nikki glanced up at Tawnie, noticing the bulge in her cheek and an inkling of an idea forming in her brain. "Are you chewing?"

"Yeah, whut about it?"

"I cannot get all the poison to drain from the leg. Would you mind spitting the rest of your wad over the wound in his leg? I have heard stories where tobacco pulls poison from wounds."

"And waste my last chaw?" Tawnie growled. "Ah, heck," she mumbled in defeat, "show me where."

After spreading the brown mess snuggly in and around the man's seeping wounds, Nikki bound his leg again. They set his broken bones, then splint them before wiping the pouring sweat from their faces.

Nikki gathered her parfleches and left the room. Grabbing a tin coffee cup from the shelf and setting it on the countertop, she opened one parfleche. Lifting out different ingredients, she crushed them into the cup.

Pouring boiling water over the leaves from a pan of hot water on the stovetop, she grabbed the cup and headed back to the bedroom to allow it to steep before encouraging the man to drink the potion. To Nikki's relief,

Mr. Nelson soon fell into a sound sleep.

Her ribcage gripping with excruciating pain, she bent forward and grabbed at her side. The pulling and snapping of Mr. Nelson's bones in place also aggravated her still-healing cracked ribs. To hide her pain, she sat in the rocking chair setting beside the bed. "I'll watch over Mr. Nelson if you want to get out of here and feed the animals."

"Don't have to tell me twice," Tawnie mumbled, heading for the door.

Kissa and Ginger had fixed a pallet on the floor near the fire and had Lizzie lying on top of it. Lizzie cuddled the newborn in her arms, her face soft with love. She glanced up, observing Kissa and Ginger pulling the birthing quilt and cloths from the tabletop, then mop the kitchen floor of blood and her broken water incident from it.

When Tawnie entered the room, a huge thankful smile swept across her mouth and Lizzie exclaimed, "Angels, you ladies are angels sent by God to help us."

The women looked at each other, then laughed.

"Ah, shucks," Tawnie mumbled, shuffling her feet, a blush rising to her face.

"We've been called many things, Lizzie, but never angels." Ginger smiled, a new warmth spreading through her. *Angels*, she thought, *what a nice thing to be called, especially after the horrible things we were called after that night.*

GOD IS SO GOOD, KISSA THOUGHT, cuddling the

sleeping baby, knowing she needed to replace him in the crib Ginger and Tawnie moved from the bedroom into the living area, but the feel of the soft body against her brought a comfort she had long been missing. She should have been happily married and pregnant with her own child by now if it hadn't been for *that night,* which had not only destroyed her dreams, but all their dreams.

Pressing a soft kiss on the baby's forehead, she reluctantly rose from the rocker and placed him in the crib, standing over him just to watch his precious sleeping face.

Lizzie was asleep, having been up with the baby most of the night. Mr. Nelson was still recovering from the infection and broken bones, but at least he was moving some now, especially since they stripped the bed and gave everything a thorough cleansing before allowing him to lie down again.

Tawnie and Nikki were in the barn, building a crutch for him, and Ginger was on horseback, wrangling some stray horses toward the barn for the night. Heavy grey clouds warned of new snow coming.

Forcing herself from the baby's side, Kissa walked toward the kitchen. She gladly accepted the cooking duty, especially after being introduced to the cellar beside the house. After being without food for so long, it was a veritable cornucopia with jars and jars of canned vegetables, barrels of sugar, flour, cornmeal, lard— everything a person could dream about and the ability to create a swath of different types of meals, especially with the icehouse and smokehouse containing different types of meat.

In many ways, she felt like she had died and gone to heaven where there was no more hunger...or pain, she quietly added. *Yes, God is good. He brought us out of the worse circumstances into a place where our problems and sorrows can rest, and we can gain strength.*

She opened the oven to check the roast, releasing the aromatic smell into the cabin, then after checking the wood, she turned to make bread dough.

Humming at first, she lifted her sweet soprano voice, softly singing, 'Outside the Gate', a favorite church song of hers. "*I stood outside the gate, a poor way-faring child; within my heart there beat a tempest loud and wild; a fear oppressed my soul that I might be too late; and, oh, I trembled sore, and prayed outside the gate.*" While she was patting down and shaping the dough in a skillet, the other women walked in the door.

Hearing her singing, Ginger hung up her coat, adding her soprano voice to hers. "*O Mercy! loud I cried.*"

As if on que, Tawnie added her alto almost baritone voice, singing with them, "*Now give me rest from sin!*" They motioned for Nikki to join them.

Hanging up her poncho on wooden peg, she shrugged and joined with her alto voice, "*I will, a voice replied.*"

With all four singing, "*And Mercy let me in: She bound my bleeding wounds and soothed my heart oppressed. She washed away my guilt and gave me peace and rest.*"

Beginning the last verse, they turned at a slight sound still singing while Lizzie helped her husband from the room they shared. "*In Mercy's guise I knew the Savior long abused, who often sought my heart and wept when I refused. Oh, what a blest return for all my years of sin! I stood outside the gate and Jesus let me in.*"

Lizzie helped her husband to sit in a chair, then joined him at the chair beside his, tears streaming down her cheeks, and his brown eyes having a strange mist within them. "I thought I was hearing angels sing when I woke up. And I was. You *are* angels!"

WITH THE ANIMALS FED AND BEDDED for the night with a heavy snow blowing in, the group sat around the table drinking coffee. Cal was now able to move about with the single crutch underneath the armpit of his unbroken arm, even taking time to examine things around the ranch, pleased with the work the women had done around the place, even fixing things he had not had time to repair. The baby was growing, happy with five mothers providing for his every need.

Lizzie rose to retrieve a platter of freshly baked cookies and placed them on the table, then patted her husband's hand. "Kissa made your favorite, Cal."

Cal took a cookie and bit into it, smiling. "I always said I married the best cook in the world, huh, Lizzie, but I gotta say, I think you may have met your match with Miss Kissa here."

Grinning, Lizzie popped him on the shoulder. "So much for love," she teased, glancing into his beloved face, his dark hair showing the first signs of grey since the accident. Even after ten years of marriage, he still had the ability to make her heart flutter with his handsomeness. Even with him being forty-one years old, his touch still thrilled her.

"Well, between the two of you cooking, I've gain so much weight, I won't be able to move soon. I'm gaining too much extra baggage." Cal glanced tenderly at his wife, his love showing through the softness of his brown eyes when looking at her beautiful face, her gentle blue eyes, and the richness of her dark brown hair.

Nikki dropped her gaze, staring down at her hands holding a cup of coffee, their loving gaze bringing a sharp arrow of pain to her heart when memories of Dane and their last night together rose through her memory.

Cal cleared his throat before speaking, "Ladies, Lizzie and I talked last night, and we've decided to ask if you ladies would like to stay here at the ranch and work for us. We'll build you your own place if you will."

Nikki lifted her eyes and met his, her voice soft, "You probably wouldn't offer a job if you knew our past, Cal."

"Why don't you tell me and let me be the judge," Cal replied, curious now.

Kissa, Ginger, and Tawnie looked toward Nikki, waiting for her to begin, but when she looked down into her empty coffee cup and did not reply, Ginger began speaking, "We're all from the Kansas Territory near Rustic. My parents are big ranchers there, Kissa's parents own the general store, Tawnie drove a mule team during the summers with her dad, and Nikki is, ah, was a farmer's daughter." She glanced at Tawnie, waiting for her to add to the story.

With a defeated shrug, Tawnie began their story. "There were four of us spendin' the night at the farm when a gang of about fifteen men, raided the farm. They killed Nikki's daddy and brother, then her mom, well, when one of the mongrels pushed her on the floor and started violatin' her and…and…she killed herself with his own gun. It was Nikki's little sister that was the hardest to see. She was a little mite, only five, when…."

Kissa took up the story when Tawnie swallowed hard, unable to continue, "The monster killed her when he defiled her, and those fifteen men took turns assaulting us. The only reason we are still alive is because a posse was close by. Kallie, my sister, she hasn't been able to speak since then and only stares into the distance."

Nikki glanced up in time to see Cal and Lizzie exchange a glance before turning their attention back to them.

"How long ago did this happened?" Cal asked, watching each of their faces.

"Early spring," Nikki answered, studying them.

"Do you know who the men were?" he asked, glancing again at this wife.

"Yes, Jock Mason's gang and the worse one is called Mad Dog." There was something about the glances between Lizzie and Cal alerting her something more was up with the questioning, more than just their story, especially when Lizzie drew in a sharp breath, her eyes widening. She watched Lizzie nod toward her husband, seemingly in confirmation.

Lizzie took Cal's hand and held it, lifting tear-filled eyes to the women, then glanced at her husband again before saying, "Those are the same men who trampled my little boy and sullied my little girl, then cut her throat. I couldn't help them 'cause they were assaulting me too. They thought they had choked me to death, but I regained conscious sometime afterwards only to find my children dead." Tears flowed freely down her cheeks, and Cal squeezed her hand and with the other, patted her thigh.

"I was in Denver on business and picking up supplies." He nodded toward the sofa, "I brought the sofa back to her for our anniversary."

The baby started fusing. Lizzie rose and took him from the crib, bringing him back to the table before opening her bodice to feed him. Guiding a nipple to the baby's mouth, she witnessed the curious, questioning looks between their guests. She glanced at her husband again while the baby happily suckled and confirmed their unspoken question. "We don't know if little Elijah here is Cal's or one of those men's."

Cal reached over and lovingly touched the baby's face before fixing each of them with his eyes, his face filled with determination and purpose. "As far as I'm concerned, I *am* the baby's father."

"I guess I should tell you about LeeAnn then." Kissa lifted tear-coated eyes to view their expressions.

Nikki shook her head and began speaking, "The Deputy U.S. Marshal, who has been following us, well me personally, sent an Indian woman with LeeAnn who had been abused by Mad Dog and became mute afterwards. He thought if I accepted the little girl, I would give up my plans to go after the outlaws. I said I would if the law did its duty. He had brought in one of the outlaws, but the courts freed him."

Ginger picked up the story, narrating a shorten version up to the present.

Nikki stared down into her empty cup before lifting her eyes to the Nelsons. "You should also know I am half Indian, Cheyenne."

Cal cleared his throat again and regarded his wife, staring into her eyes like they were speaking to each other without saying a word. With her soft nod, he turned back to the women, "Lizzie and I agree. My offer still stands. I don't care what you have done or what's been done to you, we still want you to stay here. Beside you're some of the finest people we've ever known."

It was Tawnie who surprised them all when she lifted her face, tears flowing down her cheeks. "I married a Cheyenne whilst stayin' with them, but only for the time we spent there 'cause I needed to go with Nikki."

"Congratulations," Lizzie cried, smiling.

"Yes, congratulations," Cal repeated. "If you want to bring him here with you, we'll build you a separate cabin if he doesn't mind working for a living."

Nikki abruptly left the table and picked up the hot coffeepot with a rag before moving toward the table to refill cups. She knew they were waiting for her answer; their eyes followed her, and no one spoke a word. She set the coffeepot back on the stove and sat down, took a careful sip of the hot liquid before lifting her eyes to theirs, a shadow crossing her face.

'My friends are free women. They choose their own paths, but mine has not changed. The last two outlaws left alive are Jock Mason and Mad Dog. I cannot rest until I have made them pay for what they have done to not only us, but so many other people, especially the children."

LIFE AT THE RANCH DEVELOPED in a daily routine of Ginger, Tawnie, and Nikki caring for the animals, feeding, milking, and gathering eggs, then fixing anything broken around the ranch. Kissa and Lizzie shared the cooking and cleaning chores along with taking care of the baby. Cal helped where he could and appeared to be healing nicely.

Each night after the supper dishes were cleaned and put away, Cal or Kissa read passages from Bible out loud, then a discussion always followed. Nikki usually exchanged the discussion time to play with the baby, but tonight the baby had been fussy all day, and Lizzie finally had him asleep in his crib.

When the conversation began, Nikki rose from the table and poured herself another cup of coffee, then held the pot up and motioned toward the table. After refilling Cal's cup, she placed the coffeepot back on the stove and reluctantly sat at the table. Not really listening, it was when the subject turned to the Father, the Son, and the Holy Ghost, prompting her to glance up from staring into her coffee. "I have always been curious how the church preaches one God but talks about three different beings. So how can there only be one God?"

Lizzie rose from the table, collected a small plate and an egg, and placed it in front of her before sitting. "I always explained it this way when my children asked," she started, holding the egg in her hand. "What do you call this, Nikki?"

Nikki's eyes narrowed slightly with the strange question before replying, "An egg."

Lizzie nodded, then cracked the egg over the plate, putting the shells along its sides. "And now?"

Nikki laughed, not understanding where the demonstration was going. "It is still an egg, abet a cracked egg."

"Yes," Lizzie stated, pointing to each part. "This is the shell, the whites, and the yolk. There's three parts, but as a whole it is still considered an egg."

"Yes, but you do not usually just request the yolk or

whites. You ask for an egg," Nikki argued.

"Exactly," Cal stated before placing his hand over Lizzie's and squeezing. "The Father, the Son, and the Holy Ghost are separate beings, but they have one mind, one plan. Each work separately, but they work together in perfect union and harmony, and become as one."

"I will have to think about it," Nikki replied, understanding, yet not really understanding. "It still does not explain why your God is so vengeful."

"Well, I had trouble with that one myself," Cal remarked, his brown eyes lighting up with understanding. "I had the same discussion with many men of my acquaintance, and we did some research on the issue. This is what we discovered."

He accepted a slice of cake from Lizzie, took a quick bite and a sip of coffee before finishing his conclusion, "After studying the scriptures, we discovered every time the Lord had vengeance against his or another people was for one main reason."

Taking another bite of cake, he smiled and complimented Kissa on its wonderful flavor before explaining, "Each time this happened, the people were worshipping a foreign false god or gods usually connected to Moloch or Ba'al in some form or fashion, and their main worship or practice required child sacrifice or the killing of innocent children, which angered the Lord, therefore the Lord proclaimed, *'vengeance is mine'*."

Cal took another bite of cake before leaning forward a bit. "There were many miracles during those times, and the Lord also used men to perform His will. Yet most times the men did not even realize they were doing the Lord's work. It's still happening today."

Surprise widening her eyes, and her stomach developing a weird tingly feeling while a shiver raced down her spine, Nikki leaned forward, thoughtful, mulling over the information. "Thank you."

IN A RARE MOMENT, NIKKI SAT alone at the table while everyone, except her and Lizzie, were at the barn looking over the newborn colt Ginger had help deliver during the frigid night. Lizzie sat in a rocker, the baby over her shoulder, burping him after his meal. Satisfied with his belch, she rose and placed him in the cradle. After pouring herself a cup of coffee, she sat beside Nikki.

Searching for an appropriate topic to speak, Nikki replied, "You have a beautiful home."

Lizzie laughed, motioning around the whole interior. "Yes, I do. Cal is a perfectionist and created most of what you see by his own hand. I'm from up north, near New York, and my father brought me and my mom down to Denver on the new rail train for a vacation. I was fifteen at the time I met Cal through my father. My father owns stock in several railroads, including the Union Pacific. Cal is also an investor of many of the same railroad lines."

She laughed, holding her hand over her heart. "I never saw such a handsome man in my life, but him being fifteen years older than me, I didn't think I had a snowflake's chance on a hot fire to be with him. Apparently, I was wrong since my dad agreed to his courting of me as long as he had a proper place for me to live."

Covering Nikki's hand with hers, Lizzie met her eyes, searching for answers that bothered her about Nikki.

"Cal's a big believer in the Bible and he does things strictly by the Bible."

A blush appearing on her cheeks, she confided, "I never told anyone this, but for some reason I feel compelled to tell you. On our wedding night, Cal repeated this verse to me, and I'll never forget it. He quoted Ecclesiastes 9:9 *Live joyfully with the wife whom thou lovest all the days of the life of thy vanity, which he hath given thee under the sun, all the days of thy vanity: for that is thy portion in this life, and in thy labour which thou takest under the sun.*"

Taking a shuddering breath, Lizzie tightened her grip on Nikki's hand. "While he was undressing me on our wedding night, and kissing each spot bared, he repeated another Biblical phrase, 1 Corinthians 7:4 *The wife hath not power of her own body, but the husband: and likewise also the husband hath not power of his own body, but the wife.* He taught me in order for a man and a woman to survive in this wacky world, a husband and wife must please each other in all ways and to never listen to the bigots who spout religious dogma that a man is the only one who should take pleasure, and neither are to see each other naked. As Cal always says to me, God created us in beauty, and we need to see and admire his handiwork."

Observing surprise widening Nikki's azure blue eyes, Lizzie squeezed her hand again. "I believe somehow you have only heard dogma about God's word. I just want you to know the word of the Lord goes much deeper, into all areas of our life, even on a very personal level such as the relationship between a man and woman."

Lifting her hand from Nikki's, she reached over and caressed her cheek, her eyes soften with a love that bore only love of friendship and concern for her. "You are in love with this man, the U.S. Deputy Marshal. Never be ashamed of your love or the promises it brings. I know things are hard now, but they will eventually change, but only after you have given into the tears you feel are frozen within you. Everything is not frozen in you. It lives."

Nikki lowered her eyes from the too searching ones, wondering how she knew so much about her and why she was saying the things she did. Was she also prophetic? She momentarily lifted her eyes, whispering, "Thank you," barely getting the words out before the others tramped back into the house.

Chapter 7
Death Angels

GREEN SHOOTS OF GRASS PEEKED OUT from underneath melting snow. Geese flew overhead in a V-formation, their honking announcing spring. Birds joined the sounds of rebirth with their chirping, and rabbits poked their heads from holes, their noses lifted upward to sniff the air. On their migration toward the higher reaches of the mountains, elk and deer stopped to graze in the valley. The trash pile along the edge of the forest gave evidence a bear and her cub roamed nearby.

Over the joyful sounds of spring, hammering echoed through the valley, followed by an *ah, dang*, then a muttered oath. Tawnie shook her hand, her finger throbbing. Putting the injured digit in her mouth, she glanced over the valley. A doe with its fawn grazed unconcerned along the edges of new budding trees.

She and Cal were finishing the last of the barn roof while Nikki, Ginger, and Lizzie hoed the garden plot, preparing it to plant. Little Elijah grew fat and healthy, and spoiled rotten with five mothers hovering around him.

Cal healed nicely, but he now walked with a permanent limp. Her last chaw of tobacco had succeeded in draining the poison from his leg. Their stay with the Nelsons proved to be an enjoyable time, a healing time. The women put on weight and grew stronger. The haunted look in Kissa's eyes had disappeared and her cheeks flushed apple red again.

Being closed up for months with each other, they had learned a lot about the Nelsons, and the Nelsons about them. In bits and pieces, they filled in the rest of their stories for the Nelsons. Neither Cal nor Lizzie condemned them. Instead, they were sympathetic and understanding, offering love in ways none of them had ever experienced. Maybe they needed the reassurance and the type of love requiring nothing from them, something to keep them going.

It's gonna be hard leavin', Tawnie thought, focusing on her hammering. The women had grown attached to the Nelsons and to a way of life that was peaceful and family oriented. *It fills your heart watchin' Cal and Lizzie together who display a love 'tween each other most can only dream about and few find.* Her memories turned to Young Bird, wondering if he would come live here with her. She really missed him.

Cal gave them four exceptionally fine horses for them to go after the outlaws, saying it was the least he could do after helping him and Lizzie through the winter, especially since they were going after the men who killed their children. He also knew the countryside well. From the description of the cave and landscape they gave him, he knew exactly where the women had left their saddles. Where it took them nine days of walking to the homestead, Cal made the round trip by horseback in two days to retrieve their saddles.

Tawnie wiped the perspiration from her forehead, stopping a moment longer to examine the peaceful green valley still bearing patches of snow. From the corner of her eye, she saw Nikki rise to her full height.

Casting a glance in that direction, Tawnie watched Nikki gaze over the valley, the restlessness apparent in her eyes and stance. Tawnie followed the direction Nikki's eyes lingered and noticed a rider coming toward the ranch.

"Rider comin'." Tawnie stood to her full height to get a better view.

Cal stopped hammering to watch the rider. "Farley. He's our neighbor." He finished the last nail before crawling down the ladder to meet him.

"Nelson," Farley called out, nearing the barn and eyeing Cal limping toward him. "The wife sent me to check on you. Said you had a baby due this winter."

"Farley," Cal greeted. "We had a little boy. Named him Elijah."

"Had some problems?" Farley nodded his head toward Cal's leg.

"A little. I fell off the barn a week afore the babe was born."

"See you got visitors."

Cal nodded agreement but did not comment or introduce Farley to the visitors. "Come inside the house and have a cup of coffee."

"Thanks, I'll do that." Farley dismounted and followed Cal inside the cabin.

Tawnie stared at the disappearing backs, wanting to join the men. She did not feel slighted Cal had not introduced them. A silent understanding had passed between them; he was protecting their identities. *Welp, no use thinkin' 'bout the neighbor,* Tawnie decided, lifting the hammer again.

An hour or so later, Tawnie watched Farley come out of the cabin, mount up, and ride back in the direction of his ranch. It was not until suppertime that Cal talked about his conversation with Farley.

"Farley said while he was in Red Town, he heard someone tellin' a story about two men coming out of the mountains and headin' to the stagecoach station. Said they were near-frozen and half-starved to death. Apparently, they ate at the station, then stole two stagecoach horses and headed south."

"Do you think it was Mason and Mad Dog?" Nikki asked, hope rising in her chest.

"Could be, then it could be anybody. Farley didn't have a description of 'em." Cal watched Lizzie rise from the table, an odd, wistful expression on her face. With the end of her apron, she grabbed the coffeepot and held it toward them. With a nod of his head, he tapped his cup, talking while she refilled it. "I'd think you ladies might head in that direction. If I'm any guess of people, I'd say they'd headed for either Gunnison or Pueblo."

"It's a start," Tawnie mumbled past the lump suddenly forming in her throat, the thought of leaving the Nelsons somehow not appealing to her.

"We will leave in the morning," Nikki decided for the group.

Morning came bright and early, and the women were up and ready to leave before dawn. Lizzie packed them enough supplies to keep them going for weeks. It was a teary-eyed group eating breakfast, one the women would have liked to have skipped.

"You know, I'd let you ladies stay here with Lizzie and me to run the ranch. We could use the help. I'd pay you a healthy profit from the sales. I've had men workin' for me, but you ladies work circles around 'em. I've seen it with my own eyes." Cal met each of the women's eyes to enforce his sincerity. "'Sides, those outlaws could've died in the mountains this winter. It's a miracle you ladies didn't die up there."

"We probably would of if it hadn't been for Nikki keepin' us goin'." Tawnie leaned back against the chair, covering her stomach with her spread hands. She ate so much, she wondered if she would be sick, but she knew it might be a long time before they had fresh eggs and milk again.

"We appreciate your offer, Cal, but we cannot stay. We have to know for certain whether those men lived or died. The law is not doing anything about their killing spree, so we have taken it upon ourselves to end it." Something in Nikki wanted to stay with their adopted family. It was their generosity which saw them through the winter. If luck had not been with them that day, they *might have* died in the mountains.

"I will pray for you every day." Lizzie wiped the tears from her eyes. The women had kept the winter months lively for her, providing companionship she had long been missing.

"The job will always remain open to you. And anytime you ladies need a place to stay or hide or anything, you just name it. You are always welcome." Cal held the coffee cup firmly in his hands, eyeing each of them in turn. "If it weren't for you, Lizzie and I would have died this winter, and no one would have known 'til spring."

"Your generosity and friendship mean more to us than you will ever know." Nikki cupped Lizzie's hand in hers, gently squeezing it. "You helped us too."

"Amen," Ginger agreed, wiping a stray tear from her eye.

"I will always think of you as angels." Lizzie dabbed at her nose with a handkerchief, her eyes glistening with tears. From the scarecrow women who first arrived to the beautiful women sitting around the table with her now, she did think of them as angels.

"Ah, now," Tawnie said, blushing, but in reality, no matter how many times Lizzie called them angels or how much it embarrassed her, she still liked hearing the endearment.

The Nelsons followed the women outside and hugged each of them. The only dry eye of the group was Nikki's. If tears would have come, Nikki would have cried too.

Earlier, the women had walked to the little graveyard to say their goodbyes to LeeAnn. With Lizzie's suggestion, Kissa had happily agreed to bury LeeAnn with the Nelson children, exclaiming at least LeeAnn wouldn't be lonely anymore.

Vaulting onto the only horse without a saddle, Nikki turned back once to wave goodbye, then kicked her heels in the gelding's side, whistling for *Heoohtato,* and headed toward Red Town.

RED BUILDINGS TRIMMED WITH WHITE STOOD out starkly against the greenery of mountains. The women had no doubt they had found Red Town. The women changed into skirts and went separately to buy supplies and ask questions.

"Nothing, not even a whisper," Ginger complained at their rendezvous outside of town. "Do you think Cal might be right, and Mason and Mad Dog did die up in the mountains?"

"If Tawnie comes back empty-handed, then we will head back and scout around. I cannot stop until I know for sure." Nikki fingered the gold locket at her throat, missing the bear claw necklace. The necklace was her strength, and she needed its strength now.

"Tawnie's coming, and she's riding hard." Anxiety written across her face, Kissa watched Tawnie kneed the mare with her heels and gallop toward them.

"Feels like trouble." Ginger placed her hand over her heart to still the uncomfortable beating.

Tawnie vaulted off the horse's back before it came to a full stop, several papers held in her hand. "Nikki, you ain't gonna believe this."

"What is it?"

Tawnie shoved one of the sheets of paper at her, her face tense. "You're wanted for murder up in Fairplay. Says here ya robbed and murdered the proprietor of the general store. It's got your name on this poster and a rough sketch of ya."

"What?" The three women exclaimed together.

"It's true. Look at it! There's a fifty-dollar reward for ya."

Nikki took the wanted poster from Tawnie and stared at the drawing with a rough description of her height, the color of her eyes and hair. It stated she was wanted for the murder of John Gransom, proprietor of General Store in Fairplay, Colorado Territory. "This is ridiculous! I never killed him. He held off Injun Bill and Mad Dog so I could get out of town."

"Then why would they want you for murder? Do you think Mad Dog and Injun Bill killed him?" Ginger wondered out loud. "But if they did kill Mr. Gransom, why would the law blame you?"

"I have no idea," Nikki responded, staring at the wanted poster. *How could this happen?* The proprietor had probably saved her life, and she suspected the money she gave him for the supplies was not near enough to cover their expenses. The man had been good to her, and it did not make sense someone would think she would kill him.

"Who saw you in town?" Ginger quietly asked, perplexed.

"Well, the sheriff did talk to me before I entered the general store. And there was one other customer paying for his purchases when I walked in. Who knows who else saw me? Fairplay is a busy town. It could have been anyone, but why would they think I murdered Mr. Gransom? Logically, it is farfetched and absolutely ludicrous I would harm someone who was helping me." Fear crawled along Nikki's spine, her uneasiness growing by the moment.

"Is that where you had the run-in with Mad Dog and Injun Bill?" Ginger studied Nikki's face and the confusion crossing it before turning hard.

"Yes, but…" Her eyes distant, Nikki looked toward the line of trees. "Do you think they killed Mr. Gransom? And if they did, why am I getting the blame?"

"Those whoresons framed ya, Nikki. I don't know how, but Mad Dog and Injun Bill killed Mr. Gransom and framed ya." Tawnie dropped her hand over the pistol hanging at her waist, something in the depth of her eyes making the other women almost step back from the hard determination reflected there.

"Then we better go back to Fairplay and get you cleared of the charges." Kissa stared at the poster, thinking the picture didn't look anything like Nikki.

"What chance do I have? Even though we are suspicious Mad Dog and Injun Bill killed Mr. Gransom, we have no proof. We do not even know why they are blaming me." Nikki folded the poster and placed it in her saddlebag.

"We've got to prove your innocence," Kissa cried, placing her hand on Nikki's arm.

"How, Kissa?" With a weary shake of her head, Nikki met each of their eyes. "How? We have other things to do now. We have to finish our business with the Mason gang, then we can concentrate on proving my innocence."

Tawnie handed Nikki the other papers she held in her hands. "Here's the posters on 'em. Looks like they've been on a killin' spree up and down the territory. At least your wanted poster don't say dead or alive like theirs."

Nikki crunched the posters in her hand. "Is this all you got?"

"Naw, I jawed with a old man whose stables are outside of town a piece, and he was a tellin' me 'bout two men who fit Mason and Mad Dog's description. Seems they was a wantin' to trade for a couple of horses. The old man said he told them no because he recognized the horses belongin' to the stagecoach, recognized the brand too. That was about three weeks ago. Far as I can gather, the old man said they was a headin' toward Canon City."

"It gives them a three-week head start." Nikki barely glanced at the faces on the posters before slipping them into her saddlebags. She did not need the posters to help her remember the outlaws' faces. "Let us put distance between us and Red Town."

NIKKI SPRINTED ACROSS THE SPARSELY COVERED land, crouching low until she was near the draw the outlaws were using as a windbreak. The wind swept across her back and rain came in a burst, then quickly left. Her wet clothes clinging to her and caked with mud, she dropped on hands and knees, belly-crawling toward the edge. Cautiously, she peeked over the ledge to pinpoint each outlaw's position. She knew three more horsemen had joined Mason and Mad Dog from the trail she had been following. She watched the camp a few more moments before she silently crept away.

Ginger, Tawnie, and Kissa listened carefully as Nikki described the layout of the outlaws' camp and the position of the guards. They agreed Nikki and Ginger would take out the guards first, then Kissa would guard the entrance. Tawnie would enter the draw after the watches were taken out and surprise the sleeping men near the campfire.

"Just like wolves hunting prey," Ginger commented. "I don't think those creatures deserve the right to be portrayed as a white tail deer, but…" she finished, shrugging her shoulder.

"Easy prey?" Nikki suggested. "Maybe…"

Nervous and anxious, the women silently crept to their stations to wait for the first grey fingers of dawn. Nikki climbed the odd slanting boulder and looked down at the watchman who sat with his back against the rock.

She wanted to take him out silently and quickly. From her position almost directly overhead of him, she placed one knee backward to leave and find a more suitable place to use her bow when the guard rose, stretched, then laid his rifle against the rock wall. She watched him unbutton his pants, then heard the sounds of urinating.

Creeping forward, she slipped the Bowie knife from her waist. Rising to her feet, she jumped behind him so silently, he barely heard her. Before he could stop urinating, she grabbed him around the forehead and slashed his throat. His body grew heavy, and she lowered him to the ground, then wiped the knife blade on his shirt. It took only a moment for her to position Kissa on the boulder, then slip through the tall grass into their camp.

Ginger eased her head over the ledge to look down into the draw. The guard rested against a rock, a rifle across his lap, his head leaned forward, and soft snores emanating from him.

A scraggly tree grew almost straight out of the side of the wall. With quick, silent loops of the rope, Ginger fashioned a noose, then lowered the noose around the guard's neck.

With a quick prayer, she angled the rope across the tree and jumped on the other side. The noose tightened across the guard's neck and pulled him upward with her downward momentum, hanging him on the scraggly tree.

It took all her strength to keep the guard suspended until she could tie the end around another scraggly tree. Without emotion, she watched the guard clutch at the rope around his neck, his feet kicking in the air. With another prayer the tree would hold, she drew her pistol and crept toward the fire.

With the first fingers of dawn lightening the eastern sky, Nikki fell to her stomach and belly-crawled through the brown grass toward the camp. One of the outlaws rose from his bedroll. Nikki drew an arrow and notched it. The arrow whistled through the air and clunked into the man's chest. The outlaw's eyes widened before he sank to the ground.

Pandemonium broke then. The other two outlaws, awakened by the sound of the other falling, came out of their bedrolls shooting. Nikki ducked, and a bullet sang past her ear. Pinned to the ground by the shots kicking up dust around her, she squeezed off a couple of shots without taking aim.

Tawnie knelt behind the mesquite bush, waiting for Nikki's signal. Shots rang out in a furious cadence. Peeking around the bush, she saw Jock Mason and Mad Dog concentrating all their firepower toward the opposite end of the draw.

Still firing, both men turned and ran toward the horses. Before she could react, Mad Dog spurred the horse toward the direction Kissa guarded. She shot at Mad Dog, but the bullet missed. It was Kissa's problem now, and she hoped Kissa would not let him escape.

Mason jumped onto a horse, turning to shoot in the opposite end of the draw where Nikki's head peeked above the prairie grass. Tawnie observed Nikki's sky-blue eyes widen when Mason aimed the pistol at her head and pulled the trigger. The pistol clicked, but nothing happened. Mason threw the weapon to the ground and grabbed the other pistol in his arsenal.

His actions were what Tawnie needed, and she stepped around the bush and flicked the whip toward him. The whip snaked around the barrel of the pistol and with a quick pull, she jerked it out of his hand.

Mason barely glanced at Tawnie before he kicked his heels against the horse's flanks. Tawnie again flicked the whip and wrapped it around Mason's neck. With a quick jerk of her arm, she pulled Mason from his galloping horse.

Mason fell in an untidy heap, rolling and clutching at the whip around his throat. Jerking the whip handle, Tawnie tightened it around his throat while she drew her pistol with her free hand, cocked the hammer, and aimed the weapon at Mason. "Unless ya want your teeth blown out, you'll move your hands above your head, slow and easy."

Ginger growled deep in her throat when the bullets finally stopped, allowing her to slip from her hiding place. With pistol in hand, she advanced toward Mason, pointing the barrel at his head. Tawnie moved beside her, her own pistol aimed at his heart. With Ginger's nod, Tawnie kept the pistol on him while Ginger tied his hands behind his back.

Kissa lay at an odd angle against the rock tilting in a downward slope toward the mouth of the entrance. Her footing unsure on the gravelly face, she positioned the shotgun toward the entrance and waited.

Soon, she heard gunshots and then the beat of horse hooves. With the unmistakable figure of Mad Dog rushing toward her, Kissa bit her bottom lip, leveled the shotgun at the rider, and pulled the trigger.

The gun jerked in her hands, slamming against her shoulder and propelling her off the rock. She rolled in front of the oncoming horse, her eyes widening with sudden fear. Pulling herself into a ball, she waited for the pierce of a bullet into her flesh or the shod hooves of the horse trampling her.

With a whispered prayer, she opened her eyes. All she saw was Mad Dog's scarred face leering at her and pointing the pistol at her head. A growl sounded behind her, then the pied-colored, muscular body of *Heoohtato* jumped over her. A sudden burst of pain pierced her skull, then all went black.

Nikki rose from her prone position and dusted her mud-caked clothing. A reverberating shot rang through the enclosed draw, and the galloping clatter of horse hooves grew fainter. "I am going to check on Kissa."

Worried, Nikki drew her pistol and checked the chamber. Discarding the used shells, she reloaded before heading in the direction Kissa was guarding. Cautiously, she slipped around the rock wall and peeked around the corner. Kissa lay face down in the dirt, her head bleeding profusely. *Heoohtato* sat close by her, his jaws opened and his tongue hanging out with his panting.

"Kissa!" Running toward the prone figure, Nikki holstered her pistol.

"Kissa's been shot." Nikki's voice echoed through the draw.

"Take care of the buzzard, Ginger," Tawnie drawled, running toward the exit.

Nikki knelt beside Kissa and turned her over. The blonde, curly locks were covered with red, sticky blood. "No, Kissa. You cannot be dead," Nikki cried to the still figure. With infinite care, she laid Kissa's head in her lap to examine the wound. She pushed the blood-matted hair from Kissa's face, wanting to cry when wet blood stuck to her fingers. Kissa moaned.

"Kissa?" Nikki whispered, hoping, praying the woman would answer. Separating the blood-clotted hair from the wound, Nikki examined it.

Kissa moaned again, and after a few seconds, opened her eyes to see Nikki's face close to hers.

"Kissa, you are alive. One Above, I was so afraid you were dead."

"I'm alive?" Kissa asked, surprised. "But I saw him aim the pistol at my head, then my head erupted in pain, and I don't remember anything else."

"Yes, you are alive," Nikki laughed with relief, hugging the injured woman. "His shot creased your temple, and you will have a terrible headache, but you are alive!"

Tears filled Kissa's eyes. "I thought for sure he killed me."

Galloping horse hooves resounded through the draw followed by a man's scream. Nikki lifted her head in time to see Ginger, astride the outlaw's horse, race past them, dragging Mason behind the horse. His hands were tied behind his back and his arms were drawn up to his shoulder blades with the other end of the rope looped across the saddle horn in front of Ginger.

Mason lifted terror-filled eyes, then closed them when his face swept across grass and dirt. Ginger dragged him across a cactus, then angled for another cactus before she disappeared from Nikki's view.

"Well, I be dang," Tawnie drawled, coming toward Nikki and Kissa while staring at the dust left by Ginger and the horse.

After a few stunned moments, Tawnie and Nikki

helped Kissa to camp. Tawnie brought their horses down into the draw while Nikki doctored the wound across Kissa's temple. Kissa kept her eyes closed, whimpering from a headache feeling like steel bands squeezing the sides of her head.

"I'm gonna check on Ginger," Tawnie declared, mounting her horse and guiding it toward the entrance.

Nikki nodded and began setting up camp. Within minutes, she had a fire going and was steeping some leaves to relieve Kissa's headache.

Gone only a little while, Tawnie jumped from her horse and draped the reins toward the ground. "Ginger's all right, but she won't be back for a while. She's draggin' that whoreson through every cactus patch she can find. Guess long as we hear the screamin' ain't no reason to worry 'bout her." With her last words, she unsaddled the horses.

Toward midday, Ginger reentered the draw, a subdued, angry twist about her lips. She unsaddled the horse, then wiped it down with dried grass before joining the group. "Mason's dead."

Chapter 8
A Mad Dog Must Die

THE SUN BEAT DOWN ON THE WEARY travelers in shimmering heat waves, distorting distances and images. The travelers slouched in saddles and a deep-chested, muscular, pied-colored dog ran beside the plodding horses, its tongue hanging out with its panting.

Above their heads, a bald eagle screeched before diving toward the ground. It swooped downward and flew back up, a snake caught in its claws. The eagle flew high in the sky, nearly disappearing before releasing the snake and letting it fall to earth. The snake landed close to the women, and the horses grew skittish before settling down; the snake dying upon impact on the almost barren terrain.

At a distance, the riders resembled men, but the wind pressed their shirts against them and outlined the tender curves of their breasts. Perspiration beaded their foreheads and poured into their eyes, stinging and blurring them.

Dressed in black, the leader raised her hand to stop the entourage, then jabbed her heels into the mare's side to gallop up the next hill. Dark as midnight, the rider and horse sat upon the hill. Below, a smattering of vegetation growing along its swooping sides and reaching outward, cradled a white house, a huge garden behind it, a barn, and a couple of outbuildings.

Nikki took off the wide-brimmed hat and set it on the saddle horn, her long black braid uncoiling and falling down her back while swiping moisture with her shirt sleeve from her face.

Smoke billowed from the chimney of the house, providing the first glimpse of humanity they had seen for nearly four weeks. The scorching wind carried the sounds of cows, chickens, and horses back to her.

She grabbed her hat and waved it over her head, motioning the group forward. Ginger took the lead, and Tawnie brought up the rear, leading the pack animal.

Kissa was the first to speak after they reached Nikki. "I heard a cow. Oh, what I wouldn't give for a cool glass of sweet milk."

"And fresh eggs,"

Kissa's and Ginger's wishes made the salvia run in all their mouths. It was one of the main hardships of being on the trail—the lack of fresh milk and eggs.

"Maybe the lady of the house will sell us some," Nikki hopefully replied, staring down into the peaceful valley.

"Do you think she'll welcome us? We do look disreputable." Kissa stared longingly at the scene below which eluded a homey quality, sparking homesickness within her. She wanted a place of her own similar to the one below with hordes of children.

"Isolated as the ranch is, I think she will be glad for some company." Nikki was mesmerized by the serenity below.

"Whut if there ain't a little woman of the house?"

"There is. Look at the flowers planted in front of the house, the neat garden, and the general neatness about the place. No man cares about doing those things on his own."

Nikki set the hat on her head and turned to look at each of them. "Shall we go?"

The noise of their horses brought a woman wiping her hands on the end of her apron, outside the house. She took one look at the four riders and turned back around.

"Please, ma'am. We beg a drink of water," Nikki yelled.

The woman spun back on her heel and gawked at them. "Women? All of you?"

"Yes, ma'am," Nikki answered for them, looking at the plump, solidly built woman. She liked what she saw in the woman's face; the laugh lines around her mouth creasing into a double chin, her sparkling merry blue eyes, and her mouse brown hair coiled into a tight bun at the back of her neck.

The woman's mouth and eyes crinkled in amusement. "Well, dearies, get down off those horses. You all look so tired, you'll fall off."

"Thank you, ma'am." Nikki eased off the mare and slid to the ground. Weariness took hold of her legs and trembled underneath her.

"Take your horses to the barn and give them a good measure of grain and hay. The poor animals look like they need it. There's water here by the door for you to wash up in. By the way, my name's Hope Parkinson."

Nikki made the round of introductions, including the pit bull terrier panting hard and lying on the ground at her feet.

Hope looked from one woman to another, a million questions crowding her mind. "I'll take care of your dog while you ladies take care of your horses. I'll have supper ready in a few minutes."

After currying and feeding the animals, the women scrubbed their faces and hands before entering the house. The aroma of freshly baked bread met them at the door and set all their stomachs rumbling. Hope motioned toward the table where four extra place settings were laid.

She ladled big portions of stew onto plates and sat loaves of bread, fresh butter, honey and wild plum preserves in front of them. "I've got a pitcher of fresh milk needin' to be drank. When Mr. Parkinson comes in, he'll have to milk the cows again anyway. Would you be likin' some?" The rapt longing in each of their faces was answer enough.

"We do not want to put you out none, Mrs. Parkinson." Nikki buttered her bread while looking at the woman.

"Call me Hope, dearie. You ain't puttin' me out none. It's been so long since I talked to another woman, I nearly forgot how. No, sirree, glad to have all of you. My man and youngest children will be home afore dark. My oldest children are all married or out on their own. The two children left are my son who's ten and helpin' his father with the cows and my seven-year-old daughter. Soon as the chores are done, she heads out toward the fishpond. The little rascal will do anything to get out of housework." Hope carried on a steady conversation while the women ate, her barrage needing no comment from them.

After they finished eating, Kissa and Ginger rose from the table, cleared it, and washed dishes against Hope's protest. "Please, ma'am, it's the least we can do for your hospitality," Kissa smiled.

Hope finally agreed, seeing there was no way the women would take no for an answer. She sat at the table with Nikki and Tawnie, fanning herself with the end of her apron. "Tell me, dearie, why are four young women and a dog be travelin' in this lonely country?"

All of them turned toward Nikki, waiting for her to answer. Nikki swallowed, uncertain what to say. No matter how kind the woman looked, she could not tell her the truth. She must have sat there for some time, her brain refusing to work, when Hope leaned forward and patted her hand.

"Sorry, dearie, if I'm a pryin'. Must be hard enough travelin' the way you are without a nosey old woman askin' questions."

Nikki put her hand on the woman's and squeezed, a lump forming in her throat. She was offering the first bit of kindness any of them had experienced since leaving the Nelsons. "You are very kind, Mrs. Parkinson, eh, Hope, for taking in four strangers to share your food and drink your milk. I would tell you all if I could, but some things are better left untold lest they hurt someone."

Hope looked from one woman to the other, reading more in their faces than they wished. "Poor dears, it be a hard, cruel world out there, and it seems you've experienced more than your fair share. We won't talk about it if you don't want to. Tell me instead what's happening out there in the real world. Just women talk, you hear, nothing more."

They sat around the table laughing at Hope's sharp wit and shared little tidbits of news and family stories with her. Hope read more into their tales and wistful, sad expressions than they suspected.

They were heartily laughing at one of Hope's stories when a boy rushed into the house, breathless and with tears flowing, making dirty tracks down his cheeks. "Momma, come quick. It's Sissy. Somebody's hurt her."

"Oh, Heaven help us," Hope moaned, the laughter erased from her face. They followed Hope outside and watched in stunned silence as a big man, whom they took to be her husband, walked toward them carrying the limp naked form of a small child in his arms. Shaking his head at his wife, his strong, plain face bore the marks of tears. Hope burst into racking sobs.

Ginger and Kissa put their arms around Hope while Nikki and Tawnie followed the man inside the house. He put the lifeless body on the table, then fell onto the bench and buried his face in his big hands, his broad shoulders shaking with silent sobs.

Nikki stared at the small body, déjà vu crying through her body. The little girl was naked, her lower body covered in blood, the rest of her bearing huge bruises, and her throat had been slit.

She gripped Tawnie's arm, her fingers biting into the flesh, muttering under her breath, "Mad Dog." In a moment of compassion, she grabbed several cloths hanging nearby and covered the child's abused body.

Their own faces drained of color, Kissa and Ginger helped Hope inside. The boy stood with his hands clenched at his side, bravely holding back his tears. Nikki stepped up to him and put her hand on top of his tow-colored head. "Son," she quietly addressed him.

Nikki's tender voice was too much for him. He grabbed her around the waist and hid his face against her. She put her arms around the sobbing boy and held him, crooning comfort. When his sobs lessened, she gently disengaged him and knelt in front of him. "What is your name?"

"Irving."

"Irving, you are going to have to take on a lot of responsibility from now on. Your momma and daddy need you more than ever. Can you help them through this?"

Irving straightened, wiping his nose with the back of his sleeve. "Yes, ma'am. Tell me what to do."

Nikki studied him for a few minutes. The young boy accepted the task of becoming a little man, willingly taking on the obligation—so much to lay upon a boy, but she did not let her thoughts show. It was part of growing up and forcing him to shoulder responsibility early in life. "First, tell me where your sister was found and how to get there."

"She was found near the pond that way," the boy replied, pointing toward the south.

Nikki questioned him further about the area and landscape. "I need you to ride to your closest neighbor and bring them to your momma and daddy. Can you do that?"

"Yes, ma'am," Irving straightened his back, meeting her eyes though a film of wetness still marred his.

"How far is it to your neighbors, son?"

"I'll be back with them afore dark."

Nikki nodded. "Then go now. We will clean your sister and get her ready for burial, then we have to leave, so we may not be here when you come back. We are after the man who did this to your sister, and if we leave soon, maybe we can catch him and stop him before he does it again."

THE RELENTLESS HOT WINDS BLASTING HIM, he gazed out over the savage beauty. The rock formations, resembling nature going berserk, created and destroyed architectural shapes, straining human imagination. Only when he looked closely was he able to detect animal life and the short grass tenuously growing in barren places.

The savagery of the land matched the savagery of his heart. He was a breed apart from other men, a cold-blooded murderer, killing for enjoyment and without compunction. It was suicide to face an opponent, and he elected to take the more cautious way: by ambush, a shot in the back, or killing when his adversary was unarmed. He kept his life for over forty years this way, surviving when many men had tried to outwit him.

Depravity took many forms, and he touched upon most of them, whether it was robbing innocent victims, stagecoaches, trains, or other unspeakable crimes and acts. The thirst for blood was like a strong drug to his brain. It provided excitement—a revenge against mankind.

He received sexual enjoyment from raping, whether it was mature women, fresh young virgins, or children, and sometimes males of any age if the others were unavailable. His preference was virgins for they fought the hardest to protect their precious treasure. *But then the children—a* cruel, lustful smile lit his pocked-marked, scared face, the expression daunting enough to turn honest, brave men into cringing fear.

His mind wandered, taking his mind off the parched prairie air that was hot enough to fry a man alive. He selected a rocky plateau where the overhang provided a nice shade and where he could build a small fire that would be hard to detect after the sun went down. With darkness, temperatures dropped in a very short time.

Shifting positions on the horse, he knew he was too

smart to be captured or killed. He had the instincts of a bird of prey and no man's fool. No man could catch him because he was always one jump ahead of the law and bounty hunters. He had proven he could outwit the best of them. Deputy U.S. Marshal Dane Travis had come the closest to capturing him, but even as crafty and smart as that man was, he still was not smart enough to catch him.

He unsaddled his worn mount, then sat back to eat jerky and take a sip of his precious little water, relaxing his guard. The terrain was such that neither man nor beast could follow him without detection.

Lost in his pleasurable memories, the sharp shifting of rocks interrupted him and brought up his head. Going for his gun and catching sight of his uninvited visitors, he stopped and laughed out loud.

The lowering sun, at its brightest now, outlined four beautiful young women and a huge pit bull terrier in an ethereal glow, transfiguring them into menacing angels. Colorless grey eyes lightening with amusement, he glanced from one to the other. They were armed with various weapons and stood with their feet apart, their stance proclaiming they were out for blood.

His thin, ruthless mouth widened into an amused grin. From the soft, gentle roundness of the first, to the seductiveness of the second, the golden good looks of the third, to the dark beauty of the last, each of the women represented the best of nature's cream.

The first woman's curly blond hair hung in tight ringlets past her cherub face and danced in springing curls past her shoulders. Dressed in loose blue clothes, the type a working man would wear, did not hide her pleasantly rounded figure, yet she had no extra weight on her. Her womanly curves would satisfy any man's desire. His smile widened. She held a shotgun pointed somewhat shakenly at his heart.

The red sun glistened brightly off the next woman's unruly wavy hair, the color of a well-ripened strawberry, and lighted her proud head like a flaming torch. Her heart-shaped face and sharp cheekbones emphasized the slanted green eyes. Her pink lips were narrowed in a hard line, refusing to hide the seductive curve of them. The gentle swelling of her breast was revealed by a low buttoned, lime green blouse tucked in sharply at her tiny waist and her hips flared out in the tight-fitting, dark green pants. Around her left shoulder was a coil of rope and in her small, delicate hand, she held a pearl-handled Colt .44. His eyes turned stunned; she held the pistol steadily and surely, her eyes revealing her deadly intent.

The next was the tallest and most deadly. Her wavy golden-brown hair hung down her back and her tawny eyes gleamed almost yellow in the setting sun. A powerful neck set atop broad, muscular shoulders and sinewy arms only hinted at a strength few men could match. Her large bosom pressed against a tan blouse tucked into dark brown pants. On her shapely hips hung a Samuel's Navy revolver and in her strong square hand hung the deadly length of a bullwhip. The hardness of her eyes proclaimed she was no man's plaything, but in fact, they were hers. The deadly intent on her strong, chiseled features proclaimed even if he asked for mercy, none would be given.

The last woman stood straight and tall, her coal black hair with blue highlights, hung straight to mid-calf and her high forehead encircled by a red band. The golden bronze of her oval face made her strange light blue eyes more vivid. Her curvaceous body was clothed in black relieved only by a blood-red waistband. Her pants, tight enough to hint at her shapely thighs, were tucked into knee-high moccasins.

Slung on her back was an arrow quiver, and in her firmly gripped hands was a bow, the string tautly pulled back and loaded with a red and black striped arrow. On her slender hips was a Remington .44 pistol and on the other hip, a Bowie knife encased in leather and trimmed with wolf fur, and he imagined she had a knife hidden in one of her moccasins. If it were not for her strange blue eyes, she could easily be taken for an Indian; everything about her proclaimed an Indian heritage.

The women stood in front of him like angels of death, their set faces telling him to ask for no quarter, for none would be given. They were menacing angels and they would do to him what no man ever had been able to achieve.

The dark one turned her frigid eyes on him, their very depths sending fingers of icy cold dread down his spine and spoke five simple words sounding like a death knell to his ears. Those five simple words many men had uttered, but none had been able to succeed, came out in a hiss from her grim lips. Five small words set his heart to pounding fiercely in his chest.

"You are a dead man!"

Recognition set his mouth into a tight grin when the dark one spoke those words, reverberating to over a year ago when he had heard those same words. "So, we meet again, Dark One," Mad Dog said to Nikki.

"You brought your friends with you. Expectin' anutter party?" While he talked, Mad Dog lowered his hand to his pistol, then suddenly grabbed it.

Before he could clear leather, a snap, then a sting pulled the gun from his hand. "Damn!" he cried, placing his hand to his mouth.

"Stand up, slow and easy, mister," Ginger directed.

"Ya think I'm gonna do that for you, girlie," Mad Dog growled, crossing his arms over his chest and leaning back against the rock-facing.

A tight smile curving her lips, Ginger pulled the trigger. Dust kicked up extremely near his buttocks.

"Son of a bitch," Mad Dog cried, jumping to his feet. "You nearly kilt me."

The laugh Ginger gave was anything but funny. It was more the cackle of a witch, determined and deadly. "Not yet, Mad Dog. We've more in store for you."

Tawnie jumped from the top ledge beside Mad Dog. Before he could turn around to face her, Tawnie slammed the pistol butt into the side of his head, knocking him unconscious.

"Strip him," Nikki demanded, dropping beside Tawnie. Kissa followed Nikki, then placed her shotgun against the rock wall and bent over the slumped man. She began unbuttoning his shirt.

"No," Nikki growled, handing her a Bowie knife, handle first. "Do not waste your time carefully undressing him, Kissa. He will not need his clothes after we are finished."

Kissa took the knife and cut his clothes free, almost gagging when the huge, soft form of his manhood flopped from the material she cut from him.

"Tawnie, keep your gun on him in case he regains consciousness. I will be back soon." Nikki turned and headed back to where they had left their horses.

There was a scraggily scrub oak bush near the horses. With the knife from her moccasin, she cut some of the branches into sturdy stakes. Afterwards, she found a place in the sun suited for her purpose. Pulling the knife from her moccasin, she used the knife handle to pound one stake into the ground, then dropped the other three near it.

She walked back to the horses, drew a long leather thong from her saddlebag, and cut it into four strips. Wadding them together, she placed them in a tin coffee cup.

"It is a shame to waste good water on scum like you, but…" Nikki shrugged her shoulders and poured water from her canteen over the leather thongs. The coffee cup with the wet leather thongs joined the stakes before she headed back to her group.

"Naked as a jaybird," Tawnie grinned in greeting.

"Good, drag him up here." It took all the women to tow him to the place Nikki had staked out. Mad Dog came to once, and Tawnie slammed the pistol's grip along the side of his head, near a scar above his ear where the hair had never regrown from a bullet wound, knocking him unconscious again.

Hair mingled with sweat clung to Nikki's face. She dropped Mad Dog's arm before she brushed her hair from her eyes. "This is it. We will place his manhood over the red ant bed."

Ginger laughed, the sound uncertain. "Why? Isn't that a bit drastic?"

Nikki turned serious eyes on the group. "Once a brave has spoiled a woman and then suffers this indignant torture as his punishment, he never or rarely does it again. But with Mad Dog," she nodded toward the unconscious man, "will never leave here alive."

After they positioned Mad Dog over the red ant bed, Tawnie and Nikki stretched him spreadeagle, then tied his hands and feet with the wet leather thongs. Stretching the thongs tight, they knotted the ends, then pounded the stakes behind the knots close to his wrists and feet, into the hard-packed earth.

Nikki stepped back to survey their handiwork. With a satisfied nod, she knelt beside Mad Dog and withdrew her Bowie knife. In two quick slices, she cut off Mad Dog's eyelids, and threw the flesh on the ground. "The sun will blind him," she commented, explaining her actions.

"Make camp where we discovered Mad Dog. We will finish this in the morning, then we are gone from here." Nikki stopped them a moment as a sprig of an idea crossed her mind. "One of you bring me the small amount of honey we have left."

"Why waste good honey?" Tawnie drawled.

Nikki's smile was tight. "You will see."

Ginger scratched at her arms, her flesh crawling, watching the red ants scurry over Mad Dog's body and into his lidless eyes. "I don't think I can gather firewood. My flesh is crawling just watching this."

"Ah, dang, Ginger, the fun's just beginnin'," Tawnie laughed, turning to gather firewood.

"Kissa, come with me and bring the honey back to Nikki," Ginger ordered, turning and leaving the group to gather their horses and bring them into the makeshift camp.

Nikki accepted the last bit of their precious honey and held the bottle upside down over Mad Dog's genitals for it to slowly drip and cover the monstrosity. Watching the slow crawl of the honey drip down the glass edges before the drops formed and spattered over Man Dog's oversized soft penis, a cruel, satisfied grimace swept over her face.

Red ants swarm around the drops of honey, bringing Mad Dog back to consciousness. Nikki ignored Mad Dog's cursing and questions, then gave him a tight smile when his angry words turned to screams, the red ants biting him while fighting over the honey.

He strained against his leather bounds, but the dry hot air had already dried the leather tightly around his bound wrists and ankles, keeping him securely anchored to the ground.

The horses were unsaddled, brushed, and fed before the women sat around the wood. It took only a few seconds before the dried wood caught fire and glowed orange yellow in the dying sunlight. Tawnie tossed more pieces of wood on the fire, then jumped back. "Would ya look at them scorpions run!"

Ginger and Kissa jumped to their feet, screaming. Scorpions ran out of the fire in all directions. Nikki slowly rose to her feet, her eyes lighting with an unholy light. "Gather more firewood and bring it over to Mad Dog. We are going to build small fires all around him."

"Whut are ya gonna do?" Tawnie asked, jumping aside when another scorpion ran across her booted foot.

Shrugging, Nikki stated, "I do not know what scorpions eat, but maybe they eat ants, and maybe they will eat them off Mad Dog. Even if they do not," she shrugged again.

Tawnie laughed. "This oughta be a sight to see. Come on afore it gets too dark. The whoreson ain't stopped screamin' anyhow."

Chapter 9
Sow the Wind, Reap the Whirlwind

THE SUN WAS DIRECTLY OVERHEAD in a cloudless sky. Not even a breath of wind fluttered to cool the hot land. Nikki watched Ginger pour a few drops of water over Mad Dog's mouth. The liquid trickled down his chin before his tongue came out to lick the precious liquid. She did not know if Ginger gave him water for humanitarian reasons or if she wanted to prolong his agony, and she did not ask. Already, his eyes were burned almost white, and several places on his body, including his private parts, were red and swollen beyond recognition. His screams and struggles had stopped just before daylight spread across the land.

Adjusting the saddlebag, she flipped the flap open to pull out the wanted posters. With careful diligence, she looked at each one, mentally putting the faces on the posters with the men already dead. Satisfied all the outlaws from the Mason gang had paid with their lives, she tossed the wanted posters across Mad Dog's chest and stomach. Only one poster remained, and it was the wanted poster on herself.

"It is over now." None of them had discussed what their next move would be. The sound of Mad Dog's screams kept them from talking or sleeping last night. Now, they looked at each other, helpless and uncertain.

"I think I'm goin' back to the Nelsons," Tawnie remarked after a moment. "I've been thinkin' 'bout Cal's job offer ever since."

"So have I," Ginger replied, pushing a stray strand of wavy hair from her face. "It will at least give me some time to think about the future."

Kissa shrugged, then glanced at Tawnie and Ginger. "Me too. I've nowhere else to go."

"Nikki?" Tawnie asked, turning her attention to the silent woman.

"Go to the Nelsons without me. I have business to attend. Hopefully, I will meet you there before winter sets in." Nikki crumbled the wanted poster in her hand. Somehow, someway, she had to prove her innocence, but first, she would turn herself in to Sheriff Watkins at Fairplay. That should prove her innocence. Besides, it was something she needed to do by herself.

"We can postpone going to the Nelsons, Nikki, to help you." Curiosity lighting her green eyes, Ginger refrained from asking Nikki her business. She briefly wondered if it had something to do with Dane Travis or turning herself in to the sheriff at Fairplay. Besides, the thought of leaving Nikki was not appealing. They had been together too long and been through too much for secrets to exist between them now.

Nikki shook her head. "No, go without me. There is something I must do alone."

"Whut about Mad Dog?" Tawnie moved toward the semiconscious man, hawked deep in her throat, and spat the glob in his face.

"Just leave him. He is nearly dead." Nikki stuck the

poster back into her saddlebag.

"Just one more thang," Tawnie stated, moving over to Mad Dog. She balanced a knife in the palm of her hand, then closed her fingers around the handle. Before the other women could guess her intention, she bent forward and castrated Mad Dog.

A scream erupted from Mad Dog, then turned to whimpers. "That's for Cari and LeeAnn, and all the other little girls ya hurt and killed, ya sorry whoreson." Tawnie dropped his huge penis onto his stomach, a satisfied gloat on her face.

Kissa blanched, but a glimmer of gratification flickered in her cornflower-blue eyes before she turned her face away from him toward Nikki.

With an embarrassed smile, she brought her hands around to her front, holding the robe Cloud Walker had painted for Nikki in her hands. Red sufficing her face, she moved the wolf fur aside. "I took the liberty of taking your robe this morning while you were out hunting for breakfast."

Her face turned a deeper shade of red when Nikki's eyes narrowed. Looking down at her feet, Kissa explained, "I found a straight razor in Mad Dog's things, and I sewed it along the fur. Look, it's concealed here."

Nikki accepted the robe and looked where Kissa pulled the rich red wolf fur back from the leather. She saw nothing unusual about the robe, so she pressed her fingers to where Kissa motioned. With her fingertips, she felt the straight razor underneath the leather.

Kissa grew a little bolder. "See, look. You can pull it out here." She slipped the straight razor from the ingeniously sewn pocket.

"I do not know what to say." Nikki stared at the robe in confusion.

"You're wondering why I did it." Kissa shrugged helplessly. "I can't really say. It just seemed like the thing to do… and it kept me busy."

It was Kissa's lame explanation bringing Nikki's giggle to the surface. "Kissa, you never cease to amaze me. Thank you. Your work is beautiful." Nikki wanted to say, 'if not practical', but she bit back the words.

Ginger fumbled in her pant pockets before pulling out several coins. "You'll need some money." She pressed the coins in the palm of Nikki's hand. Nikki tried to pull her hand away, but Ginger pressed her fingers around Nikki's. "No, take it. We've enough to get us to the Nelsons and then some. Besides, we have his horse and saddle to sell."

"Well, I didna make ya nothin' and I ain't got nothin' to give ya. Ya just be careful. If ya ain't at the Nelsons by snowfall, I'm a gonna come lookin' for ya." Tawnie wrapped her in a bear hug, squeezing so tight, she lifted Nikki off her feet. She quickly released her and walked away, suspiciously wiping at her eyes.

Nikki looked at her friends one last time before she placed her hand on the saddle horn, and with one foot in the stirrup, she turned her head toward them. "I will see you in a couple of months." Mounting, she kicked her heels into the mare's flanks and left the other women staring at her back.

NIKKI WANTED TO BREATHE, TO SEE THE BEAUTY of the land instead of having to hunt for outlaws. The mission was finished and yet, something within her was still incomplete. There was mild satisfaction they had bested the men who destroyed her family and took their virtue, but the satisfaction left an empty place within her.

For some reason, thoughts of Dane Travis formed in her mind until she could see his light brown hair sweat curled around his head, his piercing silver-blue eyes crinkling with his smile and the cleft in his square chin.

They might have had a chance for a life together if circumstances had been different. Something within her longed for a chance. Her revenge was complete, her hatred gone since the animals who killed her family were dead, but could she fill her heart with love again?

Something within her wanted to run, to flee from life and love. Nikki felt hollow inside, devoid of emotions, tears, compassion, and understanding. *If only I could cry…if only*—there was that phrase again which meant absolutely nothing—*if only.*

Keep going, her heart thumped. *Finish the last of your business at Fairplay, then find life. Life…One Above, what is life? How do I live with what I have done? How do any of us live with what we have done? Quit thinking about it,* she admonished herself. *It is done. Live with it.*

Heoohtato looped beside the mare, and toward midday, the canyon loomed in front of her. She found a spot where she could watch the stars, feel the hot air sweep across her face and through her hair.

Here, she decided, *maybe I can figure out my life, something I want to do.* Even though she had decided to turn herself in, she wanted to explore the person within and hopefully find her true self once again. Somewhere along the trail, she had lost the person she once was.

She gathered enough firewood for the night and set about exploring the area after sending *Heoohtato* off to hunt for his supper.

A rock face overlooking the canyon beckoned to her and she sat on top of it to admire the beauty of the canyon below her. Closing her eyes, Nikki allowed herself to become one with nature, then with the animals. She needed the strength and orientation of Mother Earth to strengthen her.

Her hand went automatically to her shirtfront. Underneath, the gold locket touched her skin, but it was not what she missed. She missed her bear claw necklace. The bear claw had always given her strength, but now it was gone.

The wind swept her hair upward and danced it around her head. She blanked her mind and allowed it to drift with the wind, searching, asking, begging for direction, strength, and comfort.

THE WATER OF THE ARKANSAS RIVER flowed over the embedded rocks and sand bed; the spring runoff slowing to the steady, leisurely pace of early fall. Already the leaves of the aspen and scrub oak were changing their green apparel in for the brilliant colors of fall. Bushes of chokecherries and gooseberries, heavy with ripe fruit, and tall buffalo grass lined the edges of the river, providing shade and food for Nikki and fodder for her horse.

The whispering water and sighing leaves seemed to talk to her, to soothe the torment within her. The soft rustles provided, as some would say, music to calm the savage beast, Nikki thought, a sardonic smile curving her grim lips.

The edge of the sun shone with a red glow over the western slope, and the lengthening shadows darkened the land, casting gloomy shapes around her. The mare shifted nervously, its snort breaking the silence of nature. *Heoohtato* growled low within his throat and ran ahead of her, searching the perimeter in front of them.

The horse shifted uneasily underneath her, and the dog's growls increased. Wary, Nikki slowly drew her pistol, searching the river bottom spanning out in front of her.

A large boulder loomed ahead, resting along the river's edge, and water swirled around its surface in a small whirlpool. A low purring growl, then high-pitched scream of a mountain lion vibrated close in front of her. Edgy, Nikki cocked her pistol's hammer and leaned forward just as the golden-brown body of a mountain lion launched upward off the boulder directly at her.

Her horse shifted, reared, then tried to run. *Heoohtato's* growl increased, and from the corner of her eye, she saw his big, muscular body jump straight for the mountain lion. The dog and the mountain lion met in midair, then fell to the ground, their barks, growls, and screams mingling with the swift movement of their fighting bodies.

Nikki fought the horse, bringing it under control. The horse reared again, whinnying its fright. Hands tightening on the reins, Nikki gained a measure of control over the horse and backed the animal away from the fighting dog and mountain lion.

Leaning forward on the saddle, she pointed the pistol at the fighting animals, hoping for a clear shot of the mountain lion. With the animals separating, Nikki aimed and fired. The horse skittishly shifted underneath her, and her shot went wild.

She threw her leg over the saddle and dismounted, holding the reins tight in her hand. "One more shot," she whispered, watching the animals fight, almost standing on their hind legs.

The dog and the mountain lion were about the same size, the golden-brown fur of the sleek mountain lion mixed with the creamy white and tan colors of the muscular dog. Both animals looked for an opening to the throat of the other, both covered with blood. She recognized right away it was a battle to the death. Neither animal would give nor run.

The animals fought closer to her, and she backed the horse further away. The horse shied, rearing on its back legs, and she pulled down on the reins to steady the horse, then positioned the pistol again at the combatant animals.

Heoohtato found an opening and his powerful jaw clamped over the mountain lion's throat. The big cat jerked and struggled against the dog before it lay still. *Heoohtato* shook the big cat several times before he was satisfied. After releasing the animal, the dog gave the big cat a couple of warning growls before turning away, taking several steps toward Nikki, and dropping to the ground, whining in pain.

Quickly hobbling the horse, Nikki grabbed her medicine bag and canteen. Within moments, she knelt beside her dog. Dropping her supplies beside her, she grabbed at her shirt and pulled the ends free from her pants to cut pieces to bathe and wrap the dog's injuries. "Brave *Heoohtato*, you saved my life."

Dismay filled her. Losing blood fast, the dog had several deep scratches and bites over him. "Let us get this bleeding stopped, *Heoohtato*, then I will move you to a better place to take care of you. Do not worry. I will stay with you until you are well enough to leave with me."

A shadow fell over Nikki; she quickly reached for her pistol, looking upward. The click of a hammer being brought back on a handgun stopped her.

"You're a hard woman to find, Nikki," the voice drawled.

She relaxed her hand and turned to face the Deputy U.S. Marshal. "Thanks, Dane. You nearly scared me to death and…" she looked at his pistol hand, "you do not need to hold a gun on me."

"I do, Dark Angel. I'm taking you in for murder."

"Dane, I do not have time for this. I am trying to save my dog's life."

"The dog's done for, Nikki. You'd be better off killing him and getting it over with."

"That is cold," she cried, turning to cleanse the dog's wounds.

A fleeting ghost of compassion crossing his stern face, Dane clicked the hammer back into position, then slid the gun back into his hostler before kneeling beside her. "No, I'm not cold, just practical."

He reached up and scratched the dog between the ears. "The dog is suffering, Nikki, and I don't like seeing animals suffer."

"He will live. I will make sure he lives." She stopped dabbing the blood on the dog's rump to meet Dane's eyes. "He saved my life and I, in return, will save his. It is the least I can do."

"You constantly surprise me, Dark Angel." He moved closer beside her.

The dog whined, pulling her attention from Dane back to him. She worked quickly to staunch the flow of blood before bandaging the dog. "I do not have time to discuss anything with you now, Dane. I am not going anywhere until *Heoohtato* is well enough to travel."

"Take care of your dog, then. I'm gonna take a look at the mountain lion, then get rid of its carcass."

Nikki had no idea how long Dane examined the carcass before he returned and knelt beside her.

"You better kill the dog or I will."

He started to pull his pistol, and Nikki placed her hand over his, stopping him. "What is the matter with you?"

Sighing, he pushed his hat back from his eyes and looked straight into hers. "I'm afraid the mountain lion might have rabies. It doesn't make sense for a mountain lion to attack like this, especially so far from the woods."

"But you do not know for sure if it had rabies, do you?"

"No, but I'm gonna burn the body just in case."

"Then how can you ask me to kill my dog if you do not know for sure?"

Nikki was right. All he had was a strong suspicion. With a weary sigh, he glanced at the injured animal. "All right. I won't argue with you if you will allow me to keep him tied up until we know for sure. Will you agree? If you don't, I'll kill him anyway."

"You are not leaving me any choice."

Taking the rope from his saddle horn, he coiled it around his shoulder before picking up the heavy dog and carrying him up the bank to the tree-shaded area. After he tied the rope around the dog's neck and the other around a tree, he set up camp at a respectable distance away from the injured animal.

After setting up camp, he returned to the mountain lion's carcass and set about burning it while the sun disappeared, and blackness moved across the land.

Nikki checked *Heoohtato* once more before she sat near the fire and accepted the cup of coffee Dane handed her. All she wanted to do was drink the coffee, then lay down to sleep.

"I've been following the Mason gang for months now with a posse of nearly thirty men. I've seen the brutality you and your friends used on Mason and Mad Dog. In fact, me and the posse watched your trail dust as you and your friends left, but we weren't interested in bringing in the outlaws' murderers."

"Then why are you here?" Nikki stared into the fire, not interested in his conversation.

"Mad Dog wasn't dead when we reached him, Nikki. I found the wanted posters of the Mason gang laying across his chest and the remains of his business. Are they all dead?" he asked, changing the subject.

"Yes, everyone."

"There are three men I cannot account for—Toad, Injun Bill, and Smith."

She shrugged but did not answer.

"I will have to say my posse admired you and your friends' handiwork. I think the comment was even an Injun couldn't of done it any better." He studied her face, but her face and eyes were blank, revealing nothing.

Shrugging again, she sarcastically asked, "So… did you throw his almost dead carcass over a horse and take him to jail?"

"And screw up your handiwork?" His laugh cynical, he declared, "To tell you the truth, we left him to die."

"Then why are you here, Dane?"

"I've already told you, I'm taking you in for murder."

"Murder? Of whom?" she asked, meeting his narrowed silver-blue eyes.

He searched her face again for some spark, some knowledge, but her expression remained bland, uninterested. "John Gransom, proprietor of the Fairplay General Store."

A sigh escaped her. "I did not kill him."

"It's for the law to decide, Dark Angel."

"Is that why you followed me? To take me in?"

Dane did not answer for a moment, searching the depth of her remarkable baby-blue eyes with the yellow flames of the fire reflecting in them. Something was missing, some light. The innocence of before was replaced by ageless wisdom, the depths filled with despair and hopelessness.

He reached out to touch her cheek, then clenched his fingers together and dropped his hand. "I tried long ago to prevent you and your friends from going after the outlaws. You're lucky none of you were killed."

Lowering her eyes, Nikki sipped the steaming coffee. *What does he want from me? Why is he always right behind me, right on my trail?* She kept her questions to herself. "So," she shrugged, "you did not answer my question."

"I wanted to bring you in before some hotheaded, trigger-happy son of a gun went after you. I've even heard rumors the sheriff is getting ready to send someone to Denver to enlist the Pinkerton Agency to go after you."

"You are very kind, but you see, I was on my way to turn myself in at Fairplay. I have nothing to hide. I did not kill the man. He helped me escape from Injun Bill and Mad Dog while I was in his store. Besides, why would I kill someone who did not need killing, especially when he helped me?"

"I don't know what happened. I just know you and your friends have made quite a name for yourselves. Rumors of your torture will spread across the country, and many a man will be looking for you and your partners in crime."

"You have a low opinion of us, do you not, Marshal?"

"Let me put it this way, Darlin', I wouldn't want to be on your hit list."

"They deserved to die. We only followed the trail of dead bodies, especially little girls, to find the scum." She glanced up from her coffee cup to meet his eyes and held his gaze before hearing him say,

"Whatever you did, Nikki, you are the one who's going to have to live with it, so it doesn't matter what I think. However, it does matter what the court thinks. It was your bear claw necklace they found in Gransom's hand. I recognized the necklace, and so did Sheriff Watkins."

Her hand automatically went to her neck. "So that is why they thought I killed Gransom. Mad Dog pulled it from my neck when I had a run-in with him in the general store."

"Suppose you tell me what happened."

Sighing, Nikki placed the coffee cup beside her. Drawing her knees to her chest and wrapping her arms around them, she stared into the fire and related that afternoon.

"Well, it does explain why you no longer have your

bear claw necklace, but it doesn't explain why the necklace was found gripped in Gransom's hand," Dane observed, "if what you are saying is truth."

"Why would I lie? Besides, I believe Mad Dog and Injun Bill killed the man and somehow framed me, but proving it is another story because they are both dead."

"So, you did kill Injun Bill then?" Dane poured himself another cup of coffee, all the while watching Nikki. Her proud face fell into grief, her eyes faraway, and her shoulders slumped in dejection.

"What happened, Nikki? There is something you're not telling me."

Instead of answering him directly, she asked, "When did you lose our trail?"

"Your…" Dane stopped, searching the bottomless eyes, seeing despair in their depths he did not understand.

"After our time with the Cheyenne when I brought you LeeAnn, I had to go back to Kansas. I picked up your trail near Red Town." Watching her, he noticed something different in her expression and it prompted him to ask, "Where is LeeAnn anyway?"

Nikki unraveled her arms from around her knees, drew a breath, then looked down into the dark liquid of her cooling coffee. She was stalling, stalling to keep from having to tell him the full story, not knowing if she could talk about LeeAnn. Hesitantly, she took her coffee cup and moved toward the fire to refill it.

Dane put his hand near the coffeepot handle, stopping her. "Nikki?"

With a ragged sigh, she sat back on her haunches while keeping her focus on the dancing flames of the fire. "LeeAnn is dead."

Stunned, he stared at her, a million questions and curses forming on his lips. He took a deep breath to calm himself. "You have some explaining to do."

This was the part she had been dreading. The wounds of losing LeeAnn still had not healed. Even torturing the outlaws for what they had done to her, her sister, and the other children could not compensate for her losses.

Keep it short and simple, she berated herself before launching into her story. "We had run onto a homestead while we were crossing the mountains. It had snowed midmorning. That's when we noticed smoke coming from the chimney, but there were no footprints in the snow. While we watched the place, Toad came out of the cabin with a catalog under his arm."

Nikki became detached as she explained the events leading up to LeeAnn's death, her low voice droning in dull monosyllables.

She glanced up at him, paused, and took a deep breath before finishing, "We had left Kissa and LeeAnn in hiding. Somehow, LeeAnn must have gone into the cabin and taken a rag doll. We had already taken precautions by boiling our clothes and bathing in the freezing river before we went into camp. I found LeeAnn already bedded for the night, but when I went to join her, I found her clutching the doll. She came down with scarlet fever not long afterwards and was too ill to move, so we set up camp. I went to Fairplay to get supplies, and there I ran into Mad Dog and Injun Bill." She shrugged helplessly. He already knew part of her story.

"I made it back to LeeAnn and my friends during a blizzard. We knew then we were snowed in for the winter. Apparently, Mad Dog informed Mason and they followed us. We were bringing down logs to build a cabin and found we needed Kissa and her horse to help us dislodge one of the fallen trees. It had been over a month since I had been in Fairplay, and it had snowed several times, but somehow, they found us. It was the only time we ever left LeeAnn by herself. Mason, Mad Dog, Injun Bill, and Smith came into our camp while we were gone."

Throwing the remains of her coffee into the fire, a hardness crossed her face. Gathering some semblance of control, she lifted hard eyes to Dane's. "Mad Dog despoiled LeeAnn, but LeeAnn died from a weak heart while he held her with a knife against her throat. They set fire to our camp. They destroyed everything, even stole our food and our pack horses, and left us there to die."

Rising to his feet, Dane moved to her side, wanting to pull her in his arms and comfort her. The hard face she turned to him, and the coldness of her eyes stopped him from reaching out for her. He swallowed hard, past the lump forming in his throat.

Nikki dropped her gaze to the ground, her voice coming out low and pain ridden. "We had promised each other if LeeAnn survived the scarlet fever, we would find a home to raise her."

The iciness gone; she momentarily lifted hurt-filled eyes to his. "We promised to forget about the outlaws, Dane, and become mothers to her."

Slipping his arms around her, Dane pulled her close, nuzzling her soft hair, his heart sympathizing for the distraught woman. "It's all right to cry," he whispered in her hair.

She pulled away from him, distress edging her voice, "I would cry if I could. I would give anything just to be able to cry."

Cupping her cheek in his hand, his own eyes mirroring the anguish in hers, he remembered long ago when Tawnie had asked him if Nikki had cried. Had she been unable to cry after all this time? With his thumb, he caressed the side of her face. He needed more information, yet it did not seem proper to bring up his questions now.

Nikki leaned her cheek against his hand, needing, wanting a little comfort. Closing her eyes a moment, she savored his strong hand against her cheek, but she knew he deserved to know the rest of the story before she gave into his comforting presence.

Placing her hand on top of his, she drew his hand away from her face and held it in her lap while staring deep into his eyes, watching how her story affected him. "I killed Smith when we surrounded the camp. Ginger captured Injun Bill and brought him back to camp. Five or six men surrounded our camp, but we did not know some of them. They were apparently new recruits. Those animals killed our daughter, and we were so angry and hurt we…" She paused, swallowed, then finished, "lost everything human about us."

Dane heard her words, her short version of the story settling a question he and his posse had when they ran onto a burned-out camp and found three bodies. Clearing his throat, he described what they found. "We found your camp, but we didn't know it was yours. We found one man's partial remains spread eagle and upside down between two trees. It looked like he had been tortured. We thought maybe Indians had found them."

Breaking her eyes from his inquiring ones, Nikki turned her attention back to the fire while he finished,

"One had a hole in his head. We suspected he had been shot. The other body appeared to have been shot in the gut. It looked like he had tried to pull himself over the stump of a tree. He was face down over the trunk and a large branch appeared to have been jammed up his rectum. His pants were down around his feet."

Nikki jerked her eyes back to his, surprise widening them.

"So, you didn't know about that one, huh?" He watched her eyes turn from surprise to introspection, a light dawning in her eyes. "Tell me what happened, Nikki?"

She could not tell him because she was only guessing who could have done something so bizarre. Hypothetically, Kissa had disappeared to find *Heoohtato* and was gone a long time, long enough for Nikki to ready LeeAnn's body for burial, then find and treat *Heoohtato* herself.

Surely not! Not Kissa! But then memories also came back of the outlaw biting Kissa on her butt cheek and then the horrible anal assault her sister, Kallie, had experienced. "I do not know who could have done it, Dane. I know I shot Smith when I came back to the camp after hearing gunfire. We saw each other at the same time, and I know I hit him. I never went back to check if he was dead because my thoughts were only on getting to LeeAnn. Tawnie said she shot one between the eyes, and you already know about Injun Bill."

For some reason, she refused to tell him about her confrontation with Mason and about LeeAnn speaking her first words since the day she lost her voice. Her words, '*Momma Nikki*' were too precious to repeat, and it filled her soul with loss and regret.

"Who did the rest of it, Nikki?" Dane prompted.

Nikki shook her head, refusing to answer. "I do not know for sure. I only suspect, and I will not tell you whom I suspect."

Chapter 10
Tears Mend the Heart

THE CHITTERING OF SQUIRRELS AND BIRD song awoke Nikki. Unwilling to face the new day, she rolled over and came face to face with Dane. Her eyes widened and his silver-blue eyes crinkled with his smile. Rising enough to lean on his hand and elbow, he faced her.

"Good morning," he said, his smile teasing and leaning toward her.

"I do not remember asking you to sleep next to me." Nikki sat straight up, angry with his presumption.

"A bit touchy this morning, Dark Angel?" He languidly rolled over onto his back, clasped his hands behind his head, and crossed his ankles, an amused smile playing about his lips.

Ignoring him, she rose to her feet, then rolled her bedroll. "I need to see about my dog."

"Not until I've checked him first." Dane did not move, and his amusement heightened when she glared down at him, angrily tapping her toe against the sandy ground.

"Well?" she queried, her brow lifting. "I would like to check him now."

"Tsk, tsk, tsk." Dane made the noises with his tongue, hoping to bring a smile to her lips, but his teasing fell short—the angry tapping of her foot had not ceased.

His humor short-lived, he growled, "Put the coffee on, Nikki, while I check your dog."

"How long do we need to keep him tied?" Nikki asked, waiting for Dane to rise from his bed. In her mind, it was cruel to keep the animal restrained. Like her, her dog needed his freedom.

"About a week, then we'll know for sure. So, we might as well settle in and get to know each other a little better." His eyebrow lifted suggestively. When she did not respond, he slowly rose and took time to arrange his bedroll in a perfect roll before he turned back toward her.

"Why, Dane? You already have a low opinion of me, so why would you want to know me a little better?" she asked him when he rose with his bedroll tucked underneath his arm and glanced at her.

Dane shrugged. Their conversation had kept him awake most of the night and he needed to clarify a few points. "I need for you to remember who might have seen you in Fairplay."

"Besides the sheriff, there was a customer in the general store paying out when I entered. Other than that, I do not remember. But why are we talking about this now?"

The angry tapping of her foot stopping, she stood motionless, watching him squat in front of the dying fire and add more wood. "What will happen if they find me guilty, Dane?"

"They'll probably send you to prison for the rest of your life or hang you, though I don't think it will ever happen since you are a woman." Holding a log over the fire, Dane stopped long enough to meet her eyes.

"Dane, I did not kill Mr. Gransom. You must believe me."

"For some reason, I do believe you, Nikki."

THE WEEK WENT BY, AND NIKKI remained silent, speaking very little, and with her withdrawal, Dane did little more than keep the fire going, take care of the animals, and check on *Heoohtato*. She did her part by cooking their meals, her coldness toward him insuring he would not try to take advantage of the situation.

Her bed was cold at night, but she needed the coldness to keep her sanity. There was too much between them, and his determination to take her to Fairplay as a fugitive from the law, kept them at a distance. It bothered her and sent her stomach fluttering in alarm—she needed to keep her original plan and turn herself in, not be forced by the Deputy U.S. Marshall.

Setting a fresh pot of coffee on the fire, she squatted in front of it, her mind questing, searching for answers.

Dane entered the campsite, finding her in the same position. "Coffee ready?"

Slowly shaking her head, she whispered, "Let me turn myself in. I did nothing wrong, and I need to be able to turn myself in so I can prove I have nothing to hide."

"Can't do it," he replied, sitting beside her. "You're wanted for murder, and my job is to take you in."

Nikki turned toward him, and Dane was taken aback by the fear shimmering in her eyes.

"I'll take you in, Dark Angel, but I will allow you to turn yourself in without me holding a gun on you or tying your hands. Will that help?"

Without answering, Nikki queried, "What if they find

me guilty for something I did not do?"

Fear trembled her words, and he turned toward her, wanting to reach out and reassure her, but there was no guarantee he could give her. "If what you say is true, I don't see how they can find you guilty, but if the court does, I will leave immediately to seek a pardon for you."

As the week ended, Nikki decided her dog had to be free of the dreaded rabies. Rising and putting away her bedroll, she walked toward the dog, intent on releasing him. *Heoohtato* lifted his massive head and growled at her. "*Heoohtato?*"

Dane followed her and planted his arm in front of her to stop her advance while drawing his pistol with his free hand. Growling, the dog ran toward them, his expression fierce and his eyes wild. He lunged at them, but the rope around his neck jerked him upright before he fell back to the ground, drool and foam covering its mouth.

Dane lifted the pistol and aimed, but before he could shoot, Nikki pushed his arm downward.

"No, Dane. *Heoohtato* is my dog. I will take care of him." A bleak expression on her face, Nikki took his pistol and aimed at the dog's head. "I am sorry, boy," she cried, pulling the trigger.

The only sound was the report of the pistol and the big dog dropping to the ground. *Heoohtato* lay motionless. With an anguished cry, Nikki fell to her knees, dropping her hand and the pistol beside her on the ground. Her dog, the last of her family, was now dead with the rest.

Tears, the first tears since her family was killed, moistened her eyes. Lowering her head almost to her chest, the tears flowed faster, coming so fast they quickly wet her shirtfront. Sobs so deep it felt like it was pulling her insides outward, racked her slender frame. The dam had finally broken, coming so fast she could barely catch her breath.

Something within Dane broke too seeing the proud, determined woman bested by her tears. He knelt beside her and enclosed her in his arms. No matter how long he lived or what he had seen in life, nothing would ever affect him like her tears were doing now. Something within him realized she had seen more than any human should. He also realized he had no right to judge or condemn her. Tears marred his own eyes while her whole frame shook within his arms. "My Dark Angel," he murmured against her hair.

Nikki cried until she hiccupped in great sobs, so tired and distraught, she could not see the gentle face in front of her.

Dane picked her up, cradled her within his arms and carried her to the campsite. Tenderly, he laid her in the grass and smoothed her hair from her face before he laid down beside her, gathering her against him, tenderly holding her until she cried herself to sleep.

Nikki awoke the next morning with eyes so red and swollen she could barely see out of them. She sat straight up and stared in the direction where her dog had been. The animal and the rope were gone.

With a muffled sob, she rose from the bedroll, packed it away, then walked toward the river. She loosened the braided strands of her hair and shook the long mass free. Bending over, she slipped off her moccasins. Her shirt and pants soon followed. She waded to the big boulder along the river's edge and sat in the swirling pool.

Dipping her fingers along the sandy bottom, she

brought her hands up and watched the wet sand drip through between her fingers. With another sob, she scrubbed her body, thinking somehow the sand could cleanse her. She scrubbed until her skin was too sore to touch.

Tears flowed down her cheeks in a continuous river even though she thought she had cried all her tears last night. Repeatedly, she slipped under the water and stayed until she came up gasping for air.

The tears finally stopped, and some measure of calmness swept over her. Letting her arms float out beside her, she closed her eyes and lifted her face to the rising warmth of the sun.

Dane watched Nikki leave the camp and her almost maddening administrations of cleansing herself. His heart skipped several beats when she slipped underwater and did not come up for air after what seemed forever. When she finally calmed, he allowed her the time to collect herself before he interrupted her. "It's time to go, Nikki."

Nikki opened her eyes and turned a tired, swollen face toward him. "I am scared, Dane," she said so softly he almost did not hear.

He thought he would never hear her say those words, and it touched another chord within him. He waded through the water, knelt beside her, and cupped her face with his hands. "Don't be, Nikki. I will be right here beside you. If you did not kill Gransom, then the court will set you free."

"You still do not believe me, do you?"

Dane shifted his eyes from hers before he met them again. "I believe you."

With her tears moistening and shining in her sky-blue

eyes, Dane caught his breath against the lost quality reflected there and pulled her into his arms.

Tenderly, softly, he kissed Nikki until she wrapped her arms around him, returning his kiss, wondering if it would be her last. Through her tears, she cried, "Make love to me, Dane. Please love me."

Dane deepened the kiss, her words reminding him of two other times and places she had cried the same words. Standing, he lifted her with him, then picked her up in his arms and carried her to the camp.

He left her momentarily to spread a bedroll, then quickly undressed until he stood naked. Pressing his warm flesh to her cold form, he lowered his mouth to hers and swept short, tender kisses along her lips.

Her arms slipped around him, and her sigh whispered across his lips. In a fluid motion, they lowered to their knees and explored each other before lying on the bedroll. With his body positioned over hers, he entered her, crying, "I love you, Nikki. No matter what has happened or will happen, I will always love you."

NIKKI STOOD IN FRONT OF THE TABLE while the judge sternly looked down at her from the bench above. Her heart beat so hard, her chest hurt. An odd ringing of her ears blurred her hearing and a sense of unreality swept over her. The blue dress Dane had bought her, bound her in ways she had long since forgotten.

"Miss Pride, the Court has heard evidence on how you went after the notorious Mason Gang and how you tortured some of their members to death. It has been determined you probably had accomplices, but it has not been firmly established. Whether the Court agrees with your method or not is not an issue of this Court today. However, in view of your ferocity toward the Mason gang, this Court has determined you had the skill and the devious mindset to commit such a heinous crime as was committed toward John Gransom of Fairplay. It also shows this Court you lack concern for human dignity."

"This Court agreed with Mr. Travis you would receive a fairer trial here in Canon City than in Fairplay since there have been rumors of a vigilante committee being formed to carry out your execution no matter what the Court decides."

"The court sympathizes with the murder of your family, but nevertheless, this Court has listened to the Deputy U.S. Marshal testify to the condition of the mutilated bodies he found after you killed the Mason gang members. He also stated you admitted to killing and torturing those men, though he stated you did not admit to the murder of John Gransom."

"This court listened to testimony from the miners who found three bodies about twenty miles from Fairplay and the conditions of their bodies. The man tied between evergreen trees, as stated, was mutilated in ways showing he had no fingers, toes, ears, or the equipment making a man different from a woman. Deputy U.S. Marshal Dane Travis also identified the partially burnt arrows found along with the mutilated bodies. Whether those men were wanted dead or alive, no one deserves such a vicious death."

"This court has determined you were seen going into the General Store by Sheriff Watkins. We heard several people's testimony seeing John Gransom load your pack animals outside the store and then reenter the establishment. Soon afterwards, you were seen riding fast out of town by Joe Louis who stopped you and told you to slow down."

"By testimony and presumption, this Court offers a scenario of the time between Mr. Gransom loading your pack animal and your leaving town. It is determined after Mr. Gransom loaded your animal and went back into the store, he turned his back to you, at which time you brutally stabbed him in the back several times. Surprised, he turned toward you, and you stabbed him in the stomach whereupon he pulled your bear claw necklace from your neck. Instead of letting the man die with some dignity, you proceeded to cut off both his ears and placed them on his cheeks. Afterwards, the bloody water in the wash basin behind the counter showed you proceeded to wash your hands and wipe the remaining blood on a new bolt of material. Then, you took the money from the cash register and left town in a hurry."

"Miss Pride, I wish to refer to the great respect men in our community have for the fairer sex, but you represent the worst in man and woman combined. Mr. Gransom had been a respected and upright member of the Fairplay community for years. The crime toward him was brutal beyond measure. In view of the evidence, though circumstantial, the jury has found you guilty of the murder of John Gransom. You will have eight months to think about your deeds and repent before you are hung by the neck until dead."

Blackness sweeping along her vision, Nikki grabbed the top of the table, her knees weakening so much she nearly fell. Her mind refused to function, refused to accept the verdict. She did not resist the deputy who pulled her arms behind her back and cuffed her wrists together. Unable to think or feel, she walked in front of the deputy to her cell. The door slammed shut behind her.

HIS HEART PAINFULLY THUMPING IN HIS CHEST, Dane waited for the deputy to unlock the cell door. His worse fears realized, he drew in a shuddering breath, uneasiness and worry deepening the lines of his face.

Nikki sat on the edge of the cot, staring straight ahead. With the door opening, he was quickly by her side, his voice stunned with reaction. "Nikki, I never thought they would find you guilty, much less sentence you to hang. I'm leaving right now for Denver to see if I can get you a pardon. Your sentence is set for the later part of June."

Nikki did not move a muscle nor acknowledge him. "After I get you a pardon, we can go to Texas or wherever you wish and start over. We can go to my ranch. It doesn't matter to me. I want you here by my side as my wife." When she did not move or look at him, he cleared his throat.

Nikki lifted hopeless eyes to his, moving for the first time. "I am your wife, Dane, and you testified against me anyway. You forced me here knowing because of the Indian blood running through my veins, I did not have a right to a fair trial. Was not my testimony disregarded, allowing Washburn to go free? No matter what I do, I am damned by your white man laws because of my blood, laws you are determined to adhere to."

Dane drew in a sharp breath, his stomach knotting. "I knew you had no chance if your true blood was known. I really believed this way you had a chance. And Nikki," he whispered, moving toward her, his gut clenching even tighter, "I could not prove our marriage. We have never lived together, and there were too many people to testify to that fact."

"You still testified against me," she softly reminded him. Lowering her gaze to the floor, she withdrew even deeper within herself. "I did not kill him."

"I believe you, Nikki, or I wouldn't try to get you a pardon."

In a faraway cry, she repeated, "I did not kill him, Dane, but they convicted me because of the bear claw necklace. The miner who stated he stopped me on my mad rush out of town had no way of knowing Mr. Gransom was holding off Mad Dog and Injun Bill to give me a head start."

"Nikki, God, what do I say." Dane ran his fingers through his hair. Not a tear wet her eyes, just lost hopelessness dulling the sky-blue orbs. "I never believed they would hang a woman. The conviction was because of your mutilation of Injun Bill, Mason, and Mad Dog."

He grabbed her shoulders, wanting to shake her, anything to evoke some type of feeling within her. "They couldn't let a woman who could torture someone like that to live."

"They were wanted dead or alive," Nikki cried, shrugging his hands from her. "You told them what the outlaws had done. You also told them you recognized the bear claw necklace. You told them about the men in the draw and Mad Dog. You told them you knew I had killed."

"I told the truth, Dark Angel."

Nikki shook her head, unwilling to accept his answer. "You do not know the truth, Dane, and because you do not know, I am convicted of a crime I did not commit."

"Don't give up. I will get a pardon for you. Just don't give up on me. If only you had listened to me and let me take care of the Mason outfit, none of this would have happened."

"How many more people, how many more children had to die before you caught up with them, Dane? We stopped it before you could have, and you know it." She stood, then turned to face him, her eyes accusing.

"You did it with too much savagery. You succeeded in scaring the male population, and they cannot allow you to live now." A streak of frightened pain flashed in her eyes and deepened the guilt eating at his heart. Dane stood with her and lifted his arms toward her, desperately wanting to hold her close.

She backed away, refusing his offer of comfort. Dropping his arms, he stood stock still. A muscle jerked in his hard jaw and his silver-blue eyes were overcast by his love, duty and now failure to protect the woman he loved.

The age-old battle raged within him: his need to hold and comfort her, his reaction of inadequacy when it came to her—how she could unman him yet make him more than a man; the complicated woman she was—gentle yet unyielding, soft yet hard, woman yet warrior, everything that was her paradoxical and multifarious self.

How could Dane tell her his heart broke with each word he spoke, how he prayed to be able to speak falsely, but the proud, honest part of him would let no falsehood pass his lips? He had truthfulness beat into him from his childhood and through the Arapaho who adopted him. Now he damned that part of his personality until he felt condemned.

If he could give his life for hers, he would. If he had the power to change past events, he would. Instead, he stood before her like an inadequate fool with no power to help her, knowing his testimony was the cause of him losing the most precious thing in his life—her.

Dane wanted to hold her, to love her one last time, but Nikki had already closed herself from him, and blamed him for her misdeeds. Hot tears formed in his eyes; ragged breath filled his lungs until he thought it would burst through the cavity for he believed he *was* responsible for her condemnation. "I'm leaving in the morning. I have eight months to get you a pardon. Don't do anything stupid before I get back. Promise me, Nikki."

Wanting to cry with the fear eating at her heart, Nikki looked into his eyes. What could she do anyway? "I will not do anything stupid, Dane."

She grabbed his arm, her fingers digging into his flesh. "Take all my things to the Nelson ranch and tell my friends what has happened. I want them to have my things, and I want them to know why I did not make it there."

"Nikki, we have more important things to consider."

"No, please. I am asking you to deliver my things to them. They have a right to know." Nikki dropped her hands and stared at the floor, withdrawing within herself and therefore closing off herself from him.

Sighing, he ached to hold her in his arms, to comfort and protect her, but she was right, it was his testimony condemning her. He fought the urge to enfold her against him, knowing she would refuse him.

Wordless, he tapped his hat against his leg. Nodding once, he yelled for the deputy. He turned back around to her after the deputy let him outside of the cell. "I promise I will be back, and I will deliver the message to your friends."

THE STEADY RAP-TAP-TAP OF A HAMMER and the carnival-like sounds beat a jarring tattoo along her nerve endings and pounded through her blood. Through the bars of the jail, Nikki watched a man test the trapdoor of the gallows. Her throat convulsively cramping, she swallowed hard against the nausea churning her stomach.

She tore her gaze away from the disturbing scene to watch people in their Sunday-go-to-meetin' clothes mill around the dirt street. Sounds of heavy traffic mingled with the murmur of voices and excited laughter as people from hundreds of miles around came to witness a woman hanged. The sounds filled her head until they blurred and dulled into one of her bizarre nightmares, refusing to go away.

"Someone to see you."

Nikki resisted turning around when metal grated against metal and the door creaked open. Evenly paced footsteps sounded on the stone floor and stopped. The cell door clanged shut, then jangling keys and the shuffling footsteps of the sheriff resounded throughout the barren cell until the sound of another door opened and closed at the other end of the corridor.

Lifting her hands to the window bars, her grip turning her knuckles white, she closed her eyes and sighed.

She knew the sound of those footsteps better than she knew the beat of her own heart. Everything about her visitor touched places in her she wished would remain dead and buried.

His body heat bathed her back and his soft breath moved the short hairs along her neck, causing chills to race along her spine. The clean fragrance of bay rum drifted in the heat to tease her heightened senses. *One Above, help me hide my weakness!*

Her throat constricting, she forced past stiff lips the question uppermost in her mind. "Did you get the pardon?"

The silence lengthened between them while she waited for his answer. Tears stung her eyes, and she blinked them back. *I will not let him see me cry or know how frightened I am!*

Rapid gunfire followed seconds later by fast galloping, rent the numb silence between them. A fly buzzed around her head with maddening persistence. Perspiration trickled between the cleavage of her breast, and she shivered even though it was over one hundred degrees outside. A burst of laughter from the front of the jail made her realize just how little anyone cared about her plight.

Blinking back stinging tears, she forced her fingers free from the hot metal and turned to face her tormentor, her shadow, her nemesis, her love. More lines fanned out from his eyes than when she had last seen him, and it was in their piercing silver-blue depths she received her answer.

A harsh, ragged breath rattled her chest. An errant tear slipped down her cheek. She dashed it away, straightened her shoulders, and defiantly met his pitying eyes. "Damn your laws, Dane. Let my ignoble death plague you until your dying day."

"Don't!" Dane implored, taking a single step toward her, then stopped dead in his tracks. "I've done all I can. We both knew it could end this way." He reached forward to caress her cheek, but she rebelliously lifted her chin. Clenching his hand into a fist, he dropped it to squeeze the rim of his hat between nervous fingers.

Nikki shook her head in denial. "How can it end this way? I did not kill Mr. Gransom." The tears misting her eyes caused his form to waver in front of her. She inhaled deeply to gather her rampant emotions in some semblance of control, but his next words nearly snapped the thin thread binding her hard-won resolve.

"Let me hold you close to my heart."

Nikki's shoulders bowed with the impact of his loving, soft-spoken words, and every fiber of her being gravitated toward the strong length of him. With a muttered sob, she turned away and stared blindly at the floor.

A cockroach ran past her foot, and she ground its life out underneath her moccasin. She spoke in low undertones. "I have become like a cockroach—dirty, dreaded, and misunderstood. They will snuff out my life just like I did to this cockroach. Right or wrong, I am not sorry for taking vengeance against those animals. It is your love that's destroying me."

"Don't do this!" Dane begged. "Love is the only right thing passing between us."

"Right thing?" Nikki scorned, turning sharply on her heel to meet his eyes with contempt. "Your love is what condemned me to hang. It is your testimony putting the noose around my neck. Is that love? *Where does your duty end and your love begin?* I curse the day you rode into my life!"

Dane stood still, a muscle jerking in his hard jaw, his silver-blue eyes overcast by his love, duty, and failure. "It could have been different, Dark Angel. We could have done it differently, and you would not be waiting for the hangman to come for you."

Nikki tugged at the uncomfortable blue sleeves of her dress, then tugged at the tight neckline where the ruffles chaffed her skin. If she noticed his anguish, she ignored it. "Could have, would have, what if—they are all words and have no meaning for me now. I did what I thought was right. I cannot change the past." *Nor would I if I had the chance*, she added in silence.

She turned to stare at the scenery through the broken vision of the steel bars, her throat growing tighter with each passing moment. "Everything is done, and I paid the price several times. This is just the icing on the cake, something to satisfy men's perverted sense of justice."

Nikki spun around toward him, leveling him with her strange ice-blue eyes. "Your sense of justice, Marshal."

Arms folded tight underneath her breasts, she fought to keep her breathing under control. The long length of her hair lay heavy against her back, her head pounded, and her eyes burned from holding back tears. Nikki kept her face defiant, determined he would not see her break. "Leave town, Marshal. I do not want your face to be the last one I see when I hang."

"I wish…

"Damn you, leave me! You have completed your duty." Nikki caught a ragged breath, ignoring the tears forming in her eyes.

"Go! I cannot stand for you to touch me, Marshal. I will fall apart if you do." Wanting to take back the last sentence, she wanted even more to erase the whine and uncertainty wavering her words.

Dane dropped his arms at his side when she turned from him to stare out the barred window. "Goodbye, Dark Angel."

Nikki heard him call for the sheriff, and to keep from turning around, she grabbed the bars of the window and laid her forehead against the stone. *One Above, help me!* She wanted to call him back, fall into his arms, and capture his love; anything to hold at bay the terror clutching at her breasts so hard, she felt faint. Only he could fulfill this painful yearning; this need to be close to another human being before the hangman did his duty. Only he could touch this cold, hard stone called a heart within her. Yet, she believed he had sold her out, and *it was his testimony that condemned her.*

Hatred rose in her throat, the bile acidic and burning. Nikki wanted to cry out, *why did you do this to me? Why did you torture me with thoughts of freedom, hopes of a pardon, and dreams of a normal life?* But what was the use? What was the purpose? Her life was over, *and* she had accomplished what she set out to do, but she had not done the crime for which she was sentenced to be hanged.

The door grated open, and she heard him walk out of her life, leaving her to her misery.

Things could have been different, should have been different, Nikki thought, but refused to daydream about the *what ifs.* She was going to die a dishonorable death, a death few women ever experienced. The dying part did not bother her. She had lived with the knowledge nearly all her life. It was the way she was going to die disturbing her.

Haunted voices and memories plaguing Nikki, she

forced them back, refusing to think about how happiness had eluded her. The desire to fall into a corner and crouch there weakened her knees.

Prayers formed on her lips, and the weight of lifetimes bowed her slender shoulders. *One Above, strengthen me, hardened my heart once again, take this fear from me, and give me the courage to face my destiny. Let me meet my ancestors proudly.*

With an effort, Nikki turned from the window and walked toward the narrow cot against the stone-grey wall. *It will not be long now. I must ready myself,* she thought, retrieving the objects the sheriff had allowed her to keep.

She had already refused the Bible man who had come to her cell earlier. She would meet her Maker on her terms, her own beliefs. With trembling hands, she smoothed the contents on the scratchy blanket.

They may make me wear a dress to my hanging, but they cannot make me forego the rest of it, Nikki decided, brushing the long length of her hair. With trembling hands, she tied a red strip of material with the red wolf tail around her forehead, then a red piece of satin material around her waist. She fingered the locket suspended between her breasts, then changed her mind about leaving it to one of her friends. It had no meaning to them, but to her, it proved she was white, too, going to a white man's justice.

Facing east, Nikki lifted her eyes toward the cracked ceiling, and, in a low, husky voice, sang her death song. The eerie sounds reverberated through the small cell and drifted out the window. Her voice rising and falling, deepening and lightening, full of the bittersweetness of life and death, she sang in words and phrases only she understood. The song ended on a crying, coyote-like note.

Nikki lifted her arms toward the window and stared at her scarred wrists below the tight sleeves of the dress. "I have no knife to offer my blood to you, *Heammawihio*. Forgive me. Shame fills me to die this way instead of the way of a warrior. Perhaps I am wrong to sing my death song."

The sound of death's footsteps scraped against the stone floor. Only after he spoke did she lower her arms.

"It's time."

The keys jangled, then grated in the lock. The sheriff swung open the door but did not meet her eyes. She looked him over from head to toe, imprinting the image of him to carry with her. Apparently, he thought she would not try to escape because he came by himself, his gun still holstered, his aged brown eyes showing respect yet resignation.

She straightened her shoulders and held her head proudly, determined these white people's depraved form of justice would not bow her. Her legs a bit unsteady, she stepped in front of the sheriff and flinched slightly when he pulled her wrists behind her back. The harsh act of the cold metal of the handcuffs clamping around her wrists contrasted sharply with the touch on her elbow.

"Come along, Ma'am," he respectfully ordered, guiding her toward the door of her cell.

Each step took an eternity, yet not long enough. They passed down the short corridor into an office containing a case filled with various weapons, a paper-strewn desk, a pot-bellied stove, and three ladder-back chairs. The windows were so dirty, the forms outside the office were barely distinguishable. She waited while he opened the door, then he took her elbow in his rough hand to guide her to the gallows at the end of the street.

The clamoring noise stopped. People lining the street turned all at once to stare at her. Nikki suppressed the hysterical desire to giggle. *Do they honor me with their silence or condemn me?*

The sidewalk boards creaked underneath their feet, hers making no sound, the sheriff's clunking with each step. He led her down the steps onto the street where the kicked-up dirt swirled around their feet, then rose in a gush of wind. People separated and opened a path for the death march, their faces and eyes a mixture of sadness, elation, dumbfoundness.

With eyes so dry they burned, she stared straight ahead, neither looking to the right nor left. The summer sun beat down on her in shimmering, heat-filled rays, and she tilted her face toward it. Horses snorted and shuffled, but the birds were strangely silent. Wind blew dirt in swirling dust devils and a sign creaked. Everything about the day was unearthly, something from a nightmare.

The big, heavy-set man standing at the top of the gallows looked down at her with compassion. That one look nearly undid her determination not to show fear. Taking a deep, shaky breath, she put her foot on the first step of the gallows, counting each one—one, two, three, four, five, six on up to thirteen. Thirteen steps, she almost wanted to laugh.

Nikki paused at the top to glance at the crowd staring up at her: miners, roughened cowboys, neatly dressed businessmen, women, and children. Ah yes, she was the entertainment today. She flashed a brilliant smile at the crowd, a small measure of perverse pleasure filling her with their collective intake of breath and the flutter of conversation before it suddenly died.

One, two, three, four more steps and she stood in front of the hangman. He took her elbow to position her in front of the hangman's knotted rope. "I will put a hood over your head, ma'am."

His voice sounded gentle, and it surprised her. "No hood. Just make sure you adjust the noose so it will snap my neck neat and clean," she answered in quiet monotones.

"Yes'am, I'll do my best." He lowered the noose around her neck, then gently lifted the heavy length of her hair over the rope.

Her eyes widened, then changed to normal. She barely heard the sheriff ask if she had anything to say. Glancing around the sea of faces staring up at her, she looked for the marshal but did not see him. Her eyes focused on a small girl clutching her mother's hand and staring up at her with wide, frightened eyes, not comprehending what was happening.

Gentleness filled her while memories overwhelmed her, coming so fast she had trouble keeping up with them, and she experienced again all the emotions seemingly for the first time. A fleeting smile crossing her firm mouth, she lifted her eyes toward the noon sun. Again, she sang her death song in an eerie, melodious voice, the words rising and falling with each beat of her heart.

Her eyes were uplifted toward the sun, and a glint caught her eye across the street. Nikki barely looked toward it, but the sight of red hair caught her attention. Ginger slightly nodded in her direction and aimed the rifle toward her.

A fleeting ray of hope entered her heart, then

disappeared. She heard the preacher intone, "May God have mercy on your soul," before the trapdoor gave way underneath her feet.

Chapter 11
Weep This Heart of Mine

THE ROPE TIGHTENED AROUND HER THROAT with a yank, then released. She fell downward, hearing at the same time the report of a rifle. Her feet landed hard against a wooden surface, and she fell to her knees, pitching forward and hitting her face against the bottom of the wagon. A *hi ya!* sounded and the floor lurched underneath her, tossing her about like a rag doll with each roll of the wagon bed.

Soft hands steadied her against the pitching wagon and the rope tugged, then loosened before being slipped over her head. Gentle hands helped her roll over onto her side, and Kissa's beloved face bent over her before she grabbed her shoulders to help her into a sitting position. "Kissa!"

Tears shining in her eyes, Kissa helped her into an upright position, a difficult feat in the pitching wagon. Hugging Nikki tightly, Kissa gently asked, "You didn't think we would let you hang, did you? We know you didn't kill Mr. Gransom."

Struggling against the metal handcuffs while everything around her swiftly passed by in a blur, Nikki did not answer. When the sheriff came to get her, he had snapped the cuffs loosely around her wrists. Squeezing her hands small as possible, Nikki slipped one wrist from the cuff, then the other. After throwing the handcuffs toward the rapidly receding road, she hugged Kissa back, too happy to comment. Glancing over her shoulder, she saw Tawnie's broad back.

Tawnie turned around and grinned at her. "Hell, Nikki, ya almost lost your head. I'm dang glad the redhead is as good of a crack shot as she's always a braggin'."

"I am happy to see you too," Nikki laughed with the relief flooding her body.

"Well, dang it, Nikki, ya really didna think we'd let ya hang? I'm just glad ya sent the marshal with your thangs to us. Even though I don't know whut ya see in him, at least he told us whut happened. It gave us plenty of time to plan your escape. Sorry we didna get ya outta there afore now."

"You took an awful chance rescuing me. Now the posse will be looking for you too." Nikki climbed up on the seat beside Tawnie, wanting to hug the big woman.

"Don't worry 'bout it. We've got it all planned out. We'll lead the posse on a wild goose chase while ya get your behind outta the country. Your thangs are waitin' up ahead. Ginger drew a map to show ya where the horses are stationed to get ya outta the country and where ya can meet us in Mexico. We won't be long in joinin' ya."

"I do not know what to say except thank you."

"Heck, ya don't even have to say that. 'Sides, it's gonna take those miners and farmers a while to figure out just whut happened, and longer still to round up a posse. We'll be long gone by then and leadin' them in all different directions," Tawnie promised, directing the wagon toward a stand of trees and pulling the horses to a stop.

Jumping from the wagon, Tawnie waited only a

moment for Nikki to join her. "Your weapons are on the back of your horse, and your clothes and medicines are in the saddlebags."

With a quick gesture, Tawnie hugged Nikki, then backed off to give Kissa a moment to hug her. They separated quickly, every nerve ending twanging with the sound of horse hooves.

"It's Ginger," Kissa breathed in relief.

Ginger pulled on the reins, stopping the horse a few feet in front of them. She grabbed her rifle, then jumped from the horse to give Nikki a quick hug. "Go now, Nikki. Ride like the wind. We will meet you soon," she said, handing her the rifle.

Nikki slid the rifle in the boot on the back of her saddle, then gathered the long skirt between her legs and placed her foot in the stirrup. With a quick glance at her friends, she mounted, then fastened the gun belt around her waist. "Soon."

Tawnie barely let her finish the word before she slapped the horse on the hind quarter. "Hija!"

The three women watched Nikki race away, then turned and hurriedly unhitched the horses from the wagon. Slipping the harness from the animals, they slapped them across the hindquarters, sending them in different directions.

Ginger unsaddled the horse she had ridden and saddled a different horse. She sent the unsaddled horse in a different direction from the other horses.

Kissa cut a tree branch, erasing their footprints from the area before the three women jumped onto the waiting horses, taking off in different directions and dragging a tree branch behind their mounts to erase hoof prints as they disappeared into the landscape.

THE BLACK GELDING RESTLESSLY STOMPED, its ears twitching. The woman on its back gazed out over the panoramic scene of the Chisos Mountains, the wind blowing the extreme length of her raven black hair across her face and front like a wildly tossed tumbleweed. The red wolf tail connected to the back of her headband lifted and dropped in graceful, acrobatic movements with each gust.

The rugged terrain, in patterns of diversified rock formations, was painted in rich hues of buff, deep brown, amber, and lavender. Unconscious of the savage beauty, Nikki closed her eyes a moment in deep thought and reverence, an intense sadness crossing her delicate features. She opened her eyes, her longing gaze fastening on the haze-covered hills of Mexico just across the Rio Grande River.

The backwash of the setting sun bathed the earth, creating shadows from the hills and changing the appearance of the land. The spectacular orange-red backdrop silhouetted the woman and horse across the lowering sun with the moon trailing behind it to bathe the woman in ethereal beauty, emphasizing the melancholy on the deeply bronzed oval face. Her solid black shirt and pants, relieved only by the blood-red sash around her waist and the red headband across her brow, added to the illusion.

Sighing, she wiped an errant tear from her cheek, then turned her mount toward the low line of scraggly mesquite bushes a short distance away.

After unsaddling the gelding, Nikki rubbed it down with dried brown grass, for the day had been brutally hot and humid, and the animal was soaked with sweat. After caring for her horse, she lit a small fire, hoping the thin covering of mesquite trees would hide the flames.

Soul weary and bone tired, she leaned back against the saddle and stared at the tin plate of beef jerky cooked in beans. She had little appetite and ate for the sole reason of necessity, each chew more effort than she wished to expend.

After cleaning her dishes and putting them away, she removed the knife case of red wolf leather from around her waist, unbuckled her gun holster and laid it beside her knife. A small arsenal of weapons, including a rifle, an arrow pouch made of wolf leather and filled with black and red striped arrows, and a pure white bow with a leather grip were laid out neatly beside her bedroll.

With a long, weary sigh, she laid her head on the saddle and closed her burning eyes, forcing disturbing memories from her mind to concentrate on the rustling of the night creatures until sleep overtook her, enveloping her in its dreamless void.

Her eyes popping open, Nikki lay totally still. Something had awakened her. The fire beside her was grey ashes over the red glow of dying embers, revealing nothing.

"Sit up slow and easy," a deep, vibrant voice ordered her.

Relief mixed with anger washed over her. "Dane, put your gun away!"

"Sorry, my love, you're not to be trusted." He nodded

toward her weapons. "Shove them over here, and then very slowly take the knife out of your moccasin."

Dane watched the arch of her slender back as she shoved the weapons toward him, then eased a well-shaped leg encased in a richly adorned knee-high moccasin toward her stomach to remove the hidden knife.

After she complied, he eased the hammer forward and holstered his pistol. "You were sleeping the sleep of the dead, my love, but my cocking this hammer brought those lovely eyes of yours open. It's not like you to sleep so heavy. You should be more careful."

Perturbed with him as well as herself for being caught unaware, her face tightened, and her rounded chin stubbornly jutted outward toward him in defiance. "One more day and I will be across the border, Dane. One more lousy day! Why did you not let me go?"

Dane squatted in front of her, his face softening. "Ah, my dark angel, I can't do it, not even this close to the border."

"I will not go back with you. You will have to kill me first."

Even though her soft voice was even and devoid of the strong emotions she harbored, her words tore through him, angering him, and an erratic tick jumped in his cheek. "Damn you for a stubborn woman, Nikki Pride. Why did you have to escape? I was climbing the scaffold with a stay of execution in my hands. It came over the telegraph wire moments before your execution. I was ready to cut the rope myself before you could be hanged. Come back with me and I promise I'll go to Washington, D.C. this time to get a full pardon for you. For the love of God, all I'm asking is just have a little faith in me."

"Faith," Nikki spat contemptuously. "I gave you my faith once, but never again. I went back with you and stood trial. Remember, Dane? They condemned me to hang for a murder I did not commit. Do you know how I felt watching them build the gallows in front of my cell window? Do you know what a rope feels like around your neck? Do you know how it feels to have the trapdoor fall from underneath your feet? Ah, no, you do not. You promised to get me a full pardon then too."

She emphatically shook her head, the strands of shining ebony hair sweeping the ground behind her. "No, Dane. They are not going to hang me for something I did not do. They can all go to your white man's hell before I go back."

She sighed heavily, so tired of life's drama, wishing she could lay down and die, anything just to release her from loving a man who was determined to take her back to hang. And she did love him, she realized. It was something she had fought against for so long, and now it came back to slap her in the face.

Shrugging her shoulders to hide the emotions streaming through her, she calmly stated, "You would have never reached me in time to cut the rope. My neck would have been broken before you got there and I would be dead if Ginger had missed the rope with her shot."

His stomach lurched in sickening tightness for she seemed to read his thoughts the second the trapdoor fell underneath her. She was right, and he knew it, had admitted it when running up the steps to the gallows, holding the papers high in his hand, and yelling to stop the hanging—just seconds before she dropped from his sight.

She would never know how he made a commotion, drawing the people's attention to him instead of the fast-moving wagon. He kept the people's focus on him while the wagon raced out of town, and afterwards led the hastily arranged posse in the wrong direction to give her time to flee.

He had surmised she would probably head toward Mexico while he encouraged the posse to head for her Indian tribe, convincing them it was where she would hide. It was too easy, he thought, when watching the sheriff with eagle eyes, assuming from the sheriff's actions, he did not want to find her only to bring her back to hang.

And her friends were smart, way too smart for women, he thought, remembering how the horses' different trails seemed to wander back toward the mountains, putting credence to his words she was headed for the Northern Cheyenne.

Dane lifted his hand to caress her cheek, then limply dropped it when she jerked away from him. "My poor, stubborn, mixed-up dark angel. What brought us to this path?"

Ashamed of the tears sparkling in her eyes and afraid to fully think about the reasons, Nikki turned her face from his. "Please let me go. I can be across the border by tomorrow and no one will be the wiser."

She hated him in that instant, hated him for making her beg. One other time she had begged, had begged for Cari's life, and afterwards she swore never to plead with anyone again. Except, how many times had she begged the man crouched in front of her? She mentally shook her head, refusing to admit to those times.

Dane shook his head, disliking himself for the pain he was causing her, but his love for her did not stop him from doing his job. "I will know, Nikki. I'm doing my job."

"Can you not give an inch? Are you afraid you will break if you do?" Nikki asked him.

"I wouldn't be doing this in the first place if you had not gone after the Mason gang. Even if you were not guilty of the crime condemning you to hang, it would never have happened if you had stayed at home and let me take care of the outlaws. Now you are an escaped prisoner." The last sentence ended with deep sorrow.

Lifting her chin a notch, Nikki shook her hair back from her face. "I did not know my friends planned my rescue. And even if I had known, I would not have done it any different."

Leaning forward to catch her softly spoken words, the shadows starkly outlining the sharp planes of his face, he started to dispute her but decided against it. Her mixed heritage created a strong and unusual person, and no matter how much he tried, he failed to understand her motives or emotions. "If you weren't so damned hardheaded!"

"I am no different from you. I did what I believed was right." Dane rose to his feet with her, watching her every movement while she paced the small area in front of the fire. "It is not fair! I had every right to do what I did. If I had been a man, you and the others would have praised me for it, but because I am a woman, you men feel threatened."

Nikki turned on her heel to face him, her hands on her hips and her eyes begging him for an answer she did not have. "Why are there two sets of rules, one for men and one for women?"

Having no answer, he lamely responded, "You were found guilty, Nikki."

"The law!" she scornfully snarled. "The law could not prevent my loved ones from being murdered." She turned her back on him, hiding the tears springing to her eyes. "I have paid dearly for what I have done. The only thing left to lose is my life, and no hangman's noose is going to claim it." The deep, unhealed hurt she carried laced each word.

Dane stared helplessly at her back, wishing to tangle his hands in her silken hair. He wanted to comfort her, to heal the festering wounds of her heart, but the knowledge of his duty kept him rooted to the spot. Raising his eyes toward the star-sprinkled heavens and asking for forgiveness, he roughly stated, "I've got to tie you up."

Nikki spun around toward him. Even though he could not see the light blue color of her eyes, the depth of them chilled him to the bones. Her beautiful, but cold orbs held all the emotions of a trapped, injured animal: fear, mistrust, hate, disgust, and consuming hurt.

Speaking softly, the timbre of her voice carrying more ammunition than a fully equipped army, she accused, "It was always me, was it not? There were four of us, but you always came after me. Why, Dane?"

Dane remained motionless, his mouth refusing to put the explanation into words, much less form them in his own mind. Instead, he noticed the dejected droop of her shoulders combined with the proud tilt of her head and how the silken tresses flowed across her face like a curtain dropped after a spellbinding performance. He reached up and moved her silken hair from her face and caressed her cheek, unable to stop himself.

She drew back from him, her voice filled with sorrow, "The hate never stops, does it, Dane? I am marked, alone, and frightened, yet you keep on, determined to take me to an ignoble death."

Nikki cupped her hands and placed them together, fingers touching fingers, wrist touching wrist, then held them out to him in submission, her eyes lifted to his and filled with determination. "Try if you must, but I promise you, wild horses cannot drag me back. I will escape or you will be forced to kill me."

It was the age-old battle warring within him which began the first time he saw her. It was not easy for him to discard firm beliefs which had been entrenched through the years. His stern upbringing and stout beliefs were constantly being put to the test with her while duty and uprightness fought within his heart. Which would win in the end? His heart or beliefs? His duty or her? Shaking his head, more at himself than anything else, he grabbed a rope from his mount's saddle horn.

"You will see it through to the bitter end, will you not? I hope you can live with yourself after it is all over." Nikki did not resist when he jerked her arms behind her and tied her hands.

Gently, he pushed her to the ground and secured the rope connected to her wrists to around her ankles. He pulled the rope until her feet were about eight inches from her hands, his voice soft in the darkness and filled with regret, "Rest well, my love, we've a long journey ahead of us."

Nikki shook the lingering emotions away, realizing it was useless to go through it all again. Everything had been said too many times and the results were always the same. "At least put my robe on top of me or would you prefer I catch my death of cold?"

He reached for the rolled blanket behind his saddle, then stopped when she growled, "I will not sleep with your blanket. If you are afraid to put my own robe around me, then I will just freeze without one."

"What tricks do you hide, Nikki? Why so insistent on your robe?" He glanced thoughtfully at the robe lying beside her; the robe with its red wolf fur around the top and the wide strips of blood-red and black stripes painted on the leather part. Painted toward the top was a big red sun on the right, and on the left side, a little lower was painted with a white moon. He picked it up and shook it hard before taking it closer to the dying fire to examine it for hidden weapons.

"Satisfied?" Nikki taunted, refusing to answer.

"Perhaps." Draping the robe over her, he watched her nuzzle her face against the soft fur.

"Sleep well, Dark Angel." He added more fuel to the fire, then spread his bedroll and laid down, falling asleep almost as soon as his head touched the ground.

Counting off the minutes, she stared at the man on the other side of the fire. The expression on her face held a tender yet confusing love she did not understand. His strong, angular features relaxed into almost boyish lines and the deep tan of his face contrasted pleasantly with the light brown of his hair. Long, lazy lashes hid those striking silver-blue eyes in sleep.

Mentally, she added the memory of the lithe length of his long body, the sinewy muscles of arms and legs, and the hardness of his stomach and chest which once offered comfort.

Her breathing increased, tearing at her heart, remembering those long, slender hands caressing her, loving her. She closed her eyes, fighting against the disturbing images and blocking him out of her vision. *I cannot!* she moaned in despair. *I cannot think about it now! I must get away!*

Earlier, Nikki watched him search her robe, holding bated breath he did not discover the straight razor hidden in a tiny pocket underneath the fur top. The seam was thick around the neck where the fur and tanned skin had been sewn, hiding the razor and protecting it against detection. Whatever had prompted Kissa to sew the ingenious pocket was a blessing, and she silently thanked her.

With her teeth, she moved the robe toward the center until she found the razor. Spitting the hair from her mouth, she glanced at Dane to make sure he still slept. He did not move, and his breathing was deep, slow, and even.

Tingling sensations shooting through her right arm, she managed with her chin, teeth, and tongue to tug the robe upward, but as soon as she released her teeth from its leather, it slipped downward, out of her reach.

Shifting so the robe was firmly tucked underneath her, she laboriously worked the razor out with her teeth. She uneasily glanced at Dane when he shifted his position. After he stilled once more, she eased up far as the tied ropes allowed, turned her head to her left side, and dropped the straight razor to the ground. She worked her whole body upward until she could grasp it with her hands.

Dane opened his eyes, and Nikki stopped her movements. Pretending not to see him, she scooted and covered the razor with her side, acting as if she were trying to ease down into the robe.

"Having trouble, love?" Dane sardonically asked.

"I am cold. The robe keeps slipping off." She nodded

toward the robe around her waist, praying he would not find her only means of escape.

Dane rose and stepped toward her. Before she knew his intention, he bent, grabbed the robe, and pulled it completely off her. Throwing it on the ground near her feet, he knelt behind her and pulled on the ropes.

"I am still tied."

"Just checking. One can never be too sure about you." He covered her once more, patting down the fur around her neck, then caressed the satiny flesh of her face. "Ah, my dark angel, how I wish I could make love to you tonight."

A seductive half smile crossed her lips, her eyes daring him. "It will not be an easy task with me tied like this."

"I suppose you would like for me to untie you, then make love to you." He smoothed the hair from her cheek, wetting his lips, weighing the pros and cons, then shook his head. "Even though I ache for you, I won't release you. Perhaps when we get closer to our destination."

"I will never forgive you for this," Nikki hissed between clenched teeth.

"For not making love to you?" Dane asked, purposely misunderstanding her.

"Go to hell."

"My, such language, Dark Angel. I've never heard you use such strong words."

Nikki closed her eyes, ignoring him, listening to him walk back to his bedroll and lying down. She waited, it seemed forever, until she was sure he was sound asleep once more. Scooting closer to the fire, she grasped the straight razor. Working at her bonds, she was aware of every sound, each time he shifted in his sleep.

GREY DAWN MELLOWED OUT THE DARKNESS. Dane rose and added more firewood to the fire. Vividly aware of Nikki's eyes on him, he set about his morning task, feeding the horses and taking food and utensils from the saddlebags. Crouching near the fire, he met her piercing baby blues and cheerfully quipped, "Good morning, my love. Sleep well?"

His smile widened when she glared at him. "You didn't?" Dane answered as if she had spoken.

"Tsk, tsk, perhaps a little kiss will make you feel better." Kneeling beside her, he planted a kiss on her cheek. She turned her head toward him, meeting his lips, hers parted and moist. Her tongue flicked across his, inviting him to do more.

Smiling conceitedly, he tangled his hand in her hair and matched her wild exploration of tongue and mouth. She strained against him, her sighs coming out in small whimpers. Lowering his hand toward her breast, his head exploded in pain, and all went black.

Nikki pushed him off her and slowly rose to her knees, dropping the rock with a shudder. Timidly touching his cheek in a form of apology, she dropped her hand to his breast and was reassured with the shallow rise and fall of his chest. Relieved he was still breathing, she relaxed momentarily to allow feeling to return to her numb body. She stretched her arms to ease the ache before she turned him over on his stomach and methodically tied him up the same way he had tied her.

Easing him onto his side, she stared at the blood

trickling down his cheek. Searching his pockets and finding a handkerchief, she wet it with water from a canteen and tenderly bathed his face, blotting away the blood. Afterwards, she rose to her feet and stared down at him, determined yet strangely reluctant to leave him this way.

Morning erupted in glorious splendor, spraying its warming rays. Dane let his eyes adjust before he turned them toward the figure standing over him. Surprised to find Nikki still there, he tugged at his hands and found them securely tied.

"It is not a pleasant sensation, is it?" Nikki gloated, then her voice turned harsh. "You could not leave well enough alone, could you? But it does not matter anymore for you see I am going across and there is nothing you can do to stop me."

She saddled her gelding, then turned to find Dane still watching her. "Nothing to say?" she asked sarcastically, mocking him. "Goodbye, Dane."

Nikki mounted, then motioned carelessly around her. "I am leaving your horse and all your possessions. I do not want anything to remind me of you nor…." She paused for emphasis, "want to be accused of stealing."

With the last parting shot, she kicked her heels in the gelding's flanks and rode away.

THE SUN'S RAYS RAPIDLY BURNED OFF the morning chill. Nikki had been riding hard, apprehensive that Dane would suddenly appear before her. Her mount was nearly winded, and she had no choice but to slow him. It had been hours since she escaped Dane, hours of lonely, hard riding through rugged, changing land.

She wondered if he had worked loose yet and turned in the saddle and glanced behind her with her thought. An explosive *damnation!* escaped from tight lips while searching the horizon once more to make sure she really saw something move in the distance. There it was again, and whoever it was, was riding fast. She instinctively knew it was Dane.

Patting the big gelding's neck, she mumbled, "Sorry, boy, no time to rest."

Sharply kicking her heels in its side, a renewed energy invigorated her body. So close, so very close to Mexico, she could see the winding Rio Grande in the distance. The silver waters beckoned her, teased her with its closeness.

Glancing behind her, she discovered Dane was even closer than before. He must have ridden extremely hard to catch up with her so soon and his horse had to be even more winded than hers. If she pushed the gelding a little harder, she could be across the border before he caught up with her!

The gelding lowered its head, whinnied, and did a series of jump-twists, popping its tail and passing wind at something startling him. Unprepared for the sudden motion, Nikki was flung from the animal's back and landed with a bone-jarring thud.

The breath knocked out of her, she laid still, fighting to get her breath back. A terrible urgency fighting with the sane workings of her mind propelled her to her knees. She brushed the hair back from her face and glanced in the direction of the horse and rider. With a frightened gasp, she saw he was closer still.

Jumping to her feet, she frantically searched for her horse. The animal had raced off, leaving her stranded. "You stupid horse!"

Turning toward the direction Dane was coming, she raised her fist and shook it at him. "You will not get me, Dane Travis!" she shouted in the wind. With another quick glance at the rider, she ran toward the rock-covered mountainside.

Her breath ragged and her sides hurting, Nikki climbed the rocky slope, scratching hands and knees, the blood from the abrasions rendering her hold tenuous. She had to stop; her breath was tearing painfully at her lungs. She ducked behind a boulder, then peeked around it. What she saw forced her to draw her pistol. Dane was already climbing the mountainside toward her.

"Go away, Dane! I will kill you if you come any closer!" Her shouted words had no effect on him. He kept coming with the determination of an ant. Nikki pulled the hammer back on the pistol, aimed at a spot close to the right of him, and squeezed off a shot.

Debris flying around him, he ducked behind some rocks before lifting his head with caution and shouting, "Throw down your weapons, Nikki. I'm coming to get you!"

"I told you last night you will have to kill me first." Tears formed in her eyes, and she angrily dashed them away, her voice carrying the pleading note she hated. "Just a little longer and I would have been safe. Just a little longer and I would have been across the border. Why could you not leave well enough alone?"

"I can't, love, not for you or for anybody. For the love of God, Nikki, throw down your weapons and come peacefully, then we can settle this like adults." He moved forward again until another well-placed shot kicked up dirt near his side.

"No, Dane. It has come down to either you killing me or me killing you." Nikki pushed her hair behind her ear, tears forming once again in her eyes. "Why can you not bend a little? Why do you have to be so upright, so honest and loyal to a duty not worth your talent? I hate you for it, you know."

"Do you, love? Do you really hate me? I don't think so. You love me as much as I love you." Dane tried to inch forward while talking, but another well-placed shot stopped his advance. To keep her occupied until he could reach her, he fired off several shots in her direction, forcing her to dodge behind the boulder.

Nikki groaned, a fiery sensation racing through her arm. She gritted her teeth against the pain and shouted, "Yes, I love you. I love you more than life itself and this is why it has to end now. You do not love me, no matter what you say, or you would not be so determined to take me back to hang."

Her voice trailed off in a sadness so deep, it ripped through his insides. She loved him! How many times had he wanted to hear her to say it before now? And why did she wait until this moment?

He heard her groan. "Nikki?"

"I am shot."

Dane shook his head, the unreality of the situation making it seem dreamlike. He had not shot directly at her. Had a bullet ricocheted and hit her? If she was hit, perhaps she would have second thoughts. If she truly loved him, she would never be able to kill him.

Certain his reasoning was correct; he lowered his pistol, replacing it in the holster before rising to his feet. "I'm coming up."

He saw her peek around the boulder with tears streaming down her high cheekbones. He watched in amazement when she aimed the pistol, cocked the hammer, and fired. Pain ripped through his side.

Gasping, he fell to his knees. "Nikki?" he asked, disbelieving. "You really are determined to kill me?" Pain seared through him as he drew his pistol, then he dropped his hand to his side, still holding the pistol.

Nikki watched the blood seep through his shirt, and agonizing pain swept through her. "Dane!"

Dropping her weapon, she stumbled and slid, descending the mountainside. Reaching him, she fell to her knees and touched his face to make sure he was still alive. "I cannot kill you, but I cannot go back with you."

Nikki grabbed at her shirt, pulling it free from her pants and tore it open, exposing proud breasts with dark rose nipples. Taking his gun hand, she lifted it and placed the pistol barrel against her breast. "Kill me, Dane. Kill me and get it over with. I cannot live anymore like this. I cannot live with this type of destructive love. Release me. Please!"

Dumbfounded, he stared at her, confused and angry she asked him to kill her, but the look in those remarkable eyes, the pain of living, the fright of going back, made him shudder.

"Please! You would put an injured animal out of its misery. Why can you not do it for me? Do it if you love me."

The sadness of her voice made his muscles move with

a will of their own. His thumb cocked the hammer.

Nikki straightened her back, the barrel of the pistol burning against her left breast, her head lifted majestically, focusing on the rugged terrain behind him, a land as desolate and fierce as she. It was a fitting place to die.

Waiting for him to pull the trigger, a beautiful smile lit her face and her eyes sparkled with the joy of finally being released from a horrible world and a love so tragic, it was slowly killing her. At least this way would be merciful.

Nikki waited for the shot to finally end her pain of living and dealing with sorrow and a love so deep and tragic it was eating her alive. She heard the hammer being released, and a shuddering sob broke through her lips when he moved the barrel from her chest. Then hands covered her breasts, and the thumbs stroked her nipples, sending unwelcome longings beating through her body.

Her breath shook within her when the edge of his hat touched her collarbone, then the warmth of his forehead between the tops of her breasts, his lips touching her skin below, and a warm wetness touching the inner sides of her breasts.

Her breath coming in deep shudders of fear, Nikki lowered her eyes to the top of his hat. Gently, she placed her hand on the crown of his Stetson and removed it from his head before dropping it beside him. He did not move, just kept stroking her nipples until they hardened with his administrations.

Her fingers crept through the sweaty locks on both sides of his hair and her thumbs rubbed along the top edges of his ears. A quivering sigh slipped past her lips when she spied the blood covering his left hand, matching and mingling with the blood from her upper right arm. Tears sprang to her eyes and tracked down her cheeks to land in his light brown hair to mingle with his sweat from the hot Texas sun.

His lips and tongue tasted her skin underneath the line of her breasts and a moan escaped her. "Dane, when does it all end? I will not make love to you in this desolate place with the knowledge you will take me back to hang. You have already hurt me by making love to me and then forcing me to stand trial. Please, just kill me. I cannot go on loving you this way only to be destroyed by your love once again."

She kept caressing his hair, holding him firmly against her, feeling the warmth of his breath when he sighed and the shudder running through his body. "No more, Dane. Either love me for who I am and let me go or kill me. I cannot do this anymore."

Another tremor swept over her, and she whispered again, "I am in love with you, but either love me or kill me."

Dane stopped moving his thumbs and lifted glistening silver-blue eyes to hers. "You're right, love. I can't kill you. I can take you in, but you would force me to kill you before I could."

Drinking in the love, longing, and distress in her remarkable sky-blue eyes, Dane did not remove his hands from her breasts. The thought of never touching her again, of never hearing her voice or seeing her beloved face, hit him like a ton of rocks falling and pounding his very soul.

"Where do we go from here?" Nikki enquired, a tremor of desire rocking her very core when his thumbs began moving again across her sensitized, hard nipples. His thumbs stopping their maddening torture, his hands slipped down her chest and stomach to the top of her pants. He unbuttoned them before slipping a hand between her legs, his thumb caressing the essence of her while a finger slipped inside her. Trembling from the longing ripping through her insides, she fought against her own yearning building within her.

"No," Nikki whispered, stopping his hand and moving it away from her, feeling suddenly bereft and in denial of the power he had over her. One touch from him and her body acted like it was starving for his touch. And it was, she realized. Her whole body and soul desired him above and beyond any other. "I will not make love with you, Dane, just to have you betray me again."

Dane reached around her and grasped her buttocks, pulling her back toward him. Lowering his head, he kissed her stomach, running his tongue across her belly button, then pushed her pants down lower on her hips toward her thighs, kissing her all the way down until his tongue found the spot at the top of her trembling flower.

Quivering with the sensation, Nikki ran her fingers through his hair, fighting against her own yearning to fulfill both their passions, yet holding his head motionless while his tongue flicked across her essence. Breathlessly, she protested, "No, Dane, please. Do not tease me so. I cannot go back with you."

He lifted his eyes toward her, murmuring against her, "I will not let you go, Dark Angel. I cannot let you go."

Tears formed in her eyes as her body quivered with his touch. "No, you are injured. Let me tend to your injury."

Pushing back from him, she sat on her knees and gently reached for his shirt where the blood was drying on the material. She bent forward, and he emitted a sharp intake of breath. Concerned, she apologized, "I did not mean to hurt you."

"You didn't hurt me, Dark Angel," he groaned, taking her left hand and placing it on the front of his pants.

The hard length of him filled her hand, and for the rest of her life, she never knew how they did it or why, but she unbuckled his holster belt and unbuttoned his pants, pulling free his throbbing length, caressing and teasing it.

Slipping her shirt off her shoulders, she gently moved against his chest and slipped the shirt behind his back, adjusting it to cover the area of his wound from the back and tying the sleeves in the front to cover the bullet entry and exit sites.

Moving backward, she nudged him to lay on his back while she shifted his pants down around his hips. Rising, she divested herself of moccasins and pants, then posed on top of him before positioning his hardness at her hungry entrance. As soon as she lowered herself on top of him, both trembled and cried out with the orgasm rocking them both.

When she moved to lift off him, he grabbed her and kept her firmly seated on his softening member. "Don't go. Not yet," he softly begged.

"Dane," she moaned, "we are both injured and bleeding."

"I'd gladly bleed to death while I am inside of you, my love. I can't let you go."

The hot sun beating uncomfortably against her back, Nikki bent over him and placed a soft kiss on his lips before speaking, "I would rather keep us both alive and well so we can do this more often, but only if you promise you will never take me back to hang."

Wrapping his arms around her, Dane pulled her head to meet his lips. His passionate kiss swept over them both, and he hardened inside of her again. "I told you before, Dark Angel, you are mine."

He rolled her over until he was on top of her, his hips moving against her, straining for another release in the comforting confines of her wet, welcoming softness. His kisses ran across her cheek to her ear and his tongue swept across the inside of her ear, sending tingling sensations along her spine, spreading in the very core of her being as he whispered, "I will not take you back to hang, my love. I will never let you go again."

He pushed deeper inside of her, hearing her soft moans. "You are mine, Dark Angel, mine until the end of time, and I promise I will never let you go again."